Footprints In The Wilderness
The Journey
Of
The Children of Israel From Egypt
To
The Promised Land:
AN Exposition
Of
Three Great Books of The Bible

Reverend Byran C. Russell

Studio of Books LLC
5900 Balcones Drive Suite 100
Austin, Texas 78731
www.studioofbooks.org
Hotline: (254) 800-1183

Ordering Information:
Special discounts are available on quantity purchases by corporations, associations, and others. For details, contact the publisher at the address above.

Printed in the United States of America.

ISBN-13: Paperback   978-1-964928-94-4
          Hardback   978-1-968491-03-1
          Ebook   978-1-964928-95-1

Library of Congress Control Number: 2025912563

FOREWORD

The journey of the Children of Israel in the Wilderness towards the Promised Land was both a literal and spiritual one, in which more than 2,000,000 people participated. More than 4,000,000 footprints were left in the Wilderness. But since Israel journeyed with their God, for them, it was a long spiritual journey as well. And although none of their footprints can now be found, it is remarkable that each and all of the Divine footprints remain with us. These are the footprints of the principles of holiness which emanated forth from the mouth of the Living God.

These principles were not only inwrought within the religious experience of the whole nation of Israel but also in time, so that the intended lessons then are the lessons for us today. As those who failed to apply those lessons then all perished in the Wilderness, so shall we all perish in this larger Wilderness if we also fail to live by the principles of holiness. These footprints are not just mere principles of Divine holiness: they hold the key to eternal life. Anyone who loses this key will be locked out of the Coming Kingdom for all eternity. The secret to possessing it forever is that we understand the true symbolisms of these principles as expressed in the rituals, ceremonies, and statutes of the Law. The Divine substance of all these symbolisms is Christ's one eternal Atonement. This one eternal Atonement is abundantly more than the equivalent of all the blood sacrifices offered under the Law.

Christians cannot now just dismiss these principles as meaningless and irrelevant. The danger is that we would have denied ourselves the privilege of a deep sense of appreciation for Christ's one and eternal Atonement, which most logically comes from an understanding of the detailed articulation of the principles of Divine Holiness expressed in the ceremonies and statutes of the Law. We take the position that details are necessary to a summary. Christ's eternal Atonement is the summary. The details and the summary of a subject matter are so intertwined that you cannot understand the one without the other. It is with this understanding that we review the Principles of Holiness articulated in the books of Exodus, Leviticus, and Numbers. The picture before us is clear and complete: the journey to the Promised Land had a specific time of departure; there was the Divine direction, the Wilderness. But this Wilderness became Earth's greatest university.

The format of review emphasizes those events of spiritual implications for us and provides the exegeses of the offerings and ceremonies of the Law. The subject matter is arranged to enable the reader to remember more readily the contents of these Books. These books are intertwined and complementary one to the other. Together, they emphasize the message of Divine Holiness. Therefore, they must be studied together in order to better grasp their essential message of Divine Holiness.

Byran C. Russell

Table of Contents

THE AUTHORIZED KING JAMES

VERSION OF THE BIBLE IS USED

IN THIS WORK

ALL SCRIPTURES ARE VERBATIM

THE BOOK OF EXODUS:
THE
DEPARTURE OF THE CHILDREN
OF ISRAEL FROM EGYPT
TO
THE PROMIED LAND

This Book expresses God's

Omnipotence

CHAPTER 1

Historic Circumstances Of The Exodus, Chapters 1-13:1-16

The circumstances of Israel's departure from Egypt are both historical and historic because they are not only recorded in sacred history but they are also worthy of their place. But the message of these circumstances is even greater than the circumstances themselves because it addresses God's eternal purpose of man's Redemption. The Call of God to Abraham was in keeping with this eternal purpose. Abraham's mission was therefore redemptive. Besides, there were certain promises God made to him which had to be fulfilled. Though Abraham faithfully fulfilled his mission, it was yet incumbent on his descendants to continue his mission.

They went to Egypt and lived there for 430 years; and while living in slavery for most of that time, they never lost their sense of Divine mission. It was naturally impossible for them to escape the slavery of Egypt. That is why it is of paramount importance that we carefully review all the circumstances of their slavery and departure from Egypt. The first twelve chapters of Exodus provide all the information as to how the impossible was made possible. With opened hearts, we must look at all the circumstances; but first, look at the slavery itself.

The Fact of Slavery, Exodus 1: 1-10:

The first ten verses give a brief history of the Children of Israel and the reasons for their bondage. The remaining twelve verses describe the nature of the bondage. Though it was the worst kind of physical bondage they could have ever experienced, they were able to insulate themselves from the mental and psychological enslavement such bondage could naturally cause. Despite the harsh reality of their bondage, they never thought that that was their destiny. And even though looked upon as inferior, they never thought of themselves as inferior. This was due to the fact of their strong faith in the God of their fathers, who was their personal God. They could not prevent their slavery but they did prevent their minds from being enslaved.

1 Now these are the names of the children of Israel, which came into Egypt; and every man and his household came with Jacob.

Jacob was the father of the twelve tribes who went to Egypt to live due to a famine they were experiencing in Canaan. Israel was the name given to Jacob by the angel with whom he wrestled in that notable spiritual experience he had while living in Canaan. One can imagine how many times Jacob told his twelve sons of that experience. The twelve sons grew up knowing that God was real and personal and that He was good to their father. It was logical to them to make the God of their father their own God.

2 Reuben, Simeon, Levi, and Judah,

3 Issachar, Zebulun, and Benjamin,

4 Dan, and Naphtali, Gad, and Asher.

5 And all the souls that came out of the loins of Jacob were seventy souls: for Joseph was in Egypt already.

6 And Joseph died, and all his brethren, and all that generation.

7 And the children of Israel were fruitful, and increased abundantly, and multiplied, and waxed exceeding mighty and the land was filled with them.

Joseph died hundreds of years before the slavery but he knew that one day his brethren would return to Canaan. He even gave them commandment concerning his bones. That was an indication of how great was the faith of the Children of Israel Their faith was also precious to them; you could take everything they had but not their faith. Pharaoh learned that from experience.

It was not a surprise that they were greatly blessed by God in many ways. They were blessed due to their father's faith and theirs as well. Besides their great prosperity, they were a distinct and distinguished people. God put His fear upon them and things were all ways going their way until a new king came to the throne.

8 Now there arose up a new king over Egypt, which knew not Joseph.

9 And he said unto his people, Behold, the people of the children of Israel are more and mightier than we:

10 Come on, let us deal wisely with them; lest they multiply, and it come to pass, that, when there falls out any war, they join also unto our enemies, and fight against us, and so get them up out of the land.

Unlike his predecessors, the new king was driven by fear and tried to establish his throne thereby. He explained it to the Egyptian people and asked for their understanding and help. They did not explain to him that it was not the right thing to do; instead, they agreed with him to a path of instability and their own destruction. This ungodly fear was responsible for the bondage of God's children.

The Nature of Slavery, Exo.1:11-22

11 Therefore they did set over them taskmasters to afflict them with their burdens. And they built for Pharaoh treasure cities, Pithom and Raamses.

This verse alone shows that they were the most exploited

people on Earth and that the slavery became personal. Taskmasters were appointed for personal direction of slavery. They were to beat them personally and at will if the Children of Israel were not performing their daily allotted task sufficiently. This was a degree of brutality meted out to them daily. Quickly they built special cities for Pharaoh. Ordinarily these cities would have cost much more to build and a longer period of time. But behind the slavery, a phenomenon was occurring; the Children of Israel were growing exceedingly.

12 But the more they afflicted them, the more they multiplied and grew. And they were grieved because of the children of Israel.

Their growth was no comfort to the Egyptians: the more they became threatened and jealous of them. Like everything else, **evil has the potential** *to grow; it does not just go away, it becomes greater until it is stopped by a greater force. Therefore the Egyptians extended the bondage to all other areas of activity.*

13 And the Egyptians made the children of Israel to serve with rigor:

14 And they made their lives bitter with hard bondage, in mortar, and in brick, and in all manner of service in the field: all their service, wherein they made them to serve, was with rigor.

When Pharaoh saw that his best effort of slavery was not able to limit the growth of the Hebrew population, he thought of and did something no other king of Egypt did.

15 And the king of Egypt spoke to the Hebrew midwives, of which the name of the one was Shiphrah, and the name of the other Puah:

16 And he said, When ye do the office of a midwife to the Hebrew women, and see them upon the stools; if it be a son, then ye shall kill him: but if it be a daughter, then she shall live.(*It is clear that Pharaoh was motivated by fear for the miraculous growth and might of the Children of Israel*).

This, though similar to modern abortion, was much worse. One reason for modern abortion is that mothers could not force themselves to murder their own children after they were born. Pharaoh had the heart to do that and commanded the midwives to kill the males immediately after birth. As the king of Egypt, he ruled over them but he could not rule over their faith. Simply, their faith could not be shaken by all the power of Pharaoh and they proved to the world that their faith in their God was greater than all the power of Egypt at Pharaoh's disposal. Faith in God will always defy the onslaught of evil, no matter how impossible it seems.

17 But the midwives feared God, and did not as the king of Egypt commanded them, but saved the men children alive.

The midwives showed the evidence of their faith; they simply disobeyed Pharaoh's command and saved the lives of the male children. And what did he do when he was confronted with the evidence of Faith? It does not seem he was able to do very much.

18 And the king of Egypt called for the midwives, and said them, Why have ye done this thing, and have saved the men children alive?

Pharaoh saw that the male children were saved alive by the midwives and demanded an answer. The midwives did not question his sovereign authority; they only questioned his moral authority which they found inadequate to demand their obedience. And what would their answer be? These midwives were true Israelites who could not be bought, nor would have sold out their righteousness for a morsel of meat. Neither would they do injury to their moral conscience. To them, to do such thing, would have been more painful than death itself. Thus, they found an answer to Pharaoh's command.

19 And the midwives said unto Pharaoh, Because the Hebrew women are not as the Egyptian women; for they are lively, and are delivered ere the midwives come in unto them.

Indeed, it was much better to fear God rather than Pharaoh. Earthly reward will not stand the test of time but rewards of righteousness will. The midwives were not motivated by any earthly rewards but they gained them while their heavenly rewards awaited them.

20 Therefore God dealt well with the midwives: and the people multiplied, and waxed very mighty.

21 And it came to pass, because the midwives feared God, that he made them houses.

Pharaoh tried time and time again in different ways to prevent God's blessings from reaching His people and found that his best efforts miserably failed each time. But will Pharaoh give up in despair and say, I have failed, I will let the Hebrews live as other human beings?

22 And Pharaoh charged all his people, saying, Every son that is born ye shall cast into the river, and every daughter ye shall save alive.

Pharaoh made one last plan to thwart God's divine plan, not knowing that the God of the Hebrews could use his own plan to defeat his selfish and evil purpose. Pharaoh did not know that he would be caught in his own craftiness. This time he would be taught a lesson that he would live to regret and never forget. The river which was to be used as a means of mass murder would now be used as the path, the Divine path, for a child of a Hebrew slave to reach the palace of Egypt.

The Birth and Miraculous Protection of Moses, Exodus 2: 1-10:

Human life has potential for infinite possibilities and that is why no one can put a human value on any life and why the time of birth is rightfully a time of celebration, when again one can express one's appreciation for life. Thus the birth of Moses was of historic significance for a most crucial time in the life of the Children of Israel. The Deliverer could not be a mere man: he had to be God-like, being the human vessel through which the power of God would shake the Egyptian civilization to its foundation. Therefore his birth had to be divinely arranged and secretly protected at the highest level. Pharaoh would have no knowledge the Deliverer would live in his own palace and be a prince of Egypt and being unknown to his own brethren. The national significance of his birth could not have been greater: the destiny of the Children of Israel depended on it.

1 And there went a man of the house of Levi, and took to wife a daughter of Levi.

The Divine plan for the deliverer of Israel and the Levitical Priesthood began to unfold. In Genesis 15, God made a promise of blessings to Abraham; but the blessings would not be without some sorrow. God promised him the land of Canaan as an inheritance to him and his seed after him and therein set the borders of that land. The bad news, humanly speaking, was that his descendants would live in a strange land, Egypt, and would be enslaved for four hundred years, after which He would deliver them and lead them to the Promised Land. While in bondage, Israel believed this promise and continued looking for their deliverer and their deliverance with all their heart.

It was not accidental that God had chosen the Deliverer from the tribe of Levi, which tribe also He had chosen for the Priesthood. The Levitical Priesthood was at the heart of Israel's Theocracy. The choice was also important for harmony and unity. Choosing Moses as deliverer and from the tribe of the Holy Priesthood guaranteed the harmony and unity needed. Moses would eventually be, not only deliverer, but also prophet and priest, a type of Christ. Israel would survive the Egyptians slavery because of their unshakable faith in God's faithfulness. While in slavery, they were all watching and waiting. Then when Moses was born, his mother had a unique perception that he was special. It was even more than a perception; yes his parents began to put their destiny and that of the whole nation on the birth of this special child.

*Some leaders are trained and some are born; but there is a difference between the two; a trained leader can never take the place of a born leader. Moses was a born leader: his place in human history could not be substituted; neither could there be the equivalent. There was only one Moses, the one Pharaoh feared and the one who endured as seeing the **invisible God.***

They, his parents, regarded not the law of Pharaoh; and so they hid him for three months.

The records show,

2 And the woman conceived and bare a son: and when shc saw him that he was a goodly child, she hid him three months.

3 And when she could no longer hide him, she took for him an ark of bulrushes, and daubed it with slime and with pitch, and put the child therein; and she laid it in the flags by the river's brink. (It is a mazing the length a mother will go to protect her child).

Faith demanded strong action but when a mother placed her entire destiny on the event of her son's birth, greater action was needed. Faith for her meant courage and determination, not a little, but all she had. After hiding her son for three months, she never gave up hope. She made one last effort, a diligent one, in making the ark of safety for him. What if Pharaoh had found out what she had done—it could have meant instant death to her and her family. She knew she brought a special child into the world at a special time and that the God of Abraham, Isaac, and Jacob was greater than Pharaoh. It so happened that she proved to be right.

Moses was saved by the ark; it was much smaller than another ark, the Ark of the Covenant. However, it was a type of the Ark of the Covenant. The Ark of the Covenant was not only a place of safety, but it saved not only Israel from annihilation but the world as a whole.

If Israel had not been saved by the Ark, The Redeemer would not have come into the world.

4 And his sister (Miriam) stood afar off, to wit what would be done to him.

But faith is not incidental: it can be contagious at times. The mother's faith and courage were seen in her daughter. At her young age she did all she could have done. She stood afar off to see what would happen. Another child would have run away to hide. She just would not accept that anything wrong could happen to her brother. Miriam was wiser than children her age.

5 And the daughter of Pharaoh came down to wash herself at the river; and her maidens walked along by the river's side; and when she saw the ark among the flags, she sent her maid to fetch it.

6 And when she had opened it, she saw the child: and, behold, the babe wept. And she had compassion on him, and said, This is one of the Hebrew's children.

This was an event that would change Pharaoh's daughter's life forever. It all began with her curiosity: a curiosity quite like that of a child. Curiosity is the beginning of knowledge, and knowledge is the path to greatness. If it can be said that Pharaoh's daughter was a great princess, this single act was the cause.

In Pharaoh's daughter reaction to this tragedy of slavery, looking at her in the eyes, we see something very beautiful – the sovereign act of God, remembering His promise to Israel. God would move her to open her heart to a helpless child. She came just at the right time when the babe was crying, quite possible for food and from discomfort. She realized that there was no human difference between an Egyptian child and a Hebrew child. They both were mothered into the world and needed the same human care, without which both would quickly die. Would she witness in her hand the death of a helpless child or would she allow him to transform her life?

7 Then said his sister to Pharaoh's daughter, Shall I go and call to thee a nurse of the Hebrew women, that she may nurse the child for thee?

We know that young Miriam was not only full of faith and courage but also of wisdom. We should not be surprised; the Bible says the fear of God is the beginning of wisdom. Even at this young age, Miriam had the wisdom which came from faith in the God of Abraham. Her wisdom allowed her to say and do the right thing.

8 And Pharaoh's daughter said to her, Go. And the maid went and called the child's mother.

The moment Pharaoh's daughter told her to call a Hebrew nurse, she knew her brother would not only be safe but would be free from the bondage of slavery as long as he lived in Egypt. She even thought her brother could be a prince of Egypt. Miriam, a child of faith, was quick to bring the word of hope and comfort to her mother. Her mother gladly offered her services.

9 And Pharaoh's daughter said unto her, Take this child away, and nurse it for me, and I will give thee thy wages. And the woman took the child, and nursed it.

10 And the child grew, and she brought him unto Pharaoh's daughter, and he became her son. And she called his name Moses: and she said, Because I drew him out of the water.

By her own words and by her action, she formerly and officially adopted the child as her own son. There and then he became a prince of Egypt. How nice it must have been to be paid by the princess of Egypt to care for your own child. She must have thought, My ways are not God's ways for His ways are higher than mine, even as the heavens are higher than the Earth. Jochebed honored her agreement with Pharaoh's daughter: keeping an agreement is an element of faith. People who cannot keep an agreement can claim to have faith but they will have very little evidence to show. At the appropriate time she returned her child to Pharaoh's daughter. She never thought by doing so, she would have lost her son forever. To her it was only a loan which would yield great returns at the appropriate time. The God of Abraham who showed her great favor during a time of slavery would accomplish His divine purpose through the life of her son. If she were not to see him again, she would have had no regrets; the faithfulness that God had shown her was enough.

Jochebed's sincerity in keeping her agreement with Pharaoh's daughter was clearly shown by her refusing even to suggest a name for this her special son. It was Pharaoh's daughter who named him, Moses. This was good enough for her as it was good enough for Pharaoh's daughter. By his name, Moses would later learn of his own miraculous deliverance.

Moses Shows signs As the Deliverer, Exodus 2:11-14:

11 And it came to pass in those days when Moses was grown, that he went out unto his brethren, and looked on their burdens: and he spied an Egyptian smiting an Hebrew, one of his brethren.

At this time, Moses was a full grown man, learned in all the wisdom of Egypt. But the interest of his learning seems to have been in his Hebrew brethren and the God of their fathers. He knew the history of his brethren and recognized the tragedy of slavery which had consumed their lives. He wanted to see for himself how they were responding and what he could do to help them. Under the circumstances there was very little he could do to help them except to show his identity with them. However, he was compelled to act when he saw a Hebrew beaten by an Egyptian.

12 And he looked this way and that way, and when he saw that there was no man, he slew the Egyptian, and hid him in the sand.

His righteousness and compassion would not allow him to remain passive; he did what he had to do.

13 And when he went out the second day, behold, two men of the Hebrews strove together: and he said to him that did the wrong, Wherefore smites thou thy fellow?

14 And he said, Who made thee a prince and judge over us? Intends thou to kill me, as thou killed the Egyptian? And Moses feared, and said, Surely this thing is known.

He was rather surprised when he learned that his action the day before became known. Though his action put his life in danger, it did show potentials of leadership. Two qualities of true leadership are compassion and a sense of justice. Though he was helpless to do anything more, he was a voice of the voiceless.

Moses Flees to Safety, Exodus 2:15-22:

15 Now when Pharaoh heard this thing, he sought to slay Moses. But Moses fled from the face of Pharaoh, and dwelt in the land of Midian: and he sat down by a well.

This verse is only a summary of what happened when Pharaoh heard of what Moses had done. It took Moses great effort to escape the king of Egypt: he had to hide among his brethren for some time, traveled by foot in the deserts of Egypt and across the Sinai Peninsula to the land of Midian. It involved many days of travel and physical exhaustion. He was only able to survive because of Divine guidance; his will and his soul were tested. That journey had a lasting effect on him. He truly saw the frailty of man and that he was only a mere lump of clay. And he had no idea that God would use him to deliver the children of Israel from their bondage.

As a member of the royal family, his action put his life in danger and he was forced to escape the wrath of Pharaoh. The land of his escape seemed to be a deliberate choice. Canaan was much nearer than the land of Midian. The nations of Canaan became extremely corrupt and were about to be expelled by God. Midian was one of the sons of Abraham and his second wife, Ketruah. He became the father of the Midianites. As the son of Abraham, he was taught the ways of God as would be expected of a righteous father. Jethro a descendant became the priest of Midian. While the nations of Canaan were corrupt, the Midianites were God-fearing, to say the least. Moses did not know what to expect but he was divinely led.

16 Now the priest of Midian had seven daughters: and they came and drew water, and filled the troughs to water their father's flock.

17 And the shepherds came and drove them away: but Moses stood up and helped them, and watered their flock.

Moses came to the right place at the right time. It shows that our choices in life will determine what we become. Again Moses's leadership qualities stood out: the qualities of justice, courage, and compassion. He protected Jethro's daughters from the unkindly actions of the shepherds and drew the water from the well for them. This water would serve as a mere introduction to a long range of water experiences Moses was yet to experience in ways he would never think possible

Will a good deed go unrewarded?

18 And when they came to Reuel their father, he said, How is it that ye are come so soon today?
19 And they said, An Egyptian delivered us out of the hand of the shepherds, and also drew water enough for us, and watered the flock.

20 And he said unto his daughters, And where is he? Why is it that ye have left him? Call him that he might eat bread.

21 And Moses was content to dwell with the man: and he gave Moses Zipporah his daughter.

Moses was rewarded for his kindly deed far beyond his imagination. Jethro recognized the goodness in Moses and invited him home. From here on everything was left up to him. He was happy to become a part of his family. He enjoyed the tranquility provided him by a grateful family and forgot the trials of Egypt. His first son, Gershom could only add to his peace of mind; yet his heart was with his brethren in Egypt. After being in Midian some forty years, it was still a strange land because he was away from his Hebrew family.

22 And she bare him a son, and he called his name Gershom: for he said, I have been a stranger in a strange land.

23 And it came to pass in process of time, that the king of Egypt died: and the children of Israel sighed by reason of the bondage, and they cried, and their cry came up unto God by reason of the bondage.

After approximately another forty years, the bondage of the Hebrews grew worse. Yet they did not forget the God of their fathers, neither did He forget them. Faith in God must be tested and must not fail the test so that in the end God will be glorified.

24 And God heard their groaning, and God remembered his covenant with Abraham, with Isaac, and with Jacob.

25 And God looked upon the children of Israel, and God had respect unto them.

This covenant was a Divine promise of mercy and blessing: one which was impossible for God to break. And why would those with whom it was made walk away from it? Israel would not walk away from it, no matter what — they kept calling out to Him under the worse human circumstances.

God remembered the faith of their fathers and had compassion on them.

Moses' First Encounter with God, Exodus 3:1-18:

1 Now Moses kept the flock of Jethro his father-in-law, the priest of Midian: and he led the flock to the backside of the desert, and came to the mountain of God, even to Horeb.

2 And the angel of the Lord appeared unto him in a flame

of fire out of the midst of a bush: and he looked, and, behold, the bush burned with fire, and the bush was not consumed.

Moses the Prince of Egypt became a shepherd. We know one thing about sheep that is they go astray often and need a shepherd. One great lesson of the sheep is that they represent human beings who often wander from God and need a shepherd. One of the responsibilities of the shepherd is to find pastures for the sheep. This caused Moses to take them to the back side of Mount Horeb. According to custom, God frequently appeared on Mount Horeb. Unknowing to Moses, he happened to lead his flock to the opposite side of the Mount. As he did, The Angel of Lord appeared in a burning fire. The Angel of the Lord here, and in other places in the Old Testament, refers to the Pre-Incarnate Christ who so often appeared in angelic form. His angelic Pre-Incarnate appearances were quite different from the experience of the Incarnation; but, nevertheless, provided a more personal encounter with man.

3 And Moses said, I will now turn aside, and see this great sight, why the bush is not burnt.

It was a strange sight such as was never seen by Moses in all the land of Egypt and in all his prior experience as a shepherd. He wanted to find out for himself why the burning fire did not consume the bush.

4 And when the Lord saw that he turned aside to see, God called unto him out of the midst of the bush, and said, Moses, Moses. And he said, Here am I.

5 And he said draw not nigh hither: put off thy shoes from off thy feet, for the place whereon you stand is holy ground.

God wanted Moses' personal attention and so He used the burning bush. Then for the first time Moses heard the voice of the Living God. Under the circumstance of revealing Himself as the God of his fathers and the God of the Universe, God's voice was made to convey that message. The impression of that voice would remain with Moses for the rest of his life. Somehow, Moses responded. Before he could get any closer to the burning bush, the Lord quickly made the distinction between Him and Moses: it was the distinction of His holy nature compared to the sinful nature of man. He wanted Moses to be used to free his people from bondage but Moses had to realize he was not worthy to come any nearer to His presence, but He could make him worthy. An acknowledgement was necessary. Moses was told to take off his shoes, indicating to leave the past behind. His message of holiness was the foundation of His covenant with Abraham, Isaac, and Jacob.

Then God delivered the urgent message of His deliverance for the children of Israel from the bondage of Egypt.

6 Moreover he said, I am the God of thy father, the God of Abraham, the God of Isaac, and the God of Jacob. And Moses hid his face; for he was afraid to look upon God.

7 And the Lord said, I have surely seen the affliction of my people which are in Egypt, and have heard their cry by reason of their taskmasters; for I know their sorrows;

8 And I am come down to deliver them out of the hand of the Egyptians, and to bring them up out of that land unto a good land and a large, unto a land flowing with milk and honey; unto the place of the Canaanites, and the Hittites, and the Amorites, and the Perizzites, and the Hivites, and the Jebusites.

9 Now therefore, behold, the cry of the children of Israel is come unto me: and I have also seen the oppression wherewith the Egyptians oppress them.

10 Come now therefore, and I will send thee unto Pharaoh, that you may bring forth my people the children of Israel out of Egypt.

Moses was literally afraid and felt unworthy to look on God's face. He was literally overwhelmed by the greatness of

God's appearance. If he could hide, he would. On the other hand, it would have been disrespectful not to have answered to God's voice. God detailed all that was involved in the deliverance of His people. But Moses was overwhelmed by all of it and felt unworthy and inadequate for the task.

11 And Moses said unto God, Who am I, that I should go unto Pharaoh, and that I should bring forth the children of Israel out of Egypt?

12 And he said, Certainly I will be with thee; and this shall be a token unto thee, that I have sent thee: When thou hast brought forth the people out of Egypt, ye shall serve God upon this mountain.

Despite God's reassurance that it was He who would deliver the children of Israel and Moses would only be the vessel of His choice, Moses still felt unworthy and incapable. He did not question the possibility but wanted more detail as to how exactly it would be done.

13 And Moses said unto God, Behold when I come unto the children of Israel, and shall say unto them, The God of thy fathers hath sent me unto you; and they shall say to me, What is his name? What shall I say unto them?

A person is recognized by his name; he knew God was a person who must have a name. So, he asked for His personal name. He was surprised to hear God's name. God has many names but He gave him the name most appropriate.

14 And God said unto Moses, **I AM THAT I AM:** and he said, Thus shalt thou say unto the children of Israel, **I AM** hath sent me unto you.

God gave Moses the name that explains His eternal self-existence. "I AM THE ONLY GOD, THAT IS WHAT I AM". Once we understand the implications of this name, we will conclude it is His rightful name and there was nothing more he could explain to make them understand who He is. Their fathers personally experienced God. Therefore, His existence was never in question.

. They would be now happy to know that their God is the ONLY GOD, the Creator of the Universe.

15 And God said moreover unto Moses, Thus shalt thou say unto the children of Israel, The Lord God of your fathers, the God of Abraham, the God of Isaac, and the God of Jacob, hath sent me unto you: this is my name forever, and this my memorial unto all generations.

God's name is derived from experience: Abraham, Isaac, and Jacob had personal experiences with God. They taught their children about those experiences. So, rightfully the God of Abraham, the God of Isaac, the God of Jacob was and is His name. God was proud of the fact these patriarchs personally experienced His mercies and blessings and wanted to be remembered for that. The Children of Israel needed to know that the God of their fathers is the LIVING GOD and He hears their cry for deliverance, and will deliver them.

Moses had experienced for himself the ONE SELF-EXISTENT GOD. There was no doubt in his mind that He was real and personal and ruled in Heaven and Earth.

16 Go, and gather the elders of Israel together, and say unto them, The Lord God of your fathers, the God of Abraham, of Isaac, and of Jacob, appeared unto me, saying, I have surely visited you, and seen that which is done to you in Egypt:

17 And I have said, I will bring you up out of the affliction of Egypt unto the land of the Canaanites, and the Hittites, and the Amorites, and the Perizzites, and the Hivites, and the Jebusites, unto a land flowing with milk and honey.

18 And they shall harken to thy voice: and thou shalt come, thou and the elders of Israel, unto the king of Egypt, and ye shall say unto him, The Lord God of the Hebrews hath met with us: and now let us go, we beseech thee, three days' journey into the wilderness, that we may sacrifice to the Lord our God.

The message to Moses ends with a call to Divine worship, it involves sacrifice unto the Lord. The idea of the sacrifice signifies lost innocence, guilt, contrition, and redemption. It was not new to the Hebrews; it was practiced by father Abraham, and the other patriarchs. The idea did not originate with man, but with God. In Genesis 15, God commanded sacrificial worship of Abraham.

Sacrifice in worship began at an earlier time, as far back as to the time of Adam and Eve. The rejection of Cain's offering seems to be due to the fact that he did not follow the Divine order, while Abel, his brother, did.

19 And I am sure that the king of Egypt will not let you go, no, not by a mighty hand.

*Verse 19 must be memorized by Theologians and all Christians alike. We see in this verse that God foreknew that Pharaoh would not willingly free the Children of Israel from bondage. Though other verses in connection to Pharaoh's stubbornness, to free the Children of Israel, say that God hardened his heart; those verses could only be a figure of speech. God could not cause him to do things so inhuman, to cause swift Divine judgment, and then righteously judge him for those things. We must, therefore, interpret those verses to mean that God allowed him the **free exercise of his will**. The purpose of the signs and wonders was to influence Pharaoh's Will in the Divine direction, and not to strengthen it in the evil practice of slavery.*

20 And I will stretch out my hand, and smite Egypt with all my wonders which I will do in the midst thereof: and after that he will let you go.

21 And I will give this people favor in the sight of the Egyptians: and it shall come to pass, that, when ye go, ye shall not go empty:

22 But every woman shall borrow of her neighbor, and of her that sojourns in her house, jewels of silver, and jewels of gold, and raiment: and ye shall put them upon your

sons, and upon your daughters; and ye shall spoil the Egyptians.

The promise of economic justice should be received with joy. After all, it would be a small token for years of slavery. At the most appropriate time all Israel would possess these blessings.

Exodus 4:1-18:

1 And Moses answered and said, But, behold, they will not believe me, nor harken unto my voice: for they will say, The Lord hath not appeared unto thee.

2 And the Lord said unto him, What is that in thine hand? And he said, A rod.

*Moses was convinced of the faithfulness and greatness of God but he was not sure his brethren in Egypt would be as convinced. It was not until God put a degree of His omnipotence upon him that he became absolutely convinced of God's promise of deliverance. God carefully chose two initial signs to convince His brethren in Egypt that the time of their deliverance had come. The sign of the serpent was to remind Moses that the Fall of man began with the evil influence of the serpent and that its evil influence was responsible for the slavery of the children of Israel. The sign of leprosy further describes the nature of sin; sin saturates all of human nature without exceptions. Nevertheless, God has the cure of sin but it is in conjunction with the **FREE CHOICE** of man. Moses' putting his hand into his bosom and taking it out and back again symbolizes the nature of sin and its Divine cure. Man cannot cure himself of sin: it can only be done by Divine initiative and man's willing cooperation.*

Sin is something of which man must be afraid and should rightly be afraid. Man can have control of sin by listening to the voice of God, the only cure for sin.

3 And he said, Cast it on the ground. And he cast it on the ground, and it became a serpent; and Moses fled from before it.

4 And the Lord said unto Moses, Put forth thine hand, and take it by the tail. And he put forth his hand, and caught it, and it became a rod in his hand:

5 That they may believe that the Lord God of their fathers, the God of Abraham, the God of Isaac, and the God of Jacob, hath appeared unto thee.

6 And the Lord said furthermore unto him, Put now thine hand into thy bosom. And he put his hand into his bosom: and when he took it out, behold, his hand was leprous as snow.

7 And he said, Put thine hand into thy bosom again. And he put his hand into his bosom again; and plucked it out of his bosom, and, behold, it was turned again as his other flesh.

8 And it shall come to pass, if they will not believe thee, neither harken to the voice of the first sign, that they will believe the voice of the latter sign.

9 And it shall come to pass, if they will not believe also these two signs, neither harken unto thy voice, that thou shalt take of the water of the river, and pour it upon the dry land: and the water which you take out of the river shall become blood upon the dry land.

In this third sign is represented the **Triune God** *and the blood of atonement which alone cleanses from sin and offsets its awful consequences.*

10 And Moses said unto the Lord, O my God, I am not eloquent, neither heretofore, nor since thou hast spoke unto thy servant: but I am slow of speech, and of a tongue.

The recognition of Moses's poor speaking ability suggests he could not take any of the glory from the deliverance of God's children from bondage. God listened to his honest confession and provided him a spokesman.

11 And the Lord said unto him, Who hath made man's mouth? Or who makes the dumb, or deaf, or the seeing, or the blind? Have not I the Lord?

12 Now therefore go, and I will be with thy mouth, and teach thee what thou shalt say.

13 And he said, O my Lord, send, I pray thee, by the hand of him whom thou wilt send.

This was enough to invoke the anger of God. God's anger put an end to the excuses. He was very much unlike Abraham who never once questioned God's command. Then he did the logical and natural thing to inform his father-in-law of God's new mission for his life.

14 And the anger of the Lord was kindled against Moses, and he said, Is not Aaron the Levite thy brother? I know that he can speak well. And also, behold he cometh forth to meet thee: and when he sees you, he will be glad in his heart.

15 And thou shalt speak unto him, and put words in his mouth: and I will be with thy mouth, and with his mouth, and will teach you what ye shall do.

16 And he shall be thy spokesman unto the people: and he shall be, even he shall be to thee instead of a mouth, and thou shalt be to him instead of God.

17 And thou shalt take this rod in thine hand, wherewith thou shalt do signs.

18 And Moses went and returned to Jethro his father-in-law, and said unto him, Let me go, I pray thee, and return unto my brethren which are in Egypt, and see whether they be yet alive. And Jethro said to Moses, Go in peace.

Moses Prepares to Return to Egypt, Exodus 4:19-26:

19 And the Lord said unto Moses in Midian, Go, return into Egypt: for all the men are dead which sought thy life.

20 And Moses took his wife, and his sons, and set them upon an ass, and he returned to the land of Egypt: and Moses took the rod of God in his hand.

21 And the Lord said unto Moses, When you go to return into Egypt, see that thou do all those wonders before Pharaoh, which I have put in thine hand: but I will harden

his heart, that he shall not let the people go.

The hardening of Pharaoh's heart is a very misunderstood statement. It means God allows him to resist as humanly possible.

22 And thou shalt say unto Pharaoh, Thus says the Lord, Israel is my son, even my firstborn:

23 And I say unto thee, Let my son go, that he may serve me: and if thou refuse to let him go, behold, I will slay thy son, even thy firstborn.

24 And it came to pass by the way in the inn, that the Lord met him, and sought to kill him.

Moses was still experiencing family problems, which put his life in danger. The danger of his life was not from his wife but from God. His wife had much to do with it but God held him responsible for his household.

25 Then Zipporah took a sharp stone, and cut off the foreskin of her son, and cast it at his feet, and said, Surely a bloody husband art thou to me.

Circumcision was a Hebrew custom which began with Abraham and was confirmed by a covenant. Abraham was 99 years old when he was circumcised. Zipporah was not happy with it and it created a problem for Moses. It was finally solved between them.

26 So he let him go: then she said, A bloody husband thou art because of the circumcision.

Aaron Becomes A Believer, Exodus 4:27-31:

27 And the Lord said to Aaron, Go into the wilderness to meet Moses. And he went, and met him in the mount of God (Horeb) and kissed him.

28 And Moses told Aaron all the words of the Lord who had sent him, and all the signs which he had commanded him.

29 And Moses and Aaron went and gathered together all the elders of the children of Israel:

Moses related to Aaron all the things God commanded him and all his experiences with God, and the rod He commanded him to use before Pharaoh. He was convinced by Moses' testimony. God told Aaron to meet Moses in the wilderness. That served to confirm Moses's testimony; he became a strong believer in the deliverance of Israel from bondage. The whole nation also became Believers.

30 And Aaron spoke all the words which the Lord had spoken unto Moses, and did the signs in the sight of the people.

31 And the people believed: and when they heard that the Lord had visited the children of Israel, and that he had looked upon their affliction, then they bowed their heads and worshipped.

The above verse shows what true worship is all about: it was singing and rejoicing; it wasn't the offering of blood sacrifices. Such manner of worship is acceptable; but at this time it was the acknowledgment of God's faithfulness and mercies with a deep sense of reverence expressed in the bowing of their heads was true worship. This act of worship was spontaneous and profound: it was not something they were asked to do. True believers know the way to worship.

Moses and Aaron Deliver God's Message to Pharaoh, Exodus 5:1-3:

1 And afterward Moses and Aaron went in, and told Pharaoh, Thus says the Lord God of Israel, Let my people go that they may hold a feast unto me in the wilderness.

2 And Pharaoh said, Who is the Lord, that I should obey his voice to let Israel go? I know not the Lord, neither will I let Israel go.

If Pharaoh had known the Lord, he would not have held them in bondage. Neither would he have freed them had he known the Lord. They were too important to the advancement of his kingdom and power. His ignorance of the existence of

God is one more evidence of spiritual blindness and the evil nature of sin. It is also indicative of the fact that sin cannot cure itself.

3 And they said, The God of the Hebrews hath met with us: Let us go, we pray thee, three days' journey into the desert, and sacrifice unto the Lord our God; lest he fall upon us with pestilence, or with the sword.

Pharaoh's Response, Exodus 5:4-14:

4 And the king of Egypt said unto them, Wherefore do ye, Moses and Aaron, let the people from their works? Get you unto your burdens.

5 And Pharaoh said, Behold the people of the land now are many, and ye make them rest from their burdens.

6 And Pharaoh commanded the same day the task masters of the people, and their officers, saying,

7 Ye shall no more give the people straw to make brick, as heretofore: let them go and gather straw for themselves.

8 And the tale of bricks, which they did make heretofore, ye shall lay upon them; ye shall not diminish aught thereof: for they be idle; therefore they cry, saying, Let us go and sacrifice unto our God.

9 Let there more work be laid upon the men, that they may labor therein; and let them not regard vain words.

10 And the taskmasters of the people went out, and their officers, and they spoke to the people, saying, Thus says Pharaoh, I will not give you straw.

11 Go ye, get you straw where ye can find it: yet not aught of your work shall be diminished.

Increasing their burden or giving them an impossible task was a further act of cruelty. It showed the evil state of Pharaoh's heart: it showed a heart that would continue to reject all Divine pleads for mercy, and not one that needed any hardening.

12 So the people were scattered abroad throughout all

the land of Egypt to gather stubble instead of straw.

13 And the taskmasters hasted them, saying, Fulfil your works, your daily tasks, as when there was straw.

14 And the officers of the children of Israel, which Pharaoh's taskmasters had set over them, were beaten, and demanded, Wherefore have ye not fulfilled your task in making brick both yesterday and today, as heretofore?

This was slavery at its worse; it robbed Pharaoh of all his humanity and he laid aside all his faculties of reasoning. The sad thing is that his heart was desperately wicked and he did not realize it.

A Response to a Response, Exodus 5: 15-19:

15 Then the officers of the children of Israel came and cried unto Pharaoh, saying, Wherefore deal you thus with your servants?

16 There is no straw given to thy servants, and they say to us, Make brick: and, behold, thy servants are beaten; but the fault is in thine own people.

17 But he said, Ye are idle, ye are idle: therefore ye say, Let us go and sacrifice to the Lord.

18 Go therefore now, and work; for there shall no straw be given you, yet shall ye deliver the tale of bricks.

*The verses above show that Pharaoh lost all moral restraints. These verses also imply that Pharaoh was a type of a greater taskmaster, Lucifer himself. Once he had someone in his slavery, he will not let go of that one until he is delivered by the **Atoning Blood.***

19 And the officers of the children of Israel did see that they were in evil case, after it was said, You shall not diminish aught from your bricks of your daily task.

The officers of the Children of Israel saw their assignment of an impossible task as a way to inflict physical punishment upon them, to abandon any hope of freedom. They needed more time to discuss with Moses the whole plan of their freedom from bondage. Moses listened to them and promised to take the matter to the Lord.

Moses intercedes with the Lord, Exodus 5:20-6: 1-30:

20 And they met Moses and Aaron, who stood in the way, as they came forth from Pharaoh:

21 And they said unto them, the Lord look upon you, and judge; because ye have made our savor to be abhorred in the eyes of Pharaoh, and in the eyes of his servants, to put a sword in their hand to slay us.

The officers of Israel and all others interpreted Moses' message as meaning instant deliverance, whereas there was nothing in that message to suggest that. As conditions became worse the children of Israel became desperate. Moses who was plainly told that Pharaoh would not willingly let Israel go was himself surprised by the worsened condition of the slavery.

22 And Moses returned unto the Lord, and said, Lord, wherefore hast thou so evil entreated this people? Why is it that thou hast sent me?

23 For since I came to Pharaoh to speak in thy name, he hath done evil to this people; neither hast thou delivered thy people at all.

*It was strange how the people lost their patience in a matter of days after waiting for hundreds of years for God's message of hope. There is one good thing which we can all learn from the situation at hand. Whenever trials **increase victory is near.** The Devil does not have a long time left to fight; but we have all **of eternity to enjoy the victory.***

6:1 Then the Lord said unto Moses, Now shalt thou see what I will do to Pharaoh: for with a strong hand shall he let them go, and with a strong hand shall he drive them out of his land.

2 And God spoke unto Moses, and said unto him, I am the Lord:

3 And I appeared unto Abraham, unto Isaac, and unto

Jacob, by the name of **God Almighty,** but by my name **JEHOVAH** was I not known to them.

4 And I have also established my covenant with them, to give them the land of Canaan, the land of their pilgrimage, wherein they were strangers.

5 And I have also heard the groaning of the children of Israel, whom the Egyptian keep in bondage; and I have remembered my covenant.

*God reminded Moses that He met with their fathers personally and revealed Himself to each of them. They all knew that He is the omnipotent God, believed and obeyed Him. Their fathers, however, did not know all about Him: they did not know Him by His name **JEHOVAH,** a name with special meaning to Israel. By His name JEHOVAH He was going to do things for His people from then on that the whole world would be talking about for ages. The world might not accept Him as their God but would not be unable to deny His eternal existence.*

6 Wherefore say unto the children of Israel, I am the Lord, and I will bring you out from under the burdens of the Egyptians, and I will rid you out of their bondage, and I will redeem you with a stretched out arm, and with great judgments:

7 And I will take you to me for a people, and I will be to you a God: and ye shall know that I am the Lord your God, which brings you out from under the burdens of the Egyptians.

8 And I will bring you in unto the land, concerning the which I did swear to give it to Abraham, to Isaac, and to Jacob; and I will give it you for an heritage: I am the lord.

In reiterating His promise of deliverance, God declared that it would be impossible for anyone, including the Egyptians, to deny that Israel was delivered from the bondage of Pharaoh by the omnipotent hand of the Eternal God. Moses was fully convinced, and had to convince all Israel of God's guarantee.

Moses Reasons with God, Exodus 6:9-30:

9 And Moses spoke so unto the children of Israel: but they hearkened not unto Moses for anguish of spirit, and for cruel bondage.

10 And the Lord spoke unto Moses, saying,

11 Go in, speak unto Pharaoh King of Egypt, that he let the children of Israel go out of his land.

12 And Moses spoke before the Lord, saying, Behold the children of Israel have not harkened unto me; how then shall Pharaoh hear me, who am of uncircumcised lips?

Moses was faithful each time in relaying God's message to the Children of Israel. Their bondage seemed too much to bear and they could not respond favorably to Moses' message. They seemed preoccupied with the hope of their immediate deliverance that they wanted to see and not to hear about it. Human nature always comes first, and only when it is forced aside by a greater power will it fall into its rightful place. Even with the best intentions, human nature needs continuous Divine help in order to succeed.

In the midst of confusion and uncertainty, Moses seemed to forget that he was not the one to do the convincing of the people or of Pharaoh. God's power was to do the convincing. Words only apply to moral reasoning; force applies to people who abandon reasoning.

13 And the Lord spoke unto Moses and unto Aaron, and gave them a charge unto the children of Israel, and unto Pharaoh King of Egypt, to bring the children of Israel out of the land of Egypt.

14 These being the heads of their fathers' houses: The sons of Reuben the first born of Israel; Hanoch, and Pallu, Hezron, and Carmi: these be the families of Reuben.

15 And the sons of Simeon; Jemuel, and Jamin, and Ohad, and Jachin, and Zohar, and Shaul the son of the Canaanitish woman: these are the families of Simeon.

16 And these are the names of the sons of Levi according

to their generations; Gershon, and Kohath, and Merari: and the years of the life of Levi were a hundred thirty and seven years.

17 The sons of Gershon; Libni, and Shimi, according to their families.

18 And the sons of Kohath; Amram, and Izhar, and Hebron, and Uzziel: and the years of the life of Kohath were an hundred thirty and three years.

19 And the sons of Merari; Mahali and Mushi: these are the families of Levi according to their generations.

20 And Amram took him Jochebed his father's sister to wife; and she bare him Aaron and Moses: and the years of the life of Amram were an hundred and thirty and seven years.

21 And the sons of Izhar; Korah, and Nepheg, and Zichri.

22 And the sons of Uzziel; Mishael, and Elzaphan, and Zithri.

23 And Aaron took him Elisheba, daughter of Amminnadab, sister of Naashon, to wife; and she bare him Nadab, and Abihu, Eleazar, and Ithamar.

24 And the sons of Korah; Assir, and Elkanah, and Abiasaph: these are the families of the Korhites.

25 And Eleazar Aaron's son took him one of the daughters of Putiel to wife; and she bare him Phinehas: these are the heads of the fathers of the Levites according to their families.

26 These are that Aaron and Moses, to whom the Lord said, Bring out the children of Israel from the land of Egypt according to their armies.

27 These are they which spoke to Pharaoh King of Egypt, to bring out the children of Israel from Egypt: these are that Moses and Aaron.

28 And it came to pass on the day when the Lord spoke unto Moses in the land of Egypt,

The occasion of the Exodus was the first time God spoke to

Moses in the land of Egypt.

29 That the Lord spoke unto Moses, saying, I am the Lord: speak thou unto Pharaoh king of Egypt all that I say unto thee.

30 And Moses said before the Lord, Behold, I am of uncircumcised lips, and how shall Pharaoh harken unto me?

The genealogy of Moses and Aaron is important to our understanding of the Levitical Priesthood. The Levitical Priesthood was at the heart of Israel's Theocracy and the tribe of Levi was chosen to minister the holy things. Aaron the High Priest and Moses the Prophet and head of Aaron and the nation were both from the tribe of Levi. Humanly speaking, both men were indispensable to the new nation.

From the genealogy we can identify the parents of Moses Aaron and Miriam. In verse 20 Amram took Jochebed for his wife who bore him Aaron and Moses (Miriam is not here mentioned). We can distinguish Gershon, Moses' predecessor from Gershom, his son (2:22). In most cases someone of one tribe gave the name of a predecessor of that tribe to his son. Moses seemed to have followed that custom in naming his first son.

Israel distinguished itself in keeping the most accurate records of its genealogy. That was why the birth of Christ could be traced back to the lineage of King David.

Moses Gains Greater Spiritual Status, Exodus 7:1-5:

1 And the Lord said unto Moses, See, I have made thee a god to pharaoh; and Aaron thy brother shall be thy prophet.

In Pharaoh's own eyes, he was the god of Egypt. It was, therefore, difficult to recognize any other God, particularly one that would encroach on his greatness and influence throughout his empire. But he would be inclined to listen to one whom he considered of his type, someone as egotistic and daring as he, may be someone who had magical powers. Seeing He did not know the difference between magic and miracle, he would recognize Moses a great magician.

God endowed Moses not with magical powers but with a token of omnipotence. This was greater than magical powers and would quickly demand his attention. So long as Moses remained obedient to his God he had the guarantee of miraculous power. God trusted him with that power and made Aaron his prophet. The Rod of God was the symbol of that power.

2 Thou shalt speak all that I have commanded thee: and Aaron thy brother shall speak unto Pharaoh, that he send the children of Israel out of his land.

3 And I will harden pharaoh's heart and multiply my signs and my wonders in the land of Egypt.

4 But Pharaoh shall not harken unto you, that I may lay my hand upon Egypt, and bring forth mine armies, and my people the children of Israel, out of the land of Egypt by great judgments.

5 And the Egyptians shall know that I am the Lord, when I stretch forth mine hand upon Egypt, and bring out the children of Israel from among them.

Moses was made to understand that God had His own schedule for Israel's deliverance; God wanted Moses to know that mere words would not be able to influence Pharaoh decision to free Israel from bondage; it would necessitate sign and miracles. Because Israel's deliverance was urgent, there was no time to waste——.Moses introduces the first miracle.

The Sign of Serpent, 1 Exodus 7:6-13

6 And Moses and Aaron did as the Lord commanded them, so did they.

7 And Moses was fourscore years old, and Aaron fourscore and three years old, when they spoke unto Pharaoh.

8 And the Lord spoke unto Moses and Aaron, saying,

9 When Pharaoh shall speak unto you, saying, Show a

miracle for you: then thou shalt say unto Aaron, Take thy rod, and cast it before pharaoh, and it shall become a serpent.

10 And Moses and Aaron went in unto Pharaoh, and they did so as the Lord had commanded: and Aaron cast down his rod before Pharaoh, and before his servants, and it became a serpent.

The first sign to Pharaoh of the serpent was intended to be an object lesson to mankind, reminding everyone of the fatal role the serpent played in the Fall of man and its continued influence over the affairs of mankind. In particular, the sign of the serpent was to inform Pharaoh that he was living under the evil influence of the serpent which represented Lucifer the creator of sin.

The sign of the serpent, therefore, initiated a series of Divine judgments. These judgments, on the one hand, describe the nature of sin; and on the other hand, the righteousness of God. The evil influence of sin on Pharaoh and the righteous ness of God created the historic circumstances of Israel's departure from Egypt. The subsequent judgments are more catastrophic, and show the catastrophic nature of sin.

The fact that the serpents of the magicians of Egypt were devoured by the sign of Moses' serpent was indicative of the fact that there were limitations to the power of the serpent. In particular the influence of the serpent over the kingdom of Egypt was going to be given a death blow by the God of a people who were enslaved in cruel bondage.

11 Then Pharaoh also called the wise men and the sorcerers: now the magicians of Egypt, they also did in like manner with their enchantments.

12 For they cast down every man his rod, and they became serpents; but Aaron's rod swallowed up their rods.

13 And he hardened Pharaoh's heart, that he harkened not unto them; as the Lord had said.

Pharaoh's heart was already hardened and God allowed

him to go as far as it was humanly possible. Because Pharaoh had decided he would not free the Children of Israel, God would intensify His signs and wonders. Some of these signs will be repeated during the coming Great Tribulation.

1. Waters Turned into Blood, Exodus 7:14-25:

14 And the Lord said unto Moses, Pharaoh's heart is hardened, he refuses to let the people go.

15 Get thee unto Pharaoh in the morning; lo, he goes out unto the water; and thou shalt stand by the river's brink against he come (until he comes); and the rod which was turned to a serpent shalt thou take in thine hand.

16 And thou shalt say unto him, The Lord God of the Hebrews hath sent me unto thee, saying, Let my people go, that they may serve me in the wilderness: and, behold, hitherto thou would not hear.

17 Thus says the Lord, in this thou shalt know that I am the Lord: behold, I will smite with the rod that is in mine hand upon the waters which are in the river, and they shall be turned to blood.

18 And the fish that is in the river shall stink; and the Egyptians shall loathe to drink of the water of the river.

19 And the Lord spoke unto Moses, Say unto Aaron, Take thy rod, and stretch out thine hand upon the waters of Egypt, upon the streams, upon their rivers, and upon their ponds, and upon all their pools of water, that they may become blood; and that there may be blood throughout all the land of Egypt, both in vessels of wood, and in vessels of stone.

20 And Moses and Aaron did so, as the Lord commanded; and he lifted up the rod and smote the waters that were in the river, in the sight of Pharaoh, and in the sight of his servants; and all the waters that were in the river were turned into blood.

21 And the fish that was in the river died; and the river

stank, and the Egyptians could not drink of the water of the river; and there was blood throughout all the land of Egypt.

Verses 14-21 show that Pharaoh was given a fair opportunity to free Israel from the bondage of slavery. In this opportunity the immediate consequences of not obeying the Divine command were clearly stated. He chose Divine Judgment instead of freeing God's people. His magician tried to compete but could not reverse God's judgment. This judgment corresponds with the judgment of two angels with the golden vials of Divine wrath in Revelation 16:3-4. The sea and rivers became blood, signifying human destruction in the latter part of the Great Tribulation.

22 And the magicians of Egypt did so with their enchantments: and Pharaoh's heart was hardened, neither did he harken unto them; as the Lord had said.

23 And Pharaoh turned and went into his house, neither did he set his heart to do this also.

24 And all the Egyptians dug round about the river for water to drink; for they could not drink of the water of the river. *This judgment of the contamination of the waters is also confirmed by the Trumpet Judgments of Revelation 8:10 which will be repeated during the Great Tribulation. Pharaoh and all the Egyptians had to live with the consequences of defying God's command. At least it taught them to appreciate the abundance of God's free gift of water. If they could, they would realize that the God of the Hebrews could have punished them at Will during all the years they willingly enslaved God's children.*

After 7 days Pharaoh shook his head and pretended nothing had happened.

2. The Plague of Frogs, Exodus 8:1-14:

1 And the Lord spoke unto Moses, Go unto Pharaoh, and say unto him, Thus says the Lord, Let my people go, that they may serve me.

2 And if thou refuse to let them go, behold, I will smite all thy borders with frogs:

3 And the river shall bring forth frogs abundantly, which shall go up and come into thine house, and into thy bed-chamber, and upon thy bed, and into the house of thy servants, and upon thy people, and into thine ovens, and into thy kneading-troughs.

4 And the frogs shall come both on thee, and upon thy people, and upon all thy servants.

5 And the Lord spoke unto Moses, Say unto Aaron, Stretch forth thine hand with thy rod over the streams, over the rivers, and over the ponds, and cause frogs to come up upon the land of Egypt.

6 And Aaron stretched out his hand over the waters of Egypt; and the frogs came up, and covered the land of Egypt.

The above six verses show how Pharaoh allowed another opportunity to go by unappreciated and the painful consequences he and his people had to endure. Again we see that his magicians competed but could not reverse the Divine judgment. Pharaoh began to look into his heart, and realized that God was a merciful God. For the first time he recognized that he needed the help of Moses and his God and promised to free Israel from bondage.

7 And the magicians did so with their enchantments, and brought up frogs upon the land of Egypt.

8 Then Pharaoh called for Moses and Aaron, and said, Entreat the Lord, that he may take away the frogs from me, and from my people; and I will let the people go, that they may do service unto the Lord.

Moses responded favorably,

9 And Moses said unto Pharaoh, Glory all over me: when shall I entreat for thee, and for thy servants, and for thy people, to destroy the frogs from thee and thy houses, that they may remain in the river only?

10 And he said, Tomorrow. And he said, Be it according to thy word: that you may know that there is none like unto the Lord our God.

Moses looked at their soon to be **DELIVERANCE** *as an opportunity to introduce the God of the Hebrews to Pharaoh. His God is the God of nature, the God of Heaven and Earth; and above all, is merciful and righteous and would not fail to judge an evil nation.*

11 And the frogs shall depart from thee, and from thy houses, and from thy servants, and from thy people; they shall remain in the river only.

12 And Moses and Aaron went out from Pharaoh: and Moses cried unto the Lord because of the frogs which he had brought against Pharaoh.

13 And the Lord did according to the word of Moses; and the frogs died out of the houses, out of the villages, and out of the fields.

14 And they gathered them together upon heaps: and the land stank.

Pharaoh experienced God's judgment but after judgment he experienced His mercy. Mercy is always God's unmerited favor. Pharaoh did not deserve God's mercy in this regard. No one deserves God's mercy; if that were not so, mercy would no more be mercy. After the Fall of man, God could to him in mercy

3. The Plague of Lice, Exodus 8:15-19:

15 But when Pharaoh saw that there was respite, he hardened his heart, and harkened not unto them; as the Lord had said.

16 And the Lord said unto Moses, Say unto Aaron, Stretch out thy rod, and smite the dust of the land, that it may become lice throughout all the land of Egypt.

17 And they did so; for Aaron stretched out his hand with his rod, and smote the dust of the earth, and it became lice

in man, and in beast; all the dust of the land became lice throughout all the land of Egypt.

18 And the magicians did so with their enchantments to bring forth lice, but they could not: so there were lice upon man and beast.

19 Then the magicians said unto Pharaoh, This is the finger of God: and Pharaoh's heart was hardened, and he harkened not unto them; as the Lord had said.

This sign, as the others, was on a national scale. Though the magicians tried, they could not duplicate it or any other. Pharaoh's attempt was to disprove the existence of the Hebrews' God. Pharaoh was angry because his authority was challenged by a greater power he could not comprehend. And again, he refused to free the children of Israel.

4. The Plague of Flies, Exodus 8:20-32:

20 And the Lord said unto Moses, Rise up early in the morning, and stand before Pharaoh; lo, he cometh forth to the water; and say unto him, Thus says the Lord, Let my people go, that they may serve me.

21 Else, if thou wilt not let my people go, behold, I will send swarm of flies upon thee, and upon thy servants, and upon thy people, and into thy houses; and the houses of the Egyptians shall be full of swarms of flies, and also the ground whereon they are.

22 And I will sever in that day the land of Goshen, in which my people dwell, that no swarms of flies shall be there; to the end you may know that I am the Lord in the midst of the earth.

23 And I will put a division between my people and thy people: tomorrow shall this sign be.

In the above verses, God was very clear and direct. Pharaoh had to know that he and his people were singled out for Divine judgment. He also had to know that the God of the Hebrews was the Supreme God of the Universe. Though he did not know Him, the Hebrews knew Him and because of their bondage they cried out to Him and He heard them. They had been in bondage for a long time and He came to end it. Pharaoh was in deep trouble with God.

24 And the Lord did so; and there came a grievous swarm of flies into the house of Pharaoh, and into his servants' houses, and into all the land of Egypt: the land was corrupted by reason of the swarm of flies.

25 And Pharaoh called for Moses and Aaron, and said, Go ye, sacrifice to your God in the land.

26 And Moses said it is not meet so to do; for we shall sacrifice the abomination of the Egyptians to the Lord our God: lo, shall we sacrifice the abomination of the Egyptians before their eyes, and will they not stone us?

27 We will go three days journey into the wilderness, and sacrifice to the Lord our God, as he shall command us.

In the above verses, as always, Moses delivered a clear response to Pharaoh's wishes and explained exactly the way of the worship of their God. They could not worship Him as they pleased; they could only worship as He commanded them. 28 And Pharaoh said, I will let you go that ye may sacrifice to the Lord your God in the wilderness; only ye shall not go very far away: entreat for me.

Pharaoh failed to realize that he was no longer in a position to set the conditions of Israel's freedom. He showed that he and his magicians could not reverse the consequences of Divine judgment. His plea to Moses for help showed that he was actually at the mercy of a God he did not really know. Yet he would conveniently use Moses and His God as long as necessary.

29 And Moses said, Behold, I go out from thee, and I will entreat the Lord that the swarms of flies may depart from Pharaoh, from his servants, and from his people, tomorrow: but let not Pharaoh deal deceitfully anymore in not letting the people go to sacrifice to the Lord.

By now Moses realized that Pharaoh's words could not be trusted. He, nevertheless, kept his promise of entreating on his behalf.

30 And Moses went out from Pharaoh, and entreated the Lord.

31 And the Lord did according to the word of Moses; and he removed the swarms of flies from Pharaoh, and from his servants, and from his people; and there remained not one.

32 And Pharaoh hardened his heart at this time also, neither would he let the people go.

With his head Pharaoh acknowledged God's mercy but with his heart was not touched, and continued as before to deny the children of Israel their freedom. He refused to learn the lesson of the signs and God continued to teach him.

5. Plague of the Animals, Exodus 9:1-7:

1 Then the Lord said unto Moses, Go in unto Pharaoh, and tell him, Thus says the Lord God of the Hebrews, Let my people go, that they may serve me.

2 For if thou refuse to let them go, and will hold them still,

3 Behold, the hand of the Lord is upon thy cattle which is in the field, upon the horses, upon the asses, upon the camels, upon the oxen, and upon the sheep: there shall be a very grievous murrain.

4 And the Lord shall sever between the cattle of Israel and the cattle of Egypt: and there shall nothing die of all that is the children's of Israel.

5 And the Lord appointed a set time, saying, Tomorrow the Lord shall do this thing in the land.

6 And the Lord did that thing on the morrow, and all the cattle of Egypt died: but of the cattle of the children of Israel died not one.

God clearly shows a distinction between Israel's animals.

7 And Pharaoh sent, and, behold, there was not one of the cattle of the Israelites dead. And the heart of Pharaoh was hardened, and he did not let the people go.

This judgment had severe economic consequences, yet again Pharaoh refused to free the Children of Israel.

6. The Boils on Man and Beast, Exodus 9:8-11:

8 And the Lord said unto Moses and unto Aaron, Take to you handfuls of ashes of the furnace, and let Moses sprinkle it toward the heaven in the sight of Pharaoh.

9 And it shall become small dust in all the land of Egypt, and shall be a boil breaking forth with blains upon man, and upon beast, throughout all the land of Egypt.

10 And they took the ashes of the furnace, and stood before Pharaoh; and Moses sprinkled it up towards heaven; and it became a boil breaking forth with blains upon man, and upon beast.

11 And the magicians could not stand before Moses because of the boils; for the boil was upon the magicians, and upon all the Egyptians.

This judgment will be repeated during the Great Tribulation (Revelation 16:2). Pharaoh was moved but remained undecided

7. The Hail of Fire, Exodus 9:12-26:

12 And the Lord hardened the heart of Pharaoh, and he harkened not unto them; as the Lord had spoken unto Moses.

13 And the Lord said unto Moses, Rise up early in the morning, and stand before Pharaoh, and say unto him, Thus says the Lord God of the Hebrews, Let My people go, that they may serve me.

14 For I will at this time send all my plagues upon thine heart, and upon thy servants, and upon thy people; that you may know that there is none like me in all the earth.

15 For now I will stretch out my hand that I may smite thee and thy people with pestilence; and thou shalt be cut off from the earth.

16 And in very deed for this cause I have raised thee up, for to show in thee my power; and that my name may be declared throughout all the earth.

17 As yet exalt yourself against my people, that thou wilt not let them go?

It was not unusual that Pharaoh had a feeling of superiority towards the Hebrews because he saw himself as the god of Egypt. This judgment revealed that his pride figured prominently into his refusal to free the children of Israel. This was the very thing that made his heart what it was; God had no need to make his heart into something it had already been. Long before God demonstrated the first sign to Pharaoh, He knew the complete state of his heart. God saw a heart of pride in Pharaoh that would resist to the end His just demands for Israel's freedom from bondage. With the arrogance of Pharaoh, God foreknew it would take no ordinary and natural effort to free Israel from his bondage. So arrogant was Pharaoh that God had no choice except to exercise His mighty power.

By submitting his people to the severe consequences of God's judgments, Pharaoh showed more cruelty to his own people than to the Children of Israel. It took God's judgments to reveal the depth of Pharaoh's heart. And yet in a way more profound, these judgments revealed God's justice and mercy. Thereby He demonstrated to the whole world not only His power but His nature. The judgments were executed upon Pharaoh and his people but the lessons are for the whole world. This judgment will be repeated during the Great Tribulation (Revelation 8:7).God did not fail to execute the Rain of Hail upon Pharaoh, hail, such as not been seen in Egypt since the foundation thereof even until now.

18 Behold, tomorrow about this time I will cause it to

rain a very grievous hail, such as not been seen in Egypt since the foundation thereof even until now.

19 Send therefore now, and gather thy cattle, and all thou hast in the field; for upon every man and beast which shall be found in the field, and shall not be brought home, the hail shall come down upon them, and they shall die.

In verse 19, God extended a hand of mercy to Pharaoh and his people.

20 He that feared the word of Lord among the servants of Pharaoh made his servants and his cattle flee into the houses:

21 And he that regarded not the word of the Lord left his servants and his cattle in the field.

22 And the Lord said unto Moses, Stretch forth thine hand toward heaven, that there may be hail in all the land of Egypt, upon man, and upon beast, and upon every herb of the field throughout the land of Egypt.

23 And Moses stretched forth his rod toward heaven: and the Lord sent thunder and hail, and the fire ran along upon the ground; and the Lord rained hail upon the land of Egypt.

Destruction of the Hail 9:24-26:

The hail of fire corresponds to the judgment of the Vial of Wrath poured by the fourth angel and also with the first Trumpet Judgment in Revelation 16:8-9; 8: 7.

24 So there was hail, and fire mingled with the hail, very grievous, such as there was none like it in all land of Egypt since it became a nation.

25 And the hail smote throughout all the land of Egypt, all that was in the field, both man and beast; and the hail smote every herb of the field, and brake every tree of the field.

26 Only in the land of Goshen, where the children of Israel were, was there no hail.

Pharaoh's Response, 9:27-33: And Pharaoh sent, and called for Moses and Aaron, and said unto them, I have sinned this time; the Lord is righteous, and I and my people are wicked.

Pharaoh acknowledged that he sinned in refusing to free Israel from bondage; acknowledged God's righteous judgments; but yet refused to repent. Again he expressed the desire for mercy but not for a right relationship with God.

28 Entreat the Lord (for it is enough) that there be no more mighty thundering and hail; and I will let you go, and ye shall stay no longer.

29 And Moses said unto him, As soon as I am gone out of the city, I will spread abroad my hands unto the Lord; and the thunder shall cease, neither shall there be any more hail; that you may know that the earth is the Lord's.

30 But as for thee and thy servants, I know that ye will not yet fear the Lord God.

Something was missing from the equation, how could it be that his slaves knew the Lord, yet the king of Egypt knew not the Lord? He sought after God by reason and not by faith. Today the majority of human beings have taken Pharaoh's approach; and, therefore, have not found God. In the meantime the desolation was all around.

31 And the flax and the barley was smitten: for the barley was in the ear, and the flax was bolled.

32 But the wheat and the rie were not smitten: for they were not grown up.

33 And Moses went out of the city from Pharaoh, and spread abroad his hands unto the Lord: and the thunders and hail ceased, and the rain was not poured upon the earth.

Pharaoh then had the time to reconsider his ways, yet refused another time to free the children of Israel.

8. The Plague of Locusts, 9: 34-10:1-15:

34 And when Pharaoh saw that the rain and the hail and the thunders were ceased, he sinned yet more, and hardened his heart, he and his servants.

35 And the heart of Pharaoh was hardened, neither would he let the children of Israel go; as the Lord had spoken by Moses.

10:1: And the Lord said unto Moses, Go in unto Pharaoh: for I have hardened his heart, and the heart of his servants, that I might show these my signs before him:

2 And that you may tell in the ears of thy son, and of thy son's son, what things I have wrought in Egypt, and my signs which I have done among them; that ye may know how that I am the Lord.

Since man cannot find God by human reasoning, in the case of Pharaoh, God took the initiative to reveal Himself, and did so in a way in which it was impossible not to accept the revelation of His eternal existence. Pharaoh who continued to sin after 9 pleas of mercy by Moses, accepted the mighty revelation of God's existence and righteousness.

This mighty revelation of God's existence by His judgments upon Pharaoh and his people was to be memorialized by the Children of Israel by telling it from one generation to the other forever. Thus not one of the Children of Israel would ever question the existence of God.

By then Pharaoh knew of God's existence but failed to show obedience to Him. Without obedience to God the revelation of His existence has little value.

Pharaoh was using God's mercies conveniently and God was displeased. Again Moses and Aaron delivered a strong warning of another impending judgment of even greater consequences than previously.

This judgment will be repeated during the Great Tribulation (Revelation 9:1-5). The exception is that during the Great Tribulation the locusts will punish humans.

3 And Moses and Aaron came in unto Pharaoh, and said

unto him, Thus says the Lord God of the Hebrews, How long wilt thou refuse to humble thyself before me? Let my people go that they may serve me.

4 Else, if thou refuse to let my people go, behold, tomorrow will I bring the locusts into thy coast:

5 And they shall cover the face of the earth, that one cannot be able to see the face of the earth: and they shall eat the residue of that which is escaped, which remain unto you from the hail, and shall eat every tree which growth for you out of the field:

6 And they shall fill thy houses, and the houses of all thy servants, and the houses of all the Egyptians; which neither thy fathers, nor thy fathers' fathers have seen, since the day that they were upon the earth unto this day. And he turned himself, and went out from pharaoh.

Pharaoh's servants had some advice for him, but would he take it?

7 And Pharaoh's servants said unto him, How long shall this man be a snare unto us? Let the men go, that they may serve the Lord their God: know you not that Egypt is destroyed?

Pharaoh was made to face the sad fact -- Egypt was being destroyed before his very eyes, yet he could not see it.

8 And Moses and Aaron were brought again unto Pharaoh: and he said unto them, Go, serve the Lord your God: but who are they that shall go?

Moses quickly rejected Pharaoh's terms and insisted on his own terms. He emphasized the two pillars of society: the family, and the means of its existence, its possessions.

9 And Moses said, We will go with our young and with our old, with our sons and with our daughters, with our flocks and with our herds will we go; for we must hold a feast unto the Lord.

10 And he said unto them, Let the Lord be so with you, as I will let you go, and your little ones: look to it; for evil is

before you.

Pharaoh did not know God when Moses first delivered God's message to him, so it was no surprise that he did not know what was evil. Quickly he showed he could not be trusted for a day:

11 Not so: go now ye that are men, and serve the Lord; for that ye did desire. And they were driven out from Pharaoh's presence.

12 And the Lord said unto Moses, Stretch forth thine hand over the land of Egypt for the locusts, that they may come upon the land of Egypt, and eat every herb of the land, even all that the hail hath left.

God had to honor His word:

13 And Moses stretched forth his rod over the land of Egypt, and the Lord brought an east wind upon the land all that day, and all that night; and when it was morning, the east wind brought the locusts.

14 And the locusts went up over all the land of Egypt, and rested in all the coasts of Egypt: very grievous were they; neither after them shall be such.

15 For they covered the face of the whole earth, so that the land was darkened; and they did eat every herb of the land, and all the fruit of the trees which the hail had left: and there remained not any green thing in the trees, or in the herbs of the field, through all the land of Egypt.

Pharaoh's Response, 10:16-19: Then Pharaoh called for Moses and Aaron in haste, and he said, I have sinned against the Lord your God and against you.

17 Now therefore forgive, I pray thee, my sin only this once, and entreat the Lord your God, that he may take away from me this death only.

Here Pharaoh acknowledged God but not the way you would expect. He acknowledged Him because there was a need for His help, a need that was greater than his capacity to handle. Again, the forgiveness he sought was to be temporary, not lasting because he was never sincere. At a time when it was most important Pharaoh could not help his people; he had to turn to Moses for help. Then he was not as great as he thought

18 And he went forth from Pharaoh, and entreated the Lord.

19 And the Lord turned a mighty strong west wind, which took away the locusts, and cast them into the Red Sea; there remained not one locust in all the coast of Egypt.

Pharaoh had time to reconsider the matter and again did not repent.

9. The Darkness, Exodus 10:20-29:

20 But the Lord hardened Pharaoh's heart, so that he would not let the children of Israel go.

21 And the Lord said unto Moses, Stretch out thine hand toward heaven, that there may be darkness over the land of Egypt, even darkness which may be felt.

22 And Moses stretched forth his hand toward heaven; and there was a thick darkness in all the land of Egypt three days:

23 They saw not one another, neither rose any from his place for three days: but all the children of Israel had light in their dwellings.

*This kind of darkness reminds us of the outer-darkness Christ speaks about in St. Matthew 25:30. This judgment corresponds to the Trumpet Judgment of the fourth angel in Revelation 8:12. The Sun, Moon, and stars withheld their light, causing darkness on the Earth. Darkness is a forewarning of **impending death.** During the Great Tribulation, God will again strike the Earth with darkness on a scale never experienced before (Revelation 16: 10-11).*

Pharaoh's Response, 10:24-29: And Pharaoh called unto Moses, and said, Go ye, serve the Lord; only let your flocks and your herds be stayed: your little ones also let go with you.

Here Pharaoh repeated his conditions for freeing the Children of Israel; and Moses countered with his own conditions. Pharaoh considered himself the god of Egypt and he had never been challenged like that before; it was difficult for him to submit to the God of the Hebrews

25 And Moses said, Thou must give us also sacrifices and burnt offerings, that we may sacrifice unto the our God.

26 Our cattle also shall go with us; there shall not an hoof be left behind; for thereof must we take to serve the Lord our God; and we know not with what we must serve the Lord, until we come thither.

27 But the Lord hardened Pharaoh's heart, and he would not let them go.

28 And Pharaoh said unto him, Get thee from me, take heed to thyself, see my face no more; for in that day you see my face you shall die.

29 And Moses said, Thou hast spoken well, I will see thy face again no more.

This was to be the final departure and in it was a spirit of goodwill. As a matter of fact, it was an ultimatum given by a king who desperately needed Moses' help. We will see how Pharaoh's ultimatum compelled God's own **ultimatum.**

10.The Death of the First Born, Exodus 11:1-12:28-42:

1 And the Lord said unto Moses, Yet I will bring one plague more upon Pharaoh, and upon Egypt; afterwards he will let you go hence: when he shall let you go, he shall surely thrust you out hence altogether.

2 Speak now in the ears of the people, and let every man borrow of his neighbor, and every woman of her neighbor's jewels of silver, and jewels of gold.

3 And the Lord gave the people favor in the sight of the Egyptians. Moreover the man Moses was very great in the land of Egypt, in the sight of Pharaoh's servants, and in the sight of the people.

*The special favors were given the people but the Egyptians did not know the Children of Israel were getting ready to leave. Without them the Egyptian empire would be diminished. In the end, we see the **immortality and the national glory** of Moses, for it was Moses who was looked upon as a god in Egypt, not that he wanted it to be so; but he tied his destiny to the destiny of the Hebrew salves.*

The Ultimatum Is Given, Exo. 11:4-10:

4 And Moses said, Thus says the Lord, About midnight I will go out into the midst of Egypt:

5 And all the first born in the land of Egypt shall die, from the first born of Pharaoh that sits upon his throne, even unto the first born of the maidservant that is behind the mill; and all the first born of beasts.

6 And there shall be a great cry throughout all the land of Egypt, such as there was none like it, nor shall be like it any more.

7 But against any of the children of Israel shall not a dog move his tongue, against man or beast: that ye may know that the Lord doth put a difference between the Egyptians and Israel.

8 And all these thy servants shall come down unto me, and bow down themselves unto me, saying, Get thee out and all the people that follow thee: and after that I will go out. And he went out from Pharaoh in a great anger.

9 And the Lord said unto Moses, Pharaoh shall not harken unto you; that my wonders may be multiplied in the land of Egypt.

10 And Moses and Aaron did all these wonders before Pharaoh: and the Lord hardened Pharaoh's heart, so that he would not let the children of Israel go out of the land.

*Moses had enough with Pharaoh; he knew something very sad was about to happen, which he did not want to see or hear – the death of all the **first born** of man and beast in the* *land of Egypt. And for the first time Moses refused to restrain his **righteous anger.***

Preparation for the Midnight Cry, Exo. 12:1-13:

1 And the Lord spoke unto Moses and Aaron in the land of Egypt, saying,

2 This month shall be unto you the beginning of months: it shall be the first month of the year to you.

3 Speak ye unto all the congregation of Israel, saying, In the tenth day of this month they shall take to them every man a lamb, according to the house of their fathers, a lamb for a house:

4 And if the house be too little for the lamb, let him and his neighbor next unto his house take it according to the number of the souls; every man according to his eating shall make your count for the lamb.

This was to be a most solemn occasion; it was to be prepared a certain time of a certain day, and of a certain kind, and its blood was to be applied a certain way. Unknowing to them, the Passover Lamb foreshadowed in all aspects another Passover Lamb, God's Only Son.

5 Your lamb shall be without blemish, a male of the first year: ye shall take it out from the sheep, or from the goats:

6 And ye shall keep it up until the fourteenth day of the same month: and the whole assembly of the congregation of Israel shall kill it in the evening.

Did not the whole nation of Israel crucify Christ at evening time, the fourteenth day of Abib?

7 And they shall take of the blood, and strike it on the two side posts and on the upper door post of the houses, wherein they shall eat it.

8 And they shall eat the flesh in that night, roast with fire and unleavened bread; and with bitter herbs they shall eat it.

The bitter herbs symbolize that Israel's future life would

not be all joy. Did not Christ observe the Passover with His disciples the last night before His death?

9 Eat not of it raw, nor sodden at all with water, but roast with fire; his head with his legs, and with the purtenance thereof.

10 And ye shall let nothing of it remain until the morning; and that which remains of it until the morning ye shall burn with fire.

11 And thus shall ye eat it; with your loins girded, your shoes on your feet, and your staff in your hand; and ye shall eat it in haste: it is the Lord's Passover.

After the Passover, did not Christ and His disciples quickly go to the garden of Gethsemane to pray?

12 For I will pass through the land of Egypt this night, and will smite all the firstborn in the land of Egypt, both man and beast; and against all the gods of Egypt I will execute judgment: I am the LORD.

13 And the blood shall be to you for a token upon the houses where ye are: and when I see the blood, I will pass over you, and the plague shall not be upon you to destroy you, when I smite the land of Egypt.

The blood of the lamb was a protection for the Children of Israel against the **DEATH ANGEL;** *the atoning blood of Christ is our protection against the consequences of sin, including eternal death.*

The Children of Israel Obeyed, Exo. 12:28-42:

28 and the children of Israel went away and did as the Lord had commanded Moses and Aaron, so did they.

29 And it came to pass, that at midnight the Lord smote all the firstborn in the land of Egypt, from the firstborn of Pharaoh that sat on his throne unto the firstborn of the captive that was in the dungeon; and all the firstborn of cattle.

30 And Pharaoh rose up in the night, he, and all his

servants, and all the Egyptians; and there was a great cry in Egypt; for there was not a house where there was not one dead

This was the tenth of a series of Divine judgments executed upon Pharaoh and his people, which brought an end to the historic circumstances of the Exodus of the Children of Israel from the bondage of Egypt. It shows the catastrophic nature of sin, and yet the righteousness and faithfulness of God. It also shows the human nature of Pharaoh: he complied to the Divine demand in order to save his live. However, he gave no indication that he wanted the God of Moses and the Hebrews to be a part of his life. Apparently his heart remained unchanged. But he never again would have the opportunity of the benefit of Moses' prayer for Divine mercy. Not one of those 10 opportunities did he use to respond to God's mercy in a personal and lasting way. Yet he could no longer question the eternal existence of God; he only felt no personal need for Him.

Besides the leprous hand of Moses, there were 12 signs altogether. The first sign to Pharaoh was the sign of the serpent. These12, signs symbolized the 12 tribes of Israel. Underneath these signs was a Divine message saying, Israel is special. These 12 signs displayed a measure of God's omnipotence. But greater still was a display of God's righteousness and faithfulness. Pharaoh felt these Divine judgments but he also saw the righteousness of God and his people's unrighteousness. Finally he bowed to God's demand

The death of the first born in Egypt was the **Midnight Cry** *heard throughout the land of Egypt. Pharaoh and his people were in a state of panic.*

31 And he called for Moses and Aaron by night, and said, Rise up, and get you forth from among my people, both ye and the children of Israel; and go, serve the Lord, as ye have said.

32 Also take your flocks and your herds, as ye have said

and be gone; and bless me also.

Sadly, Pharaoh felt the need for a Divine blessing but not the need for a right relationship with God, one which only came about by true repentance.

33 And the Egyptians were urgent upon the people, that they might send them out of the land in haste; for they said, We be all dead men.

34 And the people took their dough before it was leavened, their kneading troughs being bound up in their clothes upon their shoulders.

35 And the children of Israel did according to the word of Moses; and they borrowed of the Egyptians jewels of silver, and jewels of gold, and raiment:

36 And the Lord gave the people favor in the sight of the Egyptians, so that they lent unto them such things as they required. And they spoiled the Egyptians.

37 And the children of Israel journeyed from Rameses to Succoth, about six hundred thousand on foot that were men besides children.

Women and children were not counted. An estimate of the total Hebrew population was 2,000,000. The Egyptians that were with them were not included.

38 And a mixed multitude went up also with them; and flocks and herds, even very much cattle.

Verse 38 indicates that a number of the Egyptians went with them to the Promised Land. Look on the map and see Rameses the point of their departure.

39 And they baked unleavened cakes of the dough which they brought forth out of Egypt, for it was not leavened; because they were thrust out of Egypt, and could not tarry, neither had they prepared for themselves any victual.

40 Now the sojourning of the children of Israel, who dwelt in Egypt, was four hundred and thirty years. (*That was approximately twice the age of the United States of America.)*

41 And it came to pass at the end of the four hundred

and thirty years, even the selfsame day, it came to pass that all the hosts of the Lord went out from the land of Egypt.

42 It is a night to be much observed unto the Lord for bringing them out from the land of Egypt: this is that night of the Lord to be observed of all the children of Israel in their generations.

The Command to Observe the Passover, Exodus 12:14-20:

The event of the Passover brought the deliverance of the Children of Israel from the bondage of Egypt. By reason of its nature, the Lord commanded it to be an ordinance of the Children of Israel forever. It is described below. When Pharaoh saw the death of the first born, he was afraid for his own life and hastily commanded Israel to go and serve their own God.

14 And this day shall be to you for a memorial; and ye shall keep it a feast to the Lord throughout your generation; ye shall keep it a feast by an ordinance forever.

15 Seven days shall ye eat unleavened bread; even the first day ye shall put away leaven out of your houses: for whosoever eats leavened bread from the first day until the seventh day, that soul shall be cut off from Israel.

16 And in the first day there shall be an holy convocation, and in the seventh day there shall be an holy convocation to you; no manner of work shall be done in them, save that which every man must eat, that only may be done of you.

17 And ye shall observe the feast of unleavened bread; for in this selfsame day have I brought your armies out of the land of Egypt: therefore shall ye observe this day in your generations by an ordinance forever.

18 In the first month, on the fourteenth day of the month at even, ye shall eat unleavened bread, until the one and twentieth day of the month at even.

19 Seven days shall there be no leaven found in your

houses: for whosoever eats that which is leavened, even that soul shall be cut off from the congregation of Israel, whether he be a stranger , or born in the land.

20 Ye shall eat nothing leavened; in all your habitations

Map of Israel's Journey of the First Year

shall ye eat unleavened bread.

The Passover occurred on the fourteenth day of Abib at 3 PM. The lamb killed and its blood was daubed on the door posts and lintel. Its flesh was roasted and eaten with unleavened bread. In the yearly observance, the process must be repeated 7 days, from the fourteenth day of Abib, the New Year, to the twenty first day. The first day of the week is to be a holy assembly of the congregation, and also the twenty first day. The seven day celebration shows its importance

The Event of the Passover, Exo. 12:21-27:

21 Then Moses called for all the elders of Israel, and said unto them, Draw out and take you a lamb according to your families, and kill the Passover.

22 And ye shall take a bunch of hyssop, and dip it in the blood that is in the basin, and strike the lintel and the two side posts with the blood that is in the basin; and none of you shall go out at the door of his house until the morning.

The hyssop, a medicinal plant, was generally used for ceremonial purposes, in cleansing and purification.

23 For the Lord will pass through to smite the Egyptians; and when he sees the blood upon the lintel, and on two side posts, the Lord will pass over the door, and will not suffer the destroyer to come in unto your houses to smite you.

24 And ye shall observe this thing for an ordinance to thee and to thy sons forever.

25 And it shall come to pass, when ye be come to the land which the Lord will give you, according as he hath promised, that ye shall keep this service.

The Passover was so important that on that night the Children of Israel were told to observe it every year.

26 And it shall come to pass, when your children shall say unto you, What mean ye by this service?

27 That ye shall say, It is the sacrifice of the LORD'S Passover, who passed over the houses of the children of

Israel in Egypt, when he smote the Egyptians and delivered our houses. And the people bowed the head and worshipped.

Exceptions to the Passover, Exo. 12:43-51:

43 And the Lord said unto Moses and Aaron, This is the ordinance of the Passover: There shall no stranger eat thereof:

44 But every man's servant that is bought for money, when thou hast circumcised him, then shall he eat thereof.

45 A foreigner and an hired servant shall not eat thereof.

46 In one house shall it be eaten; thou shalt not carry forth aught of the flesh abroad out of the house; neither shall ye break a bone thereof.

47 All the congregation of Israel shall keep it.

48 And when a stranger shall sojourn with thee, and will keep the Passover to the Lord, let all his males be circumcised, and then let him come near and keep it; and he shall be as one that is born in the land: for no uncircumcised person shall eat thereof.

In Verse 46 the Pre-Incarnate Lamb is symbolized: not one bone of the Passover Lamb was to be broken. Verse 45 is the exception: foreigners and strangers were not allowed to participate except they met the condition of circumcision. By meeting this condition, they became like naturally born citizen. The emphasis here again placed by Moses on the observance of the Passover shows it importance.

49 One law shall be to him that is home-born, and unto the stranger that sojourns among you.

50 Thus did all the children of Israel; as the Lord commanded Moses and Aaron, so did they.

51 And it came to pass the selfsame day, that the Lord did bring the children of Israel out of the land of Egypt by their armies.

The Lessons of the Passover, Exodus 13:1-16:

This is the third time Moses addresses the children of Israel on the subject of the Passover. It represents all the other eleven signs shown in the land of Egypt and symbolizes, as nothing else, the Pre-Incarnate Christ's atonement. Such an event is to be memorialized by all generations of the children of Israel. There are some important lessons for them to learn and to teach their children, generation to generation. The importance of the Passover and the lessons therefrom are described below.

1.The First Born of Man and Beast Are the Lord's, Exo. 13:1-2, 11-13:

1 And the Lord spoke unto Moses, saying,

2 Sanctify unto me all the first born, whatsoever opens the womb among the children of Israel, both of man and of beast: it is mine.

11 And it shall be when the Lord shall bring thee into the land of the Canaanites, as he swore unto thee and to thy fathers, and shall give it thee,

12 That thou shalt set apart unto the Lord all that opens the matrix, and every firstling that cometh of a beast which thou hast; the males shall be the Lord's.

13 And every firstling of an ass thou shalt redeem with a lamb; and if thou wilt not redeem it, then thou shalt break his neck: and all the firstborn of man among the children shalt thou redeem.

Redemption is an Old Testament word which had its origin in the Passover. The Passover occasioned the death of the first born of man and beast of the Egyptians. From thence the Lord claimed all the first born of man and beast in Israel as His. The Lord made a way by which all the first born in Israel could be bought back or redeemed. This made it impossible for the Passover to be forgotten. The parents should anticipate questions about the Passover and the buying back of some children and some animals.

14 And it shall be when your son asks thee in time to come, saying, What is this? That thou shalt say unto him, By strength of hand the Lord brought us out from Egypt, from the house of bondage.

15 And it came to pass, when Pharaoh would hardly let us go, that the Lord slew all the firstborn in the land of Egypt, both the firstborn of man, and the first born of beast: therefore I sacrifice to the Lord all that opens the matrix, being males; but all the firstborn of my children I redeem.

16 And it shall be for a token upon thine hand, and for frontlets between thine eyes: for by strength of hand the Lord brought us forth out of Egypt.

During the commemoration of the Passover they had to wear frontlets on their foreheads with the Scriptures, or on their hands.

2. No Leavened Bread to Be Eaten, Ex. 13: 3, 7:

3 And Moses said unto the people, Remember this day, in which ye came out from Egypt, out of the house of bondage; for by strength of hand the Lord brought you out from this place: there shall no leavened bread be eaten.

7 Unleavened bread shall be eaten seven days; and there shall no leavened bread be seen with thee, neither shall there be leaven seen with thee in all thy quarters.

Life became different for the children of Israel from the very eve of the Passover. The eating of unleavened bread on the eve of the first Passover in Egypt and during its commemoration was to remind them of their freedom from the bondage of slavery. On the other the hand, the leavened bread represented the life style of Egypt.

3. Time and Duration of the Passover, Ex.13:4,5-6,10:

4 This day came ye out in the month Abib.

5 And it shall be when the Lord shall bring thee into the land of the Canaanites, and the Hittites, and the Amorites

and the Hivites, and the Jebusites, which he swore unto your fathers to give thee, a land flowing with milk and honey, that thou shalt keep this service in this month.

6 Seven days thou shalt eat unleavened bread, and in the seventh day shall be a feast to the Lord.

The Passover marks the beginning of a new life and a new year for Israel. The month, Abib was to be the first month of the New Year; on the fourteenth day, the Passover was to be celebrated; it was to be a one day celebration. Then followed the Feast of Unleavened Bread. It lasted 7 days, beginning the fifteenth day following the Passover. See Exodus 23:1-8.

10 Thou shalt therefore keep this ordinance in his season from year to year.

4. The Passover a of Memorial, Ex. 13:8-9:

8 And thou shalt show thy son in that day, saying, This is done because of that which the Lord did unto me when I came forth out of Egypt.

9 And it shall be for a sign unto thee upon thine hand, and for a memorial between thine eyes, that the Lord's law may be in thy mouth: for with a strong hand the Lord brought thee out of Egypt.

SUMMARY

We close the chapter with the most solemn Jewish ordinance of the Passover. Like nothing else, it symbolizes Israel's deliverance from the bondage of Egyptian slavery. On the other hand, it symbolizes the Eternal Passover Lamb, God's Only Son.

However, the historic circumstances of Israel's freedom from the bondage of Egypt began with the 70 Member Hebrew Family. How could one even begin to think of anything about the Exodus, unless one has an understanding of Israel's brief history provided in Exodus 1.

There we learn of God's blessings on Israel, causing them to grow exceedingly, to the amazement and wonder of the Egyptians. These Divine blessings caused jealousy and cruelty from the Egyptians. These were the elements in the foundation of the historic circumstances which could not be ignored.

A genealogy of the tribe of Levi was given from which it is learned that Moses and Aaron were from that Tribe. It is customary to associate the names of great people with the names of their parents. Amram and his wife Jochebed were the parents of these two great leaders of the Children of Israel. By the genealogy, we were able to distinguish Gershom the first son of Moses from Gershon a predecessor of Moses.

Moses' miraculous protection at birth, and his adoption by Pharaoh's daughter helped to form the historic circumstances. The 10 Divine judgment were at the heart of these circumstances, but they were only the indirect effects of Pharaoh's bondage. The 12 signs symbolize the 12 tribes of Israel. Also emphasized was the fact that Pharaoh's arrogance of heart made him the instrument for destruction, and not that he was prepared by God for the destruction of Egypt and his people. To believe otherwise is the equivalent of saying God caused people to do bad things and then punishes them severely.

In the next chapter, the complete departure of Israel from Egypt will be considered. It will show that Pharaoh was not changed by any of those 10 Divine judgements and, for the most part, was insincere about agreeing to free Israel from slavery. Today mankind has advanced in science and technology beyond belief. But, like Pharaoh, has not learned from the lessons of God's mercy and power. Mankind is still living in spiritual ignorance; and, therefore, five of the signs and judgements of Egypt will be repeated during the Great Tribulation on a worldwide scale.

The first sign of the **serpent** was a reminder that Satan is the cause of all the evils of the World. Sin has not decreased since; it has increased many times more. Mankind's spiritual ignorance will not prevent God from repeating the signs and wonders of Egypt before He ends man's reign on the Earth. Man remains ignorant because he chooses to remain ignorant.

CHAPTER 2

The Exodus Proper, Exodus 13:17-15:1-21

Israel's historic circumstances, in Egypt, were marked by a series of miracles; the Exodus proper was the crowning miracle of that series. Each miracle presented Pharaoh an opportunity to repent and to free Israel from bondage. Yet the Exodus did not cause pharaoh to repent but did produce the fear for his own life and the destruction of his nation. His fear was quickly changed into the instant pursuit of the Children of Israel to the shores of the Red Sea. At the Red Sea, God showed the omnipotence of His right hand by dividing it and brought Israel across to the other side. At this point in time, the Exodus began and the Children of Israel were on their way to the Promised Land.

The Red Sea event shows that God is slow to anger and merciful, but remains omnipotent.

Let us now look at the Departure, the Pursuit, and the Destruction of Pharaoh's Army.

The Departure, Exodus 13:17-22; 14:1-4:

17 And it came to pass, when Pharaoh had let the people go, that God led them not through the way of the Philistines, although that was near; for God said, Lest peradventure the people repent when they see war, and they return to Egypt:

18 But God led the people about, through the way of the wilderness of the Red Sea: and the children of Israel went up harnessed out of the land of Egypt.

Look on the map of the Journey of the Children of Israel from Egypt, to Rameses the point of their departure, and see how comparatively closer they were to Philistia, the land of the Philistines, than by the way of the Red Sea. Instead they journeyed southward to Succoth. From there they continued southward to Etham by the edge of the wilderness. Etham is not shown on the map. From there they continued to Pihahiroth where they encamped between Migdol and the sea beside Baalzephon by the sea. These places are not shown on the map on page 67. Apparently they were at the edge of the wilderness between two mountains. Assume that this location was at the northern end of the Red Sea. The Egyptians were pursuing them from behind, quite naturally, starting from Rameses the point of their departure. The Egyptians with their horses and chariots overtook them, and there was no way of escape naturally for them. The Egyptians were coming from behind. The mountains were on both sides, and before them was the Red Sea of death. To Israel it could only be described as the Red Sea of death.

Look on the map of the Middle East on page on 78 at the Sinai Peninsula where they encamped for approximately a year. See how close it was to the Promised Land by way of the Mediterranean Sea, had Israel gone that way.

19 And Moses took the bones of Joseph with him: for he had straightly sworn the children of Israel, saying, God will surely visit you; and ye shall carry up my bones away hence with you.

There is no natural or spiritual value of a dead man's bone, but what was important was the principle of faith and prophecy. Joseph had faith that one day God would visit the Children of Israel by way of a miraculous deliverance and take them back to the land of Canaan. By his great faith in God, he prophesied about it. The fulfillment of his prophecy was of mutual honor to Joseph and to his brethren who took with them his bones to be buried in the Promised Land. Such noble action of principle cannot be bought with the treasures of Earth. Faith is proven time and time again to be priceless.

20 And they took their journey from Succoth, and encamped in Etham, in the edge of the wilderness.

21 And the Lord went before them by day in a pillar of cloud to lead them the way; and by night in a pillar of fire to give them light; to go by day and by night.

22 He took not away the pillar of cloud by day, nor the pillar of fire by night from before the people.

In their darkest hour and the greatest time of need, God was there walking beside them. He was not there with them in spirit but His visible presence was with them every moment of this incredible journey. From Rameses to the Red Sea took many days' journey of a nation of people carrying everything they had. And there was God's own light shining so brightly upon them. As they arrived at the Red Sea a sense of hopelessness gripped their hearts. Then to them all efforts were in vain: they could not see any natural possibility. Pharaoh thought it was the time of opportunity for him to reclaim the Children of Israel for their God would not be able to help them or to save them from his revenge.

14:1-4: And the Lord spoke unto Moses, saying,

2 Speak unto the children of Israel, that they turn and encamp before Pihahiroth, between Migdol and the sea, over against Baal-zephon: before it ye shall encamp by the sea.

3 For Pharaoh will say of the children of Israel, They are entangled in the land, the wilderness hath shut them in.

4 And I will harden Pharaoh's heart, that he shall follow after them; and I will be honored upon Pharaoh, and upon all his host; that the Egyptians may know that I am the Lord. And they did so.

Because Pharaoh decided in his heart to pursue the Children of Israel, God allowed him for the reason that He would do something which Pharaoh never imagined possible. The whole world would honor Him for what He was about to do to Pharaoh and his armies. The Children of Israel were in a state of panic, not knowing what would happen next.

<u>Map of the Middle East</u>

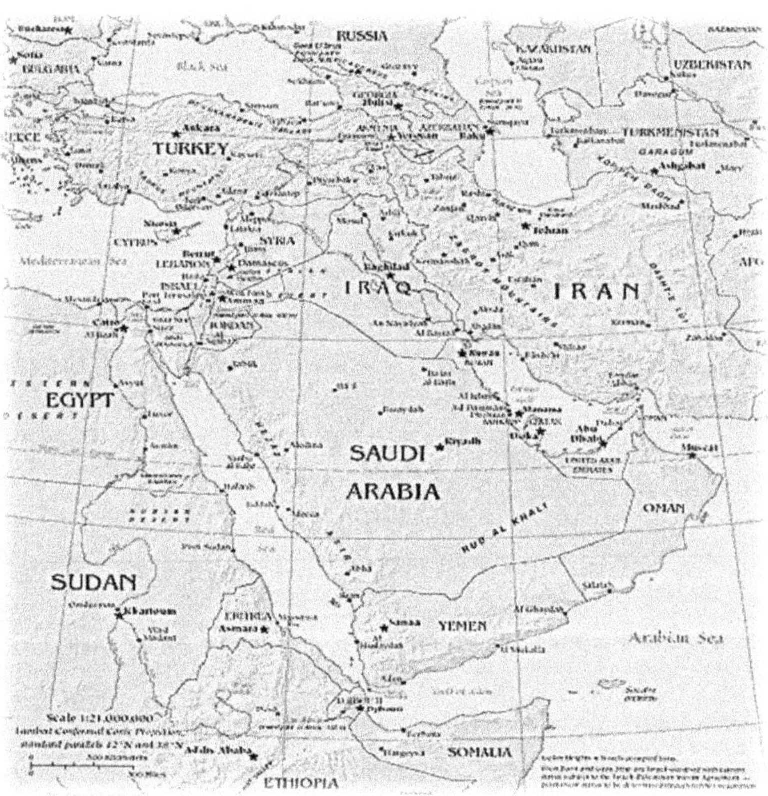

The Pursuit after Israel, Exodus 14:5-25:
    5 And it was told the king of Egypt that the people fled: and the heart of Pharaoh and of his servants was turned

against the people, and they said, Why have we done this, that we have let Israel go from serving us?

6 And he made ready his chariot, and took his people with him.

7 And he took six hundred chosen chariots, and all the chariots of Egypt, and captains over every one of them.

8 And the Lord hardened the heart of Pharaoh King of Egypt, and he pursued after the children of Israel: and the children of Israel went out with an high hand.

Pharaoh was determined to bring Israel back into slavery and God allowed him to pursue them, because He was determined to show His power through the arrogance of Pharaoh. Pharaoh thought his military power was all that was needed: there was no reason not to pursue them.

9 But the Egyptians pursued after them, all the horses and chariots of Pharaoh, and his horsemen, and his army, and overtook them encamping by the sea, beside Pihahiroth, before Baal-zephon.

10 And when Pharaoh drew nigh, the children of Israel lifted up their eyes, and, behold, the Egyptians marched after them; and they were sore afraid: and the children of Israel cried out unto the Lord.

As Pharaoh and his army approached Israel rapidly at Baalzephon before the Red Sea, they lifted up their voices and cried unto the Lord. That was commendable of them. Nevertheless, they complained against Moses, which could only make the situation worse instead of better.

11 And they said unto Moses, Because there were no graves in Egypt, hast thou taken us away to die in the wilderness? Wherefore hast thou dealt thus with us, to carry us forth out of Egypt?

12 Is not this the word we did tell thee in Egypt, saying, Let us alone, that we may serve the Egyptians? For it had been better for us to serve the Egyptians, than that we should die in the wilderness.

Complaint, instead of faith, became a second nature. A second nature was not something they could lay aside easily: it would later create future problems for them. Despite the fact of the 10 judgments God executed on the Egyptians, Israel was not prepared for the Red Sea experience. Moses, on the other hand, was the only one prepared and ready. He was prepared by his personal experience with God when he first met with Him at Mount Horeb. That experience absolutely transformed his life. He learned that God was faithful and holy and that all things were possible with Him; he had absolute faith in Him. Despite the humanly hopeless situation, he was able to inspire them with faith and courage. Moses had to be prepared by God for this moment in their existence.

13 And Moses said unto the people, Fear ye not, stand still, and see the salvation of the Lord, which he will show to you today: for the Egyptians whom ye have seen today, ye shall see them again no more forever.

14 The Lord shall fight for you, and ye shall hold your peace.

Moses assured them of complete victory and that their help was not even needed in the battle at the Red Sea because God would do all the fighting. They only needed to stand by to see the miraculous thing God was going to do for them.

15 And the Lord said unto Moses, Wherefore cry you unto me? Speak unto the children of Israel, that they go forward:

How were they to go forward under the circumstances at hand?

16 But lift up thy rod and stretch forth thine hand over the sea, and divide it: and the children of Israel shall go on dry ground through the midst of the sea.

Because God is omnipotent, He allowed Pharaoh and his army to pursue Israel into the Red Sea. In that way the whole Earth would honor Him for what He would do to Pharaoh and his army.

17 And behold, I will harden the hearts of the Egyptians

and they shall follow them: and I will get me honor upon Pharaoh, and upon all his host, upon his chariots, and upon his horsemen.

18 And the Egyptians shall know that I am the Lord when I have gotten me honor upon Pharaoh, upon his chariots.

Pharaoh's army would not be able to tell the story but those who remained alive in Egypt would know that the God of the Hebrews was the One True God.

19 And the angel of God which went before the camp of Israel, removed and went behind them; and the pillar of the cloud went from before their face, and stood behind them:

The Angel of the Lord is believed to be the Pre-Incarnate Christ, the Son of God, who in Old Testament Times, appeared as the Angel of the Lord. Here He appeared in a pillar of fire to give light to the Children of Israel.

20 And it came between the camp of the Egyptians and the camp of Israel; and it was a cloud and darkness to them, but it gave light by night to these: so that the one came not near the other all the night.

The cloud of fire which gave light to Israel removed from before them and went behind; but instead of being of light to the Egyptian, it was darkness to them and prevented them from getting too close to Israel.

21 And Moses stretched out his hand over the sea; and the Lord caused the sea to go back by a strong east wind all that night, and made the sea dry land, and the waters were divided.

22 And the children of Israel went into the midst of the sea upon the dry ground: and the waters were a wall unto them on their right hand and on their left.

This miracle was of astronomical proportion: it brings back our minds to the third day of Creation when God gathered the waters together and formed them into the seas and ocean

The Egyptians saw this miracle as an opportunity to overtake the Children of Israel stead of a warning. They thus placed themselves on the wrong side of history which was the path to their destruction.

23 And the Egyptians pursued, and went in after them to the midst of the sea, even all Pharaoh's horses, his chariots, and his horsemen.

They pursued Israel as if there were no tomorrow and thought that God had forgotten them; and might of thought that there were some limitations with God.

24 And it came to pass, that in the morning watch the Lord looked unto the host of the Egyptians through the pillar of fire and of the cloud, and troubled the host of the Egyptians,

25 And took off their chariot wheels, that they drove them heavily: so that the Egyptians said, Let us flee from the face of Israel; for the Lord fights for them against the Egyptians.

Suddenly they discovered that God had not forgotten about them and that they were in real trouble with Him; they thought of quickly retreating from their pursuit of Israel, it was too late. For the first time they were helpless against Israel. And they were all on the other side of mercy — the side of Divine wrath. This choice of Pharaoh of fighting against the Almighty is still one of the great wonders of history and a lesson for all earthly rulers

The Destruction of Pharaoh's Army, Exodus 14:26-15:1-21:

26 And the Lord said unto Moses, Stretch out thine hand over the sea, that the waters may come again upon the Egyptians, upon their chariots, and upon their horsemen.

This was not what God wanted; He tried to avoid this calamity. The previous 10 judgment signs were intended to prevent the destruction of the Egyptians at the Red Sea. To them the destruction of the first born was only a *time to recollect their thoughts as to how to make Israel pay for their desire for **freedom from bondage.** Yet there was never the thought of the greater price they could pay for refusing to free God's children from bondage.*

27 And Moses stretched forth his hand over the sea, and the sea returned to his strength when the morning appeared; and the Egyptians fled against it; and the Lord overthrew the Egyptians in the midst of the sea.

28 And the waters returned and covered the chariots, and the horsemen, and all the host of Pharaoh that came into the sea after them; there remained not so much as one of them.

Finally, at long last, the harvest from the seed of destruction was reaped, and Egypt became the poorer, and Israel the richer; righteousness and faith prevailed and evil vanquished.

29 But the children of Israel walked upon dry land in the midst of the sea; and the waters were a wall unto them on their right hand, and on their left.

30 Thus the Lord saved Israel that day out of the hand of the Egyptians; and Israel saw the Egyptians dead upon the sea shore.

31 And Israel saw that great work which the Lord did upon the Egyptians: and the people feared the Lord, and his servant Moses.

*The judgment at the Red Sea shows that Israel's salvation was not in man but in their God. Sinful nature cannot save itself; it must be delivered from by Divine intervention. Though Pharaoh accepted mercy on 10 separate occasions, he never once accepted the **God of mercy.** When people reject the God of mercy, their destruction is secured. Those who accept the God of mercy will have a song of victory and praise. God took no pleasure in destroying the Egyptians. As a matter of fact, He tried to prevent it by the miracles of mercy He demonstrated to Pharaoh.*

The Song of Moses, 15:1-21:

The song of Moses was beautifully written and well appropriate. There are three parts to this song.

Acknowledgment of God's Faithfulness and Righteousness, 15:1-13:

1 Then sang Moses and the children of Israel this song unto the Lord, and spoke, saying, I will sing unto the Lord, for he hath triumphed gloriously: the horse and his rider hath he thrown into the sea.

2 The Lord is my strength and is become my salvation: he is my God, and I will prepare him an habitation; my father's God, and I will exalt him.

3 The Lord is a man of war: the Lord is his name.

4 Pharaoh's chariots and his host hath he cast into the midst of the sea: his chosen captains also are drowned in the sea.

5 The depths have covered them: they sank into the bottom as a stone.

6 Thy right hand, O Lord, is become glorious in power: thy right hand, O Lord, hath dashed in pieces the enemy.

7 And in the greatness of thy excellency thou hast overthrown them that rose up against You: You send forth Your wrath, which consumed them as stubble.

8 And with the blast of thy nostrils the waters gathered together, the floods stood upright as an heap, and the depths were congealed in the heart of the sea.

9 The enemy said, I will pursue, I will overtake, I will divide the spoil; my lust shall be satisfied upon them; I will draw my sword, my hand shall destroy them.

10 Thou didst blow with thy wind, the sea covered them: they sank as lead in the mighty waters.

11 Who is like unto thee, O Lord, among the gods? Who is like thee, glorious in holiness, fearful in praises, doing wonders?

12 Thou stretched out thy right hand, the earth swallowed them.

13 Thou in thy mercy hath led forth thy people which thou hast redeemed: thou hast guided them in thy strength unto thy holy habitation.

Verse 2: *Israel's strength was totally insufficient to compete with the Egyptians' at a time when they needed deliverance. Their deliverance came from God and He became their salvation. They acknowledged Him while the Egyptians rejected Him as their God. Israel wanted God not for convenience but forever. Therefore they would prepare a habitation for Him in their midst.*

Verses 3-6*: By defeating Pharaoh's army in the midst of the Red Sea, Israel acknowledged Him as a God of war who is glorious in victory.* ***Verses 7-13:*** *God is the invisible God. He commanded the waters and they obeyed Him in every direction, even the bottom of the sea was made a highway for the feet of the Children of Israel. By commanding the sea the way He did, He filled the whole Earth with His praise and declared His holiness to those who looked at holiness as weakness.*

Anticipation of Victory over Future Enemies, 14-16:

14 The people shall hear and shall be afraid: sorrow shall take hold of the inhabitants of Palestina.

15 Then the dukes of Edom shall be amazed; the mighty men of Moab, trembling shall take hold upon them; all the inhabitants of Canaan shall melt away.

16 Fear and dread shall fall upon them; by the greatness of thine arm they shall be as still as a stone; till thy people pass over, O Lord, till the people pass over, which thou hast purchased.

The crossing of the Red Sea was not their only crossing: ahead was the Mighty Jordan. They would need a miracle to cross over Jordan. They would then be exposed to great dangers from their enemies who were preparing for their destruction. By the greatness of their God, they knew they would defeat all enemies. The song is closed with praises and rejoicing.

Praises and Rejoicing, 17-21:

17 Thou shalt bring them in, and plant them in the mountain of thine inheritance, in the place, O Lord, which thou hast made for thee to dwell in, in the sanctuary, O Lord, which thy hands have established.

18 The Lord shall reign for ever and ever.

19 For the horse of Pharaoh went in with his chariots and with his horsemen into the sea, and the Lord brought again the waters of the sea upon them; but the children of Israel went on dry land in the midst of the sea.

20 And Miriam the prophetess, the sister of Aaron took a timbrel in her hand; and all the women went out after her with timbrels and with dances.

21 And Miriam answered them, Sing ye to the Lord, for he hath triumphed gloriously; the horse and its rider hath he thrown into the sea.

SUMMARY

The death of the firstborn of man and beast of the Egyptians had caused Pharaoh to make a hasty decision to free Israel from the bondage of slavery. Their pursuit of Israel to the shores of the Red Sea explains the temporary nature of Pharaoh's decision. But just before Israel began their journey they did a remarkable thing which is often overlooked——they took with them the bones of Joseph. There is no natural or spiritual value of a dead man's bone, but what was important was the principle of faith and prophecy. Joseph had faith that one day God would visit the Children of Israel by way of a miraculous deliverance and take them back to the land of Canaan. By his great faith in God he prophesied about it. The fulfillment of his prophecy was of mutual honor to Joseph and to his brethren who took with them his bones to be buried in the Promised Land. Such noble action of principle cannot be bought with the treasures of Earth. Faith is proven time and time again to be priceless.

Pharaoh's pursuit of Israel shows he was determined to bring Israel back into slavery and God allowed him to pursue them because He was determined to show His power through the arrogance of Pharaoh. Pharaoh thought his military power was all that was needed: there was no reason not to pursue them. As Pharaoh pressed forward, the Children of Israel were afraid when they saw his army.

Their fear caused them to complain; complaint, instead of faith, became a second nature. A second nature was not something they could lay aside easily: it would later create future problems for them. Despite the fact of the 10 signs God showed to the Egyptians before their eyes, they were not prepared for the Red Sea experience. Moses, on the other hand, was the only one prepared and ready. He was prepared by his personal experience with God when he first met with Him at Mount Horeb. That experience absolutely transformed his life. He learned that God was faithful and holy and that all things were possible with Him; he had absolute faith in Him. Despite the humanly hopeless situation, he was able to inspire the Children of Israel with faith and courage. With faith in God, he stretched forth the rod of God towards the Red Sea and it was divided.

This miracle was of astronomical proportion: it brings back our minds to the third day of Creation when God gathered the waters together and formed them into the seas and oceans. The Egyptians saw this miracle as an opportunity instead of a warning. Thus they pursued Israel and there found themselves on the wrong side of mercy.

CHAPTER 3

Three Months' Journey, Exodus 15:22-19

The Children of Israel were living in Rameses at the time of the Passover and then journeyed to Pihahiroth between Migdol and the sea over against Baalzephon (Exodus 12:37; 13:17-22; 14:1-3,8,9). From the shores of the Red Sea, they went into the wilderness of Shur (15:22) for Divine direction and purpose. Israel who had already known about God's omnipotence would come to know about His holiness, mercy, and forgiveness.

In the wilderness, they would face humanly insurmountable challenges; they would learn that man shall not live by bread alone because their natural survival would not depend on their material means but on the very word of God that would create those miraculous provisions for their daily existence. The wilderness life would demand absolute dependence on God's word.

In the wilderness, Moses's status as a leader would be elevated to that of Prophet and Priest. His life, as the lives of all those that would follow, had to be one of faith and complete obedience to God. "By faith he forsook Egypt, not fearing the wrath of the king: for he endured, as seeing him who is invisible." It was not in Egypt he saw the Invisible God; it was in the wilderness. We must assume, therefore, that the wilderness experience was God's perfect Will for the God of the Red Sea would demonstrate that He was the God of the wilderness. The lessons in the wilderness must not go unnoticed: they can enrich our lives. And we must ask ourselves, What can we learn from the first three months of Israel's journey in the Wilderness?

From The Wilderness of Shur to Marah, Exodus 15:22-28:

22 So Moses brought Israel from the Red sea, and they went out into the wilderness of Shur; and they went three days journey in the wilderness, and found no water.

23 And when they came to Marah, they could not drink of the waters of Marah, for they were bitter: therefore the name of it was called Marah.

24 And the people murmured against Moses, saying, What shall we drink?

This was the third time the Children of Israel murmured: they murmured against Moses when he delivered the message of their deliverance, when they encamped by the Red Sea being overcome by fear, and here for thirst. Murmur replaced faith and overshadowed God's blessings, causing them to forget those rich blessings. Hearing the murmurings, Moses did what which he knew to do. He did not know how God would solve the problem but he knew He would.

25 And he cried unto the Lord; and the Lord showed him a tree, which when he had cast into the waters, the waters were made sweet: there he made for them a statute and an ordinance, and there he proved them,

God proved faithful and challenged them to complete obedience:

26 And said, If thou wilt diligently hearken to the voice of the Lord thy God, and will do that which is right in his sight, and will give ear to his commandments, and keep all his statutes, I will put none of these diseases upon thee, which I have brought upon the Egyptians: for I am the Lord that heals you.

27 And they came to Elim, where there were twelve wells

of water, and three score and ten palm trees: and they camped there by the waters.

The Divine direction took them to Elim to remind them of God's benevolence and the promise of a better land. Herein lies a symbolic message of the 12 tribes of Israel and the 70 charter members of the Nation.

From Elim to the Wilderness of Sin, Exodus 16:1-36: Murmuring, 16:1-3

And they took their journey from Elim, and all the congregation of the children of Israel came unto the Wilderness of Sin, which is between Elim and Sinai, on the fifteenth day of the second month after their departing out of the land of Egypt.

If ABIB, the first month corresponds to March or April, the fifteenth day of the second month corresponds to the fifteenth day of May. It seemed they were already murmuring while on the way from Elim because the instant they arrived at the Wilderness of Sin, the official murmurings began. This was the fourth occasion of murmurings. Undoubtedly the murmuring was so widespread that the place of their murmuring was called the Wilderness of Sin. This murmuring had a strange death wish and a desire for the flesh of Egypt:

2 And the whole congregation of the children of Israel murmured against Moses and Aaron in the wilderness:

3 And the children of Israel said unto them, Would to God we had died by the hand of the Lord in the land of Egypt, when we sat by the flesh pots, and when we did eat bread to the full; for ye have brought us forth into this wilderness, to kill this whole assembly with hunger.

What a strange death wish they had – they wished to have died in Egypt at the hand of their God. Did not they see how the Egyptians died at the hand of the Lord, the first born, and then all the Egyptians in the depths of the Red Sea? This wish must, therefore, be the most irrational and selfish wish expressed by God's people. As selfish and irrational as Pharaoh's desires were, he never expressed a death wish at the hand of the Hebrews' God. The soul is tested through the needs of the body, but the needs of the soul cannot be satisfied by bread but by the Living God. Israel saw the judgment signs on the Egyptians and their recent miracles, but allowed none of those miracles to touch their lives, inspiring faith. Therefore, they remained unchanged.

Would these daily miracles touch their lives?

Miracle of the Manna and Meat, 16:4-15:

4 Then said the Lord unto Moses, Behold, I will rain bread from heaven for you; and the people shall go out and gather a certain rate every day, that I may prove them, whether they will walk in my law, or no.

The nature of these two miracles would prove whether or not Israel would obey the Lord: faith required obedience. This was why their faith never increased and why they were characterized by murmurings and fear. If they had stopped to praise God for each blessing, there would have been no place for murmurings, and their faith would increase. They were wondering whether or not God was with them when there was no evidence to indicate otherwise. But there were no excuses, substitutes, or escape from obedience to God's word: obedience had to be tested.

Moses describes the nature of the miracles:

5 And it shall come to pass that on the sixth day they shall prepare that which they bring in; and it shall be twice as much as they gather daily.

6 And Moses and Aaron said unto all the children of Israel, At even, then ye shall know that the Lord hath brought you out from the land of Egypt:

7 And in the morning, then ye shall see the glory of the Lord; for that he hears your murmurings against the Lord: and what are we that ye murmur against us?

8 And Moses said, This shall be, when the Lord shall give you in the evening flesh to eat, and in the morning bread to the full; for that the Lord hears your murmurings which ye murmur against him: and what are we? Your murmuring is not against us, but against the Lord.

9 And Moses spoke unto Aaron, Say unto all the congregation of the children of Israel, Come near before the Lord: for he hath heard your murmurings

God was eager to provide miraculously for them as He was eager to express His displeasure with their murmurings. Moses made them understand that they were not only murmuring against him but more so against God. It was not he who brought them across Red Sea, it was their God. God's sudden appearance to them indicated His displeasure and wanted them to lay aside this besetting sin. Providing for them miraculously was not a reward for murmuring, but His sovereign duty.

10 And it came to pass as Aaron spoke unto the whole congregation of the children of Israel, that they looked toward the wilderness, and, behold, the glory of the Lord appeared in the cloud.

11 And the Lord spoke unto Moses saying,

12 I have heard the murmurings of the children of Israel: speak unto them, saying, At even ye shall eat flesh, and in the morning ye shall be filled with bread; and ye shall know that I am the Lord your God.

Israel already failed God; but being their God, He could not fail them in a single instance, and reaffirmed to Moses that He was in the process of providing for His children.

13 And it came to pass, that at even the quails came up, and covered the camp: and in the morning the dew lay round about the host.

14 And when the dew that lay was gone up, behold, upon the face of the wilderness there lay a small round thing, as small as the hoar frost on the ground.

15 And when the children of Israel saw it, they said one to another, It is manna: for they knew not what it was. And Moses said unto them, This is the bread which the Lord hath given you to eat. *God's miraculous provision occurred so fast that Israel did not fully recognize what it was that God provided for them, even though they were looking right at it. Moses told them it was the fulfillment of God's promise to them. Their obedience would be tested by the rules they needed to obey.*

Rules for the Manna and Meat, 16:16-26:
16 This is the thing which the Lord hath commanded, Gather of it every man according to his eating, an omer for every man, according to the number of your persons; take ye every man for them which are in his tents.

17 And the children of Israel did so, and gathered, some more, some less.

18 And when they did mete it with an omer, he that gathered much had nothing over, and he that gathered little had no lack; they gathered every man according to his eating.

19 And Moses said, Let no man leave of it till the morning.

Each man was to gather an omer (2 U.S. dry quarts) for his household and should not be left overnight. This rule was easily understood, yet many did not obey.

20 Notwithstanding they harkened not unto Moses; but some of them left it until the morning, and it bred worms, and stank: and Moses was wroth with them.

21 And they gathered it every morning, every man according to his eating: and when the sun waxed hot it melted.

22 And it came to pass that on the sixth day they gathered twice as much bread, two omers for one man: and all the rulers of the congregation came and told Moses.

On the sixth day each household should gather 2 omers, enough for two days' provision because on the Sabbath they were not allowed to collect the Manna. Because they were obeying God's command they were able to keep the manna until the Sabbath, without having any damage. If during the week they left any for the next day it would be spoiled, no good.

23 And he said unto them, This is that which the Lord hath said, Tomorrow is the rest of the holy Sabbath unto the Lord: bake that which ye will bake today, and seethe that ye will seethe; and that which remains over lay up for you to be kept until the morning.

24 And they laid it up till the morning, as Moses bade: and it did not stink, neither was there any worm therein.

25 And Moses said, Eat that today; for today is a Sabbath unto the Lord: today ye shall not find it in the field.

26 Six days ye shall gather it; but on the seventh day, which is the Sabbath, in it there shall be none.

27 And it came to pass, that there went out some of the people on the seventh day for to gather, and they found none.

The rule of not collecting Manna on the Sabbath was easily understood, yet many went out on the Sabbath to collect it. But then they were confounded because they found no Manna. Moses had to take them back through this rule.

28 And the Lord said unto Moses, How long refuse ye to keep my commandments and my laws?

29 See, for the Lord hath given you the Sabbath, therefore he giveth you on the sixth day the bread of two days; abide ye every man in his place, let no man go out of his place on the seventh day.

30 So the people rested on the seventh day.

They finally understood, having learned from experience.

31 And the house of Israel called the name there of Manna: and it was like coriander seed, white; and the taste

of it was like wafers made with honey.

The Manna Memorialized, 16:32-36:

32 And Moses said, This is the thing which the Lord commands, Fill an omer of it to be kept for your generations; that they may see the bread wherewith I have fed you in the wilderness, when I brought you forth from the land of Egypt.

33 And Moses said unto Aaron, Take a pot and put an omer full of mamma therein, and lay it up before the Lord, to be kept for your generations.

For forty years the Lord fed His people with Manna; it was important to memorialize the experience by securing two quarts (U.S. dry quarts) in a pot to teach the generations following how God miraculously provided for them during their forty year journey in the Wilderness.

Ordinarily, the Manna could not be left over till the morning without being spoiled; at God's command it could be kept forever without being spoiled. Unlike the Children of Israel, Moses obeyed every single word of the Lord. "Man shall not live by bread alone but by every word that proceeds from the mouth of God". To live by the word of God, one has to obey. The secret of victory and miracles is obedience for which there is no substitute.

34 As the Lord commanded Moses, so Aaron laid it up before the testimony to be kept.

35 And the children of Israel did eat Manna forty years, until they came to a land inhabited; they did eat manna, until they came unto the borders of the land of Canaan.

36 Now an omer (2 U.S. dry quarts) is the tenth part of an ephah.

For forty years God provided food without an earthly name for His children because it was not earthly but heavenly: no one was able to give it an earthly name. God's ways are past finding out, even in His material blessings.

From the Wilderness of Sin to Rephidim, Exodus 17:1-16

Murmuring, 17:1-4:

1 And all the congregation of the children of Israel journeyed from the Wilderness of Sin, after their journeys according to the commandment of the Lord, and pitched in Rephidim: and there was no water for the people to drink.

This was the fourth test since Israel began their journey to the Promised Land: from the Red Sea, to the Wilderness of Shur, to the Wilderness of Sin, and to Rephidim. God wanted to prove whether or not they trust Him for their every need or would fear the circumstances over which they had no control. Not one out of four times after their miraculous material blessings had they ever praised God. It became natural to expect them to murmur each time they were faced with a material need. One would have hoped that by now they were ready to pass any **test of trusting the Lord.** *But again they failed in their customary style of murmuring.*

2 Wherefore the people did chide with Moses, and said, Give us water that we may drink. And Moses said unto them, Why chide ye with me? Wherefore do ye tempt the Lord?

Moses endeavored to show them that the greater sin was not murmuring at him, but rather tempting their God who had never failed to provide for their needs. Although God understood their needs, He could not understand why they never praised Him for His past provisions. Murmuring was something foreign and contrary to any kind of praise.

3 And the people thirsted there for water; and the people murmured against Moses, and said, Wherefore is this that thou hast brought us up out of Egypt, to kill us and our children and our cattle with thirst?

One can understand the intensity of their thirst, but one cannot understand their murmuring and accusation against Moses. However, he did not argue with them; arguing with them would only make matters worse, and he brought the matter to the attention of the Lord.

4 And Moses cried unto the Lord, saying, What shall I do unto this people? They be almost ready to stone me.

The Miracle at Horeb, 17:5-7:

5 And the Lord said unto Moses, Go on before the people, and take with thee of the elders of Israel; and thy rod wherewith you smote the river, take in your hand and go.

6 Behold, I will stand before thee there upon the rock in Horeb; and thou shalt smite the rock, and there shall come water out of it, that the people may drink. And Moses did so in the sight of the elders of Israel.

Moses was brought back to a well familiar place. This was the place of his first encounter with God (3:1-3). In verse 12 of chapter 3, Moses' return to Horeb was to be a token that God had sent him to deliver His people from bondage. Look on the map on page 67 and see the location of the land of Midian. It is just the opposite side of the Mount Horeb which is close to Mount Sinai. It could be that some of the Midianites, including Moses's father-in-law, Jethro, migrated across and were living near Horeb. Here Moses had his first experience with God while he was tending the sheep. In order to fulfill His promise to Moses, God directed the steps of His people to Horeb.

God had another reason, unknown and undeclared to Moses, for guiding them to Mount Horeb. He foreknew that by the time they reached to Horeb on their journey, their thirst would have reached alarming degrees: God had preplanned the miracle at Horeb; He just withheld that secret from Moses. Moses had just realized what was in that token promise.

Moses then did as he was commanded and the water flowed from the rock. This was the fourth miracle since leaving the bondage of Egypt. These four miracles are to be distinguished from the signs and wonders of Egypt. These were wholly beneficial to Israel; the signs were punitive in nature with respect to Pharaoh and the Egyptians. Now an un-necessary question was answered because they always knew that their God was with them.

7 And he called the name of the place Massah, and Meribah, because of the chiding of the children of Israel, and because they tempted the Lord, saying, Is the Lord among us, or not?

They had not finished drinking the water before Amalek and his army came up against them. This was one way of telling Israel that He was not pleased with their behavior of constant murmuring. When a man's ways pleases the Lord He makes his enemies to be at peace with him. Some lessons are being taught the hard way.

The Battle with Amalek, 17:8-16:
Then came Amalek, and fought with Israel in Rephidim.

9 And Moses said unto Joshua, Choose us out men, and go out, fight with Amalek: tomorrow I will stand on the top of the hill with the rod of God in my hand.

10 So Joshua did as Moses had said to him, and fought with Amalek: and Moses, Aaron and Hur went up to the top of the hill.

While Israel had doubts and fears; Moses had faith and confidence in the God of their fathers. While Israel allowed circumstances to draw them away from God, Moses allowed those same circumstances to draw him closer to God. He saw the war with Amalek as a way of proving to Israel the greatness of God. He knew that by faith, all God's enemies would fall one by one and none would be left standing. He ordered Joshua, his general, to accept Amalek's challenge and Joshua did.

11 And it came to pass when Moses held up his hand, that Israel prevailed: and when he let down his hand, Amalek prevailed.

12 But Moses' hands were heavy; and they took a stone

and put it under him, and he sat thereon; and Aaron and Hur stayed up his hands, the one on one side, and the other on the other side; and his hands were steady until the going down of the sun.

Moses did not go to the war in person but his faith in God gave the victory to God's army. And Amalek became an example of defeat to the other enemies of God. Amalek had no good reason to war with Israel, and so his defeat was celebrated by all Israel and memorialized.

13 And Joshua discomfited Amalek and his people with edge of the sword.

14 And the Lord said unto Moses, Write this for a memorial in a book, and rehearse in the ears of Joshua: for I will utterly put out the remembrance of Amalek from under heaven.

15 And Moses built an altar and called the name of it Jehovah-nissi.

Before and after, Moses acknowledged God and in the end gave Him all the glory. He memorialized the victory by writing it in a memorial book, built an altar of worship, and named it Jehovah-nissi, The Lord Our Banner.

16 For he said, Because the Lord hath sworn that the Lord will have war with Amalek from generation to generation.

Moses Meets with His Father-in-law, 18: 1-9:

1 When Jethro, the priest of Midian, Moses' father-in-law, heard of all God had done for Moses, and for Israel his people, and that the Lord had brought Israel out of Egypt;

2 Then Jethro, Moses father-in-law, took Zipporah, Moses' wife, after he had sent her back,

3 And her two sons; of which the name of the one was Gershom; for he said I had been an alien in a strange land:

4 And the name of the other was Eliezer; for the God of my father, said, he, was my help, and delivered me from the

sword of Pharaoh.

Moses appropriately named his two sons in recognition of God's goodness and mercies   to him. Moses had sent back his family to their homeland in view of kind consideration for them. He did not want to keep them with him in Egypt where there would be that constant danger and the personal responsibility which could distract him from his mission of life of leading Israel from the bondage of Egypt. This should be seen as love for his family and obedience to God. He was simply balancing family and mission.

5 And Jethro, Moses' father-in-law, came with his sons and his wife unto Moses into the wilderness, where he encamped at the mount of God:

Undoubtedly Jethro was living in the neighborhood of Horeb and heard about the great things which God had done for the Children of Israel. It is clear they were both on good terms and were happy to see each other. Moses was especially respectful to him, and he was grateful to have a son-in-law of universal prominence. Moses had a great story to tell and Jethro listened with joy.

6 And he said unto Moses, I thy father-in-law Jethro am come unto thee, and thy wife, and her two sons with her.

7 And Moses went out to meet his father-in-law, and did obeisance, and kissed him; and they asked each other of their welfare; and they came into the tent.

8 And Moses told his father-in-law all that the Lord had done unto Pharaoh and to the Egyptians for Israel's sake, and all the travail that had come upon them by the way, and how the Lord delivered them.

9 And Jethro rejoiced for all the goodness which the Lord had done to Israel, whom he had delivered out of the hand of the Egyptians.

After listening to all the great things the Lord had done for His people, Jethro was overwhelmed with joy and drew closer to Moses to give him some fatherly advice.

Moses' Father-in-law Counsels Him, 18:10-27

10 And Jethro said, Blessed be the Lord, who hath delivered you out of the hand of the Egyptians, and out of the hand of Pharaoh, who hath delivered the people from under the hand of the Egyptians.

11 Now I know that the Lord is greater than all gods: for in the thing wherein they dealt proudly he was above them.

Obviously Jethro saw God in a way he had not seen Him before for since Creation He had not displayed such degree of omnipotence.

12 And Jethro Moses' father-in-law took a burnt offering and sacrifices for God: and Aaron came, and all the elders of Israel, to eat bread with Moscs' father-in-law before God.

It was already pointed out that Midian the father of the Midianites was the son of Abraham by Ketruah his second wife. It is assumed that Abraham taught his son the way of worship. Thus Jethro was not ignorant of the way of worship with Burnt Offering and sacrifices. It cannot be denied that people can offer Burnt Offering and sacrifices to other gods. However, there is no reason to believe that Jethro had worshipped other gods. It is noteworthy that Jethro was welcomed by the elders of Israel.

Jethro took a keen interest in Moses' work and observed him working.

13 And it came to pass on the morrow, that Moses sat to judge the people: and the people stood by Moses from the morning unto the evening.

14 And when Moses' Father-in-law saw all that he did to the people, he said, What is this thing that you do to the people? Why sit yourself alone and all the people stand by thee from morning unto even?

15 And Moses said unto his Father-in-law, Because the people come unto me to inquire of God:

16 When they have a matter, they come unto me; and I judge between one and another, and I do let them know the

statutes of God, and his laws.

Quickly Jethro saw that Moses' job was too much for any human being and was impossible for him to continue for much longer.

17 And Moses' father-in-law said unto him, The thing that you do is not good.

18 Thou wilt surely wear away, both thou, and this people that is with thee: for this thing is too heavy for thee; thou art not able to perform it thyself alone.

19 Harken now unto my voice, I will give thee counsel, and God shall be with thee: Be thou for the people to Godward, that you may bring the causes unto God:

20 And thou shalt teach them ordinances and the laws and shalt show them the way wherein they must walk, and the work that they must do.

21 Moreover thou shalt provide out of all the people able men, such as fear God, men of truth, hating covetousness; and place such over them, to be rulers of thousands, and rulers of hundreds, rulers of fifties, and rulers of tens:

22 Let them judge the people at all seasons: and it shall be, that every great matter they shall bring unto thee, but every small matter they shall judge: so shall it be easier for thyself, and they shall bear the burden with thee.

23 If thou shalt do this thing, and God command thee so, then thou shalt be able to endure, and all this people shall also go to their place in peace.

24 So Moses harkened to the voice of his father-in-law, and did all that he had said.

25 And Moses chose able men out of all Israel, and made them heads over the people, rulers of thousands, rulers of hundreds, rulers of fifties, and rulers of tens.

26 And they judged the people all seasons: the hard causes they brought unto Moses, but every small matter they judged themselves.

27 And Moses let his father-in-law depart; and he went

his way into his own land.

Jethro advises Moses to limit his job to that of a mediator by taking the great concerns of the people to God and explaining the laws to the people. He should delegate the daily responsibility of judging the people to qualified men in an orderly way. The whole job of judging would be accomplished more efficiently and all would be pleased.

Verse 23 shows that Jethro had a sense of deep humility in giving advice to such great man as Moses. Moses had displayed deep humility in accepting the advice of his father-in-law (verse 24). Many son-in-laws would have thought they needed no advice from their father-in-laws when their status was preeminently elevated above theirs. This was not so with Moses; he was eternally grateful, and showed it by immediately delegating his spiritual responsibility to the appointed leaders of the congregation.

In the end Jethro proved to be the best friend Moses ever had: inviting the weary stranger home, giving him his first daughter to wife, and bringing his daughter and grandsons to be with their incomparable husband and father. If Moses never had a great day in his life, this was it.

Jethro then departed to his own land. His own land could well be beyond the backside of Mount Horeb where Moses was tending his sheep not so long ago.

From Rephidim to Sinai, Exodus, 19:1-25:
1. An admonition, 19:1-8:
1 And in the third month, when the children of Israel were gone forth out of the land of Egypt, the same day came they into the wilderness of Sinai.

2 For they were departed from Rephidim, and were come to the desert of Sinai, and had pitched in the wilderness; and there Israel camped before the mount.

3 And Moses went up unto God, and the Lord called unto him out of the mountain, saying, Thus shalt thou say to the

house of Jacob, and tell the children of Israel;

The picture is clear: after leaving Rephidim the people encamped in the Wilderness of Sinai. Moses went up into the Mount and God gave him a message for the people:

4 Ye have seen what I did to the Egyptians, and how I bare you on eagle's wings, and brought you to myself.

5 Now therefore, if ye will obey my voice indeed, and keep my covenant, then ye shall be a peculiar treasure unto me above all people: for all the earth is mine:

6 And ye shall be unto me a kingdom of priest, and an holy nation. These are the words that ye shall speak unto the children of Israel.

This was a great message for in it was the promise of the greatness of Israel's special role in God's great plan for mankind. Moses delivers the message to the people and returns to the Mount with the response of the people.

7 And Moses came and called for the elders of the people, and laid before their faces all these words which the Lord commanded him.

8 And all people answered together, and said, All that the Lord hath spoken we will do. And Moses returned the words of the people unto the Lord. (the second time to the Mount)

On Moses' return to the Mount, the Lord gave him the reason for appearing in thick cloud to speak to him.

2. Preparing to Meet with God, 19:9-16:

9 And the Lord said unto Moses, Lo, I come unto thee in a thick cloud, that the people may hear when I speak with you, and believe you forever. And Moses told the words of the people unto the Lord.

10 And the Lord said unto Moses, Go unto the people, and sanctify them today and tomorrow, and let them wash their clothes,

11 And be ready against the third day: for the third day

the Lord will come down in the sight of all people upon mount Sinai.

12 And thou shalt set bounds unto the people round about, saying, Take heed to yourselves, that ye go not up into the mount, or touch the border of it: whosoever touches the mount shall be surely put to death:

13 There shall not an hand touch it, but he shall surely be stoned, or shot through, whether it be beast or man, it shall not live: when the trumpet sounds long, they shall come up to the mount.

14 And Moses went down from the mount unto the people, and sanctified the people; and they washed their clothes.

This was the third time Moses brought God's message to His people. They were going to meet face to face with their God. For that to happen, the preparations described above had to be made, precisely as directed. The people washed their clothes, set bounds around Mount Sinai, and the men stayed away from their wives.

God's true intentions came across upon Mount Sinai. These were the principles of holiness seen in setting the bounds around Mount Sinai and in the sanctification of the people. God could not meet with them in their present state. They had to set themselves apart for that occasion. While God was present on the Mount, they could not even touch the holy Mount. They were absolutely unworthy of the privilege of being in God's holy presence. There were too many doubts, fears, ingratitude, and murmurings among them. God had to establish His standard of holiness where death would be the sure consequence of un-holiness. God had to protect them from such death by setting the bounds around the holy Mount. Something was going to happen, which had not happened since the creation of the Universe; something their fathers never heard about nor saw.

Moses warns the people:

15 And he said unto the people, Be ready against the third day: come not at your wives.

16 And it came to pass on the third day in the morning, that there were thunders and lightning, and a thick cloud upon the mount, and the voice of the trumpet exceeding loud; so that all the people that was in the camp trembled.

God's voice sounded like a trumpet and caused the people in the camp to tremble. At that time Moses had not yet brought the people to meet with their God. God had listened to their murmurings and ingratitude all that time and now was introducing Himself to begin a discussion with them.

Moses was now ready to bring the congregation to meet with God.

3. The Congregation Meets with God, 19:17-25:

17 And Moses brought forth the people out of the camp to meet with God; and they stood at the nether part of the mount.

18 And mount Sinai was altogether on a smoke, because the Lord descended upon it in fire: and the smoke thereof ascended as the smoke of a furnace, and the whole mount quaked greatly.

19 And when the voice of the trumpet sounded long, and waxed louder and louder, Moses spoke, and God answered him by a voice.

20 And God came down on top of the mount: and the Lord called Moses up to the top of the mount; and Moses went up.

This was the third time Moses went on top of the holy Mount.

21 And the lord said unto Moses, Go down, charge the people, lest they break through unto the Lord to gaze, and many of them perish.

God knew their curiosity and that they were more interested in what He looked like than the words of life emanating from His mouth. The description of His manifestation suggests that He wanted to prevent them from making some image of what they thought He looked like.

God made no exception for the priests: they too had to sanctify themselves in order to meet with Him.

22 And let the priests also, which come near to the Lord, sanctify themselves, lest the Lord break forth upon them.

23 And Moses said unto the Lord, The people cannot come up to mount Sinai: for You charge us, saying, Set bounds about the mount, and sanctify it.

24 And the Lord said unto him, Away, get thee down, and thou shalt come up, thou, and Aaron with thee: but let not the priests and the people break through to come up unto the Lord, lest he break forth upon them.

For the fourth time Moses came down from the holy Mount. This time he was to bring Aaron to the Mount.

25 So Moses went down unto the people, and spoke unto them.

SUMMARY

Israel's three month journey took them to Pihahiroth from where they crossed over the Red Sea. At the Red Sea, they murmured against Moses, due to fear of Pharaoh and his army. This fear was conceived when Moses delivered God's message of deliverance to Pharaoh and when, as a result, Pharaoh made their bondage greater.

Fear then became a second nature and was responsible for all their murmurings. After their miraculous crossing of the Red Sea, they journeyed to the Wilderness of Shur where they found no water after journeying three days. They then came to Marah where they found water but could not drink of it because it was bitter. Then their second nature took-over and they murmured against Moses. God heard their murmur and made the waters sweet. They next journeyed to

Elim where things were beautiful, having twelve wells and seventy palm trees. This to them was a reminder that God would keep His promise to take them to the Promised Land.

Next, they journeyed to the Wilderness of Sin. Here they murmured again against Moses; hunger was the cause. God miraculously provided them with meat and Manna. Then they came to Rephidim where they murmured against Moses for thirst of water. Then God provided them with water from the rock of Horeb. Before they could finish drinking the water, Amalek engaged them in a bloody war. There, God was with them and gave them a great victory. God did not reward murmurings. Neither did He allow it to thwart His purposes. What the murmurings proved was God's great faithfulness to keep His promises.

From Rephidim they came to the Wilderness of Sinai. This proved to be their most precious experience since for the first time they met with their God, heard His voice, saw His glory, and felt His power in a most personal way. All their lingering doubts and uncertainties were swept away from their minds and hearts as to the personality of their God.

With respect to Moses, he had the most personal knowledge of his God. It was a special favor to him for his faithfulness and obedience. Of a truth, he saw the Invisible God and spoke with Him man to man, something no other human being had ever done. For him, it was worth it choosing rather to suffer affliction with the people of God than to enjoy the pleasures of Egypt for a moment.

As glorious as Israel's personal experience with their God was and as wonderful as the signs, wonders, and miracles were, we shall see that none of that did change their human nature. Therefore their dependence on God became greater by the day for His mercies and forgiveness.

CHAPTER 4

Mount Sinai, Exodus 20-24

We saw in the previous chapter that the first three months' journey took Israel to the Wilderness of Sinai and there on Mount Sinai God revealed Himself to His people in a way He never did before. All the contents of the event were not reviewed. In this chapter we shall review more of the contents of that event. There was that ineffable glory but beyond it, we saw a God who is infinitely holy. On the other hand, Israel who represented the best of **fallen humanity** fell short and woefully inadequate to relate to God on the terms of holiness. Israel could not endure that Shekinah glory for long. They could not even endure the voice of the Living God speaking to them. They were seeking for somewhere to hide as they saw how unworthy they were.

However, there was a beautiful way to commemorate Mount Sinai and that was by living by the laws which were given them from Mount Sinai. How relevant are the words of the Master: "Man shall not live by bread alone, but by every word that proceeds from the mouth of God". In the end Mount Sinai must be remembered not so much for the glory of the Eternal God, but for the laws of the Holy God. These laws encompass the whole being of man: body, soul, and spirit; social, moral, and spiritual. All the events and circumstances experienced in the Wilderness had spiritual intent. Therefore, everything can be summed up in one law, Holiness unto the Lord.

This chapter encompasses the Ten Commandments, The Judgments, and Moses' return to the top of the holy Mount.

The Ten Commandments, Exodus 20:1-18
1 And God spoke all these words, saying,

2 I am the Lord thy God, which have brought thee out of the land of Egypt, out of the house of bondage.

3 Thou shalt have no other gods before me.

4 Thou shalt not make unto thee any graven image, or any likeness of anything that is in heaven above, or that is in the earth beneath, or that is in the waters under the earth:

5 Thou shalt not bow down thyself to them, nor serve them: for I the Lord thy God am a jealous God, visiting the iniquities of the fathers upon the children of the third and forth generation of them that hate me;

6 And showing mercy unto thousands of them that love me, and keep my commandments.

7 Thou shalt not take the name of the Lord thy God in vain; for the Lord wilt not hold him guiltless that taketh his name in vain.

8 Remember the Sabbath day to keep it holy.

9 Six days shalt thou labor and do all thy work:

10 But the seventh day is the Sabbath of the Lord thy God: in it thou shalt not do any work, thou, nor thy son, nor thy daughter, thy manservant, nor thy maidservant, nor thy cattle, nor thy stranger that is within thy gates.

11 For in six days the Lord made heaven and earth, the sea and all that in them is, and rested the seventh day: wherefore the Lord blessed the Sabbath day, and hallowed it.

12 Honor thy father and thy mother: that thy days may be long upon the land which the Lord thy God giveth thee.

13 Thou shalt not kill.

14 Thou shalt not commit adultery.

15 Thou shalt not steal.

16 Thou shalt not bear false witness against thy

neighbor.

Lying is another name for false witness.

17 Thou shalt not covet thy neighbor's house, thou shalt not covet thy neighbor's wife, nor his manservant, nor his maidservant, nor his ox, nor his nor his ass, nor any that is thy neighbor's.

The Ten Commandments are the foundation of all the laws of the Old Testament. All these laws can be summed in the words of Deuteronomy 6:5, "And thou shalt love the Lord thy God with all thine heart, and with all thy soul, and with all thy might". This does not imply the elimination of all the laws because they give the knowledge of God, and loving God comes from knowing Him.

18 And all the people saw the thundering, and the lightning, and the noise of the trumpet, and the mountain smoking: and when the people saw it, they removed and stood afar off.

19. And they said unto Moses, Speak thou with us and we will hear: but let not God speak with us, lest we die.

The people responded with fear because they were not in a right relationship with their God. When God called unto Adam and Eve in the Garden they responded with the same kind of fear. Sin causes fear and severs man's relationship with God. Unlike the Children of Israel, Moses eagerly embraced the presence of God.

20 And Moses said unto the people, Fear not: for God is come to prove you, and that is fear may be before your faces, that ye sin not.

21 And the people stood afar off, and Moses drew near unto the thick darkness where God was.

God's Response, 20:22-26

22 And the Lord said unto Moses, Thus thou shalt say unto the children of Israel, Ye have seen that I have talked with you from heaven.

23 Ye shall not make with me gods of silver, neither shall ye make unto you gods of gold.

Here God opened the door of Theology to reveal His omnipresent nature to Israel and all mankind. From Heaven the special place of His manifestation, God simultaneously manifested Himself on Mount Sinai. By God's omnipresent nature, He can manifest Himself simultaneously in as many places as He chooses. The Universe cannot contain Him: He fills Heaven and Earth. The mystery is that He conceals Himself so we cannot see Him. He is right beside you while you are reading this book.

24 An altar of earth thou shalt make unto me, and shalt sacrifice thereon thy burnt offerings, and thy peace offerings, thy sheep and thine oxen: in all places where I record my name I will come unto thee, and I will bless thee.

He keeps the door of Theology opened and reveals His holy nature in stating the requirement for an altar. By lifting up a hammer on any of the stones of the altar would have defiled it, making it meaningless and unworthy.

The altar of earth was for general purpose, particularly with respect to the oxen of the sin offering. In the Levitical Priesthood the body of the Sin Offering was burnt outside the camp; and in the days of the patriarchs the altar was for general purpose and could be a combination of earth and stones. God would permit these general purpose altars wherever He appointed them. These altars were not intended to replace the Tabernacle altars; they were to be altars of convenience.

25 And if thou wilt make me an altar of stone, thou shalt not build it of hewn stone; for if thou lift up thy tool upon it, thou hast polluted it.

Here the fearsome holiness of God is reflected.

26 Neither shalt thou go up by steps unto mine altar, that thy nakedness be not discovered thereon.

Appropriate attire is important in showing of reverence in

Divine worship. God is not worshipped by the clothes we wear but He requires Christians to dress modestly. Do not save your best clothing for occasions other than Divine worship.

The Judgments, Exodus 21-23:1-13:

The judgments are a list of given circumstances of actions, their solutions, and in some cases, their consequences. These were not man's ideas; they were God's commands intended for the wellbeing and spiritual wholeness of the Nation. They also show how greatly loved and special were the Children of Israel to their God. There was nothing too small, and of such, being insignificant with God. The details are most critical to a summary because a summary is logically woven therefrom.

1. Bondservant, Ex. 21:1-6:

1 Now these are the judgments which thou shalt set before them.

2 If thou buy an Hebrew servant, six years shall he serve: and in the seventh, he shall go out free for nothing.

3 If he came in by himself, he shall go out by himself: if he were married, then his wife shall go out with him.

4 If his master have given him a wife, and she have born him sons or daughters; the wife and her children shall be her master's, and he shall go out by himself.

5 And if the servant shall plainly say, I love my master, my wife , and my children; I will not go out free:

6 Then his master shall bring him unto the judges; he shall also bring him to the door, or unto the door post; and his master shall bore his ear through with an awl; and he shall serve him forever.

2. Maidservant, Ex. 21:7-11

7 And if a man sell his daughter to be a maidservant, she shall not go out as the men servants do.

8 If she pleases not her master, who hath betrothed her to himself, then shall he let her be redeemed: to sell her unto a strange nation he shall have no power, seeing he hath dealt deceitfully with her.

9 And if he have betrothed her unto his son, he shall deal with her after the manner of daughters.

10 If he take him another wife; her food, her raiment, and her duty of marriage, shall he not diminish.

11 And if he do not these three unto her, then shall she go out free without money.

3. Murder, 21:12-15:

12 He that smites a man, so that he die, shall be surely put to death.

13 And if a man lie not in wait, but God delivers him into his hand; then I will appoint thee a place whither he shall flee.

14 But if a man come presumptuously upon his neighbor, to slay him with guile; thou shalt take him from mine altar, that he may die.

15 And he that smites his father, or his mother, shall be surely put to death.

4. Stealing and Selling a Man, 21:16:

16 And he that steals a man and sells him, or if he be found in his hand, he shall surely be put to death.

5. Cursing of Parents, 21:17: And he that curses his father, or his mother shall surely be put to death.

6. Fight Between Two Men, 21:18-19: And if men strife together, and one smite another with a stone, or with his fist, and he die not, but keeps his bed.

19 If he rise again, and walk abroad upon his staff, then shall he that smote him be quit: only he shall pay for the loss of his time, and shall cause him to be thoroughly healed.

7. Physical Conflict between Master and Servant, Ex. 21:20-21:

20 And if a man smite his servant, or his maid, with a rod, and he die under his hand; he shall be surely punished.

21 Notwithstanding, if he continue a day or two, he shall not be punished: for he is his money.

8. *Injury to a Pregnant Woman, 21:22-25:*

22 If men strive, and hurt a woman with child, so that her fruit depart from her, and yet no mischief follow: he shall be surely punished, according as the woman's husband will lay upon him; and he shall pay as the judges determine.

23 And if any mischief follow, then thou shalt give life for life,

24 Eye for eye, tooth for tooth, hand for hand, foot for foot,

25 Burning for burning, wound for wound, stripe for stripe.

9. *Injury Caused to a Servant, 21:26-27:* And if a man smite the eye of his servant, or the eye of his maid, that it perished; he shall let him go free for his eye's sake.

27 And if he smite out his manservant's tooth, or his maidservant's tooth; he shall let him go free for his tooth's sake.

10. *Injury Caused by an Ox to a Man, 21:28-32:* If an ox gore a man or a woman, that they die: then the ox shall be surely stoned, and his flesh shall not be eaten; but the owner of the ox shall be quit.

29 But if the ox were wont to push with his horn in time past, and it hath been testified to his owner, and he hath not kept him in, but that he hath killed a man or a woman; the ox shall be stoned, and his owner also shall be put to death.

30 If there be laid on him a sum of money, then he shall give for the ransom of his life whatsoever is laid upon him.

31 Whether he have gored a son, or have gored a daughter, according to this judgment shall it be done unto him.

32 If the ox shall push a manservant or a maid servant;

he shall give unto their masters thirty shekels of silver, and the ox shall be stoned.

11. Injury Caused by a Pit, 21:33-34: And if a man shall open a pit, or if a man shall dig a pit, and not cover it, and an ox or an ass fall therein;

34 The owner of the pit shall make it good, and give money unto the owner of them; and the dead beast shall be his.

12. Injury Caused by Animals to Animals, 21:35-36: And if one man's ox hurt another's, that he die; then they shall sell the live ox, and divide the money of it; and the dead ox also they shall divide.

36 Or if it be known that the ox hath used to push in times past, and his owner hath not kept him in; he shall surely pay ox for ox; and the dead shall be his own.

13. Stealing Ox or Sheep, 22:1-4:

1 If a man shall steal an ox or a sheep, and kill it, or sell it; he shall restore five oxen for an ox, and four sheep for a sheep.

2 If a thief be found breaking up, and be smitten that he die, there shall no blood be shed for him.

3 If the sun be risen upon him, there shall be no blood shed for him; for he should make full restitution; if he have nothing, then he shall be sold for his theft.

4 If the theft be certainly found in his hand alive, whether it be ox or ass, or sheep; he shall restore double.

14. Restitution of a Field, 22:5-6: If a man shall cause a field or a vineyard to be eaten, and shall put in his beast, and shall feed in another man's field; of the best of his own field, and of the best of his own vineyard, shall he make restitution.

6 If fire break out, and catch in thorns, so that the stacks of corn, or the standing corn, or the field be consumed therewith; he that kindled the fire shall surely make restitution.

15. Restitution of Money, 22:7-9: If a man shall deliver to his neighbor money or stuff to keep, and it be stolen out of the man's house; if the thief be found, let him pay double.

8 If the thief be not found, then the master of the house shall be brought unto the judges, to see whether he have put his hand unto his neighbor's goods.

This is considered a case of trespassing and in such case the consequence is that the guilty party paid a double compensation. Verse 9 explains: For all manner of trespass, whether it is for ox, for ass, for sheep, for raiment, or for any manner of lost thing, which another challenges to be his, the cause of both parties shall come before the judges; and whom the judges shall condemn, he shall pay double unto his neighbor. The trespasser was never condemned, he was commanded to make restitution with his neighbor.

16. Restitution of animals, 22:10-15: If a man deliver unto his neighbor an ass, or an ox, or a sheep, or any beast, to keep; and if it die, or be hurt, or driven away, no man sees it:

11 Then shall an oath of the Lord be between them both, that he hath not put his hand unto his neighbor's goods; and the owner of it shall accept thereof, and he shall not make it good.

12 And if be stolen from him, he shall make restitution unto the owner thereof.

13 If it be torn in pieces, then let him bring it for a witness, and he shall not make good that which was torn.

14 If a man borrow aught of his neighbor, and it be hurt, or die, the owner thereof   being not with it, he shall surely make it good.

15 But if the owner thereof be with it, he shall not make it good: if it be an hired thing, it came for his hire.

17. Man and a maid, 22:16-18: And if a man entice a maid that is not betrothed, and lie with her, he shall surely endow her to be his wife.

17 If her father utterly refuse to give her unto him, he shall pay money according to the dowry of virgins.

18 Thou shalt not suffer a witch to live.

18. Bestiality, Idolatry, 22:19-20 Whosoever lies with a beast shall surely be put to death.

20 He that sacrifices to any god, save unto the Lord only, he shall be utterly destroyed.

19. Relationship with the Poor, 22:21-28: Thou shalt neither vex a stranger, nor oppress him: for ye were strangers in the land of Egypt.

22 Ye shall not afflict any widow, or fatherless child.

23 If thou afflict them in any wise, and they cry at all unto me, I will surely hear their cry;

24 And my wrath shall wax hot, and I will kill you with the sword; and your wives shall be widows, and your children fatherless.

25 If thou lend money to any of my people that is poor by thee, thou shalt not be to him as an usurer, neither shalt thou lay upon him usury.

26 If thou at all take your neighbor's raiment to pledge, thou shalt deliver it unto him by that the sun goes down:

27 For that is his covering only, it is his raiment for his skin: wherein shall he sleep? And it shall come to pass, when he cries unto me, that I will hear; for I am gracious.

28 Thou shalt not revile the gods, nor curse the ruler of thy people.

20. The First Fruits, 22:29-31: Thou shalt not delay to offer the first of thy ripe fruits, and of thy liquors: the first born of thy sons shalt thou give unto me.

30 Likewise shalt thou do with thine oxen, and with thy sheep: seven days it shall be with his dam; on the eighth day thou shalt give it me.

31 And ye shall be holy men unto me: neither shall ye eat any flesh that is torn of beasts in the field; ye shall cast it to the dogs.

21. A False Report, 23:1-3, 6, 7: Thou shalt not raise a false report: put not thine hand with the wicked to be an unrighteous witness.

2 Thou shalt not follow a multitude to do evil; neither shalt thou speak in a cause to decline after many to wrest judgment:

3 Neither shalt thou countenance a poor man in his cause.

6 Thou shalt not wrest the judgment of the poor in his cause.

7 Keep thee far from a false matter; and the innocent and righteous slay thou not: for I will not justify the wicked.

22. Strayed Animals, 23:4-5: If thou meet thine enemy's ox or his ass going astray, thou shalt surely bring it back to him again.

5 If thou see the ass of him that hates you lying under his burden, and would forbear to help him, you shall surely help with him.

23. Perversion of Justice, 23:8-9: And thou shalt take no gift: for the gift blinds the wise, and perverts the words of the righteous.

9 Also thou shalt not oppress a stranger: for ye know the heart of a stranger, seeing ye were strangers in the land of Egypt.

All these judgments are of a social nature and are based on the commandment, Thou Shalt Love Thy Neighbor. Christ declares this commandment is second in priority to loving God. Loving God inspires love for one's neighbor.

Statutes of the Law, 23:10-19

Statutes of the Law describe celebrations and memorials, their formalities, and their appointed times. They were greatly significant for Israel to perpetuate from generation to generation. They did single out God's special mercies and blessings. These are only some of them.

1. The Sabbatical Year, Ex. 23:10-13: And six years thou shalt sow thy land, and shalt gather in the fruits thereof:

11 But the seventh year thou salt let it rest and lie still; that the poor of thy people may eat: and what they leave the beasts of the field shall eat. In like manner thou shalt deal with thy vineyard, and with thy olive-yard.

The time and reasons for the Sabbatical Year are herein clearly stated.

12 Six days thou shalt do thy work, and on the seventh day thou shalt rest: that thy ox and thine ass may rest, and the son of thine handmaid, and the stranger, may be refreshed.

13 And in all things that I have said unto you be circumspect: and make no mention of the name of other gods, neither let it be heard out of thy mouth.

2. The Feast of Unleavened Bread, Ex. 23:14-15: Three times thou shalt keep a feast unto me in the year.

15 Thou shalt keep the feast of unleavened bread: (thou shalt eat unleavened bread seven days, as I commanded you, in the time appointed of the month Abib; for in it thou came out from Egypt: and none shall appear before me empty:)

3. The Feast of the First Fruits, Ex. 23:16,19: And the feast of harvest, the first fruits of your labors, which thou hast sown in the field: and the feast of ingathering, which is in the end of the year, when thou hast gathered in your labors out of the field.

19 The first of the first fruits of thy land thou shalt bring into the house of the Lord thy God. Thou shalt not seethe a kid in his mother's milk.

4. The Feast of Ingathering, Ex. 23:16-17: And the feast of ingathering, which is in the end of the year, when thou hast gathered in your labors out of the field.)

17 Three times in the year all thy males shall appear before me the Lord God.

18 Thou shat not offer the blood of my sacrifice with leavened bread; neither shall the fat of my sacrifices remain until the morning.

These statutes are based on the first commandment. They inspired Israel's love and obedience. The Feast of Unleavened Bread reminded them of the Passover. The feasts of the First Fruits and the Ingathering were to remind them that their material blessings came from God.

All the males were to appear before the Lord during the Feast of Unleavened Bread, during the Feast of Weeks, known as Pentecost, and during the Feast of the Tabernacles (Deuteronomy 16:16).

The Pre-Incarnate Son, Their Captain to the Promised Land, Ex. 23:20-23

20 Behold, I send an Angel before thee, to keep thee in the way, and to bring thee into the place which I have prepared.

21 Beware of him, and obey his voice, provoke him not; for he will not pardon your transgressions: for my name is in him.

22 But if thou shalt indeed obey his voice, and do all that I speak; then I will be an enemy unto thine enemies, and an adversary to thine adversaries.

The Pre-Incarnate Christ appeared on a number of different occasions in Old Testament Times in angelic form. Some consider He did so in anticipation of the Incarnation. Israel needed more than a mere physical leader that's why God promised them this special angel, the Pre-Incarnate Christ. Notice the words,... "Provoke him not; for he will not pardon your transgressions: for my name is in him".

23 For mine angel shall go before thee, and bring thee unto the Amorites, and the Hittites, and the Perizzites, and the Canaanites, the Hivites, and the Jebusites: and I will cut them off.

The Blessings of Obedience, 23:24-33:

24 Thou shalt not bow down to their gods, nor serve them, nor do after their works: but thou shalt utterly overthrow them, and quite break down their images.

25 And ye shall serve the Lord your God, and he shall bless thy bread, and thy water; and I will take sickness away from the midst of thee.

26 There shall nothing cast their young, nor be barren, in thy land: the number of thy days I will fulfill.

27 I will send my fear before thee, and will destroy all the people to whom thou shalt come, and I will make all thine enemies turn their backs unto thee.

28 And I will send hornets before thee, which shall drive out the Hivite, the Canaanite, and the Hittite, from before thee.

29 I will not drive them out from before thee in one year; lest the land become desolate, and the beast of the field multiply against thee.

30 By little and little I will drive them out from before thee, until thou be increased, and inherit the land.

31 And I will set thy bounds from the Red Sea even unto the sea of the Philistines, and from the desert unto the river: for I will deliver the inhabitants of the land into your hand; and thou shalt drive them out before thee.

32 Thou shalt make no covenant with them, nor with their gods.

33 They shall not dwell in thy land, lest they make thee sin against me: for if thou serve their gods, it will surely be a snare unto thee.

These blessings were based on condition of obedience and guaranteed by the Immutable God. They were blessings of prosperity, honor, power, protection, and independence of other nations; their dependence should only be on God.

Moses Called to the top of Mount Sinai, Exodus 24

1. *Moses and the Seventy Elders called to the Mount*, *24:1-3:* And the Lord said unto Moses, Come up unto the Lord, thou, and Aaron, Nanab, and Abihu, and seventy of the elders of Israel; and worship ye a far off.

It was necessary for Israel's God to personally reveal Himself to them. He chose the time and place and how. It was to remove all lingering doubts from the minds and hearts of His people as to who He is and was. It was appropriate then that Aaron, his two sons, the 70 elders of Israel be given the privilege of going up on the holy Mount to meet with their God. Moses long had a personal experience with Him and was absolutely sure of His eternal existence. He was more than happy to guide them to the holy Mount. As a faithful and obedient servant, Moses returned from the Mount and delivered to Israel the message of the Lord. The people responded with joy.

2 And Moses alone shall come near the Lord: but they shall not come nigh; neither shall the people go up with him.

3 And Moses came and told the people all the words of the Lord, and all the judgments: and all the people answered with one voice, and said, All the words which the Lord hath said will we do.

2. Moses Offers Sacrifice unto the Lord, 24:4-8

And Moses wrote all the words of the Lord, and rose up early in the morning, and built an altar under the hill, and twelve pillars, according to the twelve tribes of Israel.

Being highly honored and favored by God, Moses became more fervent in serving and worshipping God. By the burden of love for his people, he humbly and faithfully served them against all odds. During this time of urgency and high expectation of God's people, he took time to build an altar for Divine worship. To truly worship God takes time and sacrifice. Time and formality showed reverence and recognition of God's spiritual and material blessings. In doing so, as the leader of the new nation, he sets a supreme example of the requirement of the first commandment.

5 And he sent young men of the children of Israel, which offered burnt offerings, and sacrificed peace offerings of oxen unto the Lord.

6 And Moses took half of the blood, and put it in basins; and half of the blood he sprinkled on the altar.

7 And he took the book of the covenant, and read it in the audience of the people: and they said, All that the Lord hath said will we do, and be obedient.

His other duty was to lead Israel the way to true worship. God must be worshipped in spirit and in truth. It takes cleansing and sanctification. God was dwelling on the Mount seven days. Therefore, the minds, hearts, eyes, and ears of the people had to be sanctified. There was no better way to sanctify the people than to read to them from the Book of the Covenant and to sprinkle them with the blood of the Covenant. The blood of the innocent animal reminded them of their guilt, the consequence of death, and yet the forgiveness of their sins. Therefore there was no reason to be afraid of the presence of God.

Having done that, he was ready to guide Aaron and the seventy elders of Israel to the holy Mount.

8 And Moses took the blood, and sprinkled it on the people, and said, Behold the blood of the covenant, which the Lord hath made with you concerning all these things.

3.Moses and the Seventy Elders Went up to Mount Sinai, Ex. 24:9-11:

Then went up Moses and Aaron, Nadab, and Abihu, and seventy of the elders of Israel:

The cleansing blood was symbolic of the blood of Christ, which must cleanse the believers before they can have fellowship with God.

10 And they saw the God of Israel: and there was under

His feet as it were a paved work of a sapphire stone, and as it were the body of heaven in its clearness.

11 And upon the nobles of the children of Israel he laid not his hand: also they saw God, and did eat and drink.

God's people actually saw their God. This was not all about Him; it was for their edification and wellbeing. The elders could describe with their own eyes God's feet, yet were unable to follow His footsteps in the wilderness.

4. Moses Alone went to the Top of The Mount, *24:12-18:* And the Lord said unto Moses, Come up to me into the mount, and be there: and I will give thee tables of stone, and a law and commandments which I have written; that you may teach them.

13 And Moses rose up and his minister Joshua: and Moses went up into the mount of God.

14 And he said unto the elders, Tarry ye here for us, until we come again unto you: and, behold, Aaron and Hur are with you: if any man have any matters to do, let him come unto them.

16 And the glory of the Lord abode upon mount Sinai, and the cloud covered it six days: and the seventh day he called unto Moses out of the midst of the cloud.

Moses had to experience further sanctification before he was ready to enter into the immediate presence of God. The number, 7 indicates completion. It indicated the completion of God's sovereign visitation on Mount Sinai. On the other hand, it indicated the completion of Moses' sanctification.

17 And the sight of the glory of the Lord was like devouring fire on the top of the mount in the eyes of the children of Israel

We can readily see God's reason for leading by the way of the wilderness.

18 And Moses went into the midst of the cloud, and gat him into the mount: and Moses was in the mount forty days and fort nights.

SUMMARY

In talking about Mount Sinai, the first thing that comes to mind is the Ten Commandments. The second thing that comes to mind is the Shekinah Glory. This seems to suggest that the principles of His holiness outweigh the splendor of Mount Sinai. All the laws of the Old Testament are based on the Ten Commandments and are summed up in in Deuteronomy 6:5, "And thou shalt love the Lord thy God with all thine heart, and with all thy soul, and with all thy might".

In revealing Himself so manifestly on Mount Sinai, *God* opened the door of Theology to reveal His omnipresent nature to Israel and all mankind. From Heaven the special place of His manifestation, God simultaneously manifested Himself on Mount Sinai. By God's omnipresent nature, He can manifest Himself simultaneously in as many places as He chooses. The Universe cannot contain Him: He fills Heaven and Earth. The mystery is that He conceals Himself so we cannot see Him.

The judgments issued from Mount Sinai were based on the tenth commandment, Thou shalt not covet. These judgments are directed at social justice. They are a list of given circumstances, their solutions, and in some cases, their consequences are given. These were not man's ideas; they were God's commands intended for the wellbeing and spiritual wholeness of the Nation. They also show how greatly loved and special were the Children of Israel to their God. There was, nothing too small, and of such, being insignificant with God.

There were also the Statutes of the Law. They describe celebrations and memorials, their formalities, and their appointed times. They were greatly significant for Israel in perpetuating the memory of God's blessings from generation to generation. These statutes are based on the First

Commandment. They inspired Israel's love and obedience. The Feast of Unleavened Bread reminded them of the Passover. The feasts of the First Fruits and the Ingathering were to remind them that their material blessings came from God.

Finally the elders of Israel had the most personal encounter with their God. God's people actually saw their God. This was not all about Him; it was for their edification and wellbeing. The elders could describe with their own eyes God's feet, yet were unable to follow His footsteps in the Wilderness.

CHAPER 5

The Concept of The Tabernacle, Exodus 25-27

In the previous chapter we described the Mount Sinai Experience and reviewed some of the contents of that experience. The glory of that experience is long gone. But the principles by which all mankind are expected to live remain with us.

The concept of the Tabernacle and its vessels is among the contents of the Mount Sinai Experience. The contents of the experience extend beyond this chapter to the end of the book of Exodus and beyond. This chapter encompasses only the concept of the Tabernacle and not the actual building. The actual building will be reviewed in a subsequent chapter. The gathering of the material is the first part of the concept.

Taking an Offering, Ex. 25:1-9

1 And the Lord spoke unto Moses, saying,

2 Speak unto the children of Israel, that they bring me an offering: of every man that giveth it willingly with his heart ye shall take my offering.

God commanded Moses to take an offering for the building of the Tabernacle and its instruments of Divine service. The people were to give willingly. This command would test their obedience and love for God. In most cases this freewill offering would be sacrificial. God knew if they had the Will, all that was needed would be found among the people.

He describes all that was needed:
3 And this is the offering which ye shall take of them; gold, and silver, and brass,
4 And blue, and purple, and scarlet, and fine linen, and goats hair,
5 And ram's skin dyed red, and badgers' skins, and shittim wood,
6 Oil for the light, spices for anointing oil, and for sweet incense,
7 Onyx stones, and stones to be set in the ephod, and in the breastplate.

There was a specific purpose for everything requested. The colors had special symbolic significance. The blue symbolizes holiness, Divinity. Purple the next color symbolizes the Incarnation: Divinity mingled with humanity, the Divine nature and the human nature united in the person of Christ for the purpose of cleansing humanity from sin. The third color, scarlet, symbolizes sin which necessitated the Incarnation. The fourth color, the fine linen, symbolizes the outworking of the Divine and the human process of the Incarnation. That process resulted in the righteousness of Christ and applied by faith to the Believer.

None of the colors stood alone; they were to be used together for the purpose of building the Tabernacle. Neither did any of the symbolisms stand alone; they reflect the righteous-ness in cleansing the soul from sin, which was represented by the scarlet. These colors were featured prominently in the building of the Tabernacle.

The goats' hair, the rams' skins, and the badgers' skins were to make the threefold covering of the Tabernacle.

The precious stones represented the twelve tribes of Israel. The greater significance of these stones is a reflection of God's glory in many different ways by the Believers. The twofold purpose of the holy oil to sustain the lamps of the Candlestick and to anoint the instruments and the High Priest symbolizes a separation unto God. The greater symbolism of all of this is the anointing of the Holy Spirit for the proclamation of the Gospel.

The Vessels

The Ark of the Covenant, 25:10-16:

10 And they shall make an ark of shittim wood: two cubits and a half shall be the length thereof, and a cubit and a half the breath thereof, and a cubit and a half the height thereof.

11 And thou shalt overlay it with pure gold, within and without shalt thou overlay it, and shalt make upon it a crown of gold round about.

12 And thou shalt cast four rings of gold for it, and put them in the four corners thereof; and two rings shall be it the one side of it, and two rings in the other side of it.

13 And thou shalt make staves of shittim wood, and overlay them with gold.

14 And thou shalt put the staves into the rings by the sides of the ark, that the ark may be borne by them.

15 The staves shall be in the rings of the ark: they shall not be taken from it.

16 And thou shalt put into the ark the testimony which I shall give thee.

The Ark was essentially a place of safety. One of the best illustration was the ark of little Moses; he cried in his ark but he was safe. Noah's ark is a another example. That ark alone saved humanity from absolute destruction. By the design of the Ark of the Covenant, it was the greatest place of safety for the most valuable document known to man, the Covenant of the Everlasting God with Israel. He made that same Covenant with Abraham, Isaac, and Jacob in a different form. The Covenant with them became His name: The God Abraham, The God of Isaac, and The God of Jacob (Exodus 3:15). Now in this Covenant with Israel, the words were written by the finger of God. With Israel it needed a safer place of protection, the Golden Ark.

<u>The Mercy Seat Covering the Ark of the Covenant</u>

The Mercy Seat, Ex. 25:17-22

17 And thou shalt make a mercy seat of pure gold: two cubits and a half shall be the length thereof, and a cubit and a half the breath thereof.

18 And you shall make two cherubim of gold, of beaten

work shall you make them, in the two ends of the mercy seat.

19 And make one cherub on the one end, and the other cherubim on the other end: even of the mercy seat shall ye make the cherubim on the two ends thereof.

20 And the cherubim shall stretch forth their wings on high, covering the mercy seat with their wings, and their faces shall look one to another; toward the mercy seat shall the faces of the cherubim be.

21 And thou shalt put the mercy seat above upon the ark; and in the ark thou shalt put the testimony that I shall give thee.

22 And there I will meet with thee, and I will commune with thee from above the mercy seat, from between the two cherubim which are upon the ark of the testimony, of all things which I will give thee in commandment unto the children of Israel.

The Mercy Seat was put on top of the Ark of the Covenant. It signifies that God could only relate to man in mercy. The cherubim covering the Mercy Seat signifying that man is impure and unholy to approach God on his own behalf. Even his petitions must go through the process of the Mercy Seat overshadowed by the cherubim, symbolizing that man needed a mediator. The sin nature could not have been more evident than from Israel's murmurings after God divided the Red Sea and from many occasions after He miraculously provided for them.

There had to be a bridge between the Holy God and a disobedient and rebellious people. Israel had that bridge in the instituting of the Mercy Seat.

Verse 22 seems to suggest a special privilege of access granted to Moses by which he could approach God whenever the need arose. That was not the case with Aaron; he only had access once a year. While the Ark of the Covenant was made of Shittim Wood and gold; the Mercy Seat was made of pure gold. The Candlestick was the only other instrument made of pure gold. The frame of the Tabernacle and other instruments of service were made of Shittim Wood and gold. The Shittim Wood is from a large tree family of more than a thousand species; the Shittim Wood is only one such species. It is notable for lumbering, chiefly for its preservative properties and durability. When compared with gold which was often used with it, it was, indeed, fragile. In this respect, it represents man's fragile mortality, but when clothed in gold will endure forever.

The gold not only represents immortality but everlasting righteousness as well. The purpose of Redemption is about procuring immortality for the Believers and an environment of everlasting righteousness in which they can exercise their immortality.

While the gold and the Shittim Wood could remain together forever, none of these two components would lose its identity: though the Believer will attain immortality, he will not lose his identity and change to something else. Believers will become like the angels, but will never become the angels.

The Table of the Showbread, Ex. 25:23-30

23 Thou shalt also make a table of shittim wood: two cubits shall be the length thereof, and a cubit the breath thereof, and a cubit and a half the height thereof.

24 And thou shalt overlay it with pure gold, and make thereto a crown of gold round about.

25 And thou shalt make unto it a border of an handbreath round about, and thou shalt make a golden crown to the border thereof round about.

26 And thou shalt make for it four rings of gold, and put the rings in the four corners that are on the four feet thereof.

27 Over against the border shall the rings be for places of the staves to bear the table.

28 And thou shalt make the staves of shittim wood, and overlay them with gold, that the table may be borne with them.

29 And thou shalt make the dishes thereof, and the spoons thereof, and covers thereof, and bowls thereof, to cover withal: of pure gold shalt thou make them.

The Table of the Showbread was also made with shittim wood and covered with gold. The cubit measurement used was the length from the index finger to the elbow, which

Table of the Showbread

varied from 16 to 23 inches. For simplicity, the cubit is herein considered a foot and a half. The Showbread symbolizes God's faithfulness to provide for Israel daily.

30 And thou shalt set upon the table showbread before me always.

The Candlestick, Ex. 25:31-40:

31 And thou shalt make a candlestick of pure gold: of beaten work shall the candlestick be made: his shaft, and his branches, his bowls, his knobs, and his flowers, shall be the same.

32 And six branches shall come out of the sides of it; three branches of thc candlestick out of one side, and three branches of the candlestick out of the other side:

33 Three bowls made like unto almonds, with a knob and a flower in one branch; and three bowls made like almonds in the other branch, with a knob and a flower: so in the six branches that come out of the candlestick.

34 And in the candlestick shall be four bowls made like unto almonds, with their knobs and their flowers.

35 And there shall be a knob under two branches of the same, and a knob under two branches of the same, according to the six branches that proceed out of the candlestick.

36 Their knobs and their branches shall be of the same: and it shall be one beaten work of pure gold.

37 And thou shalt make the seven lamps thereof: and they shall light the lamps thereof, that they may give light over against it.

38 And the tongs thereof, and the snuff-dishes thereof, shall be of pure gold.

39 Of a talent of pure gold shall he make it, with all these vessels.

40 And look that thou make them after their pattern, which was shown thee in the mount.

The Candlestick was a masterful work of art; it and all its accessories were made of a talent of gold (75 U.S. pounds). Its branches, knobs, and flowers symbolize the beauty of Creation. Its seven lamps symbolize the seven Spirits of God (arch angels, Rev. 3: 1; 4:5; 8: 2). Its purpose was to give light in the Sanctuary day and night. The number 7 signifies completion: God finishes what He begins; the journey would not end in the wilderness but in the Promised Land.

The Candlestick

The Candlestick symbolizes Christ the Light of the World. The World lives in the darkness caused by sin. Christ gives the opportunity to everyone to leave the darkness of sin behind.

The Tabernacle Itself, Ex. 25:8, 9; 26:1-6

8 And let them make me a sanctuary; that I may dwell among them.

9 According to all that I show thee, after the pattern of the tabernacle, and the pattern of all the instruments thereof, even so shall ye make it.

26:1 Moreover thou shalt make the tabernacle with ten curtains of twined linen, and blue, and purple, and scarlet: with cherubim of cunning work shalt thou make them.

2 The length of one curtain shall be eight and twenty cubits, and the breath of one curtain four cubits: and every one of the curtains shall have one measure.

3 The five curtains shall be coupled together one to another; and other five curtains shall be coupled one to another.

The Tabernacle was to be made of ten curtains of blue, purple, scarlet, and twined linen, symbolizing God's holiness, redemption, sin, and the outworking of redemption (twined linen, the imputed righteousness of Christ). The north side was to be made of five curtains and the south side was to be made of five curtains. Each curtain was 42 feet by 6 feet. Two of these would be connected at the length, making a length of 84 feet by 6 feet. Two of the other 3 curtains would be connected together at the length and be connected with the first two curtains on top, making a height of 12 feet (84 feet long by 12 feet high). The other curtain would be divided into two halves, connected together, and be connected to the other four curtains, making a height of 15 feet. Thus the north side would be 84 feet long by 15 feet high. The south side would be done the same as the north side. The approximate length and height of the Tabernacle would be 84 feet by 15 feet from the details herein provided.

The curtains would be connected as stated below.

4 And thou shalt make loops of blue upon the edge of one curtain from the selvedge in the coupling; and likewise shall

you make in the uttermost edge of another curtain, in the coupling of the second.

5 Fifty loops shalt thou make in the one curtain, and fifty loops shalt thou make in the edge of the curtain that is in the coupling of the second; that the loops may take hold one of another.

6 And you shall make fifty taches of gold, and couple the curtains together with the taches: and it shall be one tabernacle.

The completed Tabernacle would have a threefold covering as stated below.

Its Covering, 26:7-14: And thou shalt make curtains of goats' hair to be a covering upon the tabernacle: eleven curtains shalt thou make.

8 The length of one curtain shall be thirty cubits, and the breath of one curtain four cubits: and the eleven curtains shall be all of one measure.

9 And thou shalt couple five curtains by themselves, and six curtains by themselves, and shalt double the six curtain in the forefront of the tabernacle.

10 And thou shalt make fifty loops on the edge of one curtain that is outmost in the coupling, and fifty loops in the edge of the curtain which couples the second.

11 And thou shalt make fifty taches of brass, and put the taches into the loops, and couple the tent together, that it may be one.

12 And the remnant that remains of the curtains of the tent, the half curtain that remains, shall hang over the backside of the tabernacle.

13 And a cubit on the one side, and a cubit on the other side of that which remains in the length of the curtains of the tent, it shall hang over the sides of the tabernacle on this side and on that side, to cover it.

14 And thou shalt make a covering for the tent of rams' skins dyed red, and a covering above the badgers' skins.

Boards, Ex. 26:15-30:

15 And thou shalt make boards for the tabernacle of shittim wood standing up.

16 Ten cubits shall be the length of a board, and a cubit and a half shall be the breath of one board.

17 Two tenons shall there be in one board, set in order one against another: thus shalt thou make for all the boards of the tabernacle.

18 And thou shalt make the boards for the tabernacle, twenty boards on the south side southward.

19 And thou shalt make forty sockets of silver under twenty boards; two sockets under one board for his two tenons, and two sockets under another board for his two tenons. (a projection on the end shaped for insertion)

20 And for the second side of the tabernacle on the north side there shall be twenty boards:

There were to be 40 boards, 15 feet high (10 cubits high) by 2' 3" (1 ½ cubit).

These boards were to be placed upright, corresponding to the height of the Tabernacle, and to be used at the north and the south sides of the of the Tabernacle. In addition, there were to be 8 boards at the west side of the Tabernacle. These boards were to be reinforced with 15 bars. These boards and bars made the frame of the Tabernacle. They were all made from Shittim Wood and covered with gold. Their connections are stated below.

21 And their forty sockets of silver; two sockets under one board, and two sockets under another board.

22 And for the sides of the tabernacle westward thou shalt make six boards.

23 And two boards shalt thou make for the corners of the tabernacle in the two sides.

24 And they shall be coupled together beneath, and they shall be coupled together above the head of it unto one ring:

thus shall it be for them both; they shall be for the two corners.

25 And they shall be eight boards, and their sockets of silver, sixteen sockets; two sockets under one board, and two sockets under another board.

26 And thou shalt make bars of shittim wood; five for the boards on one side of the tabernacle,

27 And five bars for the boards of the other side of the tabernacle, and five bars for the boards of the side of the tabernacle, for the two sides westward.

28 And the middle bar in the midst of the boards shall reach from end to end.

29 And thou shalt overlay the boards with gold, and make their rings of gold for places for the bars: and thou shalt overlay the bars with gold.

30 And thou shalt rear up the tabernacle according to the fashion thereof which was shown thee in the mount.

The frame of the Tabernacle of boards and bars were made of shittim wood and covered with gold. On this golden frame the ten curtains of blue, purple, scarlet, and twined linen, and the threefold covering hanged.

Veil of the Holy of Holies, Ex. 26:31-33:

31 And thou shalt make a veil of blue, and purple, and scarlet, and fine twined linen of cunning work: with cherubim shall it be made:

32 And thou shalt hang it upon four pillars of shittim wood overlaid with gold: their hooks shall be of gold, upon the four sockets of silver.

33 And thou shalt hang up the veil under the taches, that you may bring in thither within the veil the ark of the testimony: and the veil shall divide unto you between the holy place and the most holy.

Placing the Furniture, 26: 34-35: 34 And thou shalt put the mercy seat upon the ark of the testimony in the most holy place.

The Veil was to be made with art work of cherubim. Cherubim have specific duties in worship and are often unseen guests at places of worship. The art work of the cherubim on the most holy veil suggests their important role in Divine worship. They also overshadow the Mercy Seat, showing their important role in Divine worship. The Veil that separates the most holy place, the oracle, where the Ark of the Covenant and the Mercy Seat are kept, from the Sanctuary where the Golden Altar of Incense, the Table of the Showbread, and Candlestick are placed.

<u>Holy Sanctuary Showing the Holy Veil, Candlestick, Table with the Showbread, and Golden Altar of Burnt Incense</u>

35 And thou shalt set the table without the veil, and the candlestick over against the table on the side of the tabernacle toward the south: and thou shalt put the table on the north side.

Curtain for the Door 26: 36-37: And thou shalt make an hanging for the door of the tent, of blue, and purple, and scarlet, and fine twined linen, wrought with needlework.

37 And thou shalt make for the hanging five pillars of shittim wood, and overlay them with gold, and their hooks shall be of gold: and thou shalt cast five sockets of brass for them.

The door of the Tabernacle was to be made of blue, purple, scarlet, and twined linen as the holy Veil, and the curtains of the Tabernacle.

The Burnt Altar, Ex. 27:1-8

1 And thou shalt make an altar of shittim wood, five cubits long, and five cubits broad; the altar shall be foursquare and the height thereof shall be three cubits.

2 And thou shalt make the horns of it upon the four corners thereof: his horns shall be of the same: and thou shalt overlay it with brass.

3 And thou shalt make his pans to receive his ashes, and his shovels, and his basins, and his flesh hooks, and his firepans: all the vessels thereof thou shalt make of brass.

4 And thou shalt make for it a grate of network of brass; and upon the net shalt thou make four brazen rings in the corners thereof.

5 And thou shalt put it under the compass of the altar beneath, that the net may be even to the midst of the altar.

6 And thou shalt make staves for the altar, staves of shittim wood, and overlay them with brass.

7 And the staves shall be put into the rings, and the staves shall be upon the two sides of the altar, to bear it.

8 Hollow with boards shalt thou make it: as it was shown thee in the mount, so shall they make it.

Burnt Altar: Approximate measure, 7' x 7' x 41/2'

Its grater implication is that Divine worship involves time and sacrifice. The body and blood of the dead animal represent the consequences of sin, guilt and death for which Atonement must be made. Yet the altar signifies hope and forgiveness of sins. But worship must be cleansed from all impurities of the soul.

The Court of the Tabernacle, Ex. 27:9-21:

9 And thou shalt make the court of the tabernacle: for the south side southward there shall be hangings for the court of fine twined linen of an hundred cubits long for one side:

10 And the twenty pillars thereof and their twenty sockets shall be of brass; the hooks of the pillars and their fillets shall be of silver.

11 And likewise for the north side in length there shall be hangings of an hundred cubits long, and his twenty pillars and their twenty sockets of brass; the hooks and the pillars and their fillets of silver.

12 And for the breath of the court on the west side shall be hangings of fifty cubits: their pillars ten and their sockets ten.

13 And the breath of the court on the east side eastward shall be fifty cubits.

14 The hangings of one side of the gate shall be fifteen cubits: their pillars three, and their sockets three.

15 And on the other side shall be hangings fifteen cubits: their pillars three, and their sockets three.

16 And for the gate of the court shall be an hanging of twenty cubits, of blue, and purple, and scarlet, and fine twined linen, wrought with needlework: and their pillars shall be four, and their sockets four.

17 All the pillars round about the court shall be filleted with silver; their hooks shall be of silver, and their sockets of brass.

18 The length of the court shall be an hundred cubits, and the breath fifty every-where, and the height five cubits of fine twined linen, and their sockets of brass.

19 All the vessels of the tabernacle in all the service thereof, and all the pins thereof, and all the pins of the court, shall be of brass.

20 And thou shalt command the children of Israel, that they bring thee pure oil olive beaten for the light, to cause the lamp to burn always.

21 In the tabernacle of the congregation without the veil, which is before the testimony, Aaron and his sons shall order it from evening to morning before the Lord: it shall be a statute forever unto their generations on the behalf of the children of Israel.

In the Court were the Burnt Altar and the Laver. The Court was to be 150 feet long, 75 feet wide, 7 ½ feet high with a gate 20 feet wide, made of blue, purple, scarlet, and twined linen, as the curtains and the holy veil. I am sure the Court would be used for different religious occasions.

Tabernacle and Its Court

SUMMARY

Israel was God's special people because of their spiritual relationship with Him. Before the time of the Exodus God had not personally revealed Himself to them as a nation, as He did with their fathers. He chose the Exodus to reveal His power, but the Wilderness Experience was the time to personally reveal Himself. To know God is to know His holy nature to understand the principles of holiness for maintaining their spiritual relationship with Him.

Giving them the plan to build the Tabernacle was a way of personally revealing Himself and His holy nature. The whole concept of the Tabernacle was to declare that message. Like nothing else, the colors used in the Tabernacle, on the one hand, emphasize His holy nature and the promise of Redemption. On the other hand, the colors equally emphasize the sin nature of man and what can and will happen, once the sin nature is processed by Redemption.

Indeed, man's own mortality was reflected by the shittim wood which was to be commonly used in building the

Tabernacle. It was to be covered with gold. The gold was a symbol of immortality, it will endure forever. The shittim wood by itself cannot last forever, but will when covered and protected by gold. The Tabernacle, 84 feet long, 40 feet wide, and 15 feet high, could be called the Golden Tabernacle because it had gold everywhere. Another thing about the gold is that it symbolizes everlasting righteousness, and also Israel as a royal nation and a peculiar people. And what can better reflect the Shekinah glory than Pure Gold?

The detailed concept of the Tabernacle indicates that Divine worship is the most important thing in life. The Ark of the Covenant indicates that God is faithful in keeping His promises. The Mercy Seat overshadowing the Ark of the Covenant shows that God can only relate to man through mercy. The Holy of Holies shows the infinite holiness of God who can be approached by sinful man. While the Sanctuary indicates mutual fellowship with God, The Court implies the universality of Redemption.

The Tabernacle was to be a place where God abode among His people. Today He does not dwell in temples made with hands; the Believers are the temple of God. The concept of the Tabernacle was complete, but its purpose could not be realized without the High Priest. In the next chapter, we shall review the concept of the High Priestly Office.

CHAPTER 6
The Concept of The High Priestly Office, exodus 28-31

The High Priestly Office was at the center of Israel's Theocracy. Through this agency God would draw near to His people and His people would draw near to Him; they would become His children and He their Father. They should share His nature and be more like him in the conduct of daily living. The role of the High Priest cannot be over stated. He was to approach God on behalf of the people and pronounce Divine benediction upon them, thus being a mediator between them and God.

Of necessity, the institutional requirements had to be in place for the function of the Office. In the previous chapter we saw that some of those requirements were described. In this chapter, we shall see the other requirements to complete the function and fulfillment of the High Priestly Office. The design of the holy garments and the description of the ceremonies of consecration both of the High Priest and of the instruments of services are herein given. However, the actual making of these instruments, including the Tabernacle itself, and the ceremonies will not occur until sometime later. Thus we shall only review the concept of these things.

The Holy Garments, Exodus 28:1-43

1.The Ephod, 1-14: And take thou unto thee Aaron thy brother, and his sons with him, from among the children of Israel, that he may minister unto me in the priest's office even Aaron, Nanab, and Abihu, Eleazar and Ithamar, Aaron's sons.

2 And thou shalt make holy garments for Aaron thy brother for glory and for beauty.

3 And thou shalt speak unto all that are wise-hearted, whom I have filled with the spirit of wisdom, that they may make Aaron's garments to consecrate him, that he may minister unto me in the priest's office.

The Ephod, Breastplate, and Robe

4 And these are the garments which they shall make; a breastplate and an ephod, and a robe, and a broidered coat, a miter, and a girdle: and they shall make holy garments for Aaron thy brother, and his sons, that he may minister unto me in the priest's office. *It goes without saying that these were garments of distinction and honor.*

5 And they shall take gold, and blue, and purple, and scarlet, and fine linen.

6 And they shall make the ephod of gold, of blue, and purple, of scarlet, and fine twined linen, with cunning work.

7 It shall have the two shoulder pieces thereof joined at the two edges thereof; and so it shall be joined together.

8 And the curious girdle of the ephod, which is upon it, shall be the same, according to the work thereof; even of gold, of blue, and purple, and scarlet, and fine twined linen.

9 And thou shalt take two onyx stones, and grave on them the names of the children of Israel:

10 Six of their names on one stone, and the other six names of the rest on the other stone, according to their birth.

11 With the work of an engraver in stone, like the engraving of a signet, shalt thou engrave the two stones with the names of the children of Israel: thou shalt make them to set in ouches of gold.

12 And thou shalt put the stones upon the shoulders of the ephods for stones of memorial unto the children of Israel: and Aaron shall bear their names before the Lord upon his two shoulders for a memorial.

13 And thou shalt make ouches of gold;

14 And two chains of pure gold at the ends; of wreathen work shalt thou make them, and fasten the wreathen chains to the ouches.

The usage of gold in engraving the names of the twelve tribes of Israel in the Breastplate shows the importance of its intrinsic value as well as its symbolic value. It is gold that symbolizes the Kingdom of Righteousness, being used in the vessels and boards of the Tabernacle.

2. The Breastplate, Exodus 28:15-29:

15 And thou shalt make the breastplate of judgment with cunning work; after the work of the ephod thou shalt make

it; of gold, of blue, and of purple, and of scarlet, and of fine twined linen, shalt thou make it.

16 Foursquare it shall be, being doubled; a span shall be the length thereof, and a span shall be the breath thereof. (approximately 9")

17 And thou shalt set in it settings of stones, even four rows of stones: the first row shall be a sardius, a topaz, and a carbuncle: this shall be the first row.

18 And the second row shall be an emerald, a sapphire, and a diamond.

19 And the third row a ligure, an agate, and an amythst.

20 And the fourth row a beryl, and an onyx, and a jasper: they shall be set in gold in their in-closings.

21 And the stones shall be with the names of the children of Israel, twelve, according to their names, like the engravings of a signet; every one with his name shall they be according to the twelve tribes.

Combined in the Breastplate are twelve stones engraved with the names of the twelve tribes of Israel. Every tribe is represented by a precious stone. The special significance of each stone is not known; however, there was a special significance. God always has significant reasons for doing things. Seven of these stones are identical to seven of the twelve precious stones in the foundations of the wall of the New Jerusalem. For that matter, they might all be identical, but with different names. Names of things have special meanings

22 And thou shalt make upon the breastplate chains at the ends of wreathen work of pure gold.

23 And thou shalt make upon the breastplate two rings of gold, and shalt put the two rings on the two ends of the breastplate.

24 And thou shalt put the two wreathen chains of gold in the two rings which are on the ends of the breastplate.

25 And the other two ends of the two wreathen chains

thou shalt fasten in the ouches, and put them on the shoulder pieces of the ephod before it.

26 And thou shalt make two rings of gold, and thou shalt put them upon the two ends of the breastplate in the border thereof, which is in the side of the ephod inward.

27 And two other rings of gold thou shalt make, and shalt put them on the two sides of the ephod underneath, toward the forepart thereof, over against the coupling thereof, above the curious girdle of the ephod.

28 And they shall bind the breastplate by the rings thereof unto the rings of the ephod with a lace of blue, that it may be above the curious girdle of the ephod, and that the breastplate be not loosed from the ephod.

29 And Aaron shall bear the names of the children of Israel in the breastplate of judgment upon his heart, when he goes in unto the holy place, for a memorial before the Lord continually.

The Breastplate is connected to the Ephod above the Curious Girdle and at the shoulders of the Ephod. The Urim and the Thummim are placed at the lower right end of the Breastplate, close to the heart of the High Priest.

The spiritual burden of Aaron was very heavy as represented by the Breast Plate. In it was represented the Twelve Tribes of Israel, numbering more than 2,000,000 people. All these people had inner conflicts between obedience and disobedience, between faithfulness and unfaithfulness, between unbelief and faith in an all Loving and Mighty God. They saw His manifold miracles, yet many times questioned His power. Aaron had to know all the rituals and ceremonies of all the sacrifices of the Law in order to minister them before the Lord on their behalf. These offerings of Atonement did not make them perfect. There were always the daily conflicts between the spirit and the flesh. Nevertheless, these offerings of Atonement were the only means of fellowship with God. Fellowship with God Means more than life to us.

3. The Urim and Thummim, 28:30: And thou shalt put in the breastplate of judgment the Urim and the Thummim; and they shall be upon Aaron's heart, when he goeth in before the Lord: and Aaron shall bear the judgment of the children of Israel upon his heart before the Lord continually.

In the Breastplate of Judgment the whole nation is represented. As High Priest and Mediator, Aaron awaits the decision or judgment of the Holy Judge, in which case the decision or judgment of the Holy Judge will be favorable to the mediation, not a judgment of wrath but mercy.

<u>The Urim and the Thummim</u>

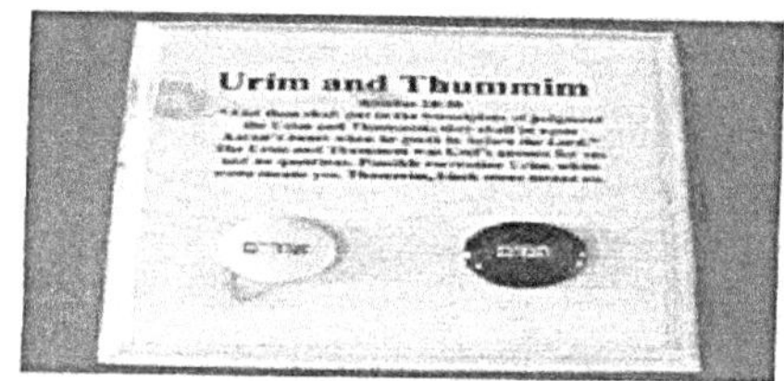

In the Breastplate the Urim and the Thummim are placed as a means of Divine communication between Aaron and the Lord. The Urim and Thummim mean truth and revelation. It seems to have been the means by which Aaron gets answers to his questions with respect to important decisions to be made on behalf of the people. It seems one gives a positive answer and the other gives a negative answer. Some suggest that they transmit messages by moving in their location or by glowing. However it may have worked, it was a sure way of revealing truth.

4. The Robe, Ex. 28:31-35: Thou shalt make the robe of the ephod of all blue.

32 And there shall be an hole in the top of it, in the midst

thereof: it shall have a binding of woven work round about the hole of it, as it were the hole of an habergeon, that it be not rent.

33 And beneath upon the hem of it thou shalt make pomegranates of blue, and of purple, and of scarlet, round about the hem thereof; and bells of gold between them round about:

34 A golden bell and a pomegranate, a golden bell and a pomegranate, upon the hem of the robe round about.

35 And it shall be upon Aaron to minister: and his sound shall be heard when he goes in unto the holy place before the Lord, and when he cometh out, that he die not.

The holy garments were made of blue, purple, scarlet, and twined linen, just as the curtains the holy veil, and the door of the Court. The message of the Tabernacle was uniformed – Holiness unto the Lord. Today the imputed righteousness of Christ to the Believers meets the requirement of Divine holiness. The twined linen linin symbolizes the outworking of Grace

The pomegranates, special fruits, symbolize God's material blessings for His people. On the other hand, the golden bells are a reminder that God expects holiness of everyone, the High Priest and every member of the congregation.

5. The Miter and Crown, Ex. 28:36-38: And thou shalt make a plate of pure gold, and grave upon it, like the engravings of a signet, HOLINESS TO THE LORD.

37 And thou shalt put in it a blue lace, that it may be upon the miter; upon the forefront of the miter it shall be.

38 And it shall be upon Aaron's forehead, that Aaron may bear the iniquity of the holy things, which the children of Israel shall hallow in all their holy gifts; and it shall be always upon Aaron's forehead, that Aaron may bear the iniquity of the holy things, which the children of Israel shall hallow in all their holy gifts; and shall be always upon

his forehead, that they may be accepted before the Lord.

The gifts of the people are holy but they represent their sins and iniquities. In presenting these gifts on behalf of the people, Aaron presents their sins as well. In that way he bears the iniquity of the holy things. The emphasis is on the sins the holy gifts represent.

The most enduring component of the Miter, the Golden Plate was inscribed with the words, HOLINESS TO THE LORD. Man must meet the condition of Divine holiness if he expects to see the Lord. The twined linin, the outworking of Redemption, implies that man can be holy and that God expects holiness of us.

6. The Linen Coat, Ex. 28:39-41: And thou shalt embroider the coat of fine linen and thou shalt make the miter of fine linen, and thou shalt make the girdle of needle work.

40 And for Aaron's sons thou shalt make coats, and thou shalt make for them girdles, and bonnets shalt thou make for them, for glory and for beauty.

41 And thou shalt put them upon Aaron thy brother, and his sons with him; and shalt anoint them, and consecrate them, and sanctify them, that they may minister to me in the priest's office.

7. The Linen Breeches, Ex. 28:42-43: And thou shalt make them linen breeches to cover their nakedness; from the loins even unto the thighs they shall reach:

43 And they shall be upon Aaron, and upon his sons, when they come in unto the tabernacle of the congregation, or when they come near unto the altar to minister in the holy place; that they bear not iniquity, and die: it shall be a statute forever unto him and his seed after him.

The message of the Tabernacle is the same as the message of the high priestly garments – Holiness is required of man. But man cannot acquire it by his own ingenuity and determination. Just as Aaron could not provide his own garments to meet Divine standard, so man can only attain holiness by means of Redemption. Man's standard is not God's standard but God's standard can become man's standard.

The priestly garments show the holiness of God, but the sacrifices of consecration show the unworthiness of man. In these sacrifices man confronts his own sin and guilt, yet the promise of forgiveness. The dead body of the innocent animal reminds him of the consequence of death which he so rightly deserves and a God whom he now faces in mercy in the hope of obviating eternal wrath.

The priestly garments are of beauty and glory because God is a God beauty and glory. The Universe speaks of His glory. We can say about the holy garments that God is interested in details and glory. The things that appear small to us may not be small with Him. However, we can say that God is interested in details, and we learn the reason that from the details came the beauty and the glory. Yet the greater message is that these garments provide complete covering, from head to foot. Self was not allowed to be exposed because such exposure would distract from God's own glory, causing man to think he was an equal partner in the provision of Redemption. Man needed to see that Redemption is a Divine act of mercy of which he is completely unworthy.

For man's own eternal wellbeing, he must submit himself to Divine consecration. With keen attention, we must now consider the consecration of the priests.

Consecration of the Priests, Sacrifices and Offerings, Exodus 29:1-46:

1 And this is the thing that you shall do unto them, to minister unto me in the priest's office: take one young bullock, and two rams without blemish,

2 And unleavened bread, and cakes unleavened tempered

with oil, and wafers unleavened anointed with oil: of wheaten flour shalt thou make them.

3 And thou shalt put them into one basket, and bring them in the basket, with the bullock and the two rams.

4 And Aaron and his sons thou shalt bring unto the door of the tabernacle of the congregation, and shalt wash them with water.

The first step in the consecration of the priests was one of separation. Aaron and his sons had to be separated from the Levites and from the whole congregation of Israel by bringing their sacrifice and offerings to the door of the tabernacle. This act of separation implies a dedication to a holy cause. Before they could be consecrated by God, they had to first surrender themselves completely. Their washing at the door of the Tabernacle was a symbol of separation by their willing desire to serve their God and their nation in the holy Priestly Office.

After washing their hands and feet, Moses was to clothe them with the holy garments and anoint them with the holy anointing oil.

5 And thou shalt take the garments, and put upon Aaron the coat, and the robe of the ephod, and the ephod, and the breastplate, and gird him with the curious girdle of the ephod.

6 And thou shalt put the miter upon his head, and put the holy crown upon the miter.

Verses 5 and 6 give the order of dressing. The linen breeches are not mentioned but it is understood that Aaron and his sons did not need Moses help in putting on the linen breeches. They would have come with the linen breeches on. Then the linen coat, the robe of the Ephod, the Ephod, the Breastplate, the Curious Girdle, and the Miter would be placed on Aaron. Then his sons would be clothed in their holy garments.

7 Then shalt thou take the anointing oil and pour it upon his head, and anoint him.

8 And thou shalt bring his sons, and put coats upon them.

9 And thou shalt gird them with girdles, Aaron and his sons, and put the bonnets on them: and the priest's office shall be theirs for a perpetual statute: and thou shalt consecrate Aaron and his sons.

The act of consecration involves the sacrifice of three animals: one for the Sin Offering, one for the Burnt Offering, and one for the Peace Offering, the Consecration Ram, with the basket of unleavened bread.

The Sacrifice and Offerings, Exodus 29:10-35:

The Sin Offering:

10 And thou shalt cause a bullock to be brought before the tabernacle of the congregation: and Aaron and his sons shall put their hands upon the head of the bullock.

11 And thou shalt kill the bullock before the Lord, by the door of the tabernacle of the congregation.

12 And thou shalt take of the blood of the bullock, and but it upon the horns of the altar with thy finger, and pour all the blood beside the bottom of the altar.

13 And you shall take all the fat that covers the inwards, and the caul that is above the liver, and the two kidneys, and the fat that is upon them, and burn them upon the altar.

14 But the flesh of the bullock, and his skin, and his dung, shalt thou burn with fire without the camp: it is a sin offering.

15 Thou shalt also take one ram; and Aaron and his sons shall put their hands upon the head of the ram.

The bullock of the Sin Offering was to be killed at the door of the congregation. Moses was to put its blood with his finger upon the horns of the Burnt Altar and pour its blood at the bottom of the Altar; burn its fat, liver, and kidney upon the Altar; and burn the remainder of the bullock outside the camp.

Verse 24 of chapter 20 provides an example of a general purpose altar where the Sin Offering would be burnt.

The Burnt Offering*: Exodus 29:16-18*
16 And thou shalt slay the ram, and thou shalt take his blood, and sprinkle it round about upon the altar.

17 And thou shalt cut the ram in pieces, and wash the inwards of him, and his legs, and put them unto his pieces and unto his head.

18 And thou shalt burn the whole ram upon the altar: it is a burnt offering unto the Lord: it is a sweet savor, an offering made by fire unto the Lord.
The blood of the Burnt Offering was to be sprinkled around and upon the altar, and the whole ram was to be cut in pieces and burned upon the altar.

The Ram of Consecration, Peace Offering Ex. 29: 19-35:
19 And thou shalt take the other ram; and Aaron and his sons shall put their hands upon the head of the ram.

20 Then shall thou kill the ram, and take of his blood, and put it upon the tip of the right ear of Aaron, and upon the tip of the right ear of his sons, and upon the thumb of their right hand, and upon the great toe of their right foot, and sprinkle the blood upon the altar round about.

21 And thou shalt take of the blood that is upon the altar, and of the anointing oil, and sprinkle it upon Aaron, and upon his garments, and upon his sons, and upon the garments of his sons with him: and he shall be hallowed, and his garments, and his sons, and his sons' garments with him.

Notice the blood of the Ram of Consecration was to be put on the tip of Aaron's right ear and also his sons'. The blood was also to be put on their right thumbs and right toes', and be sprinkled upon their garments; the remainder be poured around the altar. The anointing oil was to be sprinkled upon their garments.

Two Other Steps to Be Taken, the Wave Offering and Its Consumption:

22 Also thou shalt take of the ram the fat and the rump, and the fat that covers the inwards, and the caul above the liver, and the two kidneys, and the fat that is upon them, and the right shoulder; for it is a ram of consecration.

23 And one loaf of bread, and one cake of oiled bread, and one wafer out of the basket of the unleavened bread that is before the Lord:

24 And thou shalt put all in the hands of Aaron, and in the hands of his sons; and shalt wave them for a wave offering before the Lord.

The items of verse 22 to verse 24 were to be put in the hands of Aaron and his sons and then be waved before the Lord. Moses would receive those items from them and burn them upon the Altar of Burnt Offering.

25 And thou shalt receive them of their hands, and burn them upon the altar for a burnt offering, for a sweet savor before the Lord: it is an offering made by fire before the Lord.

The Final Step, Aaron and His Sons were to eat a portion of the Ram of Consecration, Exodus 29:26-35

26 And thou shalt take the breast of the ram of Aaron's consecration, and wave it for a wave offering before the Lord: and it shall be thy part.

This is the first mention of the Wave Offering.

27 And thou shalt sanctify the breast of the wave offering, and the shoulder of the heave offering, which is waved and which is heaved up, of the ram of the consecration, even of that which is for Aaron, and of that which is for his sons:

After the breast of the ram of consecration was waved, it was to be given to Moses to be eaten. The right shoulder of the ram of consecration was to be given Aaron and his sons after it was heaved or raised up to the Lord.

28 And it shall be Aaron's and his sons' by a statute forever from the children of Israel: for it is an heave offering: and it shall be an heave offering from the children of Israel of the sacrifice of their peace offerings, even their heave offering unto the Lord.

This is the first mention of the Peace Offering, the Wave Offering, and Heave Offering.

29 And the holy garments of Aaron shall be his sons' after him, to be anointed therein, and to be consecrated in them.

30 And that son that is priest in his stead shall put them on seven days, when he cometh into the tabernacle of the congregation to minister in the holy place.

Aaron's successor was to inherit his holy garments, instead of making new ones. These holy garments would be preserved by God's special blessings to the extent that they would be a kind of memorial to Israel.

31 And thou shalt take the ram of consecration, and seethe his flesh in the holy place.

32 And Aaron and his sons shall eat the flesh of the ram, and the bread that is in the basket, by the door of the tabernacle of the congregation.

33 And they shall eat those things wherewith the atonement was made, to consecrate and to sanctify them: but a stranger shall not eat thereof, because they are holy.

Aaron and his sons were to eat the right shoulder or Heave Offering of the ram of consecration in the holy place with unleavened bread. It was to be a most practical and rewarding way of identifying with the holy High Priestly Office. Participating in his own Atonement and consecration, Aaron symbolized the Lord's Supper. However, this was to be an exclusive privilege to Aaron and his sons and a perpetual statute.

34 And if aught of the flesh of the consecrations, or of the bread remain until the morning, then thou shalt burn the

remainder with fire: it shall not be eaten because it is holy.

35 And this shalt thou do unto Aaron, and to his sons, according to all the things which I have commanded thee: seven days shalt thou consecrate them.

Aaron and his sons were to go through the ceremony of their consecration seven days concurrently with the consecration of the Burnt Altar. Apparently the whole Tabernacle was implied. Why would a part be sanctified and not the whole?

Concurrence of Aaron's Consecration and the Burnt Altar, Exodus 29:36-46:

36 And thou shalt offer every day a bullock for a sin offering of atonement: and thou shalt cleanse the altar, when thou hast made an atonement for it, and thou shalt anoint it to sanctify it.

37 Seven days shalt thou make an atonement for the altar, and sanctify it; and it shall be an altar most holy: whatsoever touches the altar shall be holy.

The bullock of the Sin Offering was offered seven days for the consecration of Aaron and seven days for the consecration of the Burnt Altar.

By reason of serving in the High Priestly Office, the High Priest would become holy. The holy vessels were not accessible to the congregation, not even the Levites could touch the holy things. The charge of the holy things was with Aaron's sons. After the consecration of the Burnt Altar, there were to be the daily Burnt Offerings.

The Daily Burnt Sacrifice, Exodus 29:38-46

38 This is that which thou shalt offer upon the altar; two lambs of the first year day by day continually.

39 The one lamb thou shalt offer in the morning; and the other lamb thou shalt offer at even:

The Evening Lamb reminds us of Christ the Lamb of God who was crucified in the evening.

40 And with the one lamb a tenth deal of flour mingled with the fourth part of an hin (a quart) of beaten oil; and the fourth part of an hin (a quart) of wine for a drink offering.

This is the first mention of the Drink Offering. Because the wine was to be offered with the Burnt Offering, it was called a Drink Offering.

41 And the other lamb thou shalt offer at even, and shalt do thereto according to the meat offering of the morning and according to the drink offering thereof, for a sweet savor, an offering made by fire unto the Lord.

42 This shall be a continual burnt offering throughout your generations at the door of the tabernacle of the congregation before the Lord: where I will meet you, to speak there unto thee.

43 And there I will meet with the children of Israel, and the tabernacle shall be sanctified by my glory.

44 And I will sanctify the tabernacle of the congregation and the altar: and I will sanctify also both Aaron and his sons, to minister to me in the priest's office.

45 And I will dwell among the children of Israel, and will be their God.

The sacrifices and offerings of consecration had to be in place, but the act of sanctification was a Divine one; the final act of sanctification was in God's hand. Only He could sanctify the priests, the offerings alone were not sufficient.

It cannot now be said that the LIVING GOD dwells among the Children of Israel today as He originally intended. This is for the simple reason that they had failed to live by their Covenant with their God. However, it is not the end of the story. There is a time in God's schedule when His promise will become true. And at that time they will realize that God's Covenant was true.

46 And they shall know that I am the Lord their God, that brought them forth out of the land of Egypt, that I may dwell among them: I am the Lord their God.

Herein God expresses His whole purpose for delivering them from the bondage of Egypt—to know Him personally in a holy relationship.

The Golden Altar of Incense, Ex. 30:1-10:

The composition of the Golden Altar was different from the Burnt Altar and also its purpose. It was smaller in size and was positioned in the Sanctuary. Holy incense was to be burnt upon it by the High Priest and be used in the Yearly Atonement.

1 And thou shalt make an altar to burn incense upon: of shittim wood shalt thou make it.

2 A cubit shall be the length thereof, and a cubit the breath thereof; foursquare shall it be: and two cubits shall be the height thereof: the horns thereof shall be the same.

3 And thou shalt overlay it with pure gold, the top thereof and the sides thereof round about, and the horns thereof; and thou shalt make unto it a crown of gold round about.

4 And two golden rings shalt thou make to it under the crown of it, by the two corners thereof, upon the two sides of it shalt thou make it; and they shall be for places for the staves to bear it withal.

5 And thou shalt make the staves of shittim wood, and overlay them with gold.

6 And thou shalt put it between the veil that is by the ark of the testimony, before the mercy seat that is over the testimony, where I will meet with thee.

7 And Aaron shall burn thereon sweet incense every morning: when he dresses the lamps, he shall burn incense upon it.

8 And when Aaron lights the lamps at even, he shall burn incense upon it, a perpetual incense before the Lord throughout your generations.

The light of the lamps, throughout Israel's Theocracy, symbolizes Christ, the Light of the World.

9 Ye shall offer no strange incense thereon, nor burnt sacrifice, nor meat offering; neither shall ye pour drink offering thereon.

10 And Aaron shall make an atonement upon the horns of it once in a year with the blood of the sin offering of atonements: once in the year shall he make atonement upon it throughout your generations: it is most holy unto the Lord.

<u>The Holy Golden Altar of Incense</u>

The Atonement Money and Numbering, Ex. 30:11-16:

11 And the Lord spoke unto Moses, saying,

12 When you take the sum of the children of Israel after their number, then shall they give every man a ransom for his soul unto the Lord, when thou number them; that there be no plague among them, when thou number them.

13 This they shall give, every one that passes among them that are numbered, half a shekel after the shekel of the

sanctuary: (a shekel is twenty gerahs: 20x .02 ounce) an half shekel (.2 ounce, U.S.) shall be the offering of the Lord.

The Shittim Wood is best known for its preservative properties. It was used in all aspects of the Tabernacle. It was only one species from the Acacia tree family of hundreds of species

14 Every one that passes among them that are numbered, from twenty years old and above, shall give an offering unto the Lord.

The Shittim Wood

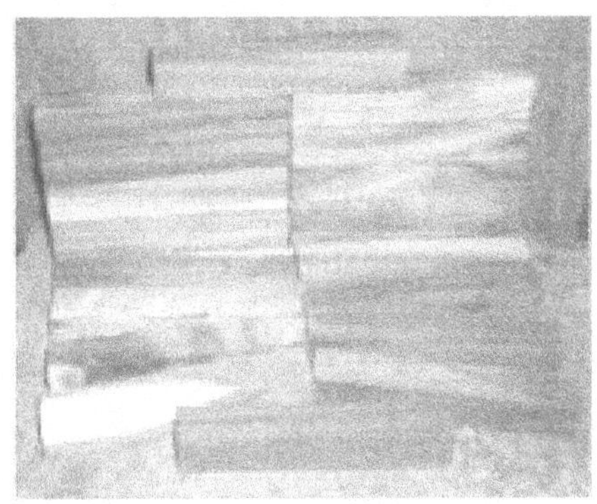

15 The rich shall not give more, and the poor shall not give less than half a shekel, when they give an offering unto the Lord, to make an atonement for your souls.

16 And thou shalt take the atonement money of the children of Israel, and shall appoint for the service of the tabernacle of the congregation; that it may be a memorial unto the children of Israel before the Lord, to make atonement for your souls. (*This numbering is mentioned in Numbers 1-4*).

This Atonement money was taken just before the work of building the Tabernacle began (Ex.38:25-28). It was half a shekel of silver from everyone who was numbered (.2 ounce). The Aonement was for an intercessory plea to establish spiritual relation with God in living holy. It involved acknowledgment of sin and the need for forgiveness. Israel could not embrace sin and expect to benefit from the blessings of God's abiding presence. But the Atonement was not to be a onetime event; it involved a life of priestly service, which necessitated the building of the Tabernacle. While the ransom money was paid unto God, it was for building the Tabernacle.

The Laver, Ex.30:17-21: And the Lord spoke unto Moses, saying,

18 Thou shalt also make a laver of brass, and his foot also of brass, to wash withal: And thou shalt put it between the tabernacle of the congregation and the altar, and thou shalt put water therein.

19 For Aaron and his sons shall wash their hands and their feet thereat:

20 When they go into the tabernacle of the congregation, they shall wash with water, that they die not; or when they come near to the altar to minister, to burn offerings made by fire unto the Lord:

21 So they shall wash their hands and their feet, that they die not: and it shall be a statute for ever to them, even to him and his seed throughout their generations.

Before Aaron could begin his daily duty, he had to wash his hands and feet at the Laver. This ritual of cleansing was a sign of separation from personal life unto his holy duties.

The Holy Anointing Oil, Composition and Purpose, Ex. 30:22-33:

22 Moreover the Lord spoke unto Moses, saying,

23 Take thou also unto thee principal spices, of pure

myrrh five hundred shekels, and of sweet cinnamon half so much, even two hundred and fifty shekels, and of sweet calamus two hundred and fifty shekels,

24 And add cassia five hundred shekels, after the shekel of the sanctuary, and of oil olive an hin: (a gallon).

A hundred shekels are one U.S. pound. The amount of spices was 5 pounds of myrrh, 2 ½ pounds of sweet cinnamon, 2 ½ pounds of sweet calamus, and 5 pounds of cassia. These elements were to be chemically blended into a holy anointing oil to anoint the High Priest and vessels of the Tabernacle as well as the Tabernacle itself. It was not to be used for any other purposes and its composition was not to be duplicated.

These items were produced by several species of the Acacia Tree Family which was one of more than 1000 species. While some species produce wood for commercial purposes, other species produce edible pods, seeds, flowers, and perfume producing fruits.

25 And thou shalt make it an oil of holy ointment, an <u>ointment compound after the art of the apothecary: it shall</u>
Foot Note: The pictures of the Tabernacle, the vessels, and the priestly garments were taken from a collection of similar pictures from the public domain, www. Goole.com. Some of the Websites are herein listed: For His Name Sake, Boomer in the Pew, A Pining, Ids.org,Temple Builders Ministry, The Seers Stone,

be an holy anointing oil

<u>The Laver</u>

26 And thou shalt anoint the tabernacle of the congregation therewith, and the ark of the testimony.

27 And the table and all his vessels, and the candlestick and his vessels, and the altar of incense,

28 And the altar of burnt offering with all his vessels, and the Laver and his foot.

29 And thou shalt sanctify them, that they may be most holy: whatsoever touches them shall be holy.

30 And thou shalt anoint Aaron and his sons, and consecrate them, that they may minister unto me in the priest's office.

31. And thou shalt speak unto the children of Israel, saying, This shall be an holy anointing oil unto me throughout your generations.

32 Upon man's flesh shall it not be poured, neither shall ye make any other like it, after the composition of it: it is holy, and it shall be holy unto you.

<u>A Species of the Acacia Tree Family</u>

33 Whosoever compounds any like it, or whosoever puts any of it upon a stranger, shall even be cut off from his people

God created all things for different reasons; He knows the potentials of all things and their best use. Some would question the possible location of the trees, for getting that He could have instantly caused them to grow for His specific purpose.

Composition of the Holy Perfume, Ex.30:34-38:

34 And the Lord said unto Moses, Take unto thee sweet spices, stacte, and onycha, and galbanum; these sweet spices with pure frankincense: of each shall there be a like weight:

35 And thou shalt make it a perfume, a confection after the art of the apothecary, tempered together, pure and holy:

36 And thou shalt beat some of it very small and put some of it before the testimony in the tabernacle of the congregation, where I will meet with thee: it shall be unto you most holy.

37 And as for the perfume which thou shalt make, ye shall not make to yourselves according to the composition thereof: it shall be unto thee holy for the Lord.

38 Whosoever shall make like unto that, to smell thereto, shall even be cut off from his people.

Some of these spices was to be put in a vessel on the Golden Altar of Incense causing a beautiful fragrance in the Sanctuary.

The Superintendent of the Works, Exodus 31:1-11:

A tabernacle of this kind was never built before. It was highly technical and demanded special understanding and skill. It could not be built by two persons but God filled two men with wisdom and understanding to lead the effort. God would not ask that something be done which was not possible

He would provide His servants with the ability.

Herein was seen a new pattern of leadership with the appointment of Bezaleel from the tribe of Judah and his assistant, Aholiab from the tribe of Dan. With them were many more willing workers anointed and ready to go building. They were to build all that was necessary.

And the Lord spoke unto Moses saying,

2 See, I have called by name Bezaleel the son Uri, the son of Hur, of the tribe of Judah:

3 And have filled him with the spirit of God, in wisdom, and in understanding, and in knowledge, and in all manner of workmanship,

4 To devise cunning works, to work in gold, and in silver, and in brass,

5 And in cutting of stones, to set them, and in carving of timber, to work in all manner of workmanship.

6 And I, behold, I have given with him Aholiab, the son of Ahisamach, of the tribe of Dan: and in the hearts of all that are wise hearted I have put wisdom, that they may make all that I have commanded thee;

7 The tabernacle of the congregation, and the ark of the testimony, and the mercy seat that is thereupon, and all the furniture of the tabernacle,

8 And the table and his furniture, and the pure candlestick with all his furniture, and the altar of incense,

9 And the altar of burnt offering with all his furniture, and the laver and his foot,

10 And the clothes of service, and the holy garments for Aaron the priest, and the garments of his sons, to minister in the priest's office,

11 And the anointing oil, and sweet incense for the holy place: according to all that I have commanded thee shall they do.

Reminder of the Sabbath, Ex. 31:12-18:

12 And the Lord spoke unto Moses, saying,

13 Speak thou also to the children of Israel, saying, Verily my Sabbaths ye shall keep: for it is a sign between me and you throughout you generations; that ye may know that I am the Lord that doth sanctify you.

14 Ye shall keep the Sabbath therefore; for it is holy unto you: every one that defiles it shall surely be put to death: for whosoever doeth any work therein, that soul shall be cut off from among his people.

15 Six days may work be done; but in the seventh is the Sabbath of rest, holy to the Lord: whosoever doeth any work in the Sabbath day, he shall surely be put to death.

16 Wherefore the children of Israel shall keep the Sabbath, to observe the Sabbath throughout their generations, for a perpetual covenant.

17 It is a sign between me and the children of Israel for ever: for in six days the Lord made heaven and earth, and on the seventh day he rested, and was refreshed.

18 And he gave unto Moses, when he had made an end of communing with him upon Mount Sinai, two tables of testimony, tables of stone, written with the finger of God.

Emphasizing the observance of the Sabbath Day indicates its importance in Israel's spiritual relationship with their God. It was important for them to acknowledge that the Universe was created by Him. If they observed the Sabbath as commanded, it would become somewhat a kind of second nature; and when tempted to go astray, it would quickly restrain them.

Footnote: The names of Aaron's sons: Nadab, Abihu, Eleazar, and Ithamar, p41. The First mention of the Ram of consecration, page 162; the first mention of the Wave Offering, page 163; the first mention of the Heave Offering, page 163; the first mention of the Peace Offering, page 164; the first mention of the Drink Offering, page 166; and the numbering of Israel, p 169.

SUMMARY

The concept of the High Priestly Office was to complement the concept of the Tabernacle. The message and purpose of both were one and the same of the spiritual reality which could not be ignored—God was on a mission of restoring humanity. The representations and symbols, though material, reflected so glaringly that spiritual reality.

First, the colors of the holy garments, of blue, purple, scarlet and white twined linen, reflected the spiritual reality with a certain guaranteed outcome. Indeed, blue was symbolic of the holiness of God, which was the cornerstone of the spiritual reality. God was immutable in His holy nature; man had fallen from his holy original state, as represented by the scarlet, sin. Sin is more than human weakness. It was an act which became a principle. As a principle, it has eternal consequences. It will not just go away or disappear with time. It could not even be expunged by the blood sacrifices. It can only be forgiven by God.

The purple was symbolic of the Redeemer, the Incarnation in which the Divinity of Christ was mingled with His humanity: His blood transforming the blue into purple. The gulf created by sin between man and God became so great that it became impossible for mere human effort to bridge. On the other hand, a holy God would have only caused it to become greater were He to attempt to bridge it because His holiness would have only pushed sinful man farther away from Him. The truth of this was evident from His manifestation on Mount Sinai. The setting of the boundaries around the holy Mount clearly showed the distance between God and Israel. Despite that distance between them and God, they insisted it was not far enough and wished not to hear God's voice any longer.

Bridging that gulf necessitated the union of the Divine and the human nature of Christ. From the Divine side of His nature, He reached up to the heights of Heaven and brought God down to the meeting place of His cross; and from His humanity, He reached into the depth of sin and depravity and brought man to the meeting ground of His cross, thus brining God and man together in reconciliation——there God dwells. Such an effort is called the righteousness of Christ.

When guilty man appropriates Christ's righteousness, he becomes the twined linen, the outworking of Redemption. The general use of gold throughout the Tabernacle, and in particular, in the engraving of the names of the twelve tribes of Israel in the Breastplate of the Ephod symbolizes God's eternal kingdom of righteousness. The twelve precious stones in the Breastplate symbolize the twelve precious stones in the walls of the New Jerusalem. The holy garments of Aaron indicated that man's own garments were not good enough to appear before God's holy presence.

The sacrifices offered in the consecration of the priests indicated that without the aid of Divine consecration, man was of no good in God's service. The Burnt Offering symbolized man's highest level of relationship with God. It symbolized the spirit of man's threefold nature, body, soul, and spirit. In the Burnt Offering the whole offering was consumed by fire, becoming spiritualized, identifying with the spirit of man in worship.

The principle of the offerings was the Innocent for the Guilty. This principle was yet based on a greater principle: the Atoning Blood of Christ, the Lamb slain before the foundation of the World. When the guilty sinner offered his blood sacrifice, God looked at the blood and saw the Atoning Blood of His Son and forgave him of his sins. In the blood sacrifices, the animals were innocent but were far inferior to the guilty sinners for whom they were offered. So they could have only atoned for guilty man on the principle of Christ's Atoning Blood.

CHAPTER 7
The Golden Calf, Exodus 32-33

The Golden Calf was contrary to all God's intentions and purposes; the idea came suddenly and out of nowhere. It was prompted by the blind impulses of impatience and a rebellious nature to an Ever Loving God. There was no logical explanation for its necessity, but it did show how far God would go to forgive His people. On the other hand, it showed the righteous anger of Moses who loved his brethren with all that was humanly possible.

We shall see in this chapter the steps taken to bridge an impassable gulf between the holy nature of God and the rebellious and sinful nature of Israel. And we shall see not His omnipotence at work, but his infinite mercy. So the lesson of the path of the Wilderness to the Promised Land is that God who is omnipotent is infinitely merciful and faithful. The fact is that God knew Israel but Israel did not Him. For the relationship to be lasting, it was necessary that Israel knew God's inner nature.

Making and Worshiping the Golden Calf, Ex. 32:1-6

1 And when they saw that Moses delayed to come down out of the mount, the people gathered themselves together unto Aaron, and said unto him, Up make us gods, which shall go before us; for as for this Moses, the man that brought us up out of the land of Egypt, we wot not what is become of him.

Moses loved his people with his whole heart but he was not equally loved in return. He was more feared than loved.

2 And Aaron said unto them, Break off the golden ear rings, which are in the ears of your wives, of your sons, and of your daughters, and bring them unto me.

3 And all the people brake off the golden earrings which were in their ears, and brought them to Aaron.

4 And he received them at their hand, and fashioned it with a graving tool, after he had made it a molten calf: and they said, These be thy gods, O Israel, which brought thee up out of the land of Egypt.

5 And when Aaron saw it, he built an altar before it; and Aaron made proclamation, and said, Tomorrow is the feast to the Lord.

6 And they rose up early on the morrow, and offered burnt offerings, and brought peace offerings; and the people sat down to eat and to drink, and rose up to play.

Verse 1 shows how spiritually destructive impatience can be: it caused Israel to do the unthinkable — they commanded Aaron to make them gods. While they were in bondage, they never thought of making themselves gods of gold because they knew that would only make their bondage worse, instead of helping. They were in bondage for many years praying for deliverance. Therefore their behavior here was not something that can be understood. Did they really think that gods of gold could help them in any way in the wilderness and take them to the Promised Land?

Their demand for gods of gold could only be seen as an act to show displeasure with Moses for his absence of forty days. This shows more dependence on Moses and less on God. It also shows that their heart was not at the right place for their faith was in Moses and not in God; they were living by sight and not by faith. This spiritual rebellion contrasts the styles of two leaderships, that of Moses and that of Aaron. They commanded Aaron and he obeyed them; they had never attempted to command Moses because they knew they would not succeed. They murmured against him many times, but murmuring was different from commanding him. When Aaron had the greatest opportunity to lead, he utterly failed himself, the people, and his God. Aaron was really a miserable failure. He never attempted to console them in a time of need or discourage them from doing the unthinkable – he urged them unto spiritual suicide. He urged them to bring him all their golden earrings of women and children. They gave him all and he crafted the **GOLDEN CALF.**

Aaron went further in breaking the first and second commandments and ascribing to the **Golden Calf** *all the praise for delivering the Children of Israel from the bondage of Egypt. To complete his idolatry and that of the people, he built an altar of worship unto it. Then together they worshipped the* **GOLDEN CALF** *with their Burnt Offering and Peace Offering.*

Aaron was more concerned about pleasing the people than pleasing God. Moses took a completely different path, that of pleasing God first and then the people. One wonders, Was this a deliberate attempt by Aaron to wrestle the leadership of the people from Moses, due to some kind of jealousy? Aaron was eloquent but he did not have the heart of a leader: the faith, the patience, the wisdom, the courage, and the humility of Moses.

This spiritual rebellion quickly got God's attention.

God's Attention is Directed at the Golden Calf, Ex. 32:7-10: 7 And the Lord said unto Moses, Go get thee down; for thy people, which you brought out of the land of Egypt have corrupted themselves.

God here dismisses the fact that they were His people by saying to Moses "thy people". In reality God's people would not have done what they did.

8 They have turned aside quickly out of the way which I commanded them: they have made them a molten calf, and have worshipped it, and have sacrificed thereunto, and

said, These be thy gods, O Israel, which have brought thee up out of the land of Egypt.

9 And the Lord said unto Moses, I have seen this people, and, behold, it is a stiff-necked people.

10 Now therefore let me alone, that my wrath may wax hot against them, and that I may consume them: and I will make of thee a great nation.

In verse 7 the Lord uses a most revealing word to describe Israel's spiritual state – the word, corrupted. The word brings to mind the corruption of man's holy original nature in the Garden of Eden. That original sin not only corrupted Adam and Eve but the entire human race. That corruption was seen in the bondage of Egypt and now seen in their open rebellion against the Holy God. Corruption means that the entire human nature is saturated by sin which left us the legacy of death.

Corruption by idolatry meant a new and daring dimension to an already corrupted nature. It meant that Israel became corrupted by the sin of idolatry and they would not be able to conveniently forget about it: It would become a part of their spiritual nature and would afflict them for years to come. There would be occasions when they would turn to idolatry as the answer to all of their problems.

In God's holy anger, He wanted to consume them instantly; yet the problem would not be solved. Their bodies could instantly perish, but their souls would live on forever. And that would not be all: their souls would be lost for all eternity. In His holy anger, He made Moses the promise of making of him a great nation in the place of the rebellious people. Moses declined and insisted on mercy and forgiveness of His people.

Moses Intercedes, 32:11-14: 11 And Moses besought the Lord his God, and said, Lord, why doth thy wrath wax hot against thy people, which thou hast brought forth out of the land of Egypt with great power, and with a mighty hand?

12 Wherefore should the Egyptians speak, and say, For mischief did he bring them out, to slay them in the mountains, and to consume them from the face of the earth? Turn from thy fierce wrath, and repent of this evil against thy people.

13 Remember Abraham, Isaac, and Israel, thy servants, to whom thou swore by thine own self, and sadist unto them, I will multiply thy seed as the stars of heaven, and all this land I have spoken of will I give unto your seed, and they shall inherit it forever.

14 And the Lord repented of the evil which he thought to do unto his people.

Though Moses' intercession was about sparing Israel from instant annihilation, it was also about God's great glory. When He brought Israel from the bondage of Egypt by His mighty power, the whole world came to attention in awe of Him. Moses explained that the whole world would then go in the opposite direction and would speak disparagingly of a God who did not fulfill His promises. And what would Abraham, Isaac, and Jacob think if they were to look and see the carcasses of the whole nation covering the wilderness? They would have considered their covenant with God nullified. And in astonishment would have put their hands on their mouths and say, "The Promised Land remains but there are no people to inherit it".

God was not at all surprised by Moses' intercession for He knew of what Moses was made as a chosen leader. He quietly put aside His holy anger and forgave His people. Moses then returned from the Mount.

Moses Returns from the Mount, Exodus 32:15-29:

15 And Moses turned, and went down from the mount, and the two tables of the testimony were in his hand: the tables were written on both their sides; on the one side and on the other were they written.

16 And the tables were the work of God, and the writing was the writing of God, graven upon the tables.

17 And when Joshua heard the noise of the people as they shouted, he said unto Moses, There is a noise of war in the camp.

18 And he said, It is not the voice of them that shout for mastery, neither is it the voice of them that cry for being overcome: but the voice of them that sing do I hear.

19 And it came to pass, as soon as he came nigh unto the camp, that he saw the calf and the dancing: and Moses anger waxed hot, and he cast the tables out of his hands, and break them beneath the mount.

20 And he took the calf which they had made, and burnt it in fire, and ground it to power, and strawed it upon the water and made the children of Israel drink of it.

While Moses was coming down from the Mount with the two tables of the Testimony written by God himself, he thought everything would be settled in a quiet way until he heard and saw for himself what the people had done because they were worshipping with jubilation, only that it was not God but a golden calf. He then broke the tables because of his righteous anger. Then he could understand the holy anger of God but not before. He felt the people were not worthy to read the writing of God. His action to restore spiritual sanity to the people showed he was not afraid to do what was right.

Aaron Questioned, Ex. 32:21-24: 21 And Moses said unto Aaron, What did this people unto thee, that thou hast brought so great a sin upon them?

22 And Aaron said, Let not the anger of my lord wax hot: you know the people, that they are set on mischief.

23 For they said unto me, Make us gods, which shall go before us: for as for this Moses, the man that brought us up out of the land of Egypt, we wot not what is become of him.

24 And I said unto them, Whosoever hath any gold, let them break it off. So they gave it me: then I cast it into the fire, and there came out this calf.

Here he placed the blame squarely upon the shoulders of Aaron, allowing him to know he was the cause of a great sin. But like Adam and Eve, Aaron tried to deflect the blame on the people. The people wanted gods but they did not make the golden calf and it did not make itself. There was no place for Aaron to hide from his sin of idolatry.

Moses, however, was more interested in the solution instead of prolonging the problem. Quick action was needed.

Action of Sanctification Taken, Ex. 32:25-29: 25 And when Moses saw that the people were naked; (for Aaron had made them naked unto their shame among their enemies:)

26 Then Moses stood in the gate of the camp, and said, Who is on the Lord's side? Let him come unto me. And all the sons of Levi gathered themselves together unto him.

27 And he said unto them, Thus says the Lord God of Israel, Put every man his sword by his side, and go in and out from gate to gate throughout the camp, and slay every man his brother, and every man his companion, and ever man his neighbor.

28 And the children of Levi did according to the word of Moses: and there fell of the people that day about three thousand men.

29 For Moses had said, Consecrate yourselves today to the Lord, even every man upon his son, and upon his brother; that he may bestow upon you a blessing this day.

There was something shameful about the spiritual rebellion because the people were naked. It seemed share madness, the singing, the dancing and the nakedness. They needed to sanctify themselves unto the Lord but apparently refused to heed Moses' call. Moses wanted to make sure that his call to repentance was understood and asked those who were sorry to separate themselves unto him. The Levites separated themselves from the rebellion and came over to Moses. That day 3,000 of them were slain. Then all Israel realized how far they had wandered from God.

In Moses' mind the matter was not quite settled, so he decided to go to the Lord in intercession.

Moses Returns to the Mount to Intercede, 32:30-35:

30 And it came to pass on the morrow, that Moses said unto the people, Ye have sinned a great sin: and now I will go up unto the Lord; peradventure I shall make an atonement for your sin.

At first on the mountain top, Moses saw sin from a distance but when he came down he faced sin face to face. The reality of hearing about sin and the reality of looking at it were two different things. Seeing sin at its worst caused him to break the two tables of the Testimony, to burn the golden calf to dust and scatter it upon the water, and to cause the people to drink it. But that was not enough to purge away the sin of idolatry from Israel; he ordered the Levites to kill those who refused to separate themselves unto God. Still that was not enough to guarantee spiritual restoration.

*Moses began to realize that God's holy anger was justified and that Israel had forfeited all their claims of all the promises made by God to their fathers. From this quick review, he concluded the idol of the golden calf was a great sin and needed special intercession. The exercise of his personal intercession would have been meaningless unless the people had realized the depth of their idolatry. They needed to acknowledge that their sin was on the **border of unforgiveness.** Then he could make a bold attempt at interceding for them.*

31 And Moses returned unto the Lord, and said, Oh, this people have sinned a great sin and have made them gods of gold.

32 Yet now, if thou wilt forgive their sin; and if not, blot me, I pray thee, out of thy book which thou hast written.

33 And the Lord said unto Moses, Whosoever hath sinned against me, him will I blot out of my book.

As the chosen leader of God's people, Moses acknowledged and confessed the sin of the people unto God. He was not sure if his intercession was going to be accepted and was willing to cast in his lot with his brethren. It is difficult to understand the depth of his love for righteousness and for his brethren. He would have preferred his name to be blotted out of the Book of Life than God's refusal to forgive His people. We do not question his sincerity; we are only amazed by it. How could a human being be so spiritually great, one may ask? The better question is, Are there any limits to God's forgiveness and love?

In answer to Moses' question, God allowed him to know that He could not remove his name from the Book of Life or charge him with the sin of the people. People cannot keep sinning and expect their names to remain in the Book of Life. God can only do things in keeping with His holy nature.

Before Moses ended his intercession, God granted forgiveness to His people.

34 Therefore now go, lead the people unto the place of which I have spoken unto thee: behold, mine Angel shall go before thee: nevertheless in the day when I visit I will visit their sin upon them.

We are sure that God forgives sins but there are consequences, and sooner than later one will face those consequences. However, God began anew from the point of forgiveness. Here he made a new promise that His Angel would go ahead and guide them. This reference to "mine Angel" implies the leadership of the Pre-Incarnate Christ who made a number of Pre-Incarnate appearances in angelic form.

Here is the promise of guidance of the Pre-Incarnate Christ.

35 And the Lord plagued the people, because they made the calf, which Aaron made.

Not long after, the people began to face the consequences of their sin of the Golden Calf. Forgiveness did not prevent the consequences.

Moses Returns from the Mount, Ex. 33

Departing Words, verses 1-5. And the Lord said unto Moses, Depart, and go up hence, thou and the people which thou hast brought up out of the land of Egypt, unto the land which I swore unto Abraham, to Isaac, and to Jacob, saying, Unto thy seed will I give it:

2 And I will send an angel before thee; and I will drive out the Canaanite, the Amorite, and the Hittite, and the Perizzite, the Hivite, and the Jebuzite:

3 Unto a land flowing with milk and honey: for I will not go up in the midst of thee; for thou art a stiff-necked people: lest I consume thee in the way.

4 And when the people heard these evil tidings, they mourned: and no man did put on him his ornaments.

5 For the Lord had said unto Moses, Say unto the children of Israel, Ye are a stiff-necked people: I will come up in the midst of thee in a moment, and consume thee: therefore now put off thy ornaments from thee, that I may know what to do unto thee.

The Wilderness was never intended to be their destination; it was only a path to the Promised Land. A new start to the old journey began at the point of the golden calf, in which the people had to be told the truth, in the hope of reconciling with it to make it work. They had to acknowledge what they were, a rebellious people. As a rebellious people, they forfeited the special favor of God's abiding presence when confronting their enemies. However, He had not abandoned them: He promised them the help of an angel. The angel here seems not to be in reference to the Pre- Incarnate Christ, but a regular angel. Nonetheless, they thought that God was abandoning them and began to mourn. They realized that their ornaments were standing between them and their God, and repentance removed from them.

Moses Takes Further Action of Sanctification, Ex. 33:6-8

6 And the children of Israel stripped themselves of their ornaments by the mount Horeb.

7 And Moses took the tabernacle and pitched it without the camp afar off from the camp, and called it the Tabernacle of the congregation. And it came to pass, that everyone which sought the Lord went out unto the tabernacle of the congregation, which was without the camp.

Mount Horeb is not shown on the map but is believed to be relatively near to Mount Sinai. Here the people left their ornaments. But Moses was not satisfied with them, they needed to prove their sincerity. By going out to the tabernacle without the camp to seek the Lord showed the kind of sincerity needed.

Removing the Tabernacle and pitching it without the camp showed a new spiritual beginning and the seriousness of the sin of the golden calf. Moses did not want to identify with the sin of the old congregation; he wanted them to begin anew. This Tabernacle was a temporary meeting place: the pattern of the one given to Moses was not yet built. There seemed to be a new spiritual renewal, reverence and gratitude.

8 And it came to pass, when Moses went out unto the tabernacle, that all the people rose up, and stood every man at his tent door, and looked after Moses, until he was gone into the tabernacle.

Compromising the truth or trying to gain the approval of the people is not what will gain their respect. By standing up for God's righteousness, Moses became a spiritual hero and in the end won back their hearts to God. They might still stumble along the way, but they would never be the same again. In the end what counts is God's approval.

God Approves, 33:9-11: 9 And it came to pass, as Moses entered into the tabernacle, the cloudy pillar descended, and stood at the door of the tabernacle, and the Lord talked with Moses.

10 And all the people saw the cloudy pillar stand at the tabernacle door: and all the people rose up and worshipped, every man in his tent door.

The appearing of the glory of God was the evidence of pardon and forgiveness, renewal and approval. The glory of God returned to the Tabernacle and the people worshipped the Lord. God's presence is important to true worship.

Moses Requests a Special Favor of God, 33:11-23:

11 And the Lord spoke unto Moses face to face, as a man speaks to his friend. And he returned again into the camp: but his servant Joshua, the son of Nun, a young man, departed not out of the tabernacle.

12 And Moses said unto the Lord, See, Thou saith unto me, Bring up this people: and Thou hast not let me know whom thou wilt send with me. Yet thou hast said, I know thee by name, and thou hast also found grace in my sight.

13 Now therefore, I pray thee, if I have found grace in thy sight, show me now thy way, that I may know thee, that I may find grace in thy sight: and consider that this nation is thy people:

14 And he said, My presence shall go with thee, and I will give you rest.

15 And he said unto him, If thy presence go not with me, carry us not up hence.

16 For wherein shall it be known here that I and thy people have found grace in thy sight? Is it not in that You go with us? So shall we be separated, I and thy people, from all the people that are upon the face of earth.

Verse 12 refers not to human help but angelic. At first, he was given Aaron as his spokes-man. In verses 20-23 of chapter 23 and in verse 34 of chapter 33, the Pre-Incarnate Christ is implied. Here Moses was requesting to know the name of the "Angel of the Lord" which was not told to him.

Knowing that he was highly favored, he felt that a fuller manifestation of God to him would prove all things. He had been in His presence numerous times and spoke with Him daily but had never seen His face. Moses wanted the special honor of seeing His face, if possible. He argued the fact that Israel was special above all other peoples and that he was His faithful servant. There was only one problem with Moses' request – mortal eye cannot see the Immortal God and remain alive. This law could not be changed for Moses or for any human being. God must live by His own laws, and so must everyone.

17 And the Lord said unto Moses, I will do this thing also that thou hast spoken: for thou hast found grace in my sight, and I know thee by name.

Moses was honored to have found special favors with God. He did not receive special favors just by wanting those favors but by loving God with all his heart and soul and by serving God's people at a time when his service was needed most. In considering Moses' request, God found a way to give him a clearer manifestation of Himself without breaking His law. There was a reason for this law.

18 And he said, I beseech thee, show me thy glory.

19 And he said, I will make all my goodness pass before thee, and I will proclaim the name of the Lord before thee; and will be gracious to whom I will be gracious, and will show mercy on whom I will show mercy.

20 And he said, Thou canst not see my face: for there shall no man see me and live.

21 And the Lord said, Behold, there is a place by me, and thou shalt stand upon a rock:

22 And it shall come to pass, while my glory passes by, that I will put thee in a cleft of the rock, and will cover thee with my hand while I pass by:

23 And I will take away mine hand, and thou shalt see my back parts: but my face shall not be seen.

Moses had shown in his early life and in his first encounter with God that he was not an ordinary man. Most of God's servants were chosen before they were born for the mission of their life. The circumstances of Moses' birth indicated that he was not an ordinary man. And there was not an event in his life that did not reflect greatness. This request to see God's face was another evidence of spiritual greatness. The problem with this request was that it transcended the limits of mortality. Moses was not an ordinary man but he had to live within the limits of mortality.

It was sin that brought mortality to life. Without sin man would live forever even if he had not eaten of the Tree of Life. The fruit of the Tree of Knowledge of Good and Evil brought death. The purpose of the Tree of Life was to guarantee immortality so that it would be impossible for man to die after eating it. Sin and mortality are inseparable, as mortality bears the mark of sin. As sin is the opposite of holiness, mortality is the opposite of immortality. The two cannot coexist, at least, not on the same plane of reality.

To be brought on the same plane of reality means that immortality, the greater of the two, will certainly extinguish mortality. You see, sin was not meant to be; neither was mortality. Mortality bears the mark of sin, something that Moses did not cause and could not change. Sin is represented by mortality but unfriendly to immortality and an alien to God's holiness. Holiness and immortality are represented by the face of God. Sin and mortality were represented by the face of Moses. These two representations could not be reconciled in the coincidence of facing each other. God would remain infinitely holy and immortal and Moses would have gone to the opposite extreme, death by sin. Death marks the end of the road for mortality. Therefore, the coincidence of the meeting between Immortality and mortality would not have a happy ending, at least not for Moses, because it would cause the instant end to his mortality which he was not expecting.

The Golden Calf

There was a built-in protection for mortality against instant death in the coincidence of mortal man coming into the immediate presence of The Immortal God. The awesome sense of being in the immediate presence of the Eternal God causes one to want to hide somewhere, instead of wanting to look into the eyes of God. In Moses' first encounter with God, when he heard the voice of God saying, Take off thy shoes from off thy feet for you are sanding on holy ground, Moses tried to look and realized the brightness of God's glory was beyond the capacity of mortal eye. He did then what came natural and that was to hide his face to protect his sight. But more than sight was at stake; Moses mortal life was at stake.

The principle of sin which caused death was already at work and God could not arbitrarily prevent it from having its effect. Death reveals the limitation to mortal life. Many different events can stimulate death, taking one to the end of mortal life. Seeing the face of the Immortal God is one such event but Moses did not know that. His request indicates his spiritual growth and, at the same time, its limit, for he could not grow beyond that point.

The only happy meeting between Immortality and mortality, and between sin and holiness, is by the process of Redemption. Man must first be elevated to immortality when all impurities and imperfections are removed, when man regains his original holy nature. The privilege of immortality cannot be bestowed on mortal man at an inappropriate time. To do so would have rendered the whole plan of Redemption meaningless and without purpose.

In order to prevent instant death to Moses and to grant his special request, God extended special love and mercy to him by preparing a place for him in the cleft of the rock where He could protect him from the glory of His immortality. In that way Moses could see His back while He was passing.

Do angels and arch angels see God's face? They do but they are immortal beings. Their nature allows them to dwell in

His presence and see His face perfectly. Flesh and blood cannot endure the glory of God's face.

SUMMARY

The Golden Calf is not something we want to remember, yet it is one thing which shows, above all others, the depth of God's love and forgiveness. The journey to the point of the Golden Calf was tempestuous, yet there were glorious moments. The Golden Calf reveals most glaringly the destructive nature of impatience. It certainly caused Israel to do the unthinkable. Their demand for gods of gold could only be seen as an act to show displeasure with Moses for his absence of forty days. It showed more dependence on Moses and less on God. It also showed that their heart was not at the right place for their faith was in Moses and not in God.

This spiritual rebellion contrasts the styles of two leaderships, that of Moses and that of Aaron. The people commanded Aaron and he obeyed them; they had never attempted to command Moses because they knew they would not succeed. They murmured against him many times, but murmuring was different from commanding him; they feared him because they knew God spoke through him. When Aaron had the greatest opportunity to lead, he utterly failed himself, the people, and his God. Aaron was really a miserable failure. He never attempted to console them in a time of need or discouraged them from doing the unthinkable——he urged them unto spiritual suicide. He urged them to bring him all their golden earrings of women and children. They gave him all and he crafted the **Golden Calf.**

The Golden Calf proceeded, not preceded, God's miraculous providential care of water, Manna, and flesh, and the greatest manifestation of God on Mount Sinai. They saw the glory of God and heard the voice of the Living God. Yet that great sin seemed to undo all of that for the memory lingered with them.

At first on the mountain top, Moses saw sin from a distance, but when he came down he faced sin face to face. The reality of hearing about sin and the reality of looking at it were two different things. Seeing sin at its worst caused him to break the two tables of the Testimony, burned the golden calf to dust, scattered it upon the water, and caused the people to drink it. But that was not enough to purge away the sin of idolatry from Israel; he ordered the Levites to kill those who refused to separate themselves unto God. Still that was not enough to guarantee spiritual restoration.

Moses began to realize that God's holy anger was justified and that Israel had forfeited all their claims of all the promises made by God to their fathers. From this quick review, he concluded the idol of the golden calf was a great sin and needed special intercession. The exercise of his personal intercession would have been meaningless unless the people had realized the depth of their idolatry. They needed to acknowledge that their sin was on the **border of un-forgiveness**. Only then he could make a bold attempt at interceding for them. By interceding for his people, he showed his love for God, for righteousness, and for his people. The people had corrupted themselves and a new spiritual beginning was needed. Thus Moses removed the tabernacle and pitched it outside of the camp. Moses did not want to identify with the sin of the old congregation; he wanted them to begin anew. This Tabernacle was a temporary meeting place: the pattern of the one given to Moses was not yet built. There seemed to be a new spiritual renewal, reverence and gratitude.

CHAPTER 8

Covenant Renewed, Exodus 34-35

The Covenant between God and Israel went back to the days of Abraham, Isaac, and Jacob. During their lifetime, they faithfully kept their commitment to it and God kept His commitment. The Covenant could justly be nullified if either party failed in his obligation. At Mount Sinai it was renewed for it was abruptly broken by Israel, which by its very nature freed God from fulfilling His obligation. If the Covenant was to be restored, it would necessitate an act of Divine mercy. Quite appropriately the Mercy Seat was to be placed on top of the Ark of the Covenant, signifying that God could only honor it through mercy.

At this point, the Covenant remained unfulfilled and God and Israel must, therefore, honor their obligations. Time was important and none of it could be wasted. Moses was in a hurry to go back to the top of Mount Sinai.

Moses Prepares to return to the Top of Mount Sinai, Ex. 34:1-4:

1 And the Lord said unto Moses, Hew thee two tables of stone like unto the first: and I will write upon these tables the words that were in the first tables, which you break.

God did not rebuke Moses for breaking the Tables of stone with the ten commandments. He knew Moses was justly angry and could not prevent it. It was then behind them and they both needed to move forward. God was ready to descend again on Mount Sinai and the boundaries had to be reestablished. One would have thought God's manifestation of Himself would have removed all lingering doubts but it did not.

2 And be ready in the morning, and come up in the morning unto Mount Sinai, and present thyself there to me in the top of the mount.

3 And no man shall come up with thee, neither let any man be seen throughout all the mount; neither let the flocks nor herds feed before that mount.

4 And he hewed two tables of stone like unto the first; and Moses rose up early in the morning, and went up unto Mount Sinai, as the Lord had commanded him, and took in his hand the two tables of stone.

This was about the seventh time Moses returned to the top of Mount Sinai: the first, Exodus 19:1-7; the second, Exodus 19:8-10; the third, Exodus 19:14-20; the fourth, Exodus 19:24-20:21; the fifth, Exodus 24:1-18; the sixth, Exodus 32:30-35; the seventh, Exodus 34:1-8.

The first two tables were hewed out of the rock by God. At this time Moses had to prepare his own tables. As he was spiritually motivated, he arose early and went to the top of Mount Sinai.

Moses' Desire Granted, Ex. 34:5-10:

5 And the Lord descended in the cloud, and stood with him there, and proclaimed the name of the Lord.

6 And the Lord passed by before him, and proclaimed, The Lord, The Lord God, merciful and gracious, longsuffering, and abundant in goodness and truth,

7 Keeping mercy for thousands, forgiving iniquity and transgression and sin, and that will by no means clear the guilty; visiting the iniquity of the fathers upon the children, and upon the children's children unto the third and to the fourth generation.

Moses' appointment with God on the top of Mount Sinai was for two purposes. First, it was to restore the Covenant and to rewrite the Ten Commandments. Second, He was to reveal Himself to Moses in a fuller revelation. He distinctly proclaimed His righteousness in verses 6-7. The latter or greater part of verse 7 seems to indicate that God recognizes a difference between His forgiving of sins and the natural consequences of sins. Though He forgives sins in His sovereign act of mercy, its consequences cannot go answered. Though He did forgive Adam and Eve of their sins, the consequences had to be accounted for: death still reigned over mankind from Adam to Moses.

The forgiven sins of Israel, particularly that of the Golden Calf, were all forgiven, but the consequences would not just go away unanswered. That was one reason that only two people of the generation that left Egypt entered the Promised Land. They all perished in the Wilderness. Moses was not allowed to go to the Promised Land: he stood afar off on the top of Mount Pisgah and viewed it. Visiting the iniquities of the fathers means that God will not prevent the consequences of sin from taking effect.

8 And Moses made haste, and bowed his head toward the earth, and worshipped.

As soon as Moses heard God's voice declaring His righteousness, he quickly bowed to the Earth in reverence of God's presence and worshipped Him. His priority was to look at God's face or His personal form. He had forgotten all about that to do what was most important —the worship of God. "God is a Spirit and they that worship Him must worship Him in spirit and in truth". Moses did not have to see His face in order to worship Him. Worship is an expression of gratitude to God for the privilege of life. God is perceived with the soul and spirit, not with the senses. Moses' priority was completely changed to what was most important. It was not anymore about personal ambition; it was now about God's people and their eternal destiny.

9 And he said, If now I have found grace in thy sight, O Lord, let my Lord, I pray thee, go among us; for it is a stiff neck people and pardon our iniquity and our sin, and take us for Thine inheritance

Moses' priority now was that God's presence be with His people all the way. He sought not to separate himself from the sin of his people; instead, he identified with and treated their sin as his very own. Then it was time to gaze on God's majesty. With a spiritually transformed leader and a forgiven people, God was ready to restore the Covenant.

10 And he said, Behold, I make a covenant: before all thy people I will do marvels, such as have not been done in all the earth, nor in any nation: and all the people among which thou art shall see the work of the Lord: for it is a terrible thing that I will do with thee.

The Covenant, Ex. 34:11-28:

11 Observe thou that which I command you this day: behold, I drive out before thee the Amorite, and the Canaanite, and the Hittite, and the Perizzite, and the Hivite, and the Jebusite.

12 Take heed to thyself, lest thou make a covenant with the inhabitants of the land whither you go, lest it be for snare in the midst of you:

13 But ye shall destroy their altars, break their images, and cut down their groves:

God solemnly promised to drive out all Israel's enemies to give them free access to the Promised Land. This part of the New Covenant was unconditional. Attached to this unconditional Covenant was a strong warning not to enter into any alliance with the inhabitants of the Promised Land.

14 For thou shalt worship no other god: for the Lord whose name is Jealous, is a jealous God:

15 Lest thou make a covenant with the inhabitants of the

land, and they go a-whoring after their gods, and do sacrifice unto their gods, and one call thee, and thou eat of his sacrifice;

16 And thou take of their daughters unto thy sons, and their daughters go a-whoring after their gods, and make thy sons go a-whoring after their gods.

17 Thou shalt make thee no molten gods.

Intermarriage was forbidden for it would be used as an entrapment to turn them away from serving their God. Emphases were placed on the Feast of Unleavened Bread, God's right to the Firstborn, the Sabbath Day, the Feasts of Weeks, the Appearance of the Males before the Lord, and Rules of Sacrifice.

The Feast of Unleavened Bread, Ex. 34:18: The feast of unleavened bread shalt thou keep. Seven days thou shalt eat unleavened bread, as I commanded thee, in the time of the month Abib: for in the month Abib you came out from Egypt.

The Feast of Unleavened Bread was preceded by the Passover. The Passover was celebrated on the 14th day in the month, Abib as commanded. It commemorated the destruction of the firstborn in the land of Egypt and the deliverance of Israel from the bondage of Egypt

The Right to the Firstborn, Ex. 34:19-20:19 All that opens the matrix is mine; and every firstling among thy cattle, whether of ox or sheep, that is male.

20 But the firstling of an ass thou shalt redeem with a lamb: and if thou redeem him not, then shalt thou break his neck. All the first born of thy sons thou shalt redeem. And none shall appear before me empty.

God's claim of the firstborn was to always remind Israel of their miraculous deliverance from Egypt and that the firstborn of what they had was to be given to the Lord in recognition of the Passover.

The Sabbath Day, 34:21: 21 Six days thou shalt work, but on the seventh day thou shalt rest: in earing time and in harvest thou shalt rest

The Sabbath Day was to remind Israel that God created the Universe. They were to rest on the Sabbath Day to ponder the wonders of Creation. Creation is a revelation of God. They did not need to see the face of God to believe in His existence.

The Feast of Weeks, 34:22: 22 And thou shalt observe the feast of weeks, of the first-fruits of wheat harvest, and the feast of ingathering at the year's end.

The feast of Weeks was to be observed seven Sabbaths from the first harvest in the Promised Land. This is recognized as the Feast of Pentecost. The Feast of Weeks is spelled out in Leviticus 23:10-21.

The Appearance of the Males, 34:23 Thrice in the year shall all your men-children appear before the Lord God, the God of Israel.

These three times are clearly stated in Deuteronomy 16:16, Three times in a year shall all thy males appear before the Lord thy God in the place which he shall choose; in the feast of unleavened bread, and in the feast of weeks, and in the feast of tabernacles: and they shall not appear before me empty.

24 For I will cast out the nations before thee, and enlarge thy borders: neither shall any man desire thy land, when thou shalt go up to appear before the Lord thy God thrice in the year.

Rules of Sacrifice, 34:25:

25 Thou shalt not offer the blood of my sacrifice with leaven; neither shall the sacrifice of the feast of the Passover be left unto the morning.

The leaven represented the Egyptian culture, a life of sin; the Children of Israel were to be different. None of the Passover lamb was to be left until the morning. It would thereby become second-place. The symbolism is that Christ

our Passover Lamb would not remain on the Cross until the next morning.

26 The first of the first fruits of thy land thou shalt bring unto the house of the Lord thy God. Thou shalt not seethe a kid in his mother's milk.

27 And the Lord said unto Moses, Write thou these words: for after the tenor of these words I have made a covenant with thee and with Israel.

28 And he was there with the Lord forty days and forty nights; he did neither eat bread, nor drink water. And he wrote upon the tables the words of the covenant, the ten commandments.

The sin of the Golden Calf had completely nullified the Covenant. The Covenant was the foundation for all the laws, statutes, and ceremonies. All that was said to Moses, during the first forty days on the Mount and before, was about the Covenant. Without the formal renewal of the Covenant, all that would have been meaningless. Nothing new was necessary to renew the Covenant. Emphasizing some of the things of the Old Covenant was sufficient to reinstate it with the unconditional promise of driving out Israel's enemies from before them.

Moses left the presence of The Holy One with the assurance that Israel's spiritual relationship with their God was renewed, the evidence being the two tables with the Ten Commandments, in God's own writing.

Moses Descends from Mount Sinai, Ex. 34:29-35

29 And it came to pass when Moses came down from mount Sinai with the two tables of testimony in Moses' hand, when he came down from the mount, that Moses knew not that the skin of his face shone while he talked with him.

Moses' pure desire to literally see God's face was of human curiosity. It had nothing to do with his belief in God's existence. In his first encounter with Him, he was absolutely convinced of the eternal existence of God. God spoke to him in a literal way and he felt His power. He was later used in all the signs and wonders shown in Egypt. Progressively, his faith and confidence grew by the day. Seeing God's face would not add to his faith; and not seeing His face would not decrease his faith.

When the time came for him to observe God's personal manifestation, he turned away and did what was more important: he quickly bowed his head to the ground and worshipped God on hearing His voice. In his forty days of communication, nothing more was said of his desire to look in God's face. Strangely, though, on coming down from the Mount and talking to the congregation, he realized that his face began to shine. It became a phenomenon because the congregation was not able to look him in the face. He had to put a veil on his face when communicating with them.

God taught him by object lesson that the glory of His face would be too glorious for mortal eyes to endure: literally he could not remain alive after looking in His face. Moses learned that the Children of Israel could not look him in the face and that he would not be able to look at the face of Eternal God and live. The line between immortality and mortality was drawn for a good reason.

30 And when Aaron and all the children of Israel saw Moses, behold, the skin of his face shone; and they were afraid to come nigh him.

31 And Moses called unto them; and Aaron and all the rulers of the congregation returned unto him: and Moses talked with them.

32 And afterward all the children of Israel came nigh: and he gave them in commandment all that the Lord had spoken

33 And till Moses hand done speaking with them, he put a veil on his face.

34 But when Moses went in before the Lord to speak with him, he took the veil off, until he came out. And he came

out, and spoke unto the children of Israel that which he was commanded.

35 And the children of Israel saw the face of Moses, that the skin of Moses face shone: and Moses put the veil upon his face again, until he went in to speak with him.

In the end the glory of Moses' face did show us what immortality will be like. The Bible does say the righteous shall shine forth in God's kingdom as the brightness of the firmament.

Moses Assembles the People, Ex. 35:1-4:

1 And Moses gathered all the congregation of the children of Israel together, and said unto them, These are the words which the Lord hath commanded, that ye should do them.

2 Six days shall work be done but on the seventh day there shall be to you an holy day, a Sabbath of rest to the Lord: whosoever doeth work therein shall be put to death.

3 Ye shall kindle no fire throughout your habitations upon the Sabbath day.

4 And Moses spoke unto the congregation of the children of Israel, saying, This is the thing which the Lord commanded, saying

The Sabbath was to be a reminder to Israel that God created the Universe. They were to learn from it that God had a plan and they were a part of that plan. The immediate plan was to build the holy Tabernacle for His abiding presence.

Moses Asks for an Offering, Ex. 35:5-9:

5 Take ye from among you an offering unto the Lord: whosoever is of a willing heart, let him bring it, an offering of the Lord; gold, and silver, and brass,

6 And blue, and purple, and scarlet, and fine linen, and goats hair,

7 And rams' skins dyed red, and badgers' skins, and shittim wood,

8 And oil for the light, and spices for anointing oil, and for the sweet incense,

9 And onyx stones, and stones to be set for the ephod, and for the breastplate.

Nothing was changed in the Covenant; the requirements of the offering to build the Tabernacle remained the same. Every one of them was welcomed to give whatever they had: material, time, and talent. Moses then gave them a list of what was to be done.

Willing Workers Needed, Ex. 35:10-20

10 And every wise-hearted among you shall come, and make all that the Lord hath commanded;

11 The tabernacle, his tent, and his covering, his taches, and his boards, his bars, his pillars, and his sockets,

12 The ark, and the staves thereof, with the mercy seat, and the veil of the covering,

13 The table, and his staves, and all his vessels, and the showbread,

14 The candlestick also for the light, and his furniture, and his lamps, with the oil for the light,

15 And the incense altar, and his staves, and the anointing oil, and the sweet incense, and the hanging for the door at the entering in of the tabernacle.

16 The altar of burnt offering, with his brazen grate, his staves, and all his vessels, the laver, and his foot,

17 The hangings of the court, his pillars, and their sockets, and the hanging for the door of the court,

18 The pins of the tabernacle, and the pins of the court, and their cords,

19 The clothes of service, to do service in the holy place, the holy garments for Aaron the priest, and the garments of his sons, to minister in the priest's office.

20 And all the congregation of the children of Israel departed from the presence of Moses.

The People Respond, Ex. 35:21-29

21 And they came every one whose heart stirred him up, and every one whom his spirit made him willing, and they brought the Lord's offering to the work of the tabernacle of the congregation, and for all his service, and for the holy garments.

22 And they came, both men and women, as many as were willing hearted, and brought bracelets, and earrings, and tablets, all jewels of gold: and every man that offered, offered an offering of gold unto the Lord.

23 And every man with whom was found blue, and purple, and scarlet, and fine linen, and goats' hair, and red skins of rams, and badgers' skins, brought them.

24 Every one that did offer an offering of silver and brass brought the Lord's offering: and every man with whom was found shittim wood for any work of the service, brought it.

25 And all the women that were wise-hearted did spin with their hands, and brought that which they had spun, both of blue, and of purple, and of scarlet, and of fine linen.

26 And all the women whose heart stirred them up in wisdom spun goats' hair.

27 And the rulers brought onyx stones, and stones to be set, for the ephod, and for the breastplate;

28 And spice, and oil for the light, and for anointing oil, and for the sweet incense.

29 The children of Israel brought a willing offering unto the Lord, every man and woman, whose heart made them willing to bring for all manner of work, which the Lord had commanded to be made by the hand of Moses.

The overwhelming response from the people to building the Tabernacle indicated the renewal of the Covenant. It could be called a great spiritual revival. All that was brought to Moses; and all the skilled workers committed themselves to the work of the Tabernacle. It was then necessary to appoint someone to supervise the work.

Superintendent Appointed, Ex. 35:30-35

30 And Moses said unto the children of Israel, See, the Lord hath called by name Bezaleel the son of Uri, the son of Hur, of the tribe of Judah;

31 And he hath filled him with the spirit of God, in wisdom, in understanding, and in knowledge, and in all manner of workmanship;

32 And to devise curious works, to work in gold, and in silver, and in brass,

33 And in cutting of stones, to set them, and in carving of wood, to make any manner of cunning work.

34 And he hath put in his heart that he may teach, both he and Aholiab, the son of Ahisamach, of the tribe of Dan.

35 Them hath he filled with wisdom of heart, to work all manner of work, of the engraver, and of the cunning workman, and of the embroiderer, in blue, and in purple, and in scarlet, and in fine linen, and of the weaver, even them that do any work, and those that devise cunning work.

Moses appointed Bezaleel of the tribe of Judah to be superintendent of the work. He appointed Aholiab of the tribe of Dan to be his assistant. It is important to observe the early leadership position given to the tribe of Judah. Bezaleel leadership was not acquired. He was singled out and anointed by God to direct the building of the Tabernacle.

SUMMARY

The renewal of the Covenant was in Israel's best interest, on the one hand. And on the other hand, was in the best interest of humanity. Therefore, the renewal of the Covenant was in keeping with God's eternal purpose. While the Golden Calf was an astonishing surprise to us, God long foreknew that Israel would quickly make and worship it while in His presence. Equally we were astonished at God's love and mercy in forgiving Israel and moving forward to the Promised Land.

We saw the worst in man, but we also saw the best in man. It was Moses who brought to light the nobility of the human soul. He refused to falter in the face of human insurmountable difficulties, revealing the potentials of mortal man. He not only spoke with God, but saw the Invisible God and came down from Mount Sinai with the full restoration of the Covenant. He did not fail his God and he did not fail his people during the most spiritually destructive experience of their existence. From that experience, he was able to show the symbol of immortality to everyone who looked at him.

As important as that symbol was, Moses realized that immortality could only be experienced by faithfully obeying every word which came from the mouth of God. To him, his greatest responsibility was to place the commandments of God in the hands, ears, and hearts of the people. There were some things the congregation should never forget. They should never forget the observance of the Passover, God's right to the Firstborn, the Sabbath Day, the Feast of Weeks, the Appearance of the Males before God thrice a year, and the Rules of the Sacrifices. The people were renewed and ready to build the Tabernacle.

CHAPTER 9
Building The Tabernacle, Exodus 36-40

In previous chapters, among other things, we have considered the Divine service of the Priesthood, the Golden Calf, and the Renewal of the Covenant. In this chapter, we shall move from concept to the actual building of the Tabernacle and the realization of a fully functioning Theocracy. Theocracy was God's ideal form of government for His people. Today there are other different forms of governments.

At the heart of this truly great Theocracy was Divine worship, underpinned by the Divine desire for a holy relationship with Israel. Nothing could have been more important to God's eternal plan of man's Redemption than His covenant relationship with Israel through whom the Redeemer would come. His eternal plan was represented in all the symbolisms of the Tabernacle, which apply to Israel, but to a greater degree, to all mankind. These symbolisms have been already explained, particularly in chapters 5 and 6.

In this chapter of the actual building of the Tabernacle, we want to see that the Tabernacle was built according to its concept, first given before the sin of the Golden Calf. The building of the Tabernacle was the strongest evidence that the Covenant was restored. It shows that Divine worship is at the center of the Universe and that the tangible things are directed to the spiritual reality of worship. The means cannot be greater than its ends, the ends are always greater. All things were created for

God's honor. Now the Tabernacle must be built to honor Him: first the Tabernacle itself, then its vessels, and the priestly garments.

The Work Begins, Exodus 36: 1-7:

1 Then wrought Bezaleel and Aholiab, and every wise-hearted man, in whom he Lord put wisdom and understanding to know how to work all manner of work for the service of the sanctuary, according to all that the Lord had commanded.

2 And Moses called Bezaleel and Aholiab, and every wise-hearted man, in whose heart the Lord had put wisdom, even every one whose heart stirred him up to come unto the work to do it:

3 And they received of Moses all the offering, which the children of Israel had brought for the work of the service of the sanctuary, to make it withal. And they brought yet unto him free offerings every morning.

Building the Tabernacle was a difficult task and no one had any previous experience. Everything had to be according to the plan; therefore, God filled Bezaleel and Aholiab with wisdom and knowledge as well as all those who were willing to work, including women. To make the things of gold, silver, and bronze demanded the wisdom and knowledge from above. The curtains of blue, purple, scarlet, and linen demanded many skill women to make. All the workers which were needed made themselves available. Then Moses gave to them all the material he collected from the congregation.

4 And all the wise men, that wrought all the work of the sanctuary, came every man from his work which they made;

5 And they spoke unto Moses saying, The people bring much more than enough for the service of the work, which the Lord commanded to make.

The superabundance of the material given had a spiritual cause. The people gave from their love for God and from the willingness of their hearts. They were not aware that they had given more than was necessary because they were thinking not about the gifts but the cause for the gifts. When people think about the cause of their giving, it will exceed what is required.

6 And Moses gave commandment, and they caused it to be proclaimed throughout the camp, saying, Let neither man nor woman make any more work for the offering of the sanctuary. So the people were restrained from bringing.

7 For the stuff they had was sufficient for all the work to make it, and too much.

The Curtains, Ex. 36:8-13:

8 And every wise-hearted man among them that wrought the work of the tabernacle made ten curtains of fine twined linen, and blue, and purple, and scarlet: with cherubim of cunning work made he them.

The use of the curtains and the design of the Tabernacle made for quick mobility as Israel were on a journey. The mention of the art work of cherubim on the curtains of the Tabernacle suggests they have specific duty in worship or at least their Divine assignment has to do with worship. It seems to be that they are a special class of angels who are assigned to the throne of God. The art work was especially evident on the holy veil between the Holy of Holies and the Sanctuary.

9 The length of one curtain was twenty and eight cubits, and the breath of one curtain four cubits: the curtains were all of one size. (42'x 6')

10 And he coupled the five curtains one unto another: and the other five curtains he couple one unto another.

One side of the Tabernacle was 84' long by 15' high.

11 And he made loops of blue on the edge of one curtain from the selvedge in the coupling: likewise he made in the uttermost side of another curtain, in coupling of the second.

12 Fifty loops made he in one curtain, and fifty loops made he in the edge of the curtain, which was in the coupling of the second: the loops held one coupling to another.

13 And he made fifty taches of gold, and coupled the curtains one unto to another with the taches: so it became one tabernacle.

By the loops and taches both sides of the Tabernacle were coupled at the top. It became necessary for it to be covered.

On the Mount of Transfiguration Peter said to the Lord, "Let us make three Tabernacles: one for Thee, one for Moses, and one for Elijah". We will be wise to remember that there is only one Church whose foundation is Christ Himself.

The Covering of the Tabernacle, Ex. 36:14-19:

14 And he made curtains of goats' hair for the tent over the tabernacle: eleven curtains he made them.

15 The length of one curtain was thirty cubits, and four cubits was the breath of one curtain: the eleven curtains were of one size. (45'x6')

16 And he coupled five curtains by themselves, and six curtains by themselves.

One side of the covering was 90'x 15'; the other was 90'x 18'. The two sides of the covering were joined together making one covering.

17 And he made fifty loops upon the uttermost edge of the curtain in the coupling, and fifty loops made he upon the edge of the curtain which couples the second.

18 And he made fifty taches of brass to couple the tent together, that it might be one.

19 And he made a covering for the tent of rams' skins dyed red, and a covering of badgers' skins above that.

The nature of the coverings made them stronger than the other curtains of the Tabernacle, and thus protected them from the external elements.

All three coverings were identical in size. This threefold covering symbolizes the Trinity, Father, Son, and Holy Spirit.

The Boards, Ex. 36:20-36:

20 And he made for the tabernacle of shittim wood, standing up.

21 The length of a board was ten cubits, and the breath of a board was one cubit and a half.

22 One board had two tenons, equally distant one from another: thus did he make for all the boards of the tabernacle.

23 And he made boards for the tabernacle; twenty boards for the south southward:

24 And forty sockets of silver he made under the twenty boards; two sockets under one board for his two tenons, and two sockets under another board for his two tenons. (*tenon, a projection on the end of a piece of wood shaped for insertion into a mortise to make a joint*).

25 And for the other side of the tabernacle, which is toward the north corner, he made twenty boards,

26 And their forty sockets of silver; two sockets under one board, and two sockets under another board.

27 And for the sides of the tabernacle westward he made six boards.

28 And two boards made he for the corners of the tabernacle in the two sides.

29 And they were coupled beneath, and coupled together at the head thereof, to one ring: thus he did to both of them in both the corners.

30 And there were eight boards; and their sockets were sixteen sockets of silver, under every board two sockets.

The boards were 10 cubits high (15 feet high, that is to say the Tabernacle was 15 feet high). There were 8 boards at the west end: Less than half of what was used at the north or the

south side. This would imply that the width of the Tabernacle was about 40 feet since its length was about 84 feet.

31 And he made bars of shittim wood; five for the boards of the one side of the tabernacle,

32 And five bars for the boards on the other side of the tabernacle, and five bars for the boards of the tabernacle for the sides westward.

33 And he made the middle bar to shoot through the boards from the one end to the other.

34 And he overlaid the boards with gold, and made their rings of gold to be places for the bars, and overlaid the bars with gold.

The boards and bars made of Shittim Wood and gold were used as the frame of the Tabernacle. The vessels were also made with gold and Shittim Wood; it was a golden tabernacle, the signal of God's kingdom of everlasting righteousness.

35 And he made a veil of blue, and purple, and scarlet, and fine twined linen: with cherubim made he it of cunning work.

36 And he made thereunto four pillars of shittim wood, and overlaid them with gold: their hooks were of gold; and he cast for them four sockets of silver.

The holy Veil indicates that fallen man needs a mediator to approach God on his behalf.

Curtains for the Tabernacle Door, Ex. 36:37-38:

37 And he made hanging for the tabernacle door of blue, and purple, and scarlet, and fine twined linen, of needlework;

38 And the five pillars of it with their hooks: and he overlaid their chapiters and their fillets with gold: but their five sockets were of brass.

The curtains for the door of the Tabernacle indicate that man can only enter into God's presence through the one door of righteousness; in our case, through Jesus Christ, the Door.

The Ark, Ex. 37:1-5:

1 And Bezaleel made the ark of shittim wood: two cubits and a half was the length of it, and a cubit and a half the breath of it, and a cubit and a half the height of it:

2 And he overlaid it with pure gold within and without, and made a crown of gold round about it.

3 And he cast for it four rings of gold, to be set by the four corners of it; even two rings upon the one side of it,

4 And he made staves of shittim wood, and overlaid them with gold.

5 And he put the staves into the rings by the side of the ark, to bear the ark.

The Ark of the Covenant indicates that God holds man responsible to obey His commandments.

The Mercy Seat, Ex. 37:6-9:

6 And he made the mercy seat of pure gold: two cubits and a half was the length thereof, and one cubit and a half was the breath thereof.

7 And he made two cherubim of gold, beaten out of one piece made he them, on the two ends of the mercy seat;

8 One cherub on the end of this side, and another cherub on the other end of that side: out of the mercy seat made he the cherubim on the two ends thereof.

9 And the cherubim spread out their wings on high, and covered with their wings over the mercy seat, with their faces one to another; even to the mercy seat-ward were the faces of the cherubim.

The Mercy Seat with the overshadowing cherubim placed upon the Ark indicates that God can only relate to man through mercy.

The Table of Showbread, Ex. 37:10-16:

10 And he made the table of shittim wood: two cubits was

the length thereof, and a cubit the breath thereof, and a cubit and a half the height thereof:

11 And he overlaid it with pure gold, and made thereunto a crown of gold round about.

12 Also he made thereunto a border of an hand-breath round about; and made a crown of gold for the border thereof round about.

13 And he cast for it four rings of gold, and put the rings upon the four corners that were in the four feet thereof.

14 Over against the borders were the rings, the places for the staves to bear the table.

15 And he made the staves of shittim wood, and overlaid them with gold, to bear the table.

16 And he made the vessels which were upon the table, his dishes, and his spoons, and his bowls, and his covers to cover withal, of pure gold.

The Table of the Showbread symbolizes Christ the Bread of Life.

The Candlestick, the Menorah, Ex. 37:17-24:

17 And he made the candlestick of pure gold: of beaten work made he the candlestick; his shaft, and his branch, his bowls, his knobs, and his flowers, were of the same:

18 And six branches going out the sides thereof; three branches of the candlestick out of the one side thereof, and three branches of the candlestick out of the other side thereof:

19 Three bowls made after the fashion of almonds in one branch, a knob and a flower; and three bowls made like almonds in another branch, a knob and a flower: so through- out the six branches going out of the candlestick.

20 And in the candlestick were four bowls made like almonds, his knob, and his flowers:

21 And a knob under two branches of the same, and a knob under two branches of the same, and a knob under

two branches of the same, according to the six branches going out of it.

22 Their knobs and their branches were of the same: all of it was one beaten work of pure gold.

23 And he made his seven lamps, and his snuffers, and his snuff-dishes, of pure gold.

24 Of a talent of pure gold made he it, and all the vessels thereof.

The Candlestick symbolizes Christ the light of the world.

The Golden Incense Altar, Ex. 37:25-28:

25 And he made the incense altar of shittim wood: the length of it was a cubit, and the breath of it a cubit; it was foursquare; and two cubits was the height of it; the horns thereof were of the same.

26 And he overlaid it with pure gold, both the top of it, and the sides thereof round about, and the horns of it: also he made unto it a crown of gold round about.

27 And he made two rings of gold for it under the crown thereof, by the two corners of it, upon the two sides thereof, to be places for the staves to bear it withal.

28 And he made the staves of shittim wood, and overlaid them with gold.

The Golden Incense Altar symbolizes purification, the fragrance of Amazing Grace. The prayers of the saints ascend as a sweet fragrance into God's presence. Purification removes the barrier of sin between man and God.

The Holy Anointing Oil and Sweet Incense, Ex. 37:29; 30:23-25, 34-38:

29 And he made the holy anointing oil, and the pure incense of sweet spices, according to the work of the apothecary.

Verses 23-25,34-38 of chapter 30 fully describe the composition of the holy anointing oil and the sweet perfume.

Their composition and God's command made them holy. These products could not be used for common purposes.

The Altar of Burnt Offering, Ex. 38:1-7

1 And he made the altar of burnt offering of shittim wood: five cubits was the length thereof , and five cubits the breath thereof; it was foursquare; and three cubits the height thereof.

2 And he made the horns thereof on the four corners of it; the horns thereof were of the same: and he overlaid it with brass.

3 And he made all the vessels of the altar, the pots, and the shovels, and the basins, and the flesh hooks, and the firepans: all the vessels thereof made he of brass.

4 And he made for the altar a brazen grate of network under the compass thereof beneath unto the midst of it.

5 And he cast four rings for the four ends of the grate of brass, to be places for the staves.

6 And he made the staves of shittim wood, and overlaid them with brass.

7 And he put the staves into the rings on the sides of the altar, to bear it withal; he made the altar hollow with boards.

The burnt Altar symbolizes purity and cleansing of the spirit of man; the blood of the sacrifices indicates the cleansing of the soul.

The Laver, Ex. 38:8:

8 And he made the laver of brass, and the foot of it of brass, of the looking glasses of the women assembling, which assembled at the door of the tabernacle of the congregation.

The Laver was also a symbol of cleansing which was available to everyone

The Court of the Tabernacle, Ex. 38:9-20:

9 And he made the court: on the south side southward

the hangings of the court were of fine twined linen, an hundred cubits:

10 Their pillars were twenty, and their brazen sockets twenty; the hooks of the pillars and their fillets were made of silver.

11 And for the north side the hangings were an hundred cubits, their pillars were twenty, and their sockets of brass twenty; the hooks of the pillars and their fillets of silver.

12 And for the west side were hangings of fifty cubits, their pillars ten, and their sockets ten; the hooks of the pillars and their fillets of silver.

13 And for the east side eastward fifty cubits.

14 The hangings of the one side of the gate were fifteen cubits; their pillars three, and their sockets three.

15 And for the other side of the court gate, on this hand, and on that hand, were hangings of fifteen cubits; their pillars three, and their sockets three.

16 All the hangings of the court roundabout were of fine twined linen.

17 And the sockets for the pillars were of brass; the hooks of the pillars and their fillets of silver; and the overlaying of their chapiters of silver; and all the pillars of the court were filleted with silver. (chapiter, a molding at the top of an art work)

18 And the hanging for the gate of the court was needlework, of blue, and purple, and scarlet, and fine twined linen: and twenty cubits was the length, and the height in the breath was five cubits, answerable to the hangings of the court.

19 And their pillars were four, and their sockets of brass four; their hooks of silver, and the overlaying of their chapiters and their fillets of silver.

20 And all the pins of the tabernacle and of the court round-about were of brass.

The Court of the Tabernacle indicates the universality of

God's righteousness. All nations were to be the recipients, not just Israel.

Cost: Gold, Silver, Brass, Ex. 38:21-31:

Building the tabernacle cost much in those days; but all the material of gold and silver was collected by Moses from the congregation. In addition, the Ransom money of half shekel of silver from all males from 20 years old was collected. The people gave willingly and above what was required. It was pleasing to God when He saw every one giving to a holy cause. We see how united they were in giving and we also see the fruits of obedience.

It took great skill in making all things required of them. God gave them the wisdom and understanding needed. He anointed two men under whose leadership the whole work was successfully completed. The account is stated thus:

21 This is the sum of the tabernacle, even of the tabernacle of testimony, as it was counted, according to the commandment of Moses, for the service of the Levites, by the hand of Ithamar, son to Aaron the priest.

Ithamar one of Aaron's sons had the special responsibility for the material.

22 And Bezaleel the son of Uri, the son of Hur, of the tribe of Judah made all that the Lord commanded Moses.

23 And with him was Aholiab, the son of Ahisamach, of the tribe of Dan, an engraver, and a cunning workman, and an embroiderer in blue, and in purple, and in scarlet, and fine linen.

Bezaleel and Ahisamach were singled out and anointed by God to direct the building of the Tabernacle. The others diligently followed their guidance.

24 All the gold that was occupied for the work in all the work of the holy place, even the gold of the offering, was twenty and nine talents, and seven hundred and thirty shekels, after the shekel of the sanctuary (2182.333 lbs.).

25 And the silver of them that were numbered of the congregation was an hundred talents, and a thousand seven hundred and threescore and fifteen shekels, after the shekel of the sanctuary (7,588.75 pounds of silver collected for building the Tabernacle).

26 A bekah (.2 ounce U.S.) for every man, that is half a shekel, after the shekel of the sanctuary, for every one that went to be numbered, from twenty years old and upward, for six hundred thousand and three thousand and five hundred and fifty men.

In Exodus 30 Moses was commanded to take the ransom money of the Children of Israel from twenty years and older at the time of their numbering. This was the age when men were selected for military service.

27 And of the hundred talents of silver were cast the sockets of the sanctuary, and sockets of the veil; an hundred sockets of the hundred talents, a talent for a socket.

28 And of the thousand seven hundred seventy and five shekels he made hooks for the pillars, and overlaid their chapiters, and filleted them.

29 And the brass of the offerings was seventy talents, and two thousand and four hundred shekels (5270 pounds).

30 And therewith he made the sockets to the door of the tabernacle of the congregation, and the brazen altar, and the brazen grate for it, and all the vessels of the altar,

31 And the sockets of the court round about, and the sockets of the court gate, and the pins of the tabernacle, and all the pins of the court round about.

The cost of building the Tabernacle indicates that Redemption was not freely provided; the whole price was paid by the death of Son of God which is beyond earthly value. In turn Redemption demands our complete devotion.

The Ephod of the Priestly Garments, Ex. 39:1-7:
1 And of blue, and purple, and scarlet, they made cloths

of service, to do service in the holy place, and made the holy garments for Aaron; as the Lord commanded Moses.

2 And he made the ephod of gold, blue, and purple, and scarlet, and fine twined linen.

3 And they did beat the gold into thin plates, and cut it into wires, to work in the blue, and in the purple, and in the scarlet, and in the fine linen, with cunning work.

4 They made shoulder-pieces for it, to couple it together: by the two edges was it coupled together.

5 And the curious girdle of his ephod, that was upon it, was of the same, according to the work thereof; of gold, blue, and purple, and scarlet, and fine twined linen; as the Lord commanded Moses.

6 And they wrought onyx stones enclosed in ouches of gold, graven as signets are graven, with the names of the children of Israel.

7 And he put them on the shoulders of the ephod, that they should be stones for a memorial to the children of Israel, as the Lord commanded Moses.

The Ephod was in more than one sense the master piece of the High Priestly Garment and reflected the fact that worship is not accidental, it is man's solemn duty to God. It also embodies the Breastplate with more details about Divine worship. Divine worship cannot be done in ignorance.

The Breastplate, Ex. 39:8-21:

8 And he made the breastplate of cunning work, like the work of the ephod; of gold, blue, and purple, and scarlet, and fine twined linen.

9 It was foursquare; they made the breastplate double: a span was the length thereof, and a span the breath thereof, being doubled. (9"x 9").

10 And they set it in four rows of stones: the first row was sardius, a topaz, and a carbuncle: this was the first row.

11 And the second row, an emerald, a sapphire, and a

diamond.

12 And the third row, a ligure, an agate, and an amethyst.

13 And the fourth row, a beryl, an onyx, and a jasper: they were enclosed in ouches of gold in their enclosing.

14 And the stones were according to the names of the children of Israel, twelve according to their names, like the engravings of a signet, everyone with his name, according to the twelve tribes.

15 And they made upon the breastplate chains at the ends, of wreathen work of pure gold.

16 And they made two ouches of gold, and two gold rings; and put the two rings in the two ends of the breastplate.

17 And they put the two wreathen chains of gold in the two rings on the ends of the breastplate.

18 And the two ends of the two wreathen chains they fastened in the two ouches, and put them on the shoulder-pieces of the ephod, before it.

19 And they made two rings of gold, and put them on the two ends of the breastplate, upon the border of it, which was on the side of the ephod inward.

20 And they made two other golden rings, and put them on the two sides of the ephod underneath, towards the forepart of it, other against the other coupling thereof, above the curious girdle of the ephod.

21 And they did bind the breastplate by his rings unto the rings of the ephod with a lace of blue, that it might be above the curious girdle of the ephod, and that the breast-plate might not be loosed from the ephod, as the Lord commanded Moses.

The Breastplate, with names of the twelve tribes of Israel represented by the twelve precious stones, suggests that God has a purpose for every-thing He created. Some of these purposes are hidden to us but they are still there. And there is a special purpose for every life.

The Robe, Ex. 39:22-26:

22 And he made the robe of the ephod of woven work, all of blue.

23 And there was a hole in the midst of the robe, as the hole of an habergeon, with a band round about the hole, that it should not rend.

24 And they made upon the hems of the robe pomegranates of blue, and purple, and scarlet, and twined linen.

25 And they made bells of pure gold, and but the bells between the pomegranates upon the hem of the robe, round about between the pomegranates;

26 A bell and pomegranate, a bell and pomegranate, round about the hem of the robe to minister in; as the Lord commanded Moses.

The blue robe of the Ephod indicates the holiness of God. The fact that Aaron had to wear it suggests that God expects man to be holy.

Linen Coats, Ex. 39:27

27 And they made coats of fine linen of woven work for Aaron, and for his sons,

The linen coats indicate the outworking of Redemption, the application of Christ's righteousness to the penitent sinner.

Miter and Crown, Ex. 39:28, 30, 31

28 And a miter of fine linen, and goodly bonnets of fine linen, and linen breeches of fine twined linen,

30 And they made the plate of the holy crown of pure gold, and wrote upon it a writing, like to the engravings of a signet, **HOLINESS TO THE LORD.**

31 And they tied unto it a lace of blue, to fasten it on high upon the miter; as the Lord commanded Moses.

The Miter and Crown suggest that man must be wholly clothed in God's righteousness. The flesh must not be exposed in God's presence; man cannot be praised for bringing sin into

the World.

The Curious Girdle, Ex. 39: 29; 28:8, 27

29 And a girdle of fine twined linen, and blue, and purple, purple, and scarlet, of needle work; as the Lord commanded
Moses.

28:8 And the curious girdle of the ephod, which is upon it, shall be of the same, according to the work thereof; even of gold, blue and purple, and scarlet, and fine twined linen.

28:27 And two other rings of gold thou shalt make, and shalt put them on the two sides of the ephod underneath, toward the forepart thereof, over against the other coupling thereof, above the curious girdle of the ephod.

The Curious Girdle indicates that the threefold nature of man must be held together by the truth of God's word.

Moses Inspects the Completion of the Work, 39:32-40:

32 Thus was all the work of the tabernacle of the tent of the congregation finished: and the children of Israel did according to all the Lord commanded Moses, so did they.

33 And they brought the tabernacle unto Moses, the tent, and all his furniture, his taches, his boards, his bars, and his sockets,

34 And the covering of rams' skin dyed red, and the covering of badgers' skins, and the veil of the covering,

35 The ark of the testimony and the staves thereof, and the mercy seat,

36 The table, and all the vessels thereof, and the showbread,

37 The pure candlestick, with the lamps thereof, even with the lamps to be set in order, and all the vessels thereof, and the oil for the light,

38 And the golden altar, and the anointing oil, and the sweet incense, and the hanging for the tabernacle door, and

all his vessels, the laver and his foot,

40 The hangings of the court, his pillars, and his sockets, and the hanging for the court gate, his cords, and his pins and all the vessels of the service of the tabernacle, for the tent of the congregation,

At the completion of the Tabernacle, the Children of Israel brought it to Moses for his inspection. The Tabernacle includes everything. It is made of very large curtains (exodus 36:14-19), long boards for it wooden frame (Exodus 26:20-36), curtains for its doors (Exodus 36:37-38), the Ark of the Covenant (Exodus 37:1-5), the Mercy Seat (Exodus 37:6-9), the Table of the Showbread (Exodus 3nt 7:10-16), the Golden Candlestick (Exodus 37:17-24), the Golden Altar of Incense (Exodus 37:25-28), the Altar of Burnt Offering (Exodus 38:1-7), the Laver (Exodus 38:8), and the Court of the Tabernacle (Exodus 38:9-20). The Tabernacle also includes the Holy Anointing Oil and the Priestly Garments

Moses was commanded to build the Tabernacle. God provided all the material and all the workers needed. Moses delegated the work to Bezaleel and Aholiab. They saw that everything was done as commanded by the Lord. Moses inspected the work and found that it was done as commanded. He then inspected the holy garments.

Moses Inspects the Garments, Ex. 39:41-43:

41 The cloths of service to do service in the holy place and the holy garments for Aaron the priest, and his sons' garments, to minister in the priest's office.

42 According to all that the Lord commanded Moses, so the children of Israel made all the work.

43 And Moses did look upon all the work, and, behold, they had done it as the Lord had commanded, even so had they done it: and Moses blessed them.

Moses inspected the holy garments and found that they were made as commanded. He was pleased with all that was

done and with all the workers. He turned to them and blessed them. This was a time for him to be happy, considering all the things he endured with them.

The instruments of Divine service remained to be put in their appointed places.

The Instruments of Service Installed, Ex. 40:1-11:

Without the installation of these instrument the services of the Tabernacle could not be performed.

1 And the Lord spoke unto Moses, saying,

2 On the first day of the first month shalt thou set up the tabernacle of the tent of the congregation.

3 And thou shalt put therein the ark of the testimony, and cover the ark with the veil.

4 And thou shalt bring in the table, and set in order the things that are to be set in order upon it; and thou shalt bring in the candlestick, and light the lamps thereof.

5 And thou shalt set the altar of gold for the incense between the ark of the testimony, and put the hanging of the door to the tabernacle.

6 And thou shalt set the altar of burnt offering before the door of the tabernacle of the tent of the congregation.

7 And thou shalt set the laver between the tent of the congregation and the altar (of burnt offering) and shalt put water therein.

8 And thou shalt set up the court round about, and hang up the hanging at the court gate.

9 And thou shalt take the anointing oil, and anoint the tabernacle, and all that is therein, and shalt hallow it, and all the vessels thereof: and it shall be holy.

10 And thou shalt anoint the altar of burnt offering, and all his vessels, and sanctify the altar: and it shall be an altar most holy.

11 And thou shalt anoint the laver and his foot, and sanctify it.

The anointing of the Tabernacle and its vessels was a part of the process of sanctification. The other part of the process was the offering of the blood sacrifices in the 7 day process ordered in Exodus 29. Though the blood sacrifices were not here mention, it must be assumed that they were offered, followed by the anointing.

Aaron and His Sons Inaugurated Ex. 40:12-16

12 And thou shalt bring Aaron and his sons unto the door of the tabernacle of congregation and wash them with water.

13 And thou shalt put upon Aaron the holy garments, and anoint him, and sanctify him; that he may minister to me in the priest's office.

14 And thou shalt bring his sons, and clothe them with coats:

15 And thou shalt anoint them as thou didst anoint their father, that they minister to me in the priest's office: for their anointing shall surely be an everlasting priesthood throughout their generations.

16 Thus did Moses according to all that the Lord commanded him, so did he.

This anointing of Aaron and his sons was only a part of the complete ceremony. The greater part was the offering of the blood sacrifices unto the Lord on their behalf. This is recorded in Exodus 29. Since it was described in details there, it is not necessary to be here repeated; and since it was the greater part of the inauguration, we must assume it was performed as commanded.

Erection Completed, Ex. 40:17-33:

In the previous verses Moses was commanded to install all the instruments of Divine service. Here we are seeing the actual execution of the Divine command.

17 And it came to pass in the first month of the second year, on the first day of the month, that the tabernacle was reared up.

18 And Moses reared up the tabernacle, and fastened his sockets, and set up the boards thereof, and put in the bars thereof, and reared up his pillars.

19 And he spread abroad the tent over the tabernacle, and put the covering over the tent above upon it; as the Lord commanded Moses.

20 And he took and put the testimony into the ark, and set the staves on the ark, and put the mercy seat above upon the ark:

21 And he brought the ark into the tabernacle, and set up the veil of covering, and covered the ark of the testimony; as the Lord commanded Moses.

22 And he put the table in the tent of the congregation, upon the side of the tabernacle northward, without the veil.

23 And he set the bread in order upon it before the Lord; as the Lord had commanded Moses.

24 And he put the candlestick in the tent of the congregation, over against the table, on the side of the tabernacle southward.

25 And he lighted the lamps before the Lord; as the Lord commanded Moses.

26 And he put the golden altar in the tent of the congregation before the veil:

27 And he burnt sweet incense thereon; as the Lord commanded Moses.

28 And he set up the hanging at the door of the tabernacle.

29 And he put the altar of burnt offering by the door of the tabernacle of the tent of the congregation, and offered upon it burnt offering and the meat offering; as the Lord commanded Moses.

30 And he set the laver between the tent of the congre

gation and the altar, and put water there, to wash withal.

31 And Moses and Aaron and his sons washed their hands and their feet thereat.

32 When they went into the tent of the congregation, and when they came near unto the altar, they washed; as the Lord commanded Moses.

33 And he reared up the court round about the tabernacle and the altar, and set up the hanging of the court gate. So Moses finished the work.

A year after leaving the bondage of Egypt, Moses had finished building the Tabernacle. He did all that the Lord commanded him, nothing was forgotten. It was an accomplishment. With God we can accomplish the impossible. God was pleased with the work of the Tabernacle, with Moses, and with the congregation. Can it be said of the Church that God is pleased? And can it be said of us that God is pleased with what we have done for Him? If He is pleased He will bless us and we will recognize it.

Blessings on the Erection, Ex. 40:34-38:

34 Then a cloud covered the tent of the congregation, and the glory of the Lord filled the tabernacle.

35 And Moses was not able to enter into the tent of the congregation, because the cloud abode thereon, and the glory of the Lord filled the tabernacle.

Because God was pleased with the work of the Tabernacle He filled it with His glory. This was the richest blessings of all. When we do what God requires of us, He will not forget to <u>*bless us.*</u>

Footnote: Old Testament weights and measures.
1 Ephah, 5.8 U.S. gallon; 1 Epha, 20 dry quarts; cubit, 17 – 21 inches; Bekah, ½ Shekle Gerah, .02 U.S. ounce;   Homer, 6 bushels U.S.; Omer, 2 dry quarts U.S.; Hin, 1 gallon U.S.; Mite, ¼ cent U.S.; Shekel, .4 ounce U.S.; Shekles, 100, I pound; Span, 9 inches; Talent, 75lbs U.S.

36 And when the cloud was taken up the children of Israel went onward in all their journeys

37 But if the cloud were not taken up, then they journeyed not till the day that it was taken up.

38 For the cloud of the Lord was upon the tabernacle by day, and fire was on it by night, in the sight of all the house of Israel, throughout all their journeys.

Despite all that was happening, there was the assurance of Divine guidance. Every human being needs Divine guidance to prevent eternal disaster.

SUMMARY

The Tabernacle was 84 feet long, forty feet wide, and 15 feet high. Its Court was 150 feet long and its width was 75 feet. The Tabernacle was made of curtains of blue, purple, scarlet, and fine twined linen. Its vessels, with the exception of the Burnt Altar, and the Laver, were made of Shittim Wood and gold. Its Court was made of fine twined linen with its door made of blue, purple, and scarlet.

The Tabernacle represented the abiding presence of God among His people. On the other hand, it was the place where Israel worshipped God during their wandering in the Wilderness. But there was a greater message to the Tabernacle, which had to do with the wider world of mankind. This message was declared in the symbolisms of the colors of the curtains, by the combination of the Shittim Wood and gold in the vessels of the Tabernacle, and in the boards of its frame.

These symbolisms were sufficiently explained in chapters 5 and 6.

We have moved from the concepts of the Tabernacle and the High Priestly Office to the completion and erection of the Tabernacle, the installation of its vessels of Divine services and the completion of the High Priestly Garments. These garments were characterized by the symbolisms of the Tabernacle and, therefore, addressed the greater message of God's eternal plan as it relates, not just to Israel, but the wider World of mankind.

It must be suggested that by the very nature of the material, the Tabernacle was given three dimensions: the Holy of Holies, the Sanctuary, and the Court. The term "dimension" is used to suggest that all three aspects of the Tabernacle represented a complete whole, as distinct from "divisions" which would suggest that each division could have independently stood alone, or that one was most important, when in fact the message of all these symbolisms is one——God is on a mission of making man holy by redeeming him. One must never overlook the special significance of the Tabernacle as related to Israel. Indeed they were the people through whom God would reach the other nations of the Earth. Their failures were not inspiring but they reveal the mercy and love of God for all mankind.

In conclusion, the Book of Exodus introduces God's omnipotence to the World and later reveals God's holiness. It shows that there is a kind of infinity to sin which had to be limited by Divine mercy and love in order for the Universe to serve God's eternal purpose. Accordingly, the Book of Exodus is the foundation on which Leviticus and Numbers rest. Where these two books differ, is only in a complementary way by providing the exegeses on some of the matters raised in the Book of Exodus. There are, however, some new subject matters, but they are based on the grand theme of God's holiness and man's relationship with Him through mercy and forgiveness. To a large extent, Leviticus and Numbers describe the implementation of those obligations required of Israel in Exodus by the ceremonies, and rituals of the Law. The Divine requirement of holiness by man pervades all three books, making them inseparable.

THE BOOK OF LEVITICUS: THE LEVITICAL PRIESTHOOD EXPRESSES THE HOLINESS OF GOD AND SYMBOLIZES CHRIST'S ATONEMENT

- *The Levitical Offerings, Chapters 1-7*

- *The Consecration of the Priests, Chapters 8-10*

- *The Social Compact, Chapters 11-15, 18, 20*

- *The Year of Atonemeant, Chapters 16-17*

- *Principles of Righteous Living Chapter 19*

- *The Social Compact with the Priests, Chapters 21-22*

- *The Yearly Feasts, Chapters 23-24*

- *The Year of Jubilee, Chapter 25*

- *Things To Remember, Chapter 26-27*

CHAPTER 10
The Levitical Offerings, Chapters 1-7

It took Israel three months after crossing the Red Sea to reach Mount Sinai where they remained for more than nine months, built and erected the Tabernacle the first month, Abib, of the second year. In Israel's Theocracy, the building of the Tabernacle was indispensable to the priesthood; the priesthood was indispensable to the blood sacrifices, and the blood sacrifices indispensable to Divine worship. The Fall of man had caused a breach of relationship with God. Sacrifice in worship was not a new phenomenon; neither was it peculiar to Israel. Its exegesis can be traced back to Genesis, immediately after the Fall. The example could be seen when God clothed Adam and Eve in coats of skin. In Genesis Noah offered burnt offering to the Lord; and in Genesis 15 Abraham worshipped the Lord with sacrifices.

It is obvious that with the early dawn of human history, offering of sacrifice was fundamental to Divine worship. So pervasive was the offering of sacrifices in worship that the heathen offered sacrifices to their gods. This is no surprise to those who know that sin originated with Lucifer. His desire to be worshipped caused the first sin. As the creator of sin, Lucifer and his angels compete with God for the worship of mankind. If there were benefits derived from worshiping the forces of darkness, that is not here relevant because in the end, those who worship Lucifer will lose their eternal souls. Here we are concerned about the meaning and purpose of the Levitical Offerings. They established right relationship with the Creator, which is the purpose of life. These offerings made the spiritual reality of worship both tangible and holy. The evidence is that when those sacrifices were offered, the penitent were forgiven of their sins and entered into a holy relationship with God.

The Burnt Offering was one of the primary offerings. This offering was an expression of worship, of thanks and gratitude to God for His blessings. However, it was a recognition of the need for Ament for him on whose behalf it was offered. There are three kinds of Burnt Offering: the bullock, the male goat or the lamb, and the turtledove or pigeon. It is important to understand the threefold symbolism of the blood sacrifice. The dead animal symbolizes death, the consequence of sin. The dead animal reminded the penitent that it had to bear the consequence of his sin. In the second place, its blood atoned for the sin of the soul, the principle being the blood of the innocent animal for the Atonement of the soul. In the third place, the sacrifice was consumed by fire, symbolizing the restoration of man's spirit in fellowship with God. Accordingly, the threefold nature of man is restored in right relationship with God.

We recognize that all the animals, whose sacrifices were offered on behalf of the guilty, were inferior to guilty man for whom they were offered. We must assume that the Atonement effected by those sacrifices could only be principled on a higher principle, with a nobler character. Indeed, the Atonement under the Law was principled on the Atoning Blood of the Son of God, the Lamb slain from the foundation of the world. Having known that man would have fallen from his original holy nature, He offered Himself to die in man's place. This was the eternal principle of the Atonement under the Law.

After a year's journey in the wilderness, the Tabernacle was completed. Before the service of Tabernacle could begin, the required blood sacrifices or offerings of Atonement were declared by God in concise but comprehensive terms. It was important that these sacrifices be fully understood by the priests who were to administer them. These sacrifices were exclusive to Israel. But we must now see how these offerings reflect in detail Christ's eternal Atonement. Though these offerings vary in nature, they reflect all aspects of Christ's Atonement.

1. The Burnt Offering, Leviticus 1

God is now speaking to Moses from the newly erected Tabernacle about the offerings that He requires of Israel,

The Bullock, Lev. 1:1-9:

1 And the Lord called unto Moses, and spoke unto him out of the tabernacle of the congregation, saying,

2 Speak unto the children of Israel, and say unto them, If any man of you bring an offering unto the Lord, ye shall bring your offering of the cattle, even of the herd, and of the flock.

3 If his offering be a burnt sacrifice of the herd, let him offer a male without blemish: he shall offer it of his own voluntary will at the door of the tabernacle of the congregation before the Lord.

4 And he shall put his hand upon the head of the burnt offering; and it shall be accepted for him to make atonement for him.

5 And he shall kill the bullock before the Lord: and the priests, Aaron's sons, shall bring the blood, and sprinkle the blood round about upon the altar that is by the door of the tabernacle of the congregation.

6 And he shall flay the burnt offering, and cut it into his pieces.

7 And the sons of Aaron the priest shall put fire upon the altar, and lay the wood in order upon the fire.

8 And the priests, Aaron's sons, shall lay the parts, head, and the fat, in order upon the wood that is on the fire which is upon the altar:

9 But his inwards and his legs shall he wash in water: and the priest shall burn all on the altar, to be a burnt sacrifice, an offering made by fire, of a sweet savor unto the Lord.

The bullock is brought before the Tabernacle and is killed by the offeror. The priest sprinkles its blood upon the Burnt Altar; cuts it into pieces; puts its head and fat upon the altar; washes its inwards and legs; and burns the whole bullock. The bullock of the Sin Offering is burnt without the camp; only its fats and inwards are burnt upon the Burnt Altar.

The Male Goat/Lamb, Lev. 1:10-13:

10 And if his offering be of the flocks, namely of the sheep, or of the goats, for a burnt sacrifice; he shall bring it a male without blemish.

11 And he shall kill it on the side of the altar northward before the Lord: and the priests Aaron's sons shall sprinkle his blood round about upon the altar.

12 And he shall cut it into his pieces, with his head and his fat: and the priest shall lay them in order on the wood that is on the fire which is upon the altar:

13 But he shall wash the inwards and the legs with water: and the priest shall bring it all, and burn it upon the altar: it is a burnt sacrifice, an offering made by fire, of a sweet savor unto the Lord.

The goat/ lamb is treated in the same manner as the bullock of the Burnt Offering. The whole offering is burnt upon the Burnt Altar.

The Turtledove /Pigeon Lev. 1:14-17:14 And if the burnt sacrifice for his offering to the Lord be of fowls, then he shall bring his offering of turtledoves, or of young pigeons.

15 And the priest shall bring it unto the altar, and ring off his head, and burn it on the altar; and the blood thereof shall be wrung out at the side of the altar:

16 And he shall pluck away his crop with his feathers, esthe ashes:

17 And he shall cleave it with the wings thereof, but shall not divide it asunder: and the priest shall burn it upon the altar, upon the wood that is upon the fire: it is a burnt sacrifice, an offering made by fire, of a sweet savor unto the Lord.

The bird, turtledove or pigeon is killed by the priest; its blood is poured out at the side of the Burnt Altar; it is now put upon the Burnt Altar; its feathers and its crop are removed and placed with the ashes of the burnt Altar, which will be later removed and burnt; and the whole offering is burnt. With the Burnt Offering, the blood is not taken into the Tabernacle, as the blood from the bullock of the Sin Offering. The Burnt Offering also symbolizes gratitude to the Lord. On the other hand, it represents purity.

Law of the Burnt Offering, Leviticus Lev. 6:8-13; 7:8:

8 And the Lord spoke unto Moses, saying,

9 Command Aaron and his sons, saying, This is the law of the burnt offering: it is the burnt offering, because of the burning upon the altar all night unto the morning, and the fire of the Lord shall be burning in it.

10 And the priest shall put on his linen garment, and his linen breeches shall he put upon his flesh, and take up the ashes which the fire hath consumed with the burnt offering on the altar, and he shall put them beside the altar.

11 And he shall put off the garments, and put on other garments, and carry forth the ashes forth without the camp unto a clean place.

12 And the fire upon the altar shall be burning in it; it shall not be put out: and the priest shall burn wood on it

every morning, and lay the burnt offering in order upon it; and he shall burn thereon the fat of the peace offerings.

13 The fire shall ever be burning upon the altar; it shall never go out.

7:8 And the priest that offers any man's burnt offering, even the priest shall have to himself the skin of the burnt offering which he hath offered.

The Law of the Burnt Offering is very revealing. The fire of the Burnt Offering burns throughout the night; in the morning the priest removes the ashes from the Burnt Altar; he only needs his linen garments to do that; he then puts on his regular clothes and removes the ashes without the camp; and puts wood on the fire to keep it burning. To complete the process of the burnt sacrifice the priest takes possession of the skin of the offering.

2. The Meat Offering, Leviticus 2

The Meat Offering is the only one of the five principal offerings, not offered with blood. It symbolizes fellowship with God. There are two kinds which are agriculture in nature, being made from flour: baked and unbaked.

Unbaked Meat Offering 2:1-3:

1 And when any will offer a meat offering unto the Lord, his offering shall be of fine flour; and he shall pour oil upon it, and put frankincense thereon:

2 And he shall bring it to Aaron's sons, the priests: and he shall take there-out his handful of the flour thereof, and of the oil thereof, with all the frankincense thereof; and the priest shall burn the memorial of it upon the altar, to be an offering made by fire, a sweet savor unto the Lord:

3 And the remnant of the meat offering shall be Aaron's and his sons' : it is a thing most holy of the offerings of the Lord made by fire

The fine flour is prepared with oil and frankincense. The

oil symbolizes the anointing of the Lord and the frankincense symbolizes cleansing and purity. The lose nature of the offering reflects the spiritual nature of man, which is thereby brought into fellowship with God. A handful of the offering is burnt upon the Burnt Altar. The remainder is given to the Priest.

Meat Offering Baked, Lev. 2: 4-11:

4 And if thou bring an oblation of a meat offering baked in the oven, it shall be unleavened cakes of fine flour mingled with oil, or unleavened wafers anointed with oil.

5 And if thy oblation be a meat offering baked in a pan, it shall be of fine flour unleavened, mingled with oil.

6 Thou shalt part it in pieces, and pour oil thereon: it is a meat offering.

7 And if thy oblation be a meat offering baked in the frying-pan, it shall be made of fine flour with oil.

8 And thou shalt bring the meat offering that is made of these things unto the Lord: and when it is presented unto the priest, he shall bring it unto the altar.

9 And the priest shall take from the meat offering a memorial thereof, and shall burn it upon the altar: it is an offering made by fire, of a sweet savor unto the Lord.

10 And that which is left of the meat offering shall be Aaron's and his sons' : it is a thing most holy of the offerings of the Lord made by fire.

11 No meat offering, which ye shall bring unto the Lord, shall be made with leaven: for ye shall burn no leaven, nor any honey in any offering of the Lord made by fire.

The baked offering is made with oil and is without leaven and honey. It is brought to the priest. He takes a portion of it and burns it upon the Burnt Altar. What remains of the offering is given to the priest.

Meat Offering of the First Fruits, Lev. 2:12-16

12 As for the oblation of the first fruits, ye shall offer them unto the Lord: but they shall not be burnt on the altar for a sweet savor.

13 And every oblation of thy meat offering shalt thou season with salt; neither shalt thou suffer the salt of the covenant of thy God to be lacking from thy meat offering: with all thine offerings thou shalt offer salt.

14 And if thou offer a meat offering of thy first fruits unto the Lord, thou shalt offer for the meat offering of thy first fruits green ears of corn dried by the fire, even corn beaten out of full ears.

15 And thou shalt put oil upon it, and lay frankincense thereon: it is a meat offering.

16 And the priest shall burn the memorial of it, part of the beaten corn thereof, with all the frankincense thereof: it is an offering made by fire unto the Lord.

From the first fruits of the ears of corn a Meat Offering is made. The corn is dried by fire and mixed with oil and frankincense. It is brought to the priest, he takes a handful and burns it upon the Burnt Altar. The remainder is given to the priest. The baked offerings of the flour and of the corn suggest that God's children must be molded into His holy image.

The Law of the Meat Offering, Lev. 6:14-18; 7:9-10

14 And this is the law of the meat offering: the sons of Aaron shall offer it before the Lord, before the altar.

15 And he shall take of it his handful, of the flour of the meat offering, and of the oil thereof, and all the frankincense which is upon the meat offering, and shall burn it upon the altar for a sweet savor, even the memorial of it, unto the Lord.

16 And the remainder thereof shall Aaron and his sons eat: with unleavened bread shall it be eaten in the holy place; in the court of the tabernacle of the congregation they

shall eat it.

17 It shall not be baked with leaven. I have given it to them for their portion of my offerings made by fire; it is most holy, as is the sin offering, and as the trespass offering.

18 All the males among the children of Aaron shall eat of it.It shall be a statute forever in your generations concerning the offerings of the Lord made by fire: everyone that touches them shall be holy.

7:9 And all the meat offering that is baked in the oven, and all that is dressed in the frying-pan, and in the pan, shall be the priest's that offers it.

10 And every meat offering mingled with oil, and dry, shall all the sons of Aaron have, one as much as the other.

The law of the Meat Offering is concise and clearly understood. It is offered by the sons of Aaron, the High Priest. A handful of it is taken and offered upon the Burnt Altar. The remainder is eaten with unleavened bread by Aaron and his sons in the Court of the Tabernacle. The remainder of the unbaked offering shall not be baked with leaven. All the males among the children of Aaron shall eat of all the kinds of the Meat offering because they are holy.

The Meat Offering at the Priests' Consecration, 6:19-23:

19 And the Lord spoke unto Moses, saying,

20 This is the offering of Aaron and of his sons, which they shall offer unto the Lord in the day when he is anointed; the tenth part of an ephah of fine flour (2 quarts) for a meat offering perpetual, half of it in the morning, and half thereof at night.

21 In a pan it shall be made with oil; and when it is baked, thou shalt bring it in: and the baked pieces of the meat offering shalt thou offer for a sweet savor unto the Lord.

22 And the priest of his sons that is anointed in his stead shall offer it: it is a statute forever unto the Lord; it shall be

wholly burnt.

23 For every meat offering for the priest shall be wholly burnt: it shall not be eaten.

The law of the Meat Offering of the consecration of the succeeding priest is different in two respects from the law of the Meat Offering with respect to the congregation. It must be wholly burnt upon the Altar of Burnt Offering and none of it must be eaten by the priest. Also, half of it must be burnt in the morning and the other half must be burnt at night.

3. The Peace Offering, Lev. 3

The Peace Offering symbolizes peace with God. The enmity caused by sin is given a death blow by the atoning blood of the sacrifice and the penitent is at full peace with God. There are three kinds of Peace Offering: by the Bullock, the lamb and male goat. The procedure is the same for all three kinds.

The Bullock, 3:1-5:

1 And if his oblation be a sacrifice of peace offering, if he offer it of the herd; whether it be male or female, he shall offer it without blemish before the Lord.

2 And he shall lay his hand upon the head of his offering, and kill it at the door of the tabernacle of the congregation: and Aaron's sons the priests shall sprinkle the blood upon the altar round about.

The offeror shall kill it at the door of the Tabernacle. In this way death, the consequence of sin, becomes very personal.

3 And he shall offer of the sacrifice of the peace offering an offering made by fire unto the Lord; the fat that covers the inwards, and all the fat that is upon the inwards,

4 And the two kidneys, and the fat that is upon them, which is by the flanks, and the caul above the liver, with the kidneys, it shall he take away.

The fats and the kidneys are removed and burned upon the Burnt Altar by the priests. The bread and the right

shoulder are the Priests'

5 And Aaron's sons shall burn it on the altar upon the burnt sacrifice, which is upon the wood that is on the fire: it is an offering made by fire, of a sweet savor unto the Lord.

The Male Lamb, Lev. 3:6-11

6 And if his offering for a sacrifice of peace offering unto the Lord be of the flock; male or female, he shall offer it without blemish.

7 If he offer a lamb for his offering, then shall he offer it before the Lord.

8 And he shall lay his hand upon the head of his offering, and kill it before the tabernacle of the congregation: and Aaron's sons shall sprinkle the blood thereof round about upon the altar.

9 And he shall offer of the sacrifice of the peace offering an offering made by fire unto the Lord; the fat thereof, and the whole rump, it shall he take off hard by the backbone; and the fat that covers the inwards, and all the fat that is upon the inwards.

10 And the two kidneys, and the fat that is upon them, which is by the flanks, and the caul above the liver, with the kidneys, it shall he take away.

11 And the priest shall burn it upon the altar: it is the food of the offering made by fire unto the Lord.

The breast and right shoulder of the Peace Offering are given to the priests for their food. All else is burnt on the Burnt Altar, an offering made by fire unto the Lord. This blessing granted to the priest also has special spiritual significance.

The Goat, Lev. 3:12-17

12 And if his offering be a goat, then he shall offer it before the Lord.

13 And he shall lay his hand upon the head of it, and kill

it before the tabernacle of the congregation: and the sons of Aaron shall sprinkle the blood thereof upon the altar round about.

14 And he shall offer thereof his offering, even an offering made by fire unto the Lord; the fat that covers the inward, and all the fat that is upon the inwards,

15 And the two kidneys, and the fat that is upon them, which is by the flanks, and the caul above the liver, with the kidneys, it shall he take away.

16 And the priest shall burn them upon the altar: it is the food of the offering made by fire for a sweet savor: all the fat is the Lord's.

17 It shall be a perpetual statute for your generations throughout all your dwellings, that ye eat neither fat nor blood.

The breast and the right shoulder are given to the priests for their food. The rest is burnt with, the fats, and kidneys on the Burnt Altar.

Law of the Peace Offering, Lev. 7:11-13

11 And this is the law of the sacrifice of peace offerings, which ye shall offer unto the Lord.

When the Peace Offering is offered as thanksgiving, there is additional requirement:

12 If he offer it for a thanksgiving, then he shall offer with the sacrifice of thanksgiving unleavened cakes mingled with oil, and unleavened wafers anointed with oil, and cakes mingled with oil, of fine flour, fried.

13 Besides the cakes, he shall offer for his offering leavened bread with the sacrifice of thanksgiving of his peace offering.

The Heave Offering, Lev. 7:14-16, 28-38

When one of the three offerings is chosen as the Peace Offering, the right shoulder is given to the priest for a Heave

Offering. This portion is to be eaten by the priest the same day of the Peace Offering of thanksgiving. If the Peace Offering is offered as a vow, it can be eaten on the first and the second day after the offering is offered. But if any of it remains until the third day, it must be burnt.

14 And of it he shall offer one out of the whole oblation for a heave offering unto the Lord, and it shall be the priest's that sprinkles the blood of the peace offerings.

15 And the flesh of the sacrifice of his peace offerings for thanksgiving shall be eaten the same day that it is offered; he shall not leave any of it until the morning.

16 But if the sacrifice of his offering be a vow, or a voluntary offering, it shall be eaten the same day that he offers his sacrifice: and on the morrow also the remainder of it shall be eaten:

The Consequence of eating ... after the Third day, Lev. 7:17-21

17 But the remainder of the flesh of the sacrifice on the third day shalt be burnt with fire.

18 And if any of the flesh of the sacrifice of his peace offerings be eaten at all on the third day, it shall not be accepted, neither shall it be imputed unto him that offers it: it shall be an abomination, and the soul that eats of it shall bear his iniquity.

There are some dangers with eating of the sacrifice of the Peace Offering:

19 And the flesh that touches any unclean thing shall not be eaten; it shalt be burnt with fire: and as for the flesh, all that be clean shall eat thereof.

20 But the soul that eats of the flesh of the sacrifice of peace offerings, that pertain unto the Lord, having his uncleanness upon him, even that soul shall be cut off from his people. *This verse shows the very special privilege of the priests. they were allowed to eat of most of the offerings.*

21 Moreover the soul that shall touch any unclean thing, as the uncleanness of a man, or any unclean beast, or any abominable unclean thing, and eat of the flesh of the sacrifice of peace offerings, which pertain unto the Lord, even that soul shall be cut off from his people.

The Wave Breast and Heave Shoulder, Lev. 7:28-38

The offeror of the Peace Offering has this obligation in offering his offering:

28 And the Lord spoke unto Moses, saying,

29 Speak unto the children of Israel saying, he that offers the sacrifice of his peace offerings unto the Lord shall bring his oblation unto the Lord of the sacrifice of his peace offerings.

30 his own hands shall bring the offerings of the Lord made by fire, the fat with the breast, it shall he bring, that the breast may be waved for a wave offering before the Lord.

The priest then waves the breast and burns the fats upon the Burnt Altar. The priest also raises or heaves the right shoulder to the Lord. Both the breast and right shoulder are given to the priests to be eaten in the court of the Tabernacle.

31 And the priest shall burn the fat upon the altar: but the breast shall be Aaron's and his sons.

32 And the right shoulder shall ye give unto the priest for an heave offering of the sacrifices of your peace offerings.

33 He among the sons of Aaron, that offer the blood of the peace offerings, and the fat, shall have the right shoulder for his part.

34 For the wave breast and the heave shoulder have I taken of the children of Israel from off the sacrifices of their peace offerings, and have given them to Aaron the priest and unto his sons by a statute forever from among the children of Israel.

35 This is the portion of the anointing of Aaron, and of the anointing of his sons, out of the offerings of the Lord

made by fire, in the day when he presented them to minister unto the Lord in the priest's office;

36 Which the Lord commanded to be given them of the children of Israel, in the day that he anointed them, by a statute forever throughout their generations

37 This is the law of the burnt offering, of the meat offering, and of the sin offering, and of the trespass offering and of the consecrations, and of the sacrifice of peace offerings;

38 Which the Lord commanded Moses in Mount Sinai, in the day that he commanded the children of Israel to offer their oblations unto the Lord in the wilderness of Sinai.

The Wave Breast and the Heave Shoulder are eaten by Aaron and his sons. This completes the offering of the Peace Offering. The waving of the breast and the raising or heaving of the right shoulder to the Lord symbolizes peace with God. The eating of the offering by the Priests symbolizes fellowship and communion with God, since Atonement was made. Peace and fellowship with God are the results of the Atonement secured by the Peace Offering.

General Law of the Offerings, Lev. 7:22-27:

22 And the Lord spoke unto Moses, saying,

23 Speak unto the children of Israel, saying, Ye shall eat no manner of fat, of ox, or of sheep, or of goat.

24 And the fat of the beast that dies of itself, and the fat of that which is torn with beasts, may be used in any other use: but ye shall in no wise eat of it.

25 For whosoever eats the fat of the beast, of which men offer an offering made by fire unto the Lord, even the soul that eats it shall be cut off from his people.

This general law applied to the blood sacrifices and beyond. In case of the accidental death of a beast, its fat could be used in purposes other than eating thereof. Blood and fat were forbidden from eating because the blood atoned *for the soul and the fat was offered unto God. Because these parts of the sacrifices were offered unto the Lord, they were forbidden to be eaten by the people.*

26 Moreover ye shall eat no manner of blood, whether it be of fowl or of beast, in any of your dwellings.

27 Whatsoever soul it be that eats any manner of blood, even that soul shall be cut off from his people.

4. Application of the Sin Offering, Lev. 4: 1- 7

The Sin Offering was offered for sins of a general nature committed by the Children of Israel, some of which was done through ignorance. Nevertheless, those acts were recognized to be sins. The Sin Offering was applied in a fourfold manner. It applied to the priests, congregation, a ruler, and an ordinary member of the congregation.

The Sin Offering of the bullock represents complete Atonement under the Law and symbolizes Christ's Atonement. The four other principal offerings represent different aspects of Atonement, the benefits in particular. These five principal offerings symbolize the five wounds Christ suffered on the Cross.

The Priests, The First Class of People. 4:1-7

1 And the Lord spoke unto Moses, saying,
2 Speak unto the children of Israel, saying, If a soul should sin through ignorance against any of the commandments of the Lord concerning things which ought not to be done, and shall do against any of them:

This applied to all members of the congregation. Since the priest was the leader of the congregation, he was to be the example. For his Sin Offering a bullock was required. The bullock was the primary Sin Offering.,

3 If the priest which is anointed do sin according to the sin of the people; then let him bring for his sin, which he hath sinned, a young bullock without blemish unto the Lord for his sin offering.

Verse 3 refers to the high priest: he was recognized as the anointed high priest. Though anointed, he was still human and subject to failures. Here was what he had to do,

4 And he shall bring the bullock unto the door of the tabernacle of the congregation before the Lord; and shall lay his hand upon the bullock's head, and kill the bullock before the Lord.

5 And the priest that is anointed shall take of the bullock's blood, and bring it to the tabernacle of congregation:

6 And the priest shall dip his finger in the blood, and sprinkle the blood seven times before the Lord, before the veil of the sanctuary.

7 And the priest shall put some of the blood upon the horn of the altar of sweet incense before the Lord, which is in the tabernacle of the congregation; and shall pour all the blood of the bullock at the bottom of the altar of burnt offering, which is at the door of the tabernacle of the congregation.

General Law of the Offerings, Lev. 4:8- 12

The general law of the offerings had to be observed.

8 And he shall take off from it all the fat of the bullock for the sin offering; the fat that covers the inwards, and all the fat that is upon the inwards,

9 And the two kidneys, and the fat that is upon them, which is by the flanks, and the caul above the liver, with the kidneys, it shall he take away,

10 As it was taken off from the bullock of the sacrifice of the peace offerings: and the priest shall burn them upon the altar of the burnt offering.

11 And the skin of the bullock and all his flesh, with his head, and with his legs, and his inwards, and his dung,

12 Even the whole bullock shall he carry forth without the camp unto a clean place, where the ashes are poured

out, and burn him on the wood with fire: where the ashes are poured out shall he be burnt.

The sons of Aaron, the associate priests were not allowed to offer the sin offering of the bullock, only the high priest. After the kidneys, the fats, and inwards were removed from the bullock, the body was carried without the camp and burned. But the kidneys, liver and fats were burnt on the altar of Burnt Offering. The removal of the body of the bullock outside the camp symbolizes Christ who offered Himself as the Sin Offering on our behalf and was crucified on Mount Calvary.

Christ was not killed at the door of the Tabernacle but the religious authority consented to His death, which was the equivalent of being killed at the door of the Tabernacle. The blood of the Sin Offering was sprinkled seven times before the holy Veil of the Tabernacle; Christ's blood was not sprinkled seven times before the Veil, but it rends the Veil in two, signifying access to the Holy of Holies by every man who believes.

The Second Class of People, the Congregation, Lev. 4:13

13 And if the whole congregation of Israel sin through ignorance, and the thing be hid from the eyes of the assembly, and they have done somewhat against any of the commandments of the Lord concerning things which should not be done, and are guilty;

The provision of Atonement was applied to the sin of the whole congregation. If the provision of Atonement was made for the spiritual leader, the high priest, it was wise to have the same provision for the whole congregation because it was more likely that they would sin. The sin of the Golden Calf reminds us how quickly and easily the whole congregation could sin against the commandments of God. Therefore the Atonement of the bullock was provided.

The Sin Offering of the Bullock, Lev. 4:14-21:

The Atonement of the bullock was to be applied to the sin of the congregation in the identical manner as was applied to the High Priest. The High Priest who offered his own Atonement, then had to offer the Atonement of the congregation. The High Priest had to be reconciled to his holy office, God, and the congregation. The congregation had to be reconciled to the holy Tabernacle and God. Sin will not just go away by itself; it cannot even be undone, it must be forgiven by Atonement.

The implications and symbolisms were the same.

14 When the sin, which they have sinned against it, is known, then the congregation shall offer a young bullock for the sin, and bring him before the tabernacle of the congregation.

15 And the elders of the congregation shall lay their hands upon the head of the bullock before the Lord: and the bullock shall be killed before the Lord.

The killing of the bullock symbolizes the consequence of sin, **death.** *The sprinkling of the blood symbolizes the remission of sin, the cleansing of the soul. The Tabernacle itself had to be cleansed from the sin of the congregation.*

16 And the priest that is anointed shall bring of the bullock's blood to the tabernacle of the congregation:

17 And the priest shall dip his finger in some of the blood, and sprinkle it seven times before the Lord, even before the veil.

Sin will not just go away in a single instance; it must be completely obliterated by the atoning blood. The number 7 implies the completed work of Atonement. Sin is dealt a death blow and the guilty is delivered and set free. Moreover, it had to be brought to the immediate attention of the Holy God for pardon and forgiveness.

18 And he shall put some of the blood upon the horns of the altar which is before the Lord, that is in the tabernacle of

the congregation, and shall pour out all the blood at the bottom of the altar of burnt offering, which is at the door of the tabernacle of the congregation.

The pouring out of the blood of Atonement implies it was more than sufficient for all their sins. The consumption by fire of the kidneys and fats of the bullock of Atonement symbolizes spiritual restoration with God. It symbolizes that the spirit, the highest level of man's being, is restored to fellowship with God. Better yet, the spiritual restoration is free from all impurities.

19 And he shall take all his fat from him, and burn it upon the altar.

20 And he shall do with the bullock as he did with the bullock for a sin offering, so shall he do with this: and the priest shall make an atonement for them, and it shall be forgiven them.

When all else fails from solving the sin problem, the atoning blood will never fail. And remember, the blood of Jesus will never lose its power and it is more than sufficient. The impartation of new life demanded death. Christ died to give man new life. But one does not get it by wishful thinking but by meeting Christ at the Cross, making a step of faith in complete surrender.

21 And he shall carry forth the bullock without the camp, and burn him as he burned the first bullock: it is a sin offering for the congregation.

The Third Class of People, the Ruler, Lev. 4:22-26:

Sin has left its mark on all mankind, from the most noble to the most vulnerable, from the young to the old, from the poor to the rich, and from the educated to the uneducated. When Atonement was provided for the ruler: it was not a bullock but a male goat.

22 When a ruler hath sinned, and done somewhat through ignorance against of the commandments of the Lord

his God concerning things which should not be done, and is guilty;

Atonement of the Male Goat, Lev. 4:23-26

The ruler had to find the perfect offering for his Atonement: the male goat had to be perfect, no blemish could be seen. Failure to meet the condition of a perfect Atonement offering would mean the priest would reject it and it would not effect Atonement on the ruler's behalf.

23 Or if his sin, wherein he hath sinned, come to his knowledge; he shall bring his offering, a kid of the goats, a male without blemish:

By killing the goat, he would be reminded of death, the consequence of sin in the most personal way. There was Atonement for his soul, but it could not provide him the Atonement of the body. He knew there and then that the Atonement of the soul would not prevent the physical death of the body, and very soon he would be just as dead as that goat that he just killed. However, the hope the Atonement brought him was greater than the physical death of his body. He would continue to hold unto that which could not perish, the commandments of the Living God. The wise will follow the commandments of God.

24 And he shall lay his hand upon he head of the goat, and kill it in the place where they kill the burnt offering before the Lord: it is a sin offering.

25 And the priest shall take of the blood of the sin offering with his finger, and put it upon the horns of the altar of burnt offering, and shall pour out his blood at the bottom of the altar of burnt offering.

The goat was killed before the Tabernacle; its blood was put upon the horns of the Burnt Altar, and was poured out at the bottom. But it was not sprinkled before the holy Veil in the Tabernacle as the blood of the bullock of the Sin Offering was. Its fats and inwards were burnt on the Burnt Altar. But the rest of its body was to be eaten by the priest in the holy place.

26 And he shall burn all his fat upon the altar, as the fat of the sacrifice of peace offerings: and the priest shall make an atonement for him as concerning his sin, and it shall be forgiven him.

The Atonement was effective and his sin was forgiven him.

The Fourth Class of People, the Average Member..., Lev.4: 27-35:

There was a distinction with the sin of a member of the congregation with a particular kind of offering – he had to offer a female goat. A ruler had to offer for his Sin Offering a male goat; the congregation, a young bullock; and the priest had to offer for his Sin Offering a young bullock.

There was an exception to the manner in which the blood of the sin offering for a member of the congregation was treated: it was not brought in the tabernacle and put upon the horn of the Altar of Burnt Incense and sprinkled before the holy Veil. In such case the remainder of the offering was given to the priest and was eaten in the Court of the Tabernacle. The ceremonies of theLaw applied to the priests and everyone.

27 And if any one of the common people sin through ignorance, while he doeth somewhat against any of the commandments of the Lord concerning things which ought not to be done, and be guilty;

28 Or if his sin, which he hath sinned, come to his knowledge: then he shall bring his offering, a kid of the goats, a female without blemish, for his sin which he hath sinned.

29 And he shall lay his hand upon the head of the sin offering, and slay the sin offering in the place of the burnt offering.

30 And the priest shall take of the blood thereof with his finger, and put it upon the horns of the altar of burnt

offering, and shall pour out all the blood thereof at the bottom of the altar.

31 And he shall take away all the fat thereof, as the fat is taken away from off the sacrifice of the peace offerings; and the priest shall burn it upon the altar for a sweet savor unto the Lord; and the priest shall make an atonement for him, and it shall be forgiven him.

The member of the congregation had a second choice of Sin Offering. However, the procedure was the same:

32 And if he bring a lamb for a sin offering, he shall bring it a female without blemish.

33 And he shall lay his hand upon the head of the sin offering, and slay it for a sin offering in the place where they kill the burnt offering.

34 And the priest shall take of the blood of the sin offering with his finger, and put it upon the horns of the altar of burnt offering, and shall pour out all the blood thereof at the bottom of the altar:

35 And he shall take away all the fat thereof, as the fat of the lamb is taken away from the sacrifice of the peace offerings; and the priest shall burn them upon the altar, according to the offerings made by fire unto the Lord: and the priest shall make an atonement for his sin that he hath committed, and it shall be forgiven him.

The Law here, is an emphasis on all the pronouncements previously made of the Sin Offering and the conclusion. Those pronouncements amount to the Law. Here those pronouncements are stated in concise terms for clarity and emphasis.

The Law of the Sin Offering, Lev. 6:24-30:

First, the Sin Offering and the Burnt Offering are to be killed before the tabernacle:

24 And the Lord spoke unto Moses, saying

25 Speak unto Aaron and to his sons, saying, This is the law of the sin offering: in the place where the burnt offering is killed shall the sin offering be killed before the Lord: it is most holy.

Second,

26 The priest that offers it for sin shall eat it: in the holy place shall it be eaten, in the court of the tabernacle of the congregation.

Third,

27 Whatsoever shall touch the flesh thereof shall be holy: and when there is sprinkled of the blood thereof upon any garment, thou shalt wash that whereon it was sprinkled in the holy place.

28 And the earthen vessel wherein it was sodden shall be broken: and if it be sodden in a brazen pot, it shall be both scoured, and rinse in water.

Fourth,

29 All the males among the priests shall eat thereof: it is most holy.

30 And no sin offering, whereof any of the blood is brought into the tabernacle of the congregation to reconcile withal in the holy place, shall be eaten: it shall be burnt in the fire.

It is important to remember that when the blood of the Sin Offering is brought into the Tabernacle, put upon the horn of the Altar of Burnt Incense, and sprinkled 7 times before the holy Veil, the sin offering must not be eaten. This is the only exception when it must not be eaten by the priests.

5. The Trespass Offering, Leviticus 5-6:1-7:

The Trespass Offering seemed to be based on the premise of ignorance is not a good excuse.

1 And if thou sin, and hear the voice of swearing, and is a witness, whether he hath seen or known of it; if he do not utter it, then he shall bear his iniquity.

2 Or if a soul touch any unclean thing, whether it be a carcass of an unclean beast, or a carcass of unclean cattle, or the carcass of unclean creeping things, and if it be hidden from him; he also shall be unclean, and guilty.

3 Or if he touch the uncleanness of a man, whatsoever uncleanness it be that a man shall be defiled withal, and it be hid from him; when he knows of it, then he shall be guilty.

4 Or if a soul swear, pronouncing with his lips to do evil, or to do good, whatsoever it be that a man shall pronounce with an oath, and it be hid from him; when he knows of it, then he shall be guilty in one of these.

5 And it shall be, when he shall be guilty in one of these things, that he shall confess that he hath sinned in that thing:

There are three kinds of trespasses to which the Trespass Offering applies such as condoning sin, ignorance of what one ought to have known, and swearing. For any of these trespasses, the trespasser has three choices of offerings: between a female lamb and female goat, between the turtledoves and the pigeons, and the choice of the tenth part of an ephah of flour.

Choice 1, Lamb or Kid, Lev. 5:6

6 And he shall bring his trespass offering unto the Lord for his sin which he hath sinned, a female from the flock, a lamb or a kid of the goats, for a sin offering; and the priest shall make an atonement for him concerning his sin.

By this choice of Sin Offering, the trespasser would kill the offering at the door of the Tabernacle; the priest would sprinkle the blood upon the Burnt Altar and then pour it out at the bottom. The kidney, fats and inwards would be removed by the priest and burnt upon the Burnt Altar. The rest of the offering would be for the use of the Priest.

Choice 2, Two Turtledoves or Pigeons, Lev.5:7-10:

With the second choice of the Sin Offering, the procedure would be different. One of the birds would be offered for a burnt offering, and the other for a sin offering.

7 And if he be not able to bring a lamb, then he shall bring for his trespass, which he hath committed, two turtledoves, or two young pigeons unto the Lord; one for a sin offering, and the other for a burnt offering.

8 And he shall bring them unto the priest, who shall offer that which is for the sin offering first, and wring off his head from his neck, but shall not divide it asunder:

9 And he shall sprinkle of the blood of the sin offering upon the side of the altar; and the rest of the blood shall be wrung out at the bottom of the altar: it is a sin offering.

The difference with this Sin Offering of trespass is that the priest would sprinkle the blood upon the side of the Burnt altar, instead of putting it with his finger upon the horns of the Burnt Altar. One could assume that only the inward parts of the bird for the Sin Offering were burnt upon the Burnt Altar and the bird for the Burnt Offering was fully burnt. This offering brought Atonement to the trespasser.

10 And he shall offer the second for a burnt offering, according to the manner: and the priest shall make an atonement for him for his sin which he hath sinned, and it shall be forgiven him.

Choice 3, Two Quarts of fine Flour, Lev.5:11-13

With the third choice of offering, the procedure was different from any of the other two choices. But the end result was the same – atonement for the trespasser.

11 But if he be not able to bring two turtledoves, or two young pigeons, then he that sinned shall bring for his offering the tenth part of an ephah (2 quarts) of fine flour for a sin offering; he shall put no oil upon it, neither shall he put any frankincense thereon: for it is a sin offering.

The difference here between the Sin Offering and the

Meat Offering is that oil and frankincense were used with the Meat Offering but not with this sin offering. Only a memorial of it was burnt; the remainder was for the priest. The priest had the privilege of eating the remainder of the sin offerings – except for the bullock of the Sin Offering – in the holy place. In the end, the trespasser received Atonement.

12 Then shall he bring it to the priest, and the priest shall take his handful of it, even a memorial thereof, and burn it on the altar, according to the offerings made by fire unto the Lord: it is a sin offering.

13 And the priest shall make an atonement for him as touching his sin that he hath sinned in one of these, and it shall be forgiven him: and the remnant shall be the priest's, as a meat offering.

The Ram for the Forth category of Trespass,Lev.5:14-19:

14 And the Lord spoke unto Moses, saying,

15 If a soul commit a trespass, and sin through ignorance, in the holy things of the Lord; then he shall bring for his trespass unto the Lord a ram without blemish out of the flocks, with thy estimation by shekels of silver (.8 ounce), after the shekel of the sanctuary, for a trespass offering:

The sin of trespassing in the holy things of the Lord seems to suggest that someone might have accidentally touched any of the holy things located in the Court. These holy things should not be touched by anyone but the priests. One of the accessories of the Burnt Altar could be removed by someone. In such case, the cost of that thing would be assessed and a fifth added thereto. In making Atonement for this sin of trespass, the trespasser would give to the priest the cost of the sin of trespass with the added amount of a fifth. Then the priest would proceed to make Atonement for him. In this situation, the Sin Offering was a ram. The priest   then followed the procedure of the Sin Offering and made Atone-

ment for the trespasser.

16 And he shall make amends for the harm that he hath done in the holy thing, and shall add the fifth part thereto, and give unto the priest: and the priest shall make an atonement for him with the ram of the trespass offering, and it shall be forgiven him.

There was an alternate sin offering of the lamb for this trespass. The lamb had to be without blemish.

17 And if a soul sin, and commit any of these things which are forbidden to be done by the commandments of the Lord; though he knew it not, yet he is guilty, and shall bear his iniquity.

18 And he shall bring a lamb without blemish out of the flock, with thy estimation, for a trespass offering, unto the priest: and the priest shall make an atonement for him concerning his ignorance wherein he erred and knew it not, and he shall be forgiven him.

19 It is a trespass offering: he hath certainly trespassed against the Lord.

The Fifth Kind Trespass, Extortion, Lev. 6:1-3:

One sad thing about the sin of extortion was that the extortioner was very eloquent and good at making up false stories. It was these false stories quite often revealed his conduct under the Law. The Law was so written that no one was so clever to escape from being caught. Eventually the extortioner realized he was not sinning against his brethren but against God.

6:1 And the Lord spoke unto Moses, saying,

2 If a soul sin and commit a trespass against the Lord, and lie unto his neighbor in that which was delivered him to keep, or in fellowship, or in a thing taken away by violence, or hath deceived his neighbor;

3 Or have found that which was lost, and lies concerning it, and swears falsely; in any of all these things that a man

does, sinning therein:

The Consequence and the Atonement of Extortion 6:4-7

4 Then it shall be, because he hath sinned, and is guilty, that he shall restore that which he took violently away, or the thing which he hath deceitfully gotten, or that which was delivered him to keep, or the lost thing which he found,

5 Or all that about which he hath sworn falsely; he shall even restore it in the principal, and shall add a fifth part more thereto, and give unto him to whom it appertains, in the day of his trespass offering.

The condition of his atonement was that he had to restore whatever he had illegally acquired and add to it a fifth of its value before he could even consider making an atonement for his sin. He had to give this amount to the priest together with his sin offering of a spotless ram. The priest then applied the ritual of the sin offering; then he was forgiven of all that degree of sin. It did not seem fair to other transgressors but atonement was sufficient for all man's sins, great and small.

6 And he shall bring his trespass offering unto the Lord, a ram without blemish out of the flock, with thy estimation, for a trespass offering, unto the priest:

7 And the priest shall make an atonement for him before the Lord: and it shall be forgiven him for anything of all that he hath done in trespassing therein.

The Law of the Trespass Offering, Lev. 7:1-7:

1 Likewise this is the law of the trespass offering: it is most holy

2 In the place where they kill the burnt offering shall they kill the trespass offering: and the blood thereof shall he sprinkle round about upon the altar.

3 And he shall offer of it all the fat thereof; the rump, and the fat that covers the inwards.

4 And the two kidneys, and the fat that is upon them

which is by the flanks, and the caul that is above the liver, with the kidneys, it shall he take away:

5 And the priest shall burn them upon the altar for an offering made by fire unto the Lord: it is a trespass offering.

6 Every male among the priests shall eat thereof: it shall be eaten in the holy place: it is most holy.

7 As the sin offering is, so is the trespass offering: there is one law for them: the priest that makes atonement therewith shall have it.

All the pronouncements of the Trespass Offering amount to its law. Were they not followed, the offering would have had no effect. The Law here mentioned is an emphasis on all those pronouncements and the conclusion. The Sin Offering and the Trespass offering are killed before the door of the Tabernacle. The fats and the inwards are removed and burnt upon the Burnt Altar. The remainder of the offerings is given to the priests. And to complete the process of Atonement, the priests must eat it in the holy place. Thus both offerings have the same law.

The only exception to this Sin Offering was another Sin Offering of another kind in which the bullock was carried without the camp and burnt after its fats and inwards were removed. In this single instance the bullock was not eaten by the priests. Unlike the Sin Offering herein emphasized, the blood of the Sin Offering of the bullock was placed on the horn of the Burnt Altar and sprinkled 7 times before the holy Veil in the Sanctuary.

The following is a chart of all the offerings.

Chart of the Levitical Offerings, pages 266-270

The Burnt Offering
Kinds: 1.The bullock, 1:1-9; 2. the male goat, 1:10-13; 3. the turtledove or pigeon, 1:14-17.
Ceremony: 1.The bullock is killed before the door of the

Tabernacle; its blood sprinkled around and upon the Burnt Altar; its legs and inwards washed; its fats and inwards separately placed upon the altar; its body cut into pieces, and all is burnt upon the Burnt Altar.

2. The offering of goat is treated in like manner. 3. The head of the bird is ringed off; its feathers and crop removed; and the whole bird is offered upon the Burnt Altar.

The Burnt Offering is mentioned 263 times.

The Daily Burnt Offering

The Daily Burnt Offering was offered of two lambs daily. One was offered in the morning and the other was offered at evening. They were offered with their complementary Drink Offering (Numbers 28:11-15).

The Burnt offering of the Sabbath Day

The Burnt Offering of the Sabbath Day was offered of two lambs with its Drink Offering and Its Meat Offering, in addition to the Daily Burnt Offering.

The Monthly Burnt Offering

The Monthly Burnt Offering was offered at the beginning of every month. It was offered of two young bullocks, one ram, seven lambs, and one kid of the goats for a Sin Offering.

This offering was offered with its complementary Meat Offering and Drink offering, in addition to the Daily Burnt Offering. (Numbers 28:11-15)

The Drink Offering

The Drink Offering was offered with the daily Burnt offerings and the Meat offerings upon the Burnt Altar, Exodus 29:36-46. It was a quart of wine which was poured out unto the Lord upon the offering. The Drink Offering and the Meat Offering were offered with the Burnt offering and the Peace Offering.

The Drink Offering is mentioned 64 times.

The Meat Offering

Kinds: 1. Unbaked from fine flour, oil, and frankincense, 2:1-3; 2. Baked in oven, pan, and frying-pan, 2:4-11.

Ceremony: 1.A handful of the unbaked Meat Offering is taken out by the priest and offered upon the Burnt Altar. The remainder is eaten by the priest in the holy place. 2. The baked Meat offering is cut into pieces by the priest and he offers a portion upon the Burnt Altar. The rest is eaten by the priest in the holy place.

The Meat Offering is mentioned 177 times.

The Peace Offering

Kinds: 1. The bullock, 3:1-5; 2. The male lamb, 3:6-11; 3. The male goat, 3:12-17.

Ceremony: 1.The bullock is killed by the offeror before the door of the Tabernacle; its blood poured out by the priest around and upon the Burnt Altar; the fats and kidneys are removed and placed separately upon the Burnt Altar. Except for the breast and the right shoulder, the rest of the bullock is cut into pieces and burnt upon the Burnt Altar. The breast is waved to the Lord and the right shoulder is raised or heaved to the Lord. This is called the Wave Offering and the Heave Offering respectively. The wave breast and the heave shoulder are
eaten by the priest. This completes the ceremony.

2. The Peace Offering of the lamb is treated the same way as the bullock.

3. The Peace Offering of the goat is treated in the same manner as the bullock and the lamb.

The Peace Offering is mentioned 127 times

The Sin Offering

Kinds: 1.The bullock for the priest, 4:1-12; 2. the bullock for the congregation, 4:13-21; 3. the male goat for the ruler, 4:22-26; 4. the female goat for a member of the congregation, 4:27-35.

Ceremony: 1.The bullock for the priest's sin offering is killed before the door of the Tabernacle; its blood is placed upon the horns of the Burnt Altar, upon the horns of the Golden Altar of Incense and sprinkled 7 times before the holy Veil. Its fats and inwards removed and burnt upon the Burnt Altar. The whole body is taken without the camp and burnt.

2. The sin offering for the congregation is treated in the same manner. 3. The sin offering for the ruler is killed before the door of the tabernacle; its blood placed upon the horns of the Burnt Altar and poured out at the bottom. Its fats and kidneys are removed and burnt upon the Burnt Altar. Because its blood is not carried into the Tabernacle, the remainder is eaten in the holy place by the priest.
4. The sin offering for a member of the congregation is treated as the sin offering of the ruler.

The Sin Offering is mentioned 248 times

Trespass Offering Kinds: 1. Lamb or Kid 5:1-6; 2. two Turtledoves or 2 Pigeons, 5:7-10; 3. two Quarts of fine flour, 5:11-13; 4. the Ram, 5:14-19; 5. Restitution, 6:1-7

Ceremony: 1. By this choice of sin offering, the trespasser would kill the offering at the door of the Tabernacle; the priest would sprinkle the blood upon the Burnt Altar and then poured it out at the bottom. The kidney, fats and inwards would be removed by the priest and burnt upon the Burnt Altar. The rest of the offering would be for the use of the priest.   2. The first bird is offered for a sin offering; the second bird is offered for burnt offering; 3. The flour of the Trespass Offering is not mixed with oil and frankincense. From it, the priest burns a handful on the Burnt altar. 4. A ram or a lamb without blemish with an estimate of .8 ounce of silver. With this, the Priest makes an atonement for him.

5. For the trespass of extortion, the trespasser makes full restoration with a fifth additional value before the priest makes atonement with the ram of the Trespass offering. The Trespass Offering is mentioned is mentioned 58 times.

Offering of jealousy, Numbers 5:15-21
This offering was offered of the tenth part of an Ephah of barley meal for a woman suspected of adultery.
The Offering of jealousy is mentioned 3 times.

The Wave Offering/ Heave Offering, Exodus 29:22
A portion of the Meat Offering was put in the hands of Aaron and his sons at the time of their consecration before they were waved before the Lord and burned upon the Burnt Altar by Moses. Then Moses waved the breast and heaved the shoulder of the Ram of Aaron's consecration unto the Lord. The Breast was to be eaten by Moses; the shoulder was for Aaron and his sons to be eaten in the holy place. By a statute, the Heave Shoulder of all Peace offerings was Aaron's portion

The Wave Offering is mention 29 times. Atonement is mentioned 298 times..

....

SUMMARY

The Levitical Offerings were the heart of Israel's Theocracy; they were offerings of Atonement to bring all Israel into a holy relationship with God. Therefore the laws and ceremonies of these offerings were well articulated and clearly understood. For these ceremonies, some of the instruments of Divine service were used such as the Laver, Burnt Altar, and the Golden Incense Altar. There were five principal offerings: the Burnt Offering, the Meat Offering, the Peace Offering, the Sin Offering, and the Trespass Offering.

The Burnt Offering. The Burnt Offering was offered of different sacrifices, and each was completely burnt on the Burnt Altar. The sacrifice of each offering symbolizes death, the consequence of sin. It addressed the offeror in the most personal way, yet brought a sense of hope of a better tomorrow. The Burnt Offering represented the spirit of man's threefold nature which was restored and brought into fellowship with God.

The fire on the Burnt Altar was not allowed to be extinguished. The priest removed the ashes every morning and put wood on it, keeping the fire burning continuously. This continuous fire symbolizes the cleansing work of Atonement. As Christians, one can allow it to be extinguished or can keep it burning continuously. Christians today must do what is necessary to keep the holy fire of the Lord burning within the soul.

The Meat Offering. The Meat Offering was made of fine flour, oil, and frankincense. A handful of it was burnt upon the Burnt Altar; and the remainder of it was eaten by the priest in the holy place. The eating of a portion of the offerings by the priest completed the ceremony. The Meat Offering symbolized fellowship with God. Though the members of the congregation were not allowed to eat of any of the offerings, they were represented in the eating by the priest. And so they were also brought into fellowship with God.

The Peace Offering. The Peace Offering was of different sacrifices. It was killed by the offeror before the door of the Tabernacle, some of its blood was put on the Burnt Altar and the rest poured out at the bottom. Its breast and right shoulder were waved to the Lord; then were eaten by the priest. The waving to the Lord signified peace with God. The enmity between God and the penitent was removed by it and peace restored.

<u>The Sin Offering</u>. The bullock of the Sin Offering symbolizes more than anything else the Atonement of Christ. Its blood was put on the horns of Burnt Altar; then poured out at the bottom; put on the horns of the Golden Altar of Incense; sprinkled seven times before the holy Veil, making reconciliation with the Tabernacle. Then the whole bullock, except for its fats and kidneys, was carried without the camp and burned. As the Sin Offering of our Atonement, Christ was crucified on Mount Calvary without the camp. His blood was poured out at the foot of the Cross.

When the blood of the Sin Offering was carried into the Tabernacle to make reconciliation, the priest was not permitted to eat of any of it. Neither was he permitted to eat of the Burnt Offering: all was burnt.

<u>The Trespass Offering</u>. The Trespass Offering was offered for sin of ignorance. Ignorance to what one should have known was not a good excuse for sinning. Once the sin of ignorance came to light, the trespasser had to offer a sin offering for his trespass. Each sin offering only represented one sin, not many sins. Sin was not allowed to multiply unchecked. The provision of Atonement was quickly applied. The Trespass Offering indicated continuous forgiveness with God because of His great mercies.

The chart of the offerings shows the comparisons and contrasts of the offerings and their ceremonies. In many respects God gave Israel choices in their offerings of Atonement. Those were the offerings that brought them into holy relationship with Him. The Five Major Offerings of Atonement, namely, the Sin Offering, the Trespass Offering, the Burnt Offering, the Meat Offering, and the Peace Offering symbolized the Five Wounds borne by Christ the Redeemer on behalf of mankind. The Sin Offering symbolizes Christ who bore our sins at Calvary, as our Sin Offering. The Trespass Offering symbolizes the daily provision provided in

His Atonement for our trespasses. The Peace Offering symbolizes Christ our Peace who has broken down the Wall of Partition between man and God, thus ensuring peace and reconciliation with our Heavenly Father. The Meat Offering symbolizes daily fellowship with The Father by the eating of a portion by the Priest in the holy Place.

CHAPTER 11

The Consecration of The Priests, Leviticus 8-10

The consecration of the priests followed the declaration of the offerings of Atonement. These offerings were not hastily declared, but all their laws were established to ensure that their purpose of Atonement was realized. The priests had to be educated in all these laws in order to fulfill their duties. Before they began their duties, they were consecrated. The duties and responsibilities of the High Priest were exacting and overwhelming: there was no room for error; everything had to be done precisely as described.

The solemn ceremony reflected the spiritual weight of the duties of the High Priest and his associates. The spiritual foundation of the nation was well rooted in the holiness of God though there was no physical infrastructure; the nation was scattered in the Wilderness, living in tents. All this added significantly to the spiritual burden of the High Priest and his associates.

As prophet and spiritual leader, Moses had the responsibility of conducting the consecration ceremony of the High Priest and his associates. The order of the ceremony, including the offerings of Atonement, was already given by God. As always, Moses performed his duties faithfully.

Moses Presents Aaron and His Sons to the Congregation, Lev. 8:1-9

1 And the Lord spoke unto Moses, saying

2 Take Aaron and his sons with him, and the garments and the anointing oil, and a bullock for the sin offering, and two rams, and a basket of unleavened bread;

3 And gather thou all the congregation together unto the door of the tabernacle of the congregation.

Moses separated Aaron and his sons from the congregation by calling them to the Tabernacle and by assembling the people to meet with him. This was a formal introduction of Aaron to the people and the people to Aaron. He then told them the reason for the assembly.

4 And Moses did as the Lord commanded him; and the assembly was gathered together unto the door of the tabernacle of the congregation.

5 And Moses said unto the congregation, This is the thing which the Lord commanded to be done.

6 And Moses brought Aaron and his sons, and washed them with water.

7 And he put upon him the coat, and girded him with the girdle, and clothed him with the robe, and put the ephod upon him, and girded him with the curious girdle of the ephod, and bound it unto him therewith.

8 And he put the breastplate upon him: also he put in the breastplate the Urim and the Thummim.

9 And he put the miter upon his head; also upon the miter, even upon his forefront, did he put the golden plate, the holy crown; as the Lord commanded Moses.

As a sign of separation and cleansing, Moses washed Aaron with water from the Laver and put the holy garments on him. The Ephod, the girdle, the Breastplate, the Miter with the Golden Plate— all had special spiritual significance. His personal garments were not good enough to represent God's standard of holiness. When people accept Jesus Christ as their Lord and personal Savor, He takes away the old garment of sin and replaces it with garments of righteousness. His righteous garment will last for all eternity.

The Anointing, Lev. 8:10-13

10 And Moses took the anointing oil, and anointed the tabernacle and all that was therein, and sanctified them.

11 And he sprinkled thereof upon the altar seven times, and anointed the altar and all his vessels, both the laver and his foot, to sanctify them.

12 And he poured of the anointing oil upon Aaron's head, and anointed him to sanctify him.

13 And Moses brought Aaron's sons and put coats upon them, and girded them with girdles, and put bonnets upon them; as the Lord commanded Moses.

The holy anointing was a token of Aaron's consecration and his Divinely delegated authority. For a successful priesthood, Aaron had to be blessed and empowered by God. His anointing was a pattern throughout Old Testament Times. From here on, all priests, prophets, and kings were anointed with the holy anointing oil, symbolizing their Divine empowerment. The entire Tabernacle was anointed, setting apart God's dwelling place as a place of blessings and refreshing for the weary. Today the holy anointing oil is not the symbol of God's anointing. The gifts of the Holy Spirit are the symbol of God's anointing, but is inclusive of all Believers who desire God's anointing of the Holy Spirit.

The purpose of the anointing today is to break the heavy yoke of sin, to set the oppressed and captives of sin free and to give spiritual sight to the blind. With the growing world population, the need for God's anointing is greater than it had ever been. The Anointing means Divine Empowerment. It makes the proclamation of the Gospel more effective in winning souls

Aaron's consecration necessitated more than the anointing of the holy oil. He had to set the example of living by the principles of holiness by which he was expected to guide Israel. All the offerings of Atonement which applied to Israel, also applied to him, and had to be demonstrated in the very act of his consecration. The Sin Offering, the symbol of complete Atonement must first be applied to Aaron.

Offerings of consecration offered, Lev. 8:14-36

Two offerings of consecration were offered on Aaron's behalf: the Sin Offering and the Burnt Offering.

The Sin offering, Lev. 8:14-17

14 And he brought the bullock for the sin offering: and Aaron and his sons laid their hands upon the head of the bullock for the sin offering.

Aaron must learn for himself the principle of the Sin offering. The meaning of death must be understood in a personal way. As the bullock is killed, he envisions his own death, the consequence of sin. As he watches the blood being applied, he realizes that sin cannot just be forgotten, it must be atoned for, not by his efforts but by the death and blood of the innocent animal which had nothing to do with his personal sin. He stands by and absorbs the lesson of sin and Atonement as Moses his younger brother applies the blood of Atonement to the burnt Altar and pours it out at the bottom, as if to say the Atonement is sufficient for all your sins and iniquities..

15 And he slew it; and Moses took the blood, and put it upon the horns of the altar roundabout with his finger, and purified the altar, and poured the blood at the bottom of the altar, and sanctified it, to make reconciliation upon it.

That was not all, Aaron watches as Moses reaches for the fat, liver, and kidneys of his Sin Offering. He realizes the pain and agony sin causes to the heart of God. He watches as those items are consumed upon the Burnt Altar; and then the whole bullock is carried without the camp to be burnt. The obvious symbolism of this is Christ who died at Calvary,

16 And he took all the fat that was upon the inwards, and the caul above the liver, and the two kidneys, and

their fat, and Moses burned it upon the altar.

17 But the bullock, and his hide, his flesh, and his dung, he burned with fire without the camp; as the Lord commanded Moses.

At that point his consecration was not yet complete: something more had to be done.

The Ram of Burnt Offering, Lev. 8:18-21:

18 And he brought the ram for the burnt offering: and Aaron and his sons laid their hands upon the head of the ram.

19 And he killed it and Moses sprinkled the blood upon the altar round about.

20 And he cut the ram into pieces; and Moses burnt the head, and pieces, and the fat.

21 And he washed the inwards and the legs in water; and Moses burnt the whole ram upon the altar: it was a burnt sacrifice for a sweet savor, and an offering made by fire unto the Lord; as the Lord commanded Moses.

The whole ram was burnt on the Burnt Altar. The Burnt Offering symbolizes purity from sin and the restoration of the spirit to fellowship with God. That was not enough; another ram is brought into the ceremony, the ram of Consecration. This ram is applied much differently from the ram of Burnt Offering.

The Ram of consecration, Lev. 8:22-36:

22 And he brought the other ram, the ram of consecration: and Aaron and his sons laid their hands upon the head of the ram.

23 And he slew it; and Moses took the blood of it, and put it upon the tip of Aaron's right ear, and upon the thumb of his right hand, and upon the great toe of his right foot.

24 And he brought Aaron's sons, and Moses put of the blood upon the tip of their right ear, and upon the thumbs of

their right hands, and upon the great toes of their right feet: and Moses sprinkled the blood upon the altar round about.

The application of the blood also had symbolic meaning. Moses applied the blood to Aaron's right ear, right thumb, right toe, and those of his sons indicating the extent of his work. He needed to hear God's voice. He had His written word, but there were times of urgency when he needed to hear God's voice of direction. There was much work to be done, and it could only be done by the consecrated hands of Aaron. He needed to continue his journey in the wilderness for which he needed consecrated feet, but more so to follow the Lord in the paths of righteousness.

25 And he took the fat, and the rump, and all the fat that was upon the inwards, and the caul above the liver, and the two kidneys, and their fat, and the right shoulder:

26 And out of the basket of unleavened bread that was before the Lord, he took one unleavened cake, and a cake of oiled bread, and one wafer, and put them on the fat, and upon the right shoulder:

27 And he put all upon Aaron's hands, and upon his sons hands, and waved them for a wave offering before the Lord.

Before Moses offers the items of sacrifice he has collected, he places them in the hands of Aaron and his sons' to indicate their separation unto the holy things of God and unto God Himself. He then waves them to God as a wave offering and burns them upon the Burnt Altar.

28 And Moses took them from their hands, and burnt them on the altar upon the burnt offering: they were consecrations for a sweet savor: it is an offering made by fire unto the Lord.

29 And Moses took the breast, and waved it for a wave offering before the Lord: for of the ram of consecration it was Moses' part; as the Lord commanded Moses.

In this regard, Moses did not exercise any personal choice.

The Consecration of The Priests

Note that the wave breast of the consecration ram was for Moses to eat. The wave shoulder was for Aaron and his sons to eat in the holy place. The wave breast and right shoulder of the Peace Offering were for Aaron and his sons. (See Leviticus 7:32-34).

30 And Moses took of the anointing oil, and of the blood which was upon the altar, and sprinkled it upon Aaron, and upon his garments, and upon his sons, and upon his sons' garments with him; and sanctified Aaron, and his garments, and his sons, and his sons' garments with him.

The application of the holy oil and the blood to Aaron's garments made them holy.

31 And Moses said unto Aaron and his sons, Boil the flesh at the door of the tabernacle of the congregation: and there eat it with bread that is in the basket of consecrations, as I commanded, saying, Aaron and his sons shall eat it.

Aaron and his sons had to eat all of the portion that was theirs that day; anything left had to be burnt.

32 And that which remains of the flesh and of the bread shall ye burn with fire.

33 And ye shall not go out of the door of the tabernacle of the congregation in seven days, until the days of your consecration be at an end: for seven days shall he consecrate you.

34 As he hath done this day, so the Lord hath commanded to do to make an atonement for you.

35 Therefore shall ye abide at the door of the tabernacle of the congregation day and night seven days, and keep the charge of the Lord, that ye die not: for so I am commanded.

36 So Aaron and his sons did all things which the Lord commanded by the hand of Moses.

The number 7 symbolizes completion; the spiritual responsibility of the priests was great. This was reflected in their consecration. The ceremonies were repeated 7 days. During the 7 days they were separated from their families and everyone. Answering the high Calling of God involves all that one has. Aaron and his sons were no exceptions. Their dedication should challenge Christians everywhere.

Aaron Performs His First Priestly Duties, Lev. 9:1-24

The Instructions:

1 And it came to pass on the eight day, that Moses called Aaron and his sons, and the elders of Israel;

2 And he said unto Aaron, Take thee a young calf for a sin offering, and a ram for a burnt offering, without blemish, and offer them before the Lord.

After seven days of consecration, Aaron was expected to begin his duties as priest. It was a surprise that his first duty was to offer a Sin Offering and a Burnt Offering for himself. He was to be an example to the congregation. If the high priest had to offer a Sin Offering for himself, how much more it was necessary for everyone. Though the offerings were applicable to all Israel, including Moses, Moses was never asked by God to make a sin offering on his behalf. In the great sin of the Golden Calf Aaron was held responsible for his part. Certainly it was not a surprise to him that his first duty was to offer a Sin Offering for himself.

Then he was commanded to offer a Sin Offering, a Burnt Offering, a Meat Offering, and a Peace Offering on behalf of the congregation. These were four of the five principal offerings. The Wave Offering of the breast and the Heave Offering of the right shoulder were parts of the Peace Offering. After Aaron waved the breast and heaved or raised the right shoulder to the Lord, they were to be eaten by the priests and their families. That was the only time the sons and daughters of the priests ate of the holy things. This shows the unity of the family and yet symbolizes the greater family, God's family.

A portion of the Meat Offering was eaten only by the priests and the Sin offering whose blood was not carried into the Tabernacle to make reconciliation. None of the Burnt

Offering was eaten by the priests: the whole offering was burnt on the Burnt Altar. In this regard, the Burnt Offering was special

3 And unto the children of Israel thou shalt speak, saying, Take ye a kid of the goats for a sin offering; and a calf and a lamb, both of the first year, without blemish, for a burnt offering.

4 Also a bullock and a ram for peace offerings, to sacrifice before the Lord; and meat offering mingled with oil: for today the Lord will appear unto you.

The Lord never communicated with Aaron personally. All the communications to him were directed through Moses; neither did He ever appear unto him. The protocol would soon be changed: the Lord would soon begin to appear unto Aaron. Therefore, one could assume that Aaron's consecration and the personal Sin Offering he offered prepared him for a higher level of personal relationship with God.

5 And they brought that which Moses commanded before quedrew near and stood before the Lord.

6 And Moses said, This is the thing which the Lord commanded that ye should do: and the glory of the Lord shall appear unto you.

7 And Moses said unto Aaron, Go unto the altar, and offer the sin offering, and thy burnt offering, and make an atonement for thyself, and for the people: and offer the offering of the people, and make an atonement for them; as the Lord commanded.

Aaron and the congregation obeyed God's command: They were both obedient and faithful.

The Performance, Lev. 9:8-24

8 Aaron therefore went to the altar, and slew the calf of the sin offering, which was for himself.

9 And the sons of Aaron brought the blood unto him: and the dipped his finger in the blood, and put it upon the horns

of the altar, and poured out the blood at the bottom of the altar

Here was the first time Aaron's sons served as priests by presenting the blood of the Sin Offering to their father, the High Priest. Their role was to assist their father in the offerings and in the oversight of the holy things.

10 But the fat and the kidneys, and the caul above the liver of the sin offering, he burnt upon the altar; as the Lord commanded Moses.

11 And the flesh and the hide he burnt with fire without the camp.

12 And he slew the burnt offering; and Aaron's sons presented unto him the blood, which he sprinkled round about upon the altar.

13 And they presented the burnt offering unto him, with the pieces thereof, and the head: and he burnt them upon the altar.

14 And he did wash the inwards and the legs, and burnt them upon the burnt offering on the altar.

After the removal of the fats and kidneys from the Sin Offering, he burnt them upon the Burnt Altar and the rest he burnt without the camp as the sin offering of the bullock. The whole Burnt Offering was burnt upon the Burnt Altar. Here we see Israel living out the true meaning of their Theocracy: a righteous family establishing a righteous nation under God. Who can disagree that the World needs Theocracy to establish Universal Peace?

The Offering for the Congregation, Lev. 9:15-24:

15 And he brought the people's offering and took the goat, which was the sin offering for the people, and slew it, and offered it for a sin offering as the first.

Note that the Sin Offering of the goat was burnt in error without the camp. In chapter 10:16 -17, Moses sought the goat of the Sin Offering but it was burnt. Only the Burnt Offering

was to be wholly burnt. When the blood of the Sin Offering was not carried into the Tabernacle to make reconciliation, the body of the goat was to be eaten by the priests.

16 And he brought the burnt offering, and offered it according to the manner.

17 And he brought the meat offering, and took an handful thereof, and burnt it upon the altar, beside the burnt sacrifice of the morning.

18 He slew also the bullock and the ram for a sacrifice of peace offerings, which was for the people: and Aaron's sons presented unto him the blood, which he sprinkled upon the altar round about,

19 And the fat of the bullock and of the ram, the rump, and that which covers the inwards, and the kidneys, and the caul above the liver:

20 And they put the fat upon the breasts, and he burnt the fat upon the altar:

21 And the breasts and the right shoulder Aaron waved for a wave offering before the Lord; as Moses commanded.

22 And Aaron lifted up his hand toward the people, and blessed them, and came down from offering the sin offering, and the burnt offering, and the peace offerings.

23 And Moses and Aaron went into the tabernacle of the congregation, and came out, and blessed the people and the glory of the Lord appeared unto all the people.

24 And there came a fire out from before the Lord, and consumed upon the altar the burnt offering and the fat: which when all the people saw, they shouted and fell on their faces.

The miraculous fire from the Lord was a sign of approval of Aaron's consecration and the offerings on behalf of the congregation. The manifestation of God's glory caused the congregation to fall on their faces in worship and praises. That was the appearing of God, of which Moses had prophesied before Aaron offered the offerings.

Then the unexpected happened, a fatal priestly error.

A Fatal Priestly Error, Lev. 10:1-2

1 And Nadab and Abihu, the sons of Aaron, took either of them his censer, and put fire therein, and put incense thereon, and offered strange fire before the Lord, which he commanded them not.

2 And there went out fire from the Lord, and devoured them, and they died before the Lord.

We do not know whether or not Nadab and Abihu were motivated by zeal or by priestly power. Only Aaron the High Priest was commanded to burn incense upon the Golden Incense Altar. To do something they were not required to do was a breach of duty or being over-ambitious. The Trespass Offering shows that ignorance of what one should have known was not a good excuse to sin. Certainly their sin had the most serious of consequences, instant death. Their instant death caused great alarm to the congregation. Moses responded with the Word of the Lord.

Moses' Response, Lev. 10:3-11:

3 Then Moses said unto Aaron, This is it that the Lord spoke, saying, I will be sanctified in them that come nigh me, and before all the people I will be glorified. And Aaron held his peace.

Nadab and his brother did something which was the duty of the High Priest. It was no one's fault but theirs; it cost their lives. Disobedience is sin; sin reveals the holiness of God. With the knowledge of God's holiness, people must reconsider what they want to do carefully because God will not hesitate to make them a public example to others. God's holiness is to discourage sin, not to encourage it. God would not require of His children something that was impossible to do.

4 And Moses called Mishael and Elzaphan, the sons of Uziel the uncle of Aaron, and said unto them, Come near

and carry your brethren from before the sanctuary out of the camp.

5 So they went near, and carried them in their coats out of the camp, as Moses had said.

Moses chose two close relatives of Nadab and Abihu to remove their bodies from the Tabernacle to outside the camp. Mishael and Elzaphan were from the tribe of Levi. In doing so, Moses followed the right procedure. Then he told Aaron and his two remaining sons that they could not take part in the mourning formalities of the dead.

6 And Moses said unto Aaron, and unto Eleazar and unto Ithamar, his sons, Uncover not your heads, neither rend your clothes; lest ye die, and lest wrath come upon all the people: but let your brethren, the whole house of Israel, bewail the burning which the Lord had kindled.

7 And ye shall not go out from the door of the tabernacle of the congregation, lest ye die: for the anointing oil of the Lord is upon you. And they did according to the word of Moses.

The holy anointing was most sacred; it symbolized Divine authority and empowerment. Aaron and his sons were special, being anointed. They were no longer their own: they were to represent God as it pleased Him. They were no longer ordinary and should not try to be.

After Aaron's consecration, a new relationship between him and God began. Previously, God spoke to him through Moses

8 And the Lord spoke unto Aaron, saying,

9 Do not drink wine nor strong drink, thou, nor thy sons with thee, when ye go into the tabernacle of the congregation, lest ye die: it shall be a statute forever throughout your generations:

10 And that ye may put difference between holy and unholy, and between unclean and clean

11 And that ye may teach the children of Israel all the

statutes which the Lord hath spoken unto them by the hand of Moses.

Drinking of wine could affect the performance of the <u>Priestly Duties</u>. God's direct instructions were intended to protect Aaron from something that could become a serious personal problem and endanger the integrity of his holy office.

A Friendly Reminder Lev. 10:12-20:

This reminder was about the portion of the offerings which was given to the priests as a privilege for their service: of the Meat Offering and of the Wave Breast and Heave Shoulder of the Peace Offering.

12 And Moses spoke unto Aaron, and unto Eleazar and unto Ithamar, his sons that were left, Take the meat offering that remaineth of the offerings of the Lord made by fire, and eat it without leaven beside the altar: for it is most holy.

13 And ye shall eat it in the holy place, because it is thy due, and thy sons' due, of the sacrifices of the Lord made by fire: for so I am commanded.

14 And the wave breast and heave shoulder shall ye eat in a clean place; thou and thy sons and thy daughters with thee: for they be thy due, and thy sons' due, which are given out of the sacrifices of peace offerings of the children of Israel.

15 The heave shoulder and the wave breast shall they bring with the offerings made by fire of the fat, to wave it as a wave offering before the Lord; and it shall be thine, and thy sons with thee, by a statute forever; as the Lord hath commanded.

16 And Moses diligently sought the goat of the sin offering, and, behold, it was burnt: and he was angry with Eleazar and Ithamar, the sons of Aaron which were left alive, saying,

17 Wherefore have ye not eaten the sin offering in the holy place, seeing it is most holy, and God hath given it you

to bear the iniquity of the congregation, to make atonement for them before the Lord?

18 Behold, the blood of it was not brought in within the holy place: ye should indeed have eaten it in the holy place, as I commanded.

The blood of the Sin Offering of the goat was not brought into the Tabernacle to make reconciliation. Therefore it was the privilege of the priests to eat it in the holy place, not in their tents. By offering the offerings unto the Lord on behalf of the people, the priests were identified with the sins of the people and rightly bore their iniquities.

19 And Aaron said unto Moses, Behold, this day have they offered their sin offering and their burnt offering before the Lord; and such things have befallen me: and if I had eaten the sin offering today, should it have been accepted in the sight of the Lord?

20 And when Moses heard that he was content.

Aaron gave a just explanation for not eating of the Sin Offering of the goat offered on behalf of the people and Moses accepted it.

SUMMARY

The consecration of Aaron and his sons to the Priesthood was imperative to Israel's Theocracy. As prophet and leader of the nation, Moses was asked by God to do the honors. Moses was obedient and faithful in all things required of him by God. It was his joy to consecrate his own brother and nephews to the Priesthood of the Nation.

First, was the official introduction of the priests to the congregation and the congregation to the priests. As a sign of Aaron's separation unto God, Moses washed him with water from the Laver and put the holy garments on him. He anointed him with the holy anointing oil, a symbol of Divine authority and empowerment. With this aspect of Aaron's consecration, Moses also anointed Aaron's sons, the Tabernacle and its vessels.

Aaron's consecration necessitated more than the anointing of the holy oil. He had to set the example of living by the principles of holiness by which he was expected to guide Israel. All the offerings of Atonement which applied to Israel, also applied to him. Some of these offerings were offered in the very act of His consecration. The Sin Offering, the symbol of complete Atonement was first offered, followed by the Burnt Offering and the ram of consecration. The blood of the ram of consecration was applied to his right ear, his right thumb, and his right toe. Its right shoulder was eaten by Aaron and his sons in the holy place. Aaron's consecration brought him a new level of relationship with God. Before, God communicated to him through Moses; but after, He communicated directly with him.

In Aaron's first official duty, he offered a Sin Offering and a Burnt Offering for himself. Then he offered four offerings on behalf of the congregation: the Sin Offering, the Meat Offering, the Burnt Offering, and the Peace Offering. God miraculously confirmed Aaron's consecration and his first official duties by causing fire to consume the offerings. The congregation were overjoyed when they had seen the fire from God: they fell on their faces and worshipped God.

There was another miraculous fire which caused the death of two of Aaron's sons. They were burning incense upon the Golden Altar in the Tabernacle. We do not know whether or not Nadab and Abihu were motivated by zeal or by priestly power. Only Aaron the High Priest was commanded to burn incense upon the Golden Incense Altar. To do something they were not required to do was a breach of duty or being over-ambitious. The Trespass Offering shows that ignorance of what one should have known was not a good excuse to sin. There are different kinds covetousness and jealousies. It was jealousy that caused

Cain to kill his brother. There could have been spiritual jealousy among the priests. But where there was love, there was no need for jealousy or covetousness. Yet among many Christians, these sins are considered of less consequence. The instant death of Nadab and Abihu caused great alarm among the congregation. The manifestation of God's holiness was to discourage sin and to encourage holiness.

CHAPER 12
The Social Compact, Leviticus 11-15, 18, 20

The institutions of society are contingent on its growth, most of which are of a social nature. But none of them had its exegesis by a declaration of a Social Compact. The Theocracy of Israel was the only society in World History whose institutions had their origins in and by a declaration of a Social Compact by God. This Social Compact was unlike anything else in human history because of its inclusive nature and its intents. There was not a single aspect of human nature that was not affected, and no one was allowed to escape its obligations by reason of its detailed definitions which not only addressed the social consciousness of man but his heart and soul as well.

The kinds of foods, the purification of the body, the healing of the body, and the proper romantic relationships addressed not only the social needs but the spiritual also. Critical to the Social Compact were its consequences. One should not be held in the darkness as to what were the exact consequences for any breach that one might incur along the way to the full realization of its purpose. Thus the ground for deniability was completely removed.

The Social Compact brought a new awareness to the Ten Commandments. These Ten Commandments were clearly and concisely stated, and were the pillars of all the laws, particularly those of the offerings of Atonement. The Ten

Commandments say, "You must love the Lord thy God". But the Offerings of Atonement and other laws explain how one can love God. The premise of the Trespass Offering that ignorance is not a good reason to sin and loving one's neighbor necessitated the Social Compact because it has removed a whole realm of ignorance which once held the ignorant captive; and it has shown the many ways of loving one's neighbors.

The meticulous details and the scope of the Social Compact have justly compelled our attention and challenged our minds to love the Lord our God with a greater passion and sense of urgency.

God takes pleasure in the health of our body, and prescribes what is best to eat.

Animals for Food, Lev. 11

God Knew what was the best food for the health and purity of Israel and carefully chose from among His creatures the best animals, fish, and birds.

Clean Animals:

1 And the Lord spoke unto Moses and Aaron, saying unto them,

2 Speak unto the children of Israel, saying, These are the beasts which ye shall eat among all the beasts that are on the earth.

3 Whatsoever parts the hoof, and is cloven-footed, and chews the cud, among the beasts, that shall ye eat.

Unclean Animals:

4 Nevertheless these shall ye not eat of them that chew the cud, or them that divide the hoof: as the camel, because he chews the cud, but divides not the hoof; he is unclean unto you.

5 And the coney because he chews the cud, but divides not the hoof; he is unclean unto you.

6 And the hare, because he chews the cud, but divides not the hoof; he is unclean unto you.

7 And the swine, though he divides the hoof, and be cloven-footed, yet he chews not the cud; he is unclean unto you.

8 Of their flesh shall ye not eat, and their carcass shall ye not touch; they are unclean to you.

The description of the unclean animals makes it much easier to understand what is to be eaten among them.

Clean and Unclean Fish:

9 These shall ye eat of all that are in the waters: whatsoever hath fins and scales in the waters, in the seas, and in the rivers, them shall ye eat.

10 And all that have not fins and scales in the seas, and in the rivers, of all that move in the waters, and of any living thing which is in the waters, they shall be an abomination unto you:

11 They shall even be an abomination unto you; ye shall not eat of their flesh, but ye shall have their carcasses in abomination.

12 Whatsoever hath no fins nor scales in the waters, that shall be an abomination unto you.

Unclean Birds:

13 And these are they which ye shall have in abomination among the fowls; they shall not be eaten, they are an abomination: the eagle, and the ossifrage, and the ospray,

14 And the vulture, and the kite after his kind;

15 Every raven after his kind;

16 And the owl, and the night hawk, and the cuckoo, and the hawk after his kind,

17 And the little owl, and the cormorant, and the great owl,

18 And the swan, and the pelican, and the gier eagle,

19 And the stork, the heron after her kind, and the lapwing, and the bat.

20 All fowls that creep, going upon all four, shall be an abomination unto you.

Clean Birds:

Yet these may ye eat of every flying creeping thing that goes upon all four, which have legs above their feet, to leap withal upon the earth;

22 Even these of them ye may eat; the locust after his kind, and the bald locust after his kind, and the beetle after his kind, and the grasshopper after his kind.

The description of the unclean and the clean birds made it easy to understand what was to be eaten. But the unclean things should not be eaten, neither should their carcasses be touched. Those who touched the carcasses of the unclean things would themselves become unclean. And if they touched anything, or anyone, that thing or person would also become unclean until the evening. Therefore it made good sense to avoid all unclean things forbidden to eat.

23 But all other flying creeping things, which have four feet, shall be an abomination unto you.

24 And for these ye shall be unclean: whosoever touches the carcass of them shall be unclean until the even.

25 And whosoever bears aught of the carcass of them shall wash his clothes, and be unclean until the even.

26 The carcass of every beast which divides the hoof, and is not cloven-footed, nor chews the cud, are unclean unto you: everyone that touches them shall be unclean.

27 And whatsoever goes upon his paws, among all manner of beasts that go on all four, those are unclean unto you: whosoever touches their carcass shall be unclean until the even.

28 And he that bears the carcass of them shall wash his clothes, and be unclean until the evening: they are unclean

unto you.

Unclean Creeping Things:

29 These also shall be unclean unto you among the creeping things that creep upon the earth; the weasel, and the mouse and the tortoise after his kind,

30 And the ferret, and the chameleon, and the lizard, and the snail, and the mole.

31 These are unclean to you among all that creep: whosoever doth touch them, when they be dead, shall be unclean until the even.

32 And upon whatsoever any of them, when they are dead, doth fall, it shall be unclean; whether it be in any vessel or wood, or raiment, or skin, or sack, whatsoever vessel it be , wherein any work is done, it must be put into water, and it shall be unclean until the even; so it shall be cleansed.

33 And every earthen vessel, where-into any of them falls, whatsoever is in it shall be unclean; and ye shall break it.

34 Of all meat which may be eaten, that on which such water cometh shall be unclean: and all drink that may be drunk in every such vessel shall be unclean.

35 And everything whereupon any part of their carcass falls shall be unclean; whether it be oven, or ranges for pots, they shall be broken down: for they are unclean, and shall be unclean unto you.

36 Nevertheless a fountain or pit, wherein there is plenty of water, shall be unclean: but that which touches their carcass shall be unclean.

37 And if any part of their carcass fall upon any sowing seed which is to be sown, it shall be unclean.

38 But if any water be put upon the seed, and any part of their carcass fall thereon, it shall be unclean unto you.

39 And if any beast of which ye may eat, die; he that touches the carcass thereof shall be unclean until the evening.

40 And he that eats of the carcass of it shall wash his clothes, and be unclean until the evening: he also that bears the carcass of it shall wash his clothes, and be unclean until the evening.

41 And every creeping thing that creeps upon the earth shall be an abomination; it shall not be eaten.

42 Whatsoever goes upon the belly, and whatsoever goes upon all four, or whatsoever hath more feet among all creeping things that creep upon the earth, them ye shall not eat; for they are an abomination.

43 Ye shall not make yourself abominable with any creeping thing that creeps neither shall ye make yourselves unclean with them, that ye should be defiled thereby.

This aspect of the Social Compact which began with proper eating ended with ceremonial cleansing because those things forbidden to be eaten could defile a person. All it took was mere contact with the carcass of the forbidden thing. It came rather quickly to surface that any of the aspects of the Social Compact was not an end in itself, but its real intent was of a moral and spiritual nature. The Compact shows the unity of the threefold nature of man. Body, soul, and spirit had to be united in the pursuit of a holy relationship with God.

44 For I am the Lord your God: ye shall therefore sanctify yourselves, and ye shall be holy; for I am holy: neither shall ye defile yourselves with any manner of creeping thing that creeps upon the earth.

45 For I am the Lord that brought you up out of the land of Egypt, to be your God: ye shall therefore be holy, for I am holy.

The environment in Egypt did not lend itself to the establishment of a holy relationship with God on a long term basis as He would have liked. Indeed, the Children of Israel had strong faith in God while they were under the bondage of Egypt, but they never had a long term holy relationship with

God. The mere attempt at establishing such relationship would have incurred even greater bondage. The truth is they had to be literally and miraculously delivered by God in order for a holy relationship to be established between them and their God. Therefore, God brought them out of Egypt, and not hastily into Canaan, but into the Wilderness where there would be time enough to begin and establish a holy relationship with His dear people. God is holy and any relationship with His people had to be holy: it could not have been any other way.

This Social Compact was a means of establishing this holy relationship. And a distinction between the clean and the unclean was necessary to be recognized.

46 This is the law of the beasts, and of the fowl, and of every living creature that moves in the waters, and of every creature that creeps upon the earth:

47 To make a difference between the unclean and the clean, and between the beast that may be eaten and the beast that may not be eaten.

Purification after Childbirth, Lev. 12:

1 And the Lord spoke unto Moses, saying,

2 Speak unto the children of Israel, saying, If a woman hath conceived seed, and born a man child: then she shall be unclean seven days; according to the days of the separation for her infirmity shall she be unclean.

3 And in the eighth day the flesh of his foreskin shall be circumcised.

4 And she shall then continue in the blood of purifying three and thirty days; she shall touch no hallowed thing, nor come into the sanctuary, until the days of her purifying be fulfilled.

5 But if she bear a maid child, then she shall be unclean two weeks, as in her separation: and she shall continue in the blood of her purifying threescore and six days. *A mother*

who brought a child into the world, a male or a female, committed no sin in such an event, assuming she was married at the time. The Law did not say such an event was a sin. But it recognizes and acknowledges the fact that sin saturates human nature and the whole human race. To the Law, the time of birth was the appropriate time to demonstrate that fact. It therefore required a time of purification of the mother, which was 7 days of separation after the birth of a son and 33 additional days, making a total of 40 days of purification. Forty days in Biblical terms was a time of completion, fulfillment. In the eighth day, the child was circumcised. For a female child, the time of purification was twice as long. During the time of purification, the mother was not allowed into the Sanctuary. That was not all about her purification.

6 And when the days of her purifying are fulfilled, for a son, or for a daughter, she shall bring a lamb of the first year for a burnt offering, and a young pigeon, or a turtledove, for a sin offering, unto the door of the tabernacle of the congregation, unto the priest:

7 Who shall offer it before the Lord, and make an atonement for her; and she shall be cleansed from the issue of her blood. This is the law for her that hath born a male or female.

The mother who had not sinned by bringing a child into the world had to bring two offerings to the priest to be offered on her behalf: one for a Sin Offering and the other for a Burnt Offering. The Law recognized the inherent nature of sin and required these offerings, in reality, for the child, not for the mother. There was a choice of offerings due to her material means. She then brought it to the priest who made Atonement on her behalf and thereby completed the process of her purification.

8 And if she be not able to bring a lamb, then she shall bring two turtles, or two young pigeons: the one for the

burnt offering, and the other for a sin offering: and the priest shall make an atonement for her, and she shall be clean.

The Nature of Leprosy, Lev. 13:

Israel was faced with three kinds of leprosy and seven conditions of leprosy. The first kind was the one that affected the human body. The second kind affected the garment and the third kind affected the house. There were seven conditions of leprosy of the body. Leviticus 13 explains these 7 conditions and the leprosy of the garment. The primary determining factor for the case of leprosy of the body was the appearance of an abnormality which went much deeper than the surface of the skin.

The first condition of leprosy is the one which must be distinguished from the scab.

1. Leprosy in the Skin as distinguished from a Scab, Lev. 13:1-9:

1 And the Lord spoke unto Moses and Aaron, saying,

2 When a man shall have in the skin of his flesh a rising, a scab, or a bright spot, and if it be in skin of his flesh like the plague of leprosy; then he shall be brought unto Aaron the priest, or unto one of his sons the priests:

3 And the priest shall look on the plague in the skin of the flesh: and when the hair in the plague is turned white, and the plague in sight be deeper than the skin of his flesh, it is a plague of leprosy: and the priest shall look on him and pronounce him unclean.

4 If the bright spot be white in the skin of his flesh, and in sight be not deeper than the skin, and the hair thereof be not turned white; then the priest shall shut up him that hath the plague seven days:

5 And the priest shall look on him the seventh day: and, behold, if the plague in his sight be at a stay, and the plague spread not in the skin; then the priest shall shut him up

seven days more:

When the suspicion of leprosy is brought to the priest, and when he is in doubt, he shuts him up for seven days. At the end of the seven days, if he remains doubtful, he shuts him up for seven more days.

6 And the priest shall look on him again the seventh day: and, behold, if the plague be somewhat dark, and the plague spread not in the skin, the priest shall pronounce him clean: it is but a scab: and he shall wash his clothes and be clean.

There is a third process:

7 But if the scab spread much abroad in the skin, after that he hath been seen of the priest for his cleansing, he shall be seen of the priest again.

8 And if the priest see that, behold, the scab spreads in the skin, then the priest shall pronounce him unclean: it is leprosy.

The third process finally determines this condition of leprosy.

2. Old Leprosy, Lev. 13:9-11:

9 When the plague of leprosy is in a man, then he shall be brought unto the priest;

10 And the priest shall see him: and, behold, if the rising be white in the skin, and it have turned the hair white, and there be quick raw flesh in the rising;

11 It is an old leprosy in the skin of his flesh, and the priest shall pronounce him unclean, and shall not shut him up: for he is unclean.

With the sudden rising of the raw flesh in the place of the suspected leprosy, the priest is able to determine with a degree of certainty the existence of leprosy.

3. Leprosy as Distinguished from a Change of skin Color, Lev. 13:12-18:

12 And if a leprosy break out abroad in the skin, and the

leprosy cover all the skin of him that hath the plague from his head even to his foot, where-so-ever the priest looketh

13 Then the priest shall consider: and, behold, if the leprosy have covered all his flesh, he shall pronounce him clean that hath the plague: it is all turned white: he is clean.

What clearly appears to be leprosy is not, if there is no appearance of raw flesh in the skin. But if raw flesh appears it is a condition of leprosy. This condition of leprosy is the most glaring picture of the nature of sin. It shows how quickly sin can permeate the whole being of man.

14 But when raw flesh appears in him, he shall be unclean.

15 And the priest shall see the raw flesh, and pronounce him to be unclean: it is a leprosy.

The third process:

16 Or if the raw flesh turn again, and be changed unto white, he shall come unto the priest;

17 And the priest shall see him: and, behold, if the plague be turned into white; then the priest shall pronounce him clean that hath the plague: he is clean.

18 The flesh also, in which, even in the skin thereof, was a boil, and is healed,

There are three processes by which the priest determines the existence of leprosy of the third condition, as also in the case of the first condition of leprosy.

4. Leprosy from an Old Boil, Lev. 13:19-23:

19 And in the place of the boil there be a white rising, or a bright spot, white, and somewhat reddish, and it be shown to the priest;

20 And if, when the priest sees it, behold, it be in sight lower than the skin, and the hair thereof be turned white; the priest shall pronounce him unclean: it is a plague of leprosy broken out of the boil.

The second process:

21 But if the priest look on it, and, behold, there be no white hairs therein, and if it be not lower than the skin, but be somewhat dark; then the priest shall shut him up seven days:

22 And if it spread much abroad in the skin, then the priest shall pronounce him unclean: it is a plague.

23 But if the bright spot stay in his place, and spread not, it is a burning boil; and the priest shall pronounce him clean.

The second process of examination by the priest finally determines whether or not a condition of leprosy exists.

5. Leprosy from a Hot Burning, Lev. 13:24-28:

24 Or if there be any flesh, in the skin whereof there is a hot burning, and the quick flesh that burns have a white bright spot, somewhat reddish , or white;

25 Then the priest shall look upon it: and, behold, if the hair in the bright spot be turned white, and if it be in sight deeper than the skin; it is a leprosy broken out of the burning: wherefore the priest shall pronounce him unclean; it is the plague of leprosy.

26 But if the priest look on it, and, behold, there be no white hair in the bright spot, and it be no lower than the other skin, but be somewhat dark; then the priest shall shut him up seven days:

In the second scenario, the examination was inconclusive, so the priest goes through a second process which brings conclusion to one of two scenarios.

27 And the priest shall look upon him the seventh day: and if it be spread much abroad in the skin, then the priest shall pronounce him unclean: it is the plague of leprosy.

28 And if the bright spot stay in his place, and spread not in the skin, but it be somewhat dark; it is a rising of the burning, and the priest shall pronounce him clean: for it is an inflammation of the burning.

6. Leprosy of the Head, Lev. 13:29-37:

29 If a man or woman have a plague upon the head or the beard;

30 Then the priest shall see the plague: and, behold, if it be in sight deeper than the skin; and there be in it a yellow thin hair; then the priest shall pronounce him unclean: it is a dry scull, even a leprosy upon the head or beard.

31 And if the priest look on the plague of the scull, and, behold, it be not in sight deeper than the skin, and that there is no black hair in it; then the priest shall shut up him that hath the plague of the scull seven days:

Because the priest cannot instantly determine this condition of leprosy, he goes through the second process.

32 And in the seventh day the priest shall look on the plague: and, behold, if the scull spread not, and there be in it no yellow hair, and the scull be not in sight deeper than the skin;

33 He shall be shaven, but the scull shall he not shave; and the priest shall shut up him that hath the scull seven days more:

The third process:

34 And in the seventh day the priest shall look on the scull: and, behold, if the scull be not spread in the skin, nor in sight deeper than the skin; then the priest shall pronounce him clean: and he shall wash his clothes, and be clean.

35 But if the scull spread much in the skin after his cleansing;

36 Then the priest shall look on him: and, behold, if the scull be spread in the skin, the priest shall not seek for yellow hair; he is unclean.

37 But if the scull be in his sight at a stay, and that there is black hair grown up therein; the scull is healed, he is clean: and the priest shall pronounce him clean.

The third process brought final conclusion to the priest's examination.

38 If a man also or a woman have in the skin of their flesh bright spots, even white bright spots;

39 Then the priest shall look: and, behold, if the bright spots in the skin of their flesh be darkish white; it is freckled spot that growth in the skin; he is clean.

7. Leprosy of the Baldhead, Lev. 13:40-46:

40 And the man whose hair is fallen off his head, he is bald; yet is he clean.

41 And he that hath his hair fallen off from the part of his head toward his face, he is **forehead bald**: yet is he clean.

42 And if there be in the bald head, or bald forehead, a white reddish sore; it is a leprosy sprung up in his bald head, or his bald forehead.

43 Then the priest shall look upon it: and, behold, if the rising of the sore be white reddish in his bald head, or in his bald forehead, as the leprosy appears in the skin of the flesh;

44 He is a leprous man, he is unclean: the priest shall pronounce him utterly unclean; his plague is in his head.

A reddish sore in the baldhead or the bald forehead is the evidence of leprosy, and the priest declares him unclean. He must then do the following:

45 And the leper in whom the plague is, his clothes shall be rent, and his head bare, and he shall put a covering upon his upper lip, and shall cry, Unclean, unclean.

46 All the days wherein the plague shall be in him he shall be defiled; he is unclean: he shall dwell alone; without the camp shall his habitation be.

Life as a leper was miserable, lonely, and, above all, was one of shame.

The leprosy of the body is one of three kinds; another is the leprosy of the garment.

Garment of Leprosy, Lev. 13:47-59:

47 The garment also that the plague of leprosy is in, whether it be a woolen garment, or linen garment;

48 Whether it be the warp, or woof; of linen, or of woolen; whether in a skin, or in anything made of skin;

49 And if the plague be greenish or reddish in the garment, or in the skin, either in the warp or woof, or in anything of skin; it is a plague of leprosy, and shall be shown unto the priest:

50 And the priest shall look upon the plague, and shut up it that hath the plague seven days:

51 And he shall look on the plague on the seventh day: if the plague be spread in the garment, either in the warp, or in the woof, or in a skin, or in any work that is made of skin; the plague is fretting leprosy; it is un-clean.

The plague of leprosy in the garment is determined by the discoloration of the garment and by its spreading after seven days. If it is determined to be leprosy, the garment or thing in which it is found is instantly destroyed.

52 He shall therefore burn hat garment, whether warp or woof, in woolen or in linen, or anything of skin, wherein the plague is: for it is a fretting leprosy; it shalt be burnt in the fire.

53 And if the priest shall look, and, behold, the plague be not spread in the garment, either in the warp, or in the woof, or in anything of skin;

54 Then the priest shall command that they wash the thing wherein the plague is, and he shall shut it up seven days more:

55 And the priest shall look on the plague, after that it is washed: and, behold, if the plague have not changed his color, and the plague be not spread; it is unclean; thou shalt burn it in the fire; it is fret inward, whether it be bare within or without.

56 And if the priest look, and, behold, the plague be

somewhat dark after the washing of it; then he shall rend it out of the garment, or out of the skin, or out of the warp, or out of the woof:

57 And if it appear still in the garment, either in the warp, or in the woof, or in anything of skin; it is a spreading plague: thou shalt burn that wherein the plague is with fire.

58 And the garment, either warp, or woof, or whatsoever thing of skin it be, which thou shalt wash, if the plague be departed from them, then it shall be washed the second time, and shall be clean.

59 This is the law of the plague of leprosy in a garment of woolen or linen, either in the warp, or woof, or anything of skins, to pronounce it clean, or to pronounce it unclean.

The "warp" and "woof" are interchangeable terms and mean the fabric or texture of the garment. It means a stain that saturates something like a garment is rather difficult to remove. That was why the destruction of a garment of leprosy was recommended.

One who had experienced a condition of leprosy had to be cleansed through the provision under the Law in a ceremony conducted by the priest. By this ceremony he was officially introduced to society again.

Cleansing of Leprosy, Lev. 14:

The cleansing of the person healed from leprosy is twofold. First is the cleansing for the leprosy itself; second is the cleansing or the Atonement for him. Two birds are used in the cleansing for the leprosy itself and four offerings are offered. There is also a modified ceremony of Atonement for the poor to ensure that they included in the process.

Cleansing for the Leprosy Itself, Lev. 14:1-9:

1 And the Lord spoke unto Moses, saying,

2 This shall be the law of the leper in the day of his cleansing: He shall be brought unto the priest:

3 And the priest shall go forth out of the camp; and the priest shall look, and, behold, if the plague of leprosy be healed in the leper;

4 Then shall the priest command to take for him that is to be cleansed two birds alive and clean, and cedar wood, and scarlet, and hyssop:

5 And the priest shall command that one of the birds be killed in an earthen vessel over running water:

6 As for the living bird, he shall take it, and the cedar wood, and the scarlet, and the hyssop, and shall dip them and the living bird in the blood of the bird that was killed over the running water:

7 And he shall sprinkle upon him that is to be cleansed from the leprosy seven times, and shall pronounce him clean, and shall let the living bird loose into the open field.

8 And he that is to be cleansed shall wash his clothes, and shave off his hair, and wash himself in water, that he may be clean: and after that he shall come into the camp, and shall tarry abroad out of his tent seven days.

9 But it shall be on the seventh day, that he shall shave all his hair off his head and his beard and his eyebrows, even all his hair he shall shave off: and he shall wash his clothes, also he shall wash his flesh in water, and he shall be clean.

Offerings of Atonement for the Leper, Lev. 14:10-11

10 And on the eighth day he shall take two he lambs without blemish, and one ewe lamb of the first year without blemish, and three tenth deals of fine flour for a meat offering, mingled with oil, and one log of oil.

11 And the priest that makes him clean shall present the man that is to be made clean, and those things before the Lord, at the door of the tabernacle of the congregation:

One of the lambs is to be offered as a Trespass Offering; the other he lamb is to be offered as a Sin Offering. The ewe lamb is to be offered as a Burnt Offering; the three tenth deals of fine flour is to be offered for a Meat Offering.

The Trespass Offering, Lev. 14:12-18:

12 And the priest shall take one he lamb, and offer him for a trespass offering, and the log of oil, and wave them for a wave offering before the Lord:

13 And he shall slay the lamb in the place where he shall kill the sin offering and the burnt offering, in the holy place: for as the sin offering is the priest's, so is the trespass offering: it is most holy:

The offerings are killed before the Tabernacle beside the Burnt Altar. The placing of the blood of the Trespass Offering, on the right ear, right thumb, and the right toe of the person on whose behalf the Atonement is made, reminds us of the similar placing of the blood of the Ram of Consecration on Aaron. Did this imply that Aaron was not better off than a leper, or did it imply that, unknowing to Aaron, he would have one day atoned for a leper?

14 And the priest shall take some of the blood of the trespass offering, and the priest shall put it upon the tip of the right ear of him that is to be cleansed, and upon the thumb of his right hand, and upon the great toe of his right foot:

15 And the priest shall take some of the log of oil and pour it into the palm of his own left hand:

It seems that the log of oil was ordinary, not the holy anointing oil. Aaron applied the oil in the same manner as he applied the blood of the Trespass Offering.

16 And the priest shall dip his right finger in the oil that is in his left hand, and shall sprinkle of the oil with his finger seven times before the Lord:

17 And of the rest of the oil that is in his hand shall the priest put upon the tip of the right ear of him that is to be cleansed, and upon the thumb of his right hand, and upon

the great toe of his right foot, upon the blood of the trespass offering:

18 And the remnant of oil that is in the priest's hand he shall pour upon the head of him that is to be cleansed: and the priest shall make an atonement for him before the Lord.

The outpouring of the rest of oil upon the atoned symbolizes the outpouring of the Holy Spirit on the Day of Pentecost after the atoning blood of Christ was applied to the Believers. The difference is that the anointing of the Holy Spirit is unlimited. This anointing is available to all Believers.

The Sin Offering, Lev.14:19:

19 And the priest shall offer the sin offering, and make an atonement for him that is to be cleansed from his uncleanness; and afterward he shall kill the burnt offering:

Notice the order of the offerings: the Sin Offering follows the Trespass Offering; then the Burnt Offering and the Meat Offering. The Atonement under the Law was sufficient for all the needs of Israel; the Atonement of God's Son is sufficient for all the needs of the world.

The Burnt Offering and the Meat Offering:

20 And the priest shall offer the burnt offering and the meat offering upon the altar: and the priest shall make an atonement for him, and he shall be clean.

The Meat Offering was burnt upon the Burnt Altar and also the whole burnt Offering.

Special consideration was given to the poor who were unable to provide all offerings heretofore mentioned. The poor would never become invisible to the eyes of the Law.

Cleansing for the Poor:

21 And if he be poor, and cannot get so much; then he shall take one lamb for a trespass offering to be waved, to make an atonement for him, and one tenth deal of fine flour mingled with oil for a meat offering, and a log of oil.

22 And two turtledoves, or two young pigeons, such as he is able to get; and the one shall be a sin offering, and the other a burnt offering.

23 And he shall bring them on the eighth day for his cleansing unto the priest, unto the door of the tabernacle of the congregation, before the Lord.

24 And the priest shall take the lamb of the trespass offering, and the log of oil, and the priest shall wave them for a wave offering before the Lord:

25 And he shall kill the lamb of the trespass offering, and the priest shall take some of the blood of the trespass offering, and put it upon the tip of the right ear of him that is to be cleansed, and upon the thumb of his right hand, and upon the great toe of his right foot:

26 And the priest shall pour of the oil into the palm of his own left hand: *The use of the oil was very important in the rituals and ceremonies of the Law.*

27 And the priest shall sprinkle with his right finger some of the oil that is in his left hand seven times before the Lord:

28 And the priest shall put of the oil that is in his hand upon the tip of the right ear of him that is to be cleansed, and upon the thumb of his right hand, and upon the great toe of his right foot, upon the place of the blood of the trespass offering:

29 And the rest of the oil that is in the priest's hand he shall put upon the head of him that is to be cleansed, to make an atonement for him before the Lord.

30 And he shall offer the one of the turtledoves, or of the young pigeons, such as he can get;

31 Even such as he is able to get, the one for a sin offering, and the other for a burnt offering, with the meat offering: and the priest shall make an atonement for him that is to be cleansed before the Lord.

The offerings of the poor were less expensive; but they were four kinds: the Trespass Offering, the Sin Offering, the

Burnt Offering, and the Meat Offering. These offerings completed the Atonement of the one for whom they were made.

32 This is the law of him in whom is the plague of leprosy whose hand is not able to get that which pertains to his cleansing.

Leprosy of the House, Lev. 14:33-48:

The leprosy of the house was the third kind of leprosy that Israel would experience. They would not have experienced it until they were living in the land of Canaan.

33 And the Lord spoke unto Moses and unto Aaron, saying,

34 When ye come into the land of Canaan, which I give to you for a possession, and I put the plague of leprosy in a house of the land of your possession;

The plague of leprosy was not by chance; it was put upon God's people by God. We just reviewed the seven conditions of leprosy, its cleansing and offerings of Atonement. We thought it was all by chance only to realize it was on purpose. The question is, Why had God put the deadly disease of leprosy on His own people? To some it was rather cruel and unusual punishment. To others, it was a corrective measure borne out of love. One thing is clear that God loved His people more than they loved Him. It is not different with us that because we love our children, we use corrective measures to correct them from their erring ways; these worked well in the past. Today we cannot even use those measures we would like before the government jumps on our backs and begins to exact on us its own corrective punishment. There is no one who can dictate to God what corrective measures He must take to correct His erring children. What is important is that in the end those corrected will concur that the corrective measures were for their own good.

Indeed, it is obvious that all those instances of leprosy drew back those erring ones from the path of sin to the path of righteousness and fellowship with God. Truly they came back to God with their offerings of cleansing and Atonement for their sins and diseases. God wanted His children to come home to Him; so He afflicted them with disease of leprosy. God did not hide His intentions; He declared them openly for the whole world to know. Today He does not use the corrective measure of leprosy but He has other corrective measures which He will not hesitate to use when we have gone astray.

Leprosy brought pain to the leper; but it gained his spiritual attention and brought him to the place where he knew he had no one to whom to turn for healing and Atonement except God.

35 And he that owns the house shall come and tell the priest, saying, It seems to me there is as it were, a plague in the house:

36 Then the priest shall command that they empty the house, before the priest go into it to see the plague, that all that is in the house be not made unclean: and afterward the priest shall go in to see the house:

Signs of Leprosy

37 And he shall look on the plague, and, behold, if the plague be in the walls of the house with hollow strakes, greenish or reddish, which in sight are lower than the wall;

38 Then the priest shall go out of the house to the door of the house, and shut up the house seven days:

39 And the priest shall come again the seventh day, and shall look: and, behold, if the plague be spread in the walls of the house;

Costly Repairs

40 Then the priest shall command that they take away

the stones in which the plague is, and they shall cast them into an unclean place without the city:

41 And he shall cause the house to be scraped within round about, and they shall pour out the dust that they scrape off without the city into an unclean place:

42 And they shall take other stones, and put them in the place of those stones; and he shall take other mortar, and shall plaster the house.

Loss of House: 43 And if the plague come again, and break out in the house, after that he hath taken away the stones, and after he hath scraped the house, and after it is plastered;

44 Then the priest shall come and look, and, behold, if the plague be spread in the house, it is a fretting leprosy in the house: it is un-clean.

45 And he shall breakdown the house, the stones of it, and the timber thereof, and all the mortar of the house; and he shall carry them forth out of the city unto an unclean place.

46 Moreover he that goes into the house all the while that it is shut up shall be unclean until the even.

47 And he that lies in the house shall wash his clothes; and he that eats in the house shall wash his clothes.

48 And if the priest shall come in, and look upon it, and, behold, the plague hath not spread in the house, after the house was plastered: the priest shall pronounce the house clean, because the plague is healed.

Leprosy is not like a friendly neighbor; it was very much opposed to the goals and dreams of those who went astray from the paths of righteousness, whether in the case of the body, or in the case of the garment, or in the case of the house. In the case of the leprosy of the house, the repairs were costly. In some cases there was the complete loss of the house. Was not that a very harsh reality? Why did God cause, or would cause some of His children to lose their houses? Quite possible, they placed their house above God and gave Him second place. Second place was not good enough for God. By the leprosy of the house, He removed those idols from their lives, irrespective of the material cost to them. Then they saw the path of righteousness by which they returned to the God from whom all blessings flow. If they returned to righteousness, the leprosy of their houses was a good thing — God be praised.

For those who did not lose their houses, there was cleansing and forgiveness.

Cleansing of the House, 14: 49-57:

49 And he shall take to cleanse the house two birds, and cedar wood, and scarlet, and hyssop:

50 And he shall kill the one of the birds in an earthen vessel over running water:

51 And he shall take the cedar wood, and the hyssop, and the scarlet, and the living bird, and dip them in the blood of the slain bird, and in the running water, and sprinkle the house seven times:

52 And he shall cleanse the house with the blood of the bird, and with the running water, and with the living bird, and with the cedar wood, and with the hyssop, and with the scarlet:

53 But he shall let go the living bird out of the city into the open fields, and make an atonement for the house: and it shall be clean.

This was the same cleansing which was applied to the leprosy of the body.

54 This is the law for all manner of plague of leprosy, and scall,

55 And for the leprosy of a garment, and of a house.

56 And for a rising, and for a scab, and for a bright spot:

57 To teach when it is un-clean, and when it is clean: this is the law of leprosy.

The law of leprosy points the leper back to God and gives him the opportunity to correct the error of his ways. Leprosy was one of many social issues addressed in the Social Compact. There were the biological issue and that of a romantic nature.

Biological Issues, Lev. 15:

Sickness in general is somewhat unpreventable; those of a biological nature are just the same. The biological issues herein, caused more shame than pain to those who had them. Not only were they defiled by them but others with whom they had contacts were also defiled. Defilement by these issues prevented access to the Tabernacle and to the priests. They had to be healed before they were able to take their offerings of atonement to the priests.

Men, Lev. 15:1-17:

1 And the Lord spoke unto Moses and unto Aaron, saying,

2 Speak unto the children of Israel, and say unto them, When any man hath a running issue out of his flesh, because of his issue he is unclean.

3 And this shall be his uncleanness in his issue: whether his flesh run with his issue, or his flesh be stopped from his issue, it is his uncleanness.

4 Every bed whereon he lies that hath the issue, is unclean: and everything, whereon he sits, shall be unclean.

5 And whosoever touches his bed shall wash his clothes, and bathe himself in water, and be unclean until the even.

6 And he that sits on anything whereon he sat that hath the issue shall wash his clothes, and bathe himself in water, and be unclean until the even.

7 And he that touches the flesh of him that hath the issue shall wash his clothes, and bathe himself in water, and be unclean until the even.

8 And if he that hath the issue spit upon him that is clean; then he shall wash his clothes, and bathe himself in water, and be unclean until the evening.

9 And what saddle that he rides upon that hath the issue shall be unclean.

10 And whosoever touches anything that was under him shall be unclean until the evening: and he that bears any of those things shall wash his clothes, and bathe himself in water, and be unclean until the even.

11 And whomsoever he touches that hath the issue, and hath not rinsed his hands in water, he shall wash his clothes, and bathe himself in water, and be unclean until the even.

12 And the vessel of earth, that he touches which hath the issue, shall be broken: and every vessel of wood shall be rinsed in water.

That was as far as the defilement could have gone. It amounted to the defilement of a local environment. After healing occurred, the person had to wait until eight days before going with his offerings to see the priests.

13 And when he that hath an issue is cleansed of his issue; then he shall number to himself seven days for his cleansing, and wash his clothes, and bathe his flesh in running water, and shall be clean.

Offerings

14 And on the eighth day he shall take to him two turtle doves, or two young pigeons, and come before the Lord unto the door of the tabernacle of the congregation, and give them unto the priest:

15 And the priest shall offer them, the one for a sin offering, and the other for a burnt offering; and the priest shall make an atonement for him before the Lord for his issue.

The healing occurred before the offerings of Atonement; but the Atonement completed the healing process. The Atonement provided both forgiveness and healing. In the Atonement of Christ both forgiveness and healing are provided.

16 And if any man's seed of copulation go out from him, then he shall wash all his flesh in water, and be unclean until the even.

17 And every garment, and every skin, whereon is the seed of copulation, shall be washed with water, and be unclean until the even.

Women, Lev. 15:18-33:

18 The woman also with whom man shall lie with seed of copulation, they shall both bathe themselves in water, and be unclean until the even.

19 And if a woman have an issue, and her issue in her flesh be blood, she shall be put apart seven days: and whosoever touches her shall be unclean until the evening.

20 And everything that she lies upon in her separation shall be unclean: everything also that she sits upon shall be unclean.

21 And whosoever touches her bed shall wash his clothes, and bathe himself in water, and be unclean until the even.

22 And whosoever touches anything that she sat upon shall wash his clothes and bathe himself in water, and be unclean until the even.

23 And if it be on her bed, or anything whereon she sits, when he touches it, he shall be unclean until the even.

24 And if any man lie with her at all, and her flowers be upon him, he shall be unclean seven days; and all the bed whereon he lies shall be unclean.

25 And if a woman have an issue of her blood many days out of the time of her separation, or if it run beyond the time of her separation; all the days of the issue of her uncleanness shall be as the days of her separation: she shall be unclean.

26 Every bed whereon she lies all the days of her issue shall be unto her as the bed of her separation: and whatsoever she sits upon shall be unclean, as the uncleanness of her separation.

27 And whosoever touches those things shall be unclean, and shall wash his clothes, and bathe himself in water, and be unclean until the even.

28 But if she be cleansed of her issue, then she shall number to herself seven days, and after that she shall be clean.

29 And on the eighth day she shall take unto her two turtledoves, or two young pigeons, and bring them unto the priest, to the door of the tabernacle of the congregation.

30 And the priest shall offer the one for a sin offering, and the other for a burnt offering; and the priest shall make an atonement for her before the Lord for the issue of her uncleanness.

The cleansing for the woman was the same as that of the man. Eight days after her healing she had to take the offerings of Atonement to the priest to make an Atonement for her. To go to the Tabernacle in their uncleanness could cause instant death. Ignorance was not a good excuse to sin: sin had to be accounted for. In a holy relationship with God, sickness could cause defilement, and defilement could cause disharmony. However, sickness and defilement lead to Atonement. This law was not given in vain; it accomplished its purpose.

31 Thus shall ye separate the children of Israel from their uncleanness; that they die not in their uncleanness, when they defile my tabernacle that is among them.

32 This is the law of him that hath an issue, and of him whose seed goes from him, and is defiled therewith;

33 And of her that is sick of her flowers, and of him that hath an issue, of the man, and of the woman, and of him that lies with her that is unclean.

Romantic Relationship, Lev. 18:

When relationships are not according to the norms of righteousness, they are physical and sinful; when they follow the norms of righteousness, they become holy and strengthen our spiritual relationship with God. The romantic and intimate relationships of the nations of Canaan were outside of God's norms, too far to be tolerated any longer by God. Therefore, it was important for Him to set the guidelines for Israel to follow in view of the fact they were to inherit the land of those nations.

1 And the Lord spoke unto Moses, saying,

2 Speak unto the children of Israel and say unto them, I am the Lord your God.

3 After the doings of the land of Egypt, wherein ye dwelt, shall ye not do: and after the doings of the land of Canaan, whither I bring you, shall ye not do: neither shall ye walk in their ordinances.

4 Ye shall do my judgments, and keep my ordinances, to walk therein: I am the Lord your God.

5 Ye shall therefore keep my statutes, and my judgments: which if a man do, he shall live in them: I am the Lord.

Relationships

6 None of you shall approach to any that is near of kin to him, to uncover their nakedness: I am the Lord.

7 The nakedness of thy father, or the nakedness of thy mother, shalt thou not uncover: she is thy mother; thou shalt not uncover her nakedness.

8 The nakedness of thy father's wife shalt thou not uncover: it is thy father's nakedness.

9 The nakedness of thy sister, the daughter of thy father, or daughter of thy mother, whether she be born at home, or born abroad, even their nakedness shall they not uncover.

10 The nakedness of thy son's daughter, or of thy daughter's daughter, even their nakedness thou shalt not

uncover: for theirs is thine own nakedness.

11 The nakedness of thy father's wife's daughter, begotten of thy father, she is thy sister, thou shalt not uncover her nakedness.

12 Thou shalt not uncover the nakedness of thy father's sister: she is thy father near kinswoman.

13 Thou shalt not uncover the nakedness of thy mother's sister: for she is thy mother's near kinswoman.

14 Thou shalt not uncover the nakedness of thy father's brother, thou shalt not approach to his wife: she is thine aunt.

15 Thou shalt not uncover the nakedness of thy daughter-in-law: she is thy son's wife; thou shalt not uncover her nakedness.

16 Thou shalt not uncover the nakedness of thy brother's wife: it is thy brother's nakedness.

17 Thou shalt not uncover the nakedness of a woman and her daughter, neither shalt thou take her son's daughter, or her daughter's daughter, to uncover her nakedness; for they are her near kinswomen: it is wickedness.

18 Neither shalt thou take a wife to her sister, to vex her, to uncover her nakedness, beside the other in her life time.

19 Also thou shalt not approach unto a woman to uncover her nakedness, as long as she is put apart for her uncleanness.

20 Moreover thou shalt not lie carnally with thy neighbor's wife, to defile thyself with her.

21 And thou shalt not let any of thy seed pass through the fire to Molech, neither shalt thou profane the name of thy God: I am the Lord.

Molech was the god the Canaanites, to whom parents sacrificed their children.

22 Thou shalt not lie with mankind, as with womankind: it is abomination.

23 Neither shalt thou lie with any beast to defile thyself therewith: neither shall any woman stand before a beast to lie down before it: it is confusion.

Reasons for Living by the Social Order:

All the nations were doing the opposite of what God required of Israel. Therefore their lands were given to Israel. Israel had an obligation to live by the social order with respect to romantic relationship and consider God's indictment against those nations.

24 Defile not ye yourselves in any of these things: for in all these the nations are defiled which I cast out before you:

25 And the land is defiled: therefore I do visit the iniquity thereof upon it, and the land itself vomits out the inhabitants.

26 Ye shall therefore keep my statutes and my judgments, and shall not commit any of these abominations; neither any of your own nation, nor any stranger that sojourns among you:

27 (For all these abominations have the men of the land done, which were before you, and the land is defiled;)

28 That the land spew not you out also, when ye defile it, as it spewed out the nations that were before you.

29 For whosoever shall commit any of these abominations, even the souls that commit them shall be cut off from among their people.

30 Therefore shall ye keep my ordinance, that ye commit not any of these abominable customs, which were committed before you, and that ye defile not yourselves therein: I am the Lord your God. *"I am the Lord your God" is His signature to His declarations. It means that He is the Holy God and His children must be holy also.*

Consequences of Failure, Lev. 20:

Both parties to a contract are obligated to fulfill the terms of the contract. If one of the parties fails, he incurs certain consequences. The failure of Israel to their obligation to the terms of the contract incurred the stated consequences.

1. Regarding Sacrifice to Molech, 20:1-5: And the Lord spoke unto Moses saying,

2 Again, thou shalt say to the children of Israel, Whosoever he be of the children of Israel, or of the strangers that sojourn in Israel, that giveth any of his seed unto Molech; he shall surely be put to death: the people of the land shall stone him with stones.

3 And I will set my face against that man, and will cut him off from among his people; because he hath given of his seed unto Molech, to defile my sanctuary, and to profane my holy name.

4 And if the people of the land do any ways hide their eyes from the man, when he giveth his seed unto Molech, and kill him not:

5 Then I will set my face against that man, and against his family, and will cut him off, and all that go a-whoring after him, to commit whoredom with Molech, from among their people.

The offering of a human sacrifice to Molech was another way by which Satan demanded worship of mankind. Satan's desire for worship was the cause of the origin of sin. Satan has not given up that desire. In the Wilderness of Temptation he demanded worship of Jesus Christ; but he got a rebuke instead. As Christians it is not our job to find out how people can connect with the **dark world** *by which certain powers are made available to them, but we know that they can. At least we know that the sacrificing of one's son to Molech was a way of connecting with the* **dark world**. *The real danger of all of this is that when one gets connected to the* **dark world**, *he goes to the very brink of hopelessness. The heathen practice of connecting with the* **dark world** *was condemned by God in the strongest terms*

2. Regarding Familiar Spirits, Lev. 20:6-8:

6 And the soul that turns after such as have familiar spirits, and after wizards, to go a-whoring after them, I will even set my face against that soul, and will cut him off from among his people.

7 Sanctify yourselves therefore, and be ye holy: for I am the Lord your God.

8 And ye shall keep my statutes, and do them: I am the Lord which sanctify you.

People with familiar spirits could connect with the Dark World. Israel had a propensity for idolatry and could easily be persuaded to turn from God. The punishment of death for those who were involved suggests the seriousness of the sin.

The death penalty was not only for those who turned to another god but for adulterers, disobedient children, incestuous relationship, same sex relationship, and more. The prevalence of the death penalty was to prevent the sudden spiritual and moral destruction of the nation.

3. Regarding Disobedient Children, 20:9:

9 For every one that curses his father or his mother shall be surely put to death: he hath cursed his father or his mother; his blood shall be upon him.

4. Regarding Another Man's Wife:

10 And the man that commits adultery with another man's wife, even he that commits adultery with his neighbor's wife, the adulterer and the adulteress shall surely be put to death.

5. Regarding a Man's Father's Wife:

11 And the man that lies with his father's wife hath uncovered his father's nakedness: both of them shall surely be put to death; their blood shall be upon them.

6. Regarding a Man's Daughter:

12 And if a man lie with his daughter-in-law, both of them shall surely be put to death: they have wrought confusion; their blood shall be upon them.

7. Regarding Same Sex, Liv. 20: 13

13 If a man also lie with mankind, as he lies with a woman, both of them have committed abomination: they shall surely be put to death; their blood shall be upon them.

8. Regarding Incestuous Relationship:

14 And if a man take a wife and her mother, it is wickedness: they shall be burnt with fire, both he and they; that there be no wickedness among you.

9. Regarding Bestiality, Man:

15 And if a man lie with a beast, he shall surely be put to death: and ye shall slay the beast.

10. Regarding Bestiality, Woman:

16 And if a woman approaches unto any beast, and lie down thereto, thou shalt kill the woman, and the beast: they shall surely be put to death; their blood shall be upon them.

11. Regarding a Man and His Sister:

17 And if a man shall take his sister, his father's daughter, or his mother's daughter, and see her nakedness, and she see his nakedness; it is a wicked thing; and they shall be cut off in the sight of their people; he hath uncovered his sister's nakedness; he shall bear his iniquity.

12. Regarding Uncleanness:

18 And if a man shall lie with a woman having her sickness, and shall uncover her nakedness; he hath discovered her fountain, and she hath uncovered the fountain of her blood: and both of them shall be cut off from among their people.

13. Regarding a Man and His Aunt:

19 And thou shalt not uncover the nakedness of thy mother's sister, nor of thy father's sister: for he uncovers his near kin: they shall bear their iniquity.

14. Regarding a Man and His Uncle's Wife:

20 And if a man shall lie with his uncle's wife, he hath uncovered his uncle's nakedness: they shall bear their sin; and they shall die childless.

15. Regarding a Man and His Brother's Wife:

21 And if a man shall take his brother's wife, it is an unclean thing: he hath uncovered his brother's nakedness; they shall be childless.

Admonition, Lev. 20: 22-27:

22 Ye shall therefore keep all my statutes, and all my commandments, and do them: that the land whither I bring you to dwell therein, spew you not out.

23 And ye shall not walk in the manners of the nation, which I cast out before you: for they committed all these things, and therefore I abhorred them.

24 But I have said unto you, Ye shall inherit their land, and I will give it to you to possess it, a land that flows with milk and honey: I am the Lord your God, which have separated you from other people.

25 Ye shall therefore put difference between clean beasts and unclean, and between unclean fowls and clean: and ye shall not make your souls abominable by beast or by fowl, or by any manner of living thing that creeps on the ground, which I have separated from you as unclean.

The Children of Israel were not given the statutes and commandments just to read and memorize, but to live by them. By living by them they would not follow the bad examples of the heathen nations. If they did not live according to God's laws, they would have the same fate of the condemned nations. They were to recognize the difference between the clean and the unclean things. This was important because the unclean things could defile them. The knowledge of wrong and right was important; but doing the right was more important. Doing the right was what would make them holy and different from all other peoples.

26 And ye shall be holy unto me: for I the Lord am holy, and have severed you out from other people, that ye should be mine.

27 A man also or woman that hath a familiar spirit, or that is a wizard, shall surely be put to death: they shall

stone them with stones: their blood shall be upon them.

SUMMARY

The Social Compact further detailed the principles of righteousness, the observance of which would distinguish Israel from other nations. God's special relationship with Israel was based on their willingness to live by the principles of *holiness. God's holy nature cannot be changed*; their sin nature could be changed by their compliance to God's order of Atonement and obedience to all His instructions. In the Social Compact there were specific instructions clearly stated, giving them the required knowledge to be holy.

There were certain foods prescribed for them. God knew what was the best food for the health and purity of Israel and carefully chose from among His creatures the best animals, fish, and birds. The unclean animals forbidden for food were not only unhealthy but, in some way, could defile the people. In the case of defilement one was denied access to the Tabernacle. One had to be cleansed before gaining access to one's natural right.

Other things could have caused defilement of the body and prevent ready access to the Tabernacle. The birth of a child is a beautiful thing but under the Law it caused defilement of the mother and required purification. Eight days after the birth of a child, its mother had to take her offerings of cleansing to the priest and had to remain in her separation for thirty-two more days, a total of forty days. In the case of a female child the time of purification was twice as long. After the time of purification was completed, the mother had to bring a lamb for her burnt offering and a turtledove or pigeon for a sin offering.

Leprosy was another thing that caused defilement and prevented ready access to the Tabernacle. The leper had to be first healed before he could take his offerings of cleansing and Atonement to the priest. There was much stigma to the disease and the process of physical examination by the priest was not at all a simple one. There were three kinds of leprosy and seven conditions of leprosy. There were the leprosy of the body, the leprosy of garment, and the leprosy of the house. These three kinds of leprosy and the seven body conditions of leprosy made the disease a much complicated issue for the priest and everyone. After the healing of the leprosy, the healed person took his offerings of cleansing and Atonement to the priest who offered them on his behalf.

Biological issues also caused defilement of the body and prevented ready access to the Tabernacle. One had to be healed before he could take his offerings to the priest to be offered for his cleansing. His offerings were two pigeons: one for a sin offering and the other for a burnt offering.

A moral code for romantic relationships was established. It applied to all possible scenarios within the context of sexual behavior. It was important for Israel to observe this code because its observance distinguished them from the other nations of Canaan whose sexual behavior was condemned and brought an end to their society by losing their lands to Israel.

In any contract, both parties must honor all its terms. Failure to honor the terms of a contract incurs certain consequences. The Social Compact was unique in two senses in that it was detailed and comprehensive, and that it included the very consequences if Israel failed in its obligations. The Social Compact brought a wealth of knowledge which was critical to holy living. That knowledge made it most valuable.

CHAPER 13
The Year of Atonement, Leviticus 16-17

Imagine a thousand people assembled before the Tabernacle at the end of the year; imagine the many sins each of those people committed during the year of which they were all conscious. But it was not just a thousand people: it was more than 2,000,000 people gathered together around the Tabernacle for the Day of Atonement— all being conscious of their sins and the solemnity of the occasion. To understand the nature of sin is to understand the solemnity of the Day of Atonement. Sin causes a breach of fellowship with God, physical death, and eternal separation from God. Sin impairs the whole being of man: body, soul, and spirit. If the whole nation of Israel had died on the Day of Atonement and had not appropriated the provision of Atonement, every one of them would have been separated from God and lost for all eternity.

It is also helpful to understand clearly the principle of Atonement— The Innocent for the Guilty, the offering of the innocent animal for the sin of guilty man. This principle was based on the eternal principle of the Holy Son of God who in eternity offered to die on man's behalf. The Atonement under the Law was based on the Atonement of God's Son. Under the Law, God saw not the blood of the animals, but the blood of His only Son and forgave the guilty of all their sins. Therefore, under the Law, Atonement was real as the Atonement of Christ is real today. On the Day of Atonement sins were forgiven, fellowship with God was restored, and Israel experienced peace with God. To us, therefore, the Day of Atonement was a historic spiritual event in the life of the nation of Israel.

It was remarkable that everyone was personally represented on the Day of Atonement. In the Breastplate of Aaron the High Priest were the names of the twelve tribes of Israel, representing every member of the congregation of Israel. The offerings of Atonement were first to be offered for Aaron and his family and then for the whole congregation of Israel. They were to be offered simultaneously.

Aaron's Atonement, Lev.16:1-4, 6-14

1 And the Lord spoke unto Moses after the death of the two sons of Aaron, when they offered before the Lord, and died;

One reason that Moses was a great prophet was that God spoke to him often and he faithfully obeyed in everything. On this occasion He is giving him instructions regarding the Day of Atonement. It seems as though Aaron had daily access to the Holy of Holies before the untimely death of two of his sons. The instructions to Moses had changed that.

2 And the Lord said unto Moses, Speak unto thy brother, that he come not at all times into the holy place within the veil before the mercy seat, which is upon the ark; that he die not: for I will appear in the cloud upon the mercy seat.

It would appear that God's presence resided in a cloud above the Mercy Seat and that presence should not be frequently interrupted by Aaron's appearance: it would cause his death. Aaron could only enter into the Holy of Holies to offer an Atonement for himself and an Atonement for the congregation of Israel once a year.

3 Thus shall Aaron come into the holy place: with a young bullock for a sin offering, and a ram for a burnt offering.

The young bullock for Aaron's Sin Offering was the most

basic of the offerings of Atonement. It represents man's three-fold nature— body, soul, and spirit— which is severely impaired by sin. The dead bullock symbolizes the physical death of the body; the pouring out of the blood symbolizes the Atonement of the soul, the remission of sins; and the offering of its essential organs of life upon the Burnt Altar symbolizes the restoration of the spirit to fellowship with God. After the blood of the Sin Offering is brought into the Holy Place to complete the offering of Atonement, the body is carried outside the camp where it is disposed of by fire because it has no more significance. The Sin Offering naturally precedes the Burnt offering.

All the offerings which require blood represent the threefold nature of man in their application: the slain animal, its blood, and the offering of its essential organs upon the Burnt Altar. The burnt Offering is a little different; after its blood is poured out, all its body is offered upon the Burnt Altar. It basically signifies the restoration of fellowship with God and naturally follows the Sin Offering.

4 He shall put on the holy linen coat, and he shall have the linen breeches upon his flesh, and shall be girded with the linen girdle, and with the linen miter shall he be attired: these are holy garments; therefore shall he wash his flesh in water, and so put them on.

Going into the Holy of Holies was the most solemn duty and responsibility of Aaron. For the occasion, he had to dress in the holy garments including the robe of the Ephod with the golden bells at its hem (Exodus 28:31-35). While ministering, the bells were sounding to indicate that Aaron was alive.

Atonement for the Congregation, 16:5, 7-10, 15, 21, 22

5 And he shall take of the congregation of the children of Israel two kids of the goats for a sin offering, and one ram for a burnt offering.

At the consecration of the Tabernacle when it was erected, a bullock was offered as the Sin offering for the congregation. Look back on the chart of the offerings on pages 266-270- and Leviticus 4:13-21. On the Day of Atonement, two goats were required for the Sin Offering and a ram for the Burnt Offering.

6 And Aaron shall offer his bullock of the sin offering, which is for himself, and make an atonement for himself, and for his house.

7 And he shall take the two goats, and present them before the Lord at the door of the tabernacle of the congregation.

8 And Aaron shall cast lots upon the two goats; one lot for the Lord, and the other lot for the scapegoat.

9 And Aaron shall bring the goat upon which the Lord's lot fell, and offer him for a sin offering.

10 But the goat, on which the lot fell to be the scapegoat, shall be presented alive before the Lord, to make an atonement with him, and to let him go for a scapegoat into the wilderness.

Both goats were offered as a Sin Offering for the congregation but only the one on which the Lord's lot fell was killed and offered. The Scapegoat was let go into the wilderness after Aaron confessed the sins of the congregation over its head. This symbolizes Christ who bore our sins in the Wilderness of Temptation for forty days.

11 And Aaron shall bring the bullock of the sin offering, which is for himself, and shall make an atonement for himself, and for his house, and shall kill the bullock of the sin offering which is for himself.

12 And he shall take a censer full of burning coals of fire from off the altar before the Lord, and his hands full of sweet incense beaten small, and bring it within the veil:

The altar before the Lord was the Golden Altar of Incense on which Aaron burned incense morning and evening. Incense could not be burnt without the coals of fire. It was positioned before the holy Veil in the Tabernacle. Aaron was to make

Atonement on it once a year by placing the blood of the Sin Offering upon its horns (Exodus 30:1-10; pages 167-168). Aaron took the burning coal from it and some sweet incense, went into the Holy of Holies, and burned the incense upon the censor. The cloud from it covered the Mercy Seat. God already appeared in the cloud above the Mercy Seat. The cloud from the burning incense came between Aaron and the cloud of God's presence. In that way Aaron did not die. Even in the Holy of Holies the place of mercy, there was a distinction made between the Holy God and Aaron.

13 And he shall put the incense upon the fire before the Lord, that the cloud of the incense may cover the mercy seat that is upon the testimony, that he die not:

14 And he shall take of the blood of the bullock, and sprinkle it with his finger upon the mercy seat eastward; and before the mercy seat shall he sprinkle of the blood with his finger seven times.

After Aaron offered his Atonement in the Holy of Holies, he offered the Atonement of the people in like manner. The sprinkling of the blood seven times upon the Mercy Seat twice indicated the Atonement was complete for himself and for the people.

15 Then shall he kill the goat of the sin offering, that is for the people, and bring his blood within the veil, and do with that blood as he did with the blood of the bullock, and sprinkle it upon the mercy seat:

Atonement for the Holy Place, Lev. 16:16-17:

16 And he shall make an atonement for the holy place, because of the uncleanness of the children of Israel, and because of their transgressions in their sins: and so shall he do for the tabernacle of the congregation, that remains among them in the midst of their uncleanness.

The offering of the blood of the Sin Offering upon the horns of the Golden Incense Altar and the sprinkling upon the Mercy

Seat was the Atonement made for the holy place and the Tabernacle. The physical presence of any one was not allowed in the Tabernacle while Aaron was making the atonement. An act as simple and harmless as that would completely undo the purpose of the Atonement Aaron was making. God is holy and He wanted Israel to understand that and, at the same time, the catastrophic nature of sin.

17 And there shall be no man in the tabernacle of the congregation when he goes in to make an atonement in the holy place, until he come out, and have made an atonement for himself, and for his household, and for all the congregation of Israel.

Atonement for the Burnt Altar, Lev. 16:18-20:

18 And he shall go out unto the altar that is before the Lord, and make an atonement for it; and shall take of the blood of the bullock, and of the blood of the goat, and put it upon the horns of the altar round about.

In making an atonement for the Burnt Altar, Aaron sprinkled the blood of the bullock and the blood of the goat seven times each upon the Burnt Altar. That was sufficient for the atonement of the Burnt Altar: the blood was already sprinkled upon the Mercy Seat.

19 And he shall sprinkle of the blood upon it with his finger seven times, and cleanse it, and hallow it from the uncleanness of the children of Israel.

20 And when he hath made an end of reconciling the holy place, and the tabernacle of the congregation, and the altar, he shall bring the live goat:

21 And Aaron shall lay both his hands upon the head of the live goat, and confess over him all the iniquities of the children of Israel, and all their transgressions in all their sins, putting them upon the head of the goat, and shall send him away by the hand of a fit man into the wilderness:

The Scapegoat was a picture of our Lord bearing our sins

into the Wilderness to be tempted forty days by the Devil.

22 And the goat shall bear upon him all the iniquities unto a land not inhabited: and he shall let go the goat in the wilderness.

23 And Aaron shall come into the tabernacle of the congregation, and shall put off the linen garments, which he put on when he went into the holy place, and shall leave them there.

After Aaron offered the Sin Offering for himself and the people, he then offered the Burnt Offering for himself and for the people. The Burnt Offering was a way of thanking God for the forgiveness of their sins. Together with the Burnt Offering, he offered the essential organs of the Sin offerings upon the Burnt Altar. Then the bodies of the Bullock and the goat were carried outside the camp where they were burnt. One would have thought that the person who burned the bodies of the sin offerings was doing a great service. But even by burning the bodies of the Sin Offerings he became somewhat contaminated by sin: he had to bathe himself and remain outside the camp for some time before joining the congregation. It means that God does not see sin the way man sees it. It is the one thing that causes disharmony in the Universe. And one day it will be finally wiped away from the face of the Universe, not by God's omnipotence but by the Atonement of Jesus Christ; due process of time is needed.

24 And he shall wash his flesh with water in the holy place, and put on his garments, and come forth, and offer his burnt offering, and the burnt offering of the people, and make an atonement for himself, and for the people.

25 And the fat of the sin offering shall he burn upon the altar.

26 And he that let go the goat for the scapegoat shall wash his clothes, and bathe his flesh in water, and afterward come into the camp.

27 And the bullock for the sin offering, and the goat for

the Sin Offering, whose blood was brought in to make Atonement in the holy place, shall one carry forth without the camp; and they shall burn in the fire their skins and their flesh, and their dung.

28 And he that burns them shall wash his clothes, and bathe his flesh in water, and afterward he shall come into the camp.

Time of Atonement, Lev. 16:29-34

29 And this shall be a statute forever unto you: that in the seventh month, October, (counting from April) on the tenth day of the month, ye shall afflict your souls, and do no work at all, whether it be one of your own country, or a stranger that sojourns among you:

30 For on that day shall the priest make an atonement for you, to cleanse you, that ye may be clean from all your sins before the Lord.

31 It shall be a Sabbath of rest unto you, and ye shall afflict your souls, by a statute forever.

The Day of Atonement was not to be seen through the eye of the Law as a time of jubilee; It was a time to consider the destructive nature of sin and the true meaning of Atonement. As long as human nature did not change, there was the need for Atonement. How thankful we are as Christians to know that Christ's one Atonement is sufficient for time and eternity: He does not have to offer Himself twice for us.

32 And the priest whom he shall anoint, and whom he shall consecrate to minister in the priest's office in his father's stead, shall make the atonement, and shall put on the linen clothes, even the holy garments:

33 And he shall make an atonement for the holy sanctuary, and he shall make an atonement for the tabernacle of the congregation, and for the altar, and he shall make an atonement for the priests, and for all the people of the congregation.

34 And this shall be an everlasting statute unto you, to make an atonement for the children of Israel for all their sins once a year. And he did as the Lord commanded Moses.

For Israel, the Day of Atonement was everlasting in the sense that under the Law they had no other choice. But then came the Grace Age which brought an end to the Law Age and ended all the offerings of Atonement and replaced them with the **one Atonement of Christ Himself** *on behalf of all mankind.*

Guide Lines for Sacrifices, Lev. 17:

There were two main guide lines for Israel to follow in their offerings: all offerings were to be offered by the priest, and the blood of animals should not be eaten.

Strange Offerings Forbidden, 17:1-9:

1 And the Lord spoke unto Moses saying,

2 Speak unto Aaron, and unto his sons, and unto all the children of Israel, and say unto them; This is the thing which the Lord hath commanded, saying,

3 Whatever man there be of the house of Israel, that kills an ox, or a lamb, or a goat, in the camp, or that kills it out of the camp,

4 And brings it not unto the door of the tabernacle of the congregation, to offer an offering unto the Lord before the tabernacle of the Lord; blood shall be imputed unto that man; he hath shed blood; and that man shall be cut off from among his people:

There were to be no local priests, or self-appointed priests. Strict compliance to the laws of the offerings of Atonement was required. The Tabernacle and its vessels were made for purpose of sacrifices unto the Lord. There was a time when the patriarchs offered sacrifices to the Lord; as they were permitted to do that. At that time there was no Tabernacle, and a high priest.

5 To the end that the children of Israel may bring their

sacrifices, which they offer in the open field, even that they may bring them unto the Lord, unto the door of the tabernacle of the congregation, unto the priest, and offer them for peace offerings unto the Lord.

6 And the priest shall sprinkle the blood upon the altar of the Lord at the door of the tabernacle of the congregation, and burn the fat for a sweet savor unto the Lord.

The Peace Offering was voluntary, but there was a danger associated with it when people offered it themselves. And if there was a danger, it was important to prevent it. Other nations offered peace sacrifices, but they offered them unto devils.

7 And they shall no more offer their sacrifices unto devils, after whom they have gone a-whoring. This shall be a statute forever unto them throughout their generations.

8 And thou shalt say unto them, What-so-ever man there be of the house of Israel, or of the strangers which sojourn among you, that offer a burnt offering or sacrifice,

9 And bring it not unto the door of the tabernacle of the congregation, to offer it unto the Lord; even that man shall be cut off from among his people.

The penalty of death for not bringing the sacrifices unto the priest was to prevent idolatry among the children of Israel.

Blood Forbidden to be Eaten, Lev. 17:10-16:

10 And whatsoever man there be of the house of Israel, or of the stranger that sojourn among you, that eats any manner of blood; I will even set my face against that soul that eats blood, and will cut him off from among his people.

11 For the life of the flesh is in the blood: and I have given it to you upon the altar to make an atonement for your souls: for it is the blood that makes an atonement for the soul.

The blood of the innocent animal was sacred to God

because it made Atonement for the soul. It should only be used for that holy purpose. Eating it as food would make it second-place, and thus would lose its sacred value. The penalty of death was to prevent the unholy use.

12 Therefore I said to the children of Israel, No soul of you shall eat blood, neither shall any stranger that sojourns among you eat blood.

13 And whatsoever man there be of the children of Israel, or of the strangers that sojourn among you, which hunt and catch any beast or fowl that may be eaten; he shall even pour out the blood thereof, and cover it with dust.

14 For it is the life of all flesh; the blood of it is for the life thereof: therefore I said to the children of Israel, Ye shall eat the blood of no manner of flesh: for the life of all flesh is the blood thereof: whosoever eats it shall be cut off.

15 And every soul that eats that which died of itself, or that which was torn with beasts, whether it be of your own country, or a stranger, he shall both wash his clothes, and bathe himself in water, and be unclean until the evening: then shall he be clean.

16 But if he wash them not, nor bathe his flesh; then he shall bear his iniquity.

SUMMARY

The Day of Atonement shows how holy God is and how holy His people can be and ought to be. But first, sin must be recognized for what it is, and God's love and mercy cannot be taken for granted. The secret of being holy is not by knowing but, by obeying God's commandments. The Day of Atonement was a spiritually historic moment for the Children of Israel: a time of Atonement for the High Priest, the congregation, the Holy of Holies, and the Sanctuary.

The offering of Atonement for the High Priest was a young bullock which was killed before the door of the Tabernacle and its blood was brought into the Tabernacle and the Holy of Holies by Aaron the High Priest. The blood was placed upon the horns of the Golden Incense Altar and sprinkled seven times upon the Mercy Seat. Aaron took a censor of burning coal from off the Golden Incense Altar and some sweet incense which he burned in the Holy of Holies before the Mercy Seat. The cloud of God's presence was already above the Mercy Seat. The Cloud from the burning incense came between Aaron and the cloud of God's abiding presence, so that he did not die. Even in the Holy of Holies the place of mercy, there was a distinction made between the Holy God and the holy Priest.

Aaron then offered the Atonement offering for the congregation. At the consecration of the Tabernacle when it was erected a bullock was offered as the Sin offering of the congregation. Look back on the chart of the offerings on pages 266-270 and Leviticus 4:13-21. On the Day of Atonement, two goats were required for the Sin Offering and a ram for the Burnt Offering. Of the two goats, only one was killed for the Sin Offering and it was offered in the same manner as the bullock of Aaron's offering. Its blood was taken into the Tabernacle and into the Holy of Holies. Aaron put its blood upon the horns of the Golden Incense Altar and sprinkled it seven times before the Mercy Seat. Over the Scapegoat, the other goat, Aaron confessed the sins of the Children of Israel and let it go into the wilderness.

A ram for Aaron's Burnt Offering was required, and also a ram for the Burnt Offering for the congregation. Aaron offered these two offerings. The whole bodies of the Burnt offerings were offered upon the Burnt Altar; the bodies of the Sin Offerings were carried without the camp and burned.

The sprinkling of the blood of the Sin Offering upon the horns of the Golden Incense Altar and its sprinkling upon the Mercy Seat was the atonement made for the holy place and the Tabernacle. The physical presence of any one was not allowed in the Tabernacle while Aaron was making the atonement. An act as simple and harmless as that would completely undo the purpose of the Atonement Aaron was making.

In making an Atonement for the Burnt Altar, Aaron sprinkled the blood of the bullock and the blood of the goat seven times each upon the Burnt Altar. That was sufficient for the Atonement of the Burnt Altar: the blood was already sprinkled upon the Mercy Seat.

The Day of Atonement was not to be seen through the eye of the Law as a time of jubilee; It was a time to consider the destructive nature of sin and the true meaning of Atonement. As long as human nature did not change, there was the need for Atonement. For Israel, the Day of Atonement was everlasting in the sense that under the Law they had no other choice. But then came the Grace Age which brought an end to the Law Age and ended all the offerings of Atonement and replaced them with the **one Atonement of Christ Himself** on behalf of all mankind.

How thankful we are as Christians to know that Christ's one Atonement is sufficient for time and eternity: He does not have to offer Himself twice for us.

CHAPTER 14

Principles of Righteous Living, Leviticus 19

Principles of righteous living enable God's people to live righteously. These principles must be understood and faithfully obeyed. Man cannot find his way back to God; God finds him, and he must be willing to follow God's direction. But God does not lead His people blindly: He shows them the consequences that would follow if they chose not to follow His direction, He gives them a choice. Choice is not difficult to make but people quite often make the wrong choice. The principles herein stated are intended for Israel to make the right choice. These principles are based on the Ten Commandments. They asked Israel to love God and their fellowmen.

Principles of Righteous Living, Lev. 19

1 And the Lord spoke unto Moses, saying,

2 Speak unto all the congregation of the children of Israel and say unto them, Ye shall be holy: for I the Lord your God I am holy. *By the Atonement under the Law, the Children of Israel were to be holy*

3 Ye shall fear every man his mother, and his father, and keep my Sabbaths: I am the Lord your God.

Honoring one's parents is the right way of living; forsaking idols is a way of pleasing God.

4 Turn ye not unto idols, nor make to yourselves molten gods: I am the Lord your God.

Sacrifice of Peace Offering, Lev. 19:5-8:

5 And if ye offer a sacrifice of peace offering unto the Lord, ye shall offer it at your own will.

When the guilty conscience is freed from sin by Atonement, one has peace with God, and willingly offers a Peace Offering to express his gratitude to God. The Kidneys and the fat of the Peace Offering were offered unto the Lord upon the Burnt Altar. The Wave Breast and the Heave shoulder were the priest's portion of the Peace Offering and were to be eaten in the holy place. The message here to the congregation was that the rest of the Peace offering belonged to the person on whose behalf it was made. Preferably it should all be eaten the first day it was offered. No portion of it should remain until the third day. No strangers should eat of the Peace Offering (Leviticus 22:10-13). For this Peace Offering to serve its purpose, this directive had to be followed.

6 It shall be eaten the same day ye offer it, and on the morrow: and if aught remain until the third day, it shalt be burnt in the fire.

7 And if it be eaten at all on the third day, it is abominable; it shall not be accepted.

8 Therefore every one that eats it shall bear his iniquity, because he hath profaned the hallowed thing of the Lord: and that soul shall be cut off from his people.

Harvesting, Lev. 19:9-10:

Harvesting is a time of joy for the sower when the labor of sowing is forgotten; it is a time of enjoying the fruits of labor, a time of reaping everything possible. That is the time to stop and think about others, the poor, and leave something behind as an act of kindness.

9 And when ye reap the harvest of your land, thou shalt not wholly reap the corners of thy field, neither shalt thou gather the gleanings of thy harvest.

10 And thou shalt not glean thy vineyard, neither shalt

thou gather every grape of thy vineyard; thou shalt leave them for the poor and stranger: I am the Lord your God.

1. Honesty, verse 11:

Five of the Ten Commandments are about loving one's neighbor. Dealing honestly with one's neighbor is to love one's neighbor.

11 Ye shall not steal, neither deal falsely, neither lie one to another.

2. Reverence the Lord's name, verse 12:

God is holy, His name is holy; great wonders are done in His name. His name must be exalted.

12 And ye shall not swear by my name falsely, neither shalt thou profane the name of thy God: I am the Lord.

3. Honest Wages verse 13:

The laborer has spent some of his life in earning his wages. Under no circumstances, should his efforts be taken lightly, He is to be compensated promptly.

Thou shalt not defraud thy neighbor, neither rob him: the wages of him that is hired shall not abide with thee all night until the morning.

4. Cursing, verse 14:

14 Thou shalt not curse the deaf, nor put a stumbling-block before the blind, but thou shalt fear thy God: I am the Lord.

When tempted to be unkind to the deaf and the blind, one should put oneself in their place. If you did, certainly you would not want what you did to be done to you.

5. Equal Respect for Everyone, verse 15:

Ye shall do no unrighteousness in judgment: thou shalt not respect the person of the poor, nor honor the person of the mighty: but in righteousness shalt thou judge thy neighbor.

Equal respect must be shown to every one because every one was made in the image and likeness of God.

6. Being a Peace Maker, verse 16:

Thou shalt not go up and down as a talebearer among thy people: neither shalt thou stand against the blood of thy neighbor: I am the Lord.

One can find better use of one's time than making mischief among brethren.

7. Learn to Love Your Neighbor, verses 17-18:

Thou shalt not hate thy brother in thine heart: thou shalt in any wise rebuke thy neighbor, and not suffer sin upon him.

Thou shalt not avenge, nor bear any grudge against the children of thy people, but thou shalt love thy neighbor as thyself: I am the Lord.

Do not think at any time to do evil to your neighbor. Try to help him with whatever problem he may have.

8. Recognize Distinctions, verse 19:

Ye shall keep my statutes. Thou shalt not let thy cattle gender with a diverse kind: thou shalt not sow thy field with mingled seed: neither shall a garment mingled of linen and woolen come upon thee.

The other nations did those things; Israel should not follow their bad examples. The order in God's creation should remain intact. God created things the way they ought to be.

9. Respect for Your Maidservant, verses 20-22:

And whosoever lies carnally with a woman, that is a bondmaid, betrothed to a husband, and not at all redeemed, nor freedom given her; she shall be scourged; they shall not be put to death because she was not free.

21 And he shall bring his trespass offering unto the Lord, unto the door of the tabernacle of the congregation, even a ram for a trespass offering.

22 And the priest shall make an atonement for him with the ram of the trespass offering before the Lord for his sin which he hath done: and the sin which he hath done shall be forgiven him.

Lying carnally with a maidservant was something done in

the dark that came to light. It was not a righteous act, and a ram for the Trespass Offering had to be offered.

10. Uncircumcised Fruits, verses23-25:

23 And when ye shall come into the land, and shall have planted all manner of trees for food, then ye shall count the fruit thereof as uncircumcised: three years shall it be as uncircumcised unto you: it shall not be eaten of.

24 But in the fourth year all the fruit thereof shall be holy to praise the Lord withal.

25 And in the fifth year shall ye eat of the fruit thereof, that it may yield unto you the increase thereof: I am the Lord your God.

It would take three full years for the fruits of the newly planted trees to be cleansed, and another year before those fruits would become holy. In that fourth year those fruits should not be eaten: they should remain un-harvested in that way God would be honored. The fifth year was to be the time for Israel to enjoy the fruits of their labor.

11. Other Things to Consider, verses 26-37:

26 Ye shall not eat anything with blood: neither shall ye use enchantments, nor observe times.

Blood is sacred because it is that which makes Atonement for the soul. Eating it makes it second place. Using enchantments will make life harder for one because it will get one connected to the dark world where one becomes less dependent on God. Obedience to God's word will prevent unnecessary problems.

27 Ye shall not round the corners of your heads, neither shalt thou mar the corners of thy beard.

28 Ye shall not make any cuttings in thy flesh for the dead, or print any marks upon you: I am the Lord.

All those things the heathen do; appreciate your natural beauty.

29 Do not prostitute thy daughter to cause her to be a whore; lest the land fall to whoredom, and the land become

full of wickedness.

"Train a child in the way he should go, and when he is old he will not depart from it"

30 Ye shall keep my Sabbaths, and reverence my sanctuary: I am the Lord.

31 Regard not them that hath familiar spirits, neither seek after wizards, to be defiled by them: I am the Lord your God.

32 Thou shalt rise up before the hoary head, and honor the face of the old man, and fear thy God: I am the Lord.

Show respect to people who are your seniors. If you respect your parents, you should also respect old people.

33 And if a stranger sojourn with thee in your land, ye shall not vex him.

34 But the stranger that dwells with you shall be unto you as one born among you, and thou shalt love him as thyself; for ye were strangers in the land of Egypt: I am the Lord your God.

35 Ye shall do no unrighteousness in judgment, in meteyard, in weight, or in measure.

36 Just balances, just weights, a just ephah, and a just hin, shall ye have: I am the Lord your God, which brought you out of the land of Egypt.

Honesty is required in all your business dealings. If you were at the other end of the business, you would have appreciated honesty.

37 Therefore shall ye observe all my statutes, and all my judgments, and do them: I am the Lord.

SUMMARY

God's purpose in His relationship with Israel was that they be holy. They would become holy if they faithfully followed the principles of righteousness which He gave them. These principles had to do with loving God and loving their fellowmen. The Atonement under the Law was to free them from the guilt of sin. The sense of Atonement led to the offering of the Peace Offering which was a means of expressing gratitude to God. The kidneys and the fat of the Peace Offering were offered unto the Lord upon the Burnt Altar. The Wave Breast and the Heave shoulder were the priest's portion and were to be eaten in the holy place. Preferably it should all be eaten the first day it was offered. No portion of it should remain until the third day. For this Peace Offering to serve its purpose, this directive had to be followed.

When harvesting their crops, they should leave some of it behind for the poor. After planting their fruit trees in the land of Canaan, they should allow four years to pass before eating of the fruits of their labor. The fourth year after planting, the fruits would be holy and should be left un-harvested. In that way God would be honored. Not until the fifth year should they begin to enjoy the fruits of their labor.

Five of the Ten Commandments have to do with loving one's neighbor. For that reason much emphasis was placed on principles of loving one's neighbor.

Understanding the statutes and judgments of God was important, but doing them was more important. It was in doing them that holiness was acquired. God would not ask Israel to be holy if it was not possible.

CHAPTER 15

The Social Compact with The Priests, Leviticus 21-22

The Social Compact with the priests brought a new realization of holiness to reality. The priests were consecrated to be mediators between God and the people by offering the offerings of Atonement unto God on their behalf. For this reason, they were to be examples to the people. Accordingly, the Social Compact had to reflect that reality. The priests were subject to the Social Compact with the people, but the Social Compact with the priests did not apply to the people. Notwithstanding, these two compacts pointed in the direction of holiness. Another way to see the Social Compact with the priests is that it was an extension of the Social Compact with the congregation. Therefore, there was an obvious difference in the volume of details between the two social compacts. However, they were both stated in a manner that they could not be misunderstood.

The priests were not allowed to do certain things; and the qualification for the priesthood, among other things, was established.

Be not Be Defiled for the Dead, Lev. 21:1-4:

1 And the Lord said unto Moses, Speak unto the priests the sons of Aaron, and say unto them, There shall none be defiled for the dead among his people: *Heretofore we did not know that a person could be defiled by the dead.*

353

2 But for his kin, that is near unto him, that is for his mother, and for his father, and for his son, and for his daughter, and for his brother,

3 And for his sister a virgin, that is nigh unto him, which hath had no husband; for her may he be defiled.

4 But he shall not defile himself, being a chief man among his people, to profane himself.

The above verses applied not to the High Priest but to the associate priests, his sons. They were not to go to any extremities in expressing their sorrow, or even following some of the normal customs relating to the dead. Furthermore they were to limit their participation to only the closest family members.

Some of the things that mourners did, were:

5 They shall not make baldness upon their head, neither shall shave off the corner of their beard, nor make any cuttings in their flesh.

6 They shall be holy unto their God, and not profane the name of their God: for the offerings of the Lord made by fire, and the bread of their God, they do offer: therefore they shall be holy.

To do those things as priests would defile them. They were also to be an example in the selection of a wife. The daughter of the priest should be an example to other wives in her moral conduct, so that the priesthood would be free from reproach. The severest penalty was attached to such immoral conduct.

Selection of a Wife, Lev. 21:7-15:

7 They shall not take a wife that is a whore, or profane; neither shall they take a woman put away from her husband: for he is holy unto his God.

8 Thou shalt sanctify him therefore; for he offers the bread of thy God: he shall be holy unto thee: for I the Lord which sanctify you, am holy.

9 And the daughter of any priest, if she profane herself

by playing the whore, she profanes her father: she shall be burnt with fire.

The high priest was held to a higher standard than the associate priest. He could not participate in the mourning of any of his family members.

The High Priest, Lev. 21:10-15:

10 And he that is the high priest among his brethren, upon whose head the anointing oil was poured, and that is consecrated to put on the garments, shall not uncover his head, nor rend his clothes;

11 Neither shall he go in to any dead body, nor defile himself for his father, nor for his mother;

12 Neither shall he go out of the sanctuary, nor profane the sanctuary of his God; for the crown of the anointing oil of his God is upon him: I am the Lord.

13 And he shall take a wife in her virginity.

14 A widow, or a divorced woman, or profane, or an harlot, these shall he not take: but he shall take a virgin of his own people to wife.

15 Neither shall he profane his seed among his people: for I the Lord do sanctify him.

The holy anointing of the High Priest symbolized Divine authority and empowerment. It distinguished him from the associate priests and from every member of the congregation. It meant he was no more ordinary, and was not expected to act as the ordinary person. Everything about him had to be different; he could not participate in the custom of mourning. He could not go near the body of a dead son or daughter. To do so would defile the Sanctuary; and he had to marry a virgin from the tribe of Levi. To whom much is given, much more is expected.

Deformity Forbidden, Lev. 21:16-24:

All kinds of deformity were barred from the priesthood;

once the son of a priest had any kind of deformity, great or small, he was disqualified from the priesthood. If someone had any kind of deformity, he did not want it, neither did he choose it. Yet he could not even officiate in any way in the offerings of the sacrifices, neither for himself nor on behalf of others.

All have inherited a sin nature, and a physical impairment of any kind is a strong reminder of that fact. God did not want to be reminded of that fact by having a person with physical deformity offering His holy offerings unto Him. God was so angry about the fact of sin that such person needed to stay as far as possible from His holy offerings. That did not mean that He did not equally love such person. But He needed to show the difference between what the physical deformity represented and what the offerings represented. The symbolism here is what is important. Deformity is identified with the Fall and is a reminder of sin. God created Adam with a perfect body. At every opportunity, God emphasizes the gulf between sin and holiness and everything that bears the mark of sin. He will one day remove every trace of sin from the Universe. This was the message of keeping any physically impaired person from offering the holy offerings unto Him.

16 And the Lord spoke unto Moses saying,

17 Speak unto Aaron, saying, Whosoever he be of thy seed in their generations that hath any blemish, let him not approach to offer the bread of his God.

18 For whosoever man he be that hath a blemish, he shall not approach: a blind man, or a lame, or he that hath a flat nose, or anything superfluous,

19 Or a man that is broken footed, or broken handed,

20 Or crookbacked, or a dwarf, or that hath a blemish in his eye, or be scurvy, or scabbed, or hath his stones broken;

21 No man that hath a blemish of the seed of Aaron the priest shall come nigh to offer the offerings of the Lord made by fire: he hath a blemish; he shall not come nigh to offer the

bread of his God.

Though the physically impaired was barred from the priesthood, God showed His love to him by allowing him to eat of the holy things, those things that were due to the family of the priest by virtue of his service.

22 He shall eat the bread of his God, both of the most holy, and of the holy.

23 Only he shall not go in unto the veil; nor come nigh unto the altar, because he hath a blemish; that he profane not the sanctuaries: for I the Lord do sanctify them.

24 And Moses told it unto Aaron, and to his sons, and unto all the children of Israel.

Cleanliness Required Serving the Holy Things, 22:1-9:

More and more, we are seeing why the Wilderness Experience was so important to Israel. It provided them the time and place for them to learn about God's holy nature and how they too could become holy. There were many issues of a sociobiological nature that could defile a priest and prevent him ready access to the holy Sanctuary and the holy things. The priests were not allowed to think that those issues could be blended with the holy things: they had to separate them and keep them apart on a daily basis.

Being God's people brought a new realization of what it really meant to be God's people. They put God first and above selfish desires.

1 And the Lord spoke unto Moses, saying,

2 Speak unto Aaron and his sons, that they separate themselves from the holy things of the children of Israel, and that they profane not my holy name in those things which they hallow unto to me: I am the Lord.

3 Say unto them, Whosoever he be of all your seed among your generations, that goes unto the holy things, which the children of Israel hallow unto the Lord, having his uncleanness upon him, that soul shall be cut off from my presence:

I am the Lord.

Uncleanliness was a serious issue and it could cause death to the priest. And He could not eat of the holy things until he was clean. Some of the issues of uncleanliness required mere washing; others required both healing and washing. Because God was dwelling among them they had to be clean. As a human instinct, cleanliness should be developed.

4 What man so ever of the seed of Aaron is a leper, or hath a running issue; he shall not eat of the holy things, until he be clean. And whoso touches anything that is unclean by the dead, or a man whose seed goes from him;

5 Or whosoever touches any creeping thing, whereby he may be made unclean, or a man of whom he may take uncleanness, whatsoever uncleanness he hath;

6 The soul which hath touched any such thing shall be unclean until even, and shall not eat of the holy things, unless he wash his flesh with water.

7 And when the sun is down, he shall be clean, and shall afterward eat of the holy things; because it is his food.

8 That which dies of itself or is torn with beasts, he shall not eat to defile himself therewith: I am the Lord.

9 They shall therefore keep mine ordinance, lest they bear sin for it, and die thereof, if they profane it: I the Lord do sanctify them.

Strangers Forbidden to Eat of the Holy Things, 22:10-13

10 There shall no stranger eat of the holy thing: a sojourner of the priest, or an hired servant, shall not eat of the holy thing.

11 But if the priest buy any soul with his money, he shall eat of it, and he that is born in his house: they shall eat of his meat.

12 If the priest daughter also be married unto a stranger, she may not eat of an offering of the holy things.

13 But if the priest's daughter be a widow, or divorced, and have no child, and is returned unto her father's house, as in her youth, she shall eat of her father's meat: but there shall no stranger eat thereof.

Strangers were not allowed to eat of the holy things. The priest's daughter would become a stranger by marrying a stranger and would not be allowed to eat of the holy things of her father.

In Israel's Theocracy religion and culture were intertwined; one had to understand from a religious aspect why things were eaten and why things were regarded holy. Strangers did not have such knowledge and they were not allowed to eat such things ignorantly.

14 And if a man eat of the holy thing unwittingly, then he shall put the fifth part thereof unto it, and shall give it unto the priest with the holy thing.

15 And they shall not profane the holy things of the children of Israel, which they offer unto the Lord;

16 Or suffer them to bear the iniquity of trespass, when they eat their holy things: for I the Lord do sanctify them.

Freewill Offerings, Lev. 22:17-25:

Freewill offerings were sometimes offered with the vows people made unto the Lord; vows were also voluntary. The offering of preference with regards to vows was the Peace Offering. The animal of the Peace Offering offered with a vow had to be blemish-less. The freewill Burnt Offering did not have to be perfect.

17 And the Lord spoke unto Moses, saying,

18 Speak unto Aaron and to his sons, and unto all the children of Israel, and say unto them, Whatsoever he be of the house of Israel, or of the strangers in Israel, that will offer his oblation for all his vows, and for all his freewill offerings, which they will offer unto the Lord for a burnt offering; Ye shall offer at your own will a male without

blemish of the beeves, of the sheep, or of the goats.

20 But whatsoever hath a blemish, that shall ye not offer: for it shall not be acceptable for you.

21 And whosoever offers a sacrifice of peace offerings unto the Lord to accomplish his vow, or a freewill offering in beeves or sheep, it shall be perfect to be accepted; there shall be no blemish therein.

22 Blind, or broken, or maimed, or having a wen, or scurvy, or scabbed, ye shall not offer these unto the Lord, nor make an offering by fire of them upon the altar unto the Lord.

The Distinction between the offering of the Vow and the Freewill Burnt Offering verse 23:

23 Either a bullock or a lamb that hath anything superfluous or lacking in his parts, that you may offer for a freewill offering; but for a vow, it shall not be accepted.

24 Ye shall not offer unto the Lord that which is bruised, or crushed, or broken, or cut; neither shall ye make any offering thereof in your land.

25 Neither from a stranger's hand shall ye offer the bread of thy God of any of these; because their corruption is in them, and blemishes be in them: they shall not be accepted for you.

Waiting Period for Offerings, Lev. 22:26-28:

26 And the Lord spoke unto Moses, saying,

27 When a bullock, or a sheep, or a goat is brought forth, then it shall be seven days under the dam; and from the eighth day and thenceforth it shall be accepted for an offering made by fire unto the Lord.

28 And whether it be cow or ewe, ye shall not kill it and her young both in one day.

Verse 27 does not seem to indicate the age of the animal of sacrifice, but the time that should be allowed between the mother and her calf before they both could be sacrificed.

29 And when ye will offer a sacrifice of thanksgiving unto the Lord, offer it at your own will.

The word "thanksgiving" implies freewill because if someone were ordered to give God thanks, that would not have been thanksgiving.

30 On the same day it shall be eaten up; ye shall leave none of it until the morrow: I am the Lord.

31 Therefore shall ye keep my commandments, and do them: I am the Lord.

32 Neither shall ye profane my holy name; but I will be hallowed among the children of Israel: I am the Lord which hallow you,

33 That brought you out of the land of Egypt, to be your God: I am the Lord.

SUMMARY

The Social Compact with the priests helped them to live up to the High Calling of God and to lead Israel to spiritual growth in their relationship with God. It was better to be instructed a head of the consequences which could have resulted from their lack of knowledge of those sociobiological issues that could have defiled them; and being defiled, could have in turn defiled the holy things of God.

The elaborate consecration of the High Priest indicated the enormous weight of the spiritual responsibility with which he was entrusted. His holy anointing symbolized Divine authority and empowerment to fulfill the awesome responsibility of his office. He had to realize that he was no longer ordinary and was not expected to act as the ordinary person he once was. Everything about him had to be different. He could not participate in the custom of mourning for his own son or daughter. He had to be meticulous in the selection of a wife. He had to guard against the participation of strangers in eating of the holy things. Without the Social

Compact he would be ignorant of his responsibility.

There was the issue of deformity which disqualified the son of a priest from the priesthood. Any physical impairment, great or small, made one unfit for the priesthood. The physical standard of qualification did not mean that God did not equally love that person. But He needed to show the difference between what the physical deformity represented and what the offerings represented. This was the message of keeping any physically impaired person from offering the holy offerings unto Him.

The preference of the Peace Offering when a vow was made unto the Lord was important. Freewill offerings were sometimes offered with the vows people made unto the Lord; vows were also voluntary. The animal of the Peace Offering offered with a vow had to be blemish-less. Other freewill offerings were offered as Burnt Offerings. With the Burnt Offering, perfection was not required.

The conclusion is that the Social Compact shows a God whose love and tender mercies are beyond our capacity to fully understand.

CHAPTER 16
The Yearly Feasts, Leviticus 23 -24

The feasts of the Lord marked the most important events in the life of the Nation of Israel. They were the expressions of joy and gratitude unto the Lord for all that He meant to them. The idea of these feasts of celebration came from God and became a part of the Law. They were to be held at certain times of the year and different offerings were designated to them. Though the Day of Atonement was not of the true nature of a feast, it was, however, designated a feast, making a number of seven yearly memorial events.

The question is not, Which was the most important? It is not even for us to decide. Each of these feasts had its own uniqueness and beauty. And since it is human nature to be attracted to beauty, you may be attracted to some of these feasts more than the others.

We shall look at them in the order they are stated in Leviticus 23.

1. The Lord's Passover, Lev. 23:1-5:

1 And the Lord spoke unto Moses, saying,

2 Speak unto the children of Israel, and say unto them, Concerning the feasts of the Lord, which ye shall proclaim to be holy convocations, even these are my feasts.

3 Six days shall work be done: but the seventh day is the Sabbath of rest, an holy convocation; ye shall do no work therein: it is the Sabbath of the Lord in all your dwellings.

4 These are the feasts of the Lord, even holy convocations which ye shall proclaim in their seasons.

5 In the fourteenth day of the first month, Abib, at even is the Lord's Passover.

The Passover marks the birth of the nation. When all the other signs and wonders failed to secure the deliverance of Israel from the bondage of Pharaoh, the miracle of the Passover succeeded. With the first sign of the serpent and the sign of Moses' leprous hand, there were 12 signs altogether. These 12 signs symbolized the 12 tribes of Israel.

The Passover was killed on the fourteenth day of Abib, at noon. Not one bone of it was to be broken; no stranger was allowed to eat of it. It was to be an exclusive Jewish celebration. This miracle had to be taught from generation to generation; one way was by memorializing it in the first feast of the Jewish Year. As important as the Passover was, the Lord reminded them to remember to keep the Sabbath Day holy.

Immediately following the Passover is the Feast of Unleavened Bread.

2. The Feast of Unleavened Bread, Lev. 23:6-8

6 And on the fifteenth day of the same month is the feast of unleavened bread unto the Lord: seven days ye must eat unleavened bread.

7 In the first day ye shall have an holy convocation: ye shall do no servile work therein.

8 But ye shall offer an offering made by fire unto the Lord seven days: in the seventh day is an holy convocation: ye shall do no servile work therein.

On the first of Abib, I imagine, the children of Israel began looking to see if they had any leaven in their houses to remove it because the Feast of Unleavened Bread was near. The Feast of Unleavened Bread meant that people could not put any leaven in their bread during the seven days of the feast. The feast began with a call to worship and on the last day there was another call to worship.

Each day of the feast a Burnt Offering (offering made by fire) was offered unto the Lord. Although the feast was a time of joy and happiness, it was spiritual. There was spiritual joy from watching the Burnt Offering offered unto the Lord as the whole sacrifice was burnt. The Feast of Unleavened Bread was closely connected to the Passover and was an indication of their new spiritual life as distinguished from their life in bondage in Egypt.

3. The Feast of Harvest, Lev. 23:9-14:
Some of these feasts could not be celebrated in the Wilderness. The Feast of Harvest was one of them. There was much joy in the Feast of Harvest. Isaiah says, "They joy before thee according to the joy in harvest, and as men rejoice when they divide the spoil". (Isaiah 9:3). This feast lasted one day and two offerings were offered.

We know that when Israel first possessed the Promised Land and planted all their fruit trees, they could not reap them until the fifth year. The first three years after planting, the fruits were designated uncircumcised and required that time for cleansing. In the fourth year after planting, the fruits were said to be holy and were to be dedicated to the Lord. They should not be reaped until the fifth year (Leviticus 19:23-25; page, 349). This does not seem to apply to unplanted crops the Children of Israel inherited when they first possessed the land. Verse 10 seems to indicate that the law of Leviticus 19:23-25 does not apply. The Feast of Harvest is also stated in Lev. 23:10-14.The only condition seems to be that before they ever considered eating the fruits, they were to offer a Wave Offering to the Lord of the first fruits on the day after the Sabbath in the land. See page 567.

9 And the Lord spoke unto Moses, saying,

10 Speak unto the children of Israel, and say unto them, When ye come into the land which I give unto you, and shall reap the harvest thereof, then ye shall bring a sheaf of

the first-fruits of your harvest unto the priest:

11 And he shall wave the sheaf before the Lord, to be accepted for you: on the morrow after the Sabbath the priest shall wave it.

The Offerings of the Feast of Harvest, Leviticus 23:12-14:

The Burnt Offering and the Meat offering are here seen as offerings of thanksgiving and gratitude.

12 And ye shall offer that day when ye wave the sheaf an he lamb without blemish of the first year for burnt offering unto the Lord.

13 And the meat offering thereof shall be two tenth deals of fine flour mingled with oil, an offering made by fire unto the Lord for a sweet savor: and the drink offering thereof shall be of wine, the fourth part of an hin.

14 And ye shall eat neither bread, nor parched corn, nor green ears, until the selfsame day that ye have brought an offering unto your God: it shall be a statute forever throughout your generations in all your dwellings.

4. The Feast of Weeks, Pentecost, Leviticus 23:15-22:

The Feast of Weeks is also called Pentecost. It also commemorates the outpouring of the Holy Spirit upon the hundred and twenty Believers on the Day of Pentecost. It is obvious the Feast of Harvest was to be celebrated in the Promised Land. It was to be followed by the Feast of Weeks. Pentecost is said to have occurred 50 days after the Passover.

The Feast of Weeks was to be celebrated fifty days after the first Wave Offering of the first fruits unto the Lord after their possession of the Promised Land. *See page 566.*

15 And ye shall count unto you from the morrow after the Sabbath, from the day that ye brought the sheaf of the wave offering; seven Sabbaths shall be complete:

16 Even unto the morrow after the seventh Sabbath shall ye number fifty days; and ye shall offer a new meat offering unto the Lord.

During the Feast of Weeks or Pentecost, four offerings were offered: the Meat Offering, Burnt Offering, Sin Offering, and the Peace Offering. With the Meat Offering, a Burnt Offering of seven lambs, a bullock, and two rams were offered. The Drink Offering was a part of the Meat Offering. The Sin Offering of a goat, and two lambs for the Peace Offering were offered. The Wave Offering was a part of the Peace Offering by which the priest waved the breast and shoulder of the Peace Offering with the bread of the first fruits. All these offerings were offered during the Feast of Weeks, indicating the spirituality of the feast. It was evident to be a holy gathering. However, the priest proclaimed it a holy convocation (verses 17-21).

17 Ye shall bring out of your habitations two wave loaves of two tenth deals: they shall be of fine flour; they shall be baked with leaven; they are the first unto the Lord.

18 And ye shall offer with the bread seven lambs without blemish of the first year, and one young bullock, and two rams: they shall be for a burnt offering unto the Lord, with their meat offering, and their drink offerings, even an offering made by fire, of sweet savor unto the Lord.

19 Then ye shall sacrifice one kid of the goats for a sin offering, and two lambs of the first year for a sacrifice of peace offerings.

20 And the priest shall wave them with the bread of the first-fruits for a wave offering before the Lord, with the two lambs: they shall be holy to the Lord for the priest.

21 And ye shall proclaim on the selfsame day, that it may be an holy convocation unto you: ye shall do no servile work therein: it shall be a statute forever in all your dwellings throughout your generations.

Israel should not be like the Egyptians; they should show love and kindness to the poor by allowing some of their harvest to remain in the fields.

22 And when ye reap the harvest of your land, thou shalt not make clean riddance of the corners of thy field when you reap, neither shalt thou gather any gleaning of thy harvest: thou shalt leave them unto the poor, and to the stranger: I am the Lord your God.

5. The Feast of Trumpets, Lev. 23:23-25; Numbers 29:1-6

23 And the Lord spoke unto Moses, saying,

24 Speak unto the children of Israel, saying, In the seventh month, October, (counting from April) in the first day of the month, shall ye have a Sabbath, a memorial of blowing of trumpets, an holy convocation.

25 ye shall do no servile work therein: but ye shall offer an offering made by fire unto the Lord.

The Trumpet, like other instruments used in Israel's Theocracy, was a symbol of power through their Covenant with their Invisible King. Besides, there were a number of codes for its usage. These codes were taught to the Congregation. The Feast of Trumpets, therefore, was to be a time of joy, and celebration of victory over adversities.

Numbers 29 is a parallel scripture; it deals with three of the yearly feasts, yet it provides much more information about those three yearly feasts. We shall herein apply that information.

Numbers 29:1-6:

1 And in the seventh month, on the first day of the month, ye shall have an holy convocation; ye shall do no servile work: it is a day of blowing the trumpets unto you.

2 And ye shall offer a burnt offering for a sweet savor unto the Lord; one young bullock, one ram, and seven lambs of the first year without blemish:

3 And their meat offering shall be flour mingled with oil, three tenth deals for a bullock, and two tenth deals for a ram,

4 And one tenth deal for a lamb, throughout the seven

lambs:

5 And one kid of the goats for a sin offering, to make an atonement for you:

6 Beside the Burnt Offering of the month, and his Meat Offering, and the daily Burnt Offering, and his Meat Offering, and their Drink offerings, according to their manner, for a sweet savor, a sacrifice made by fire unto the Lord. This account describes the Burnt Offering; includes the Sin Offering as well as their Meat offerings and Drink offerings. Meat Offerings and Drink offerings were complementary and were offered with other offerings.

6. The Day of Atonement, 23:26-32; Numbers 29:7-11:

The Day of Atonement was more a spiritual feast than literal. It was a time of cleansing and spiritual renewal, a time when the High Priest made an atonement for himself and family, the congregation, the Tabernacle and its instruments. Aaron offered two offerings for himself and family and two offerings for the congregation: a Sin Offering and a Burnt Offering. By putting the blood of the Sin Offering upon the horns of the Golden Incense Altar, upon the Ark of the Covenant, and upon the horns of the Burnt Altar, he atoned for the Holy of Holies, the Sanctuary, and its instruments. The Day of Atonement is fully treated in chapter 13.

26 And the Lord spoke unto Moses, saying,

27 Also on the tenth day of the seventh month there shall be a day of atonement: it shall be an holy convocation unto you; and ye shall afflict your souls, and offer an offering made by fire unto the Lord.

28 And ye shall do no work in that same day: for it is a day of atonement, to make an atonement for you before the Lord your God.

*The Day of Atonement was to be a day of **national repentance.** Not only should the Children of Israel repent of their sins but they should express their repentance in ways* *that everyone could recognize. The death penalty was attached to the Day of Atonement because anyone who did not repent and truly express it would be cut off from among the congregation by God. But as the Day of Atonement had the promise of death, it also had the promise of life and spiritual renewal.*

29 for whatsoever soul it be that shall not be afflicted in that same day, he shall be cut off from among his people.

30 And whatsoever soul it be that doeth any work in that same day, the same soul will I destroy from among his people.

The Day of Atonement was to be a time of rest. This time of rest was to be a recognition that they did not get to where they were by working hard, but by faith in God, which worked miracles for them. Obedience to the Commandments was to be the key to their spiritual success and every other success.

The national repentance was to begin from 6'o clock of the previous day to 6'o clock of the Day of Atonement. If anyone was serious about repenting, that was enough time.

31 Ye shall do no manner of work: it shall be a statute forever throughout your generations in all your dwellings.

32 It shall be unto you a Sabbath of rest, and ye shall afflict your souls: in the ninth day of the month at even, from even unto even, shall ye celebrate your Sabbath.

Numbers 29:7-11:

7 And ye shall have on the tenth day of this seventh month an holy convocation; and ye shall afflict your souls: ye shall not do any work therein:

8 But ye shall offer a burnt offering unto the Lord for a sweet savor; one young bullock, one ram, and seven lambs of the first year; they shall be unto you without blemish:

9 And their meat offering shall be flour mingled with oil, three tenth deals to a bullock, and two tenth deals to a ram,

10 A several tenth deal for one lamb, throughout the seven lambs:

11 One kid of the goats for a sin offering; beside the sin offering of Atonement, and the continual burnt offering, and the meat offering of it, and their drink offerings.

This account has more information. Verse 8 shows the sacrifices which were offered as a Burnt Offering. The Meat Offering and the Drink offering were complementary sacrifices and offered with other sacrifices. These sacrifices were in addition to the daily Burnt Offering and its Meat Offering.

7. The Feast of Tabernacles, Lev. 23:33-44; Numbers 29:12-40:

Five days after the Day of Atonement, the Feast of Tabernacles was to be celebrated. Unlike the Day of Atonement, the Feast of Tabernacles was to last for seven days. On the first day the congregation gathered together and the priest offered a Burnt Offering unto the Lord. Each day of the feast, a Burnt Offering was to be offered. The feast ended the eighth day with another offering unto the Lord (verses33-38).

33 And the Lord spoke unto Moses, saying,

34 Speak unto the children of Israel, saying, The fifteenth day of this seventh month shall be the feast of tabernacles for seven days unto the Lord.

35 On the first day shall be an holy convocation: ye shall do no servile work therein.

36 Seven days ye shall offer an offering made by fire unto the Lord: on the eighth day shall be an holy convocation unto you; and ye shall offer an offering made by fire unto the Lord: it is a solemn assembly; and ye shall do no servile work therein.

37 These are the feast of the Lord which ye shall proclaim to be holy convocations, to offer an offering made by fire unto the Lord, a burnt offering, and a meat offering, a sacrifice, and drink offerings, everything upon his day:

38 Beside the Sabbaths of the Lord, and beside your

gifts, and beside all your vows, and beside all your freewill offerings, which ye give unto the Lord.

The feasts required different offerings. Besides, freewill offerings and vows were made. Two of the feasts extended beyond seven days. This would provide time for the freewill offerings, gifts, and vows to be made.

There are two accounts of the Feast of the Tabernacles: one in Leviticus and the other in Numbers. Numbers describes all the offerings during the seven days of feast.

Description of the Feast of Tabernacles, 23:39-44:

The Feast of the Tabernacle was an exclusive Jewish feast. Strangers were not allowed to participate. All the Children of Israel were to dwell in booths seven days to remind future generations that their forefathers lived in booths in the Wilderness after God brought them from the land of Egypt. The Feast of Tabernacles was a time of great joy and rejoicing.

39 Also in the fifteenth day of the seventh month, when ye have gathered in the fruit of the land, ye shall keep a feast unto the Lord seven days: on the first day shall be a Sabbath, and on the eighth day shall be a Sabbath.

40 And ye shall take you on the first day the boughs of goodly trees, branches of palm trees, and the boughs of thick trees, and willows of the brook; and ye shall rejoice before the Lord your God seven days.

41 And ye shall keep it a feast unto the Lord seven days in the year. It shall be a statute forever in your generations: ye shall celebrate it in the seventh month.

42 Ye shall dwell in booths seven days; all that are Israelites born shall dwell in booths.

43 That your generations may know that I made the children of Israel to dwell in booths, when I brought them out of the land of Egypt: I am the Lord your God.

44 And Moses declared unto the children of Israel the

feasts of the Lord.

Numbers Account

Numbers 29:12-40:

12 And on the fifteenth day of the seventh month ye shall have an holy convocation; ye shall do no servile work, and ye shall keep a feast unto the Lord seven days:

13 And ye shall offer a burnt offering, a sacrifice made by fire, a sweet savor unto the Lord; thirteen young bullocks, two rams, and fourteen lambs of the first year; they shall be without blemish:

14 And their meat offering shall be of flour mingled with oil, three tenth deals unto every bullock of the thirteen bullocks, two tenth deals to each ram of the two rams,

15 And a several tenth deal to each lamb of the fourteen lambs:

16 And one kid of the goats for a sin offering; beside the continual burnt offering, his meat offering, and his drink offering.

All these sacrifices were the offerings on the first day of the Feast of the Tabernacles. The continual Burnt Offering was of two lambs offered daily with their Meat offering and Drink Offering. One was offered in the morning and the other was offered in the evening.

17 And on the second day ye shall offer twelve young bullocks, two rams, fourteen lambs of the first year without spot:

18 And their meat offering and their drink offerings for the bullocks, for the rams, and for the lambs, shall be according to their number, after the manner:

19 And one kid of the goats for a sin offering; be the continual burnt offering, and the meat offering thereof, and their drink offerings.

Notice that on the second day there were twelve bullocks

instead of thirteen.

20 And on the third day eleven bullocks, two rams, fourteen lambs of the first year without blemish;

21 And their meat offering and their drink offerings for the bullocks, for the rams, and for the lambs, shall be according to their number, after the manner:

22 And one goat for a sin offering; beside the continual burnt offering, and his meat offering, and his drink offering.

23 And on the fourth day ten bullocks, two rams, and fourteen lambs of the first year without blemish:

24 Their meat offering and their drink offerings for the bullocks, for the rams, and for the lambs, shall be according to their number, after the manner:

25 And one kid of the goats for a sin offering; beside the continual burnt offering, his meat offering, and his drink offering.

26 And on the fifth day nine bullocks, two rams, and fourteen lambs of the first year without spot:

27 And their meat offering and their drink offerings for the bullocks, for the rams, and for the lambs, shall be according to their number, after the manner:

28 And one goat for a sin offering; beside the continual burnt offering, and his meat offering, and his drink offering.

29 And on the sixth day eight bullocks, two rams, and fourteen lambs of the first year without blemish:

30 And their meat offering and their drink offerings for the bullocks, for the rams, and for the lambs, shall be according to their number, after the manner:

31 And one goat for a sin offering; beside the continual burnt offering, his meat offering, and his drink offering.

32 And on the seventh day, seven bullocks, two rams and fourteen lambs of the first year without blemish:

33 And their meat offering and their drink offerings for the bullocks, for the rams, and for the lambs, shall be according to their number, after the manner:

34 And one goat for a sin offering; beside the continual burnt offering, his meat offering, and his drink offering.

You will notice on the seventh day the number of bullocks was reduced from 13 to 7. The rams and the lambs remained unchanged.

35 And on the eighth day ye shall have a solemn assembly: ye shall do no servile work therein:

36 But ye shall offer a burnt offering, a sacrifice made by fire, of a sweet savor unto the Lord: one bullock, one ram, seven lambs of the first year without blemish:

37 Their meat offering and their drink offerings for the bullock, for the ram, and for the lambs, shall be according to their number, after the manner:

38 And one goat for a sin offering; beside the continual burnt offering, and his meat offering, and his drink offering.

39 These things ye shall do unto the Lord in your set feasts, beside your vows, and your freewill offerings, for your burnt offerings, and for your meat offerings, and for your drink offerings, and for your peace offerings.

40 And Moses told the children of Israel according to all that the Lord commanded Moses.

The account of Numbers 29 was helpful in understanding what sacrifices that were offered during the feast of the Tabernacles. What may have been the reason? Moses is the author of all three books. He may have received the instructions about the feasts at two different times: at an earlier and at a later time. He recorded everything accurately, and when the appointed time of the feasts came, he applied all the instructions which he received from the Lord. The theme of all three books is the same

Appendage

Leviticus 24 was not connected to the yearly feasts; it is merely treated here to complete the chapter. Leviticus 24 has to do with certain provision for the service of the Tabernacle, the need to reverence the name of the Lord, and social justice.

Provision for the Service of the Tabernacle, Leviticus 24:1-9:

1 And the Lord spoke unto, Moses saying,

2 Command the children of Israel, that they bring unto thee pure oil olive beaten for the light to cause the lamps to burn continually.

In the seven branches of the Candlestick were seven lamps which were to be supplied with pure olive oil for their light. All the material to build the Tabernacle and all the labor were found among the congregation; but all was first given by the Lord. The Golden Candlestick with the lamps was placed near the door of the Tabernacle, south of the Golden Incense Altar. Aaron was to dress the lamps in the mornings and light them in the evenings to provide lights during the nights. The Show Bread was to be made as prescribed below. Undoubtedly, a portion from the Show bread was offered as a Meat Offering unto the Lord.. Two rows of twelve cakes were to be kept always on the Table of the Show Bread daily. They were to be eaten by the priests in the Tabernacle

3 Without the veil of the testimony, in the tabernacle of the congregation, shall Aaron order it from the evening unto the morning before the Lord continually: it shall be a statute forever in your generations

4 Ye shall order the lamps upon the pure candlestick before the Lord continually.

5 And thou shalt take fine flour, and bake twelve cakes thereof: two tenth deals shall be in one cake.

Footnote: The account of Numbers 29 of three of the yearly feasts was useful to the account of Leviticus. It explains the sacrifices offered during those feasts. This explains the importance of reviewing all three books together

6 And thou shalt set them in two rows, six on a row, upon the pure table before the Lord.

7 And thou shalt put pure frankincense upon each row, that it may be on the bread for a memorial, even an offering made by fire unto the Lord.

8 Every Sabbath he shall set it in order before the Lord continually, being taken from the children of Israel by an everlasting covenant.

9 And it shall be Aaron's and his sons; and they shall eat it in the holy place: for it is most holy unto him of the offerings of the Lord made by fire by a perpetual statute.

Penalty for Dishonoring the Lord's Name, Lev. 24:10-16:

The Lord's name is holy; it is not to be used without due respect. One should have a holy purpose for using the Lord's name. To do otherwise was to make it common place. This was disrespectful. Also, to speak disrespectfully of the Lord's name in cursing is the sin of blasphemy. The penalty for blasphemy was death.

10 And the son of an Israelitish woman, whose father was an Egyptian, went out among the children of Israel: and this son of the Israelitish woman and a man of Israel strove together in the camp;

11 And the Israelitish woman's son blasphemed the name of the Lord, and cursed, and they brought him unto Moses: (and his mother's name was Shelomith, the daughter of Dibri, of the tribe of Dan:)

12 And they put him in ward, that the mind of the Lord might be shown them.

When the incidence of the blasphemy was brought to Moses' attention, he inquired of the Lord what to do. God told him to stone the blasphemer to death.

Anger of whatever cause was not an excuse to blaspheme the holy name of the Lord.

13 And the Lord spoke unto Moses, saying,

14 Bring forth him that hath cursed without the camp; and let all that heard him lay their hands upon his head, and let all the congregation stone him.

15 And thou shalt speak unto the children of Israel, saying, Whosoever curses his God shall bear his sin.

16 And he that blasphemes the name of the Lord, he shall surely be put to death, and all the congregation shall certainly stone him: as well as the stranger, as he that is born in the land, when he blasphemes the name of the Lord, shall be put to death.

Equal Justice, Lev. 24:17-23:

The death penalty was established at the beginning of time. In Genesis 9:6, we read, "Whoso sheds man's blood, by man shall his blood be shed: for in the image of God made he man". Equal justice applies in all other areas of human life and is clearly spelled out below.

17 And he that kills any man shall surely be put to death.

18 And he that kills a beast shall make it good; beast for beast.

19 And if a man cause a blemish in his neighbor; as he hath done, so shall it be done unto him;

A cause is said to be greater than its effect but in this case they are equal.

20 Breach for breach, eye for eye, tooth for tooth: as he hath caused a blemish in a man, so shall it be done to him again.

21 And he that kills a beast, he shall restore it: and he that kills a man, he shall be put to death.

22 Ye shall have one manner of law, as well for the stranger, as for one of your own country: for I am the Lord your God.

23 And Moses spoke to the children of Israel, that they should bring forth him that had cursed out of the camp, and

stone him with stones. And the children of Israel did as the Lord commanded Moses.

Moses never questioned any of God's commandments. God cannot make a mistake. His judgments are righteous and holy. Today many look upon the death penalty as cruel and unusual punishment. God's word does not change; neither can anyone be as holy as God. We should follow Moses' example by not questioning God's righteous judgments.

SUMMARY

The feasts of the Lord were times of celebrating special events. These feasts became statutes of the Law, so important they were to Israel. They reflected the gratitude of a nation to their God for His Divine guidance and manifold blessings. It was as though human vocabulary lacked the capacity to express in words the appreciation of a grateful nation; and so instead, the Children of Israel expressed themselves in celebrations of joy and rejoicing. There were seven feasts celebrated by Israel: The Passover, the Feast of Unleavened Bread, the Feast of Harvest, the Feast of Weeks or Pentecost, the Feast of Trumpets, the Day of Atonement, and the Feast of Tabernacles.

The Passover marks the birth of the nation. When all the other signs and wonders failed to secure the deliverance of Israel from the bondage of Pharaoh, the miracle of the Passover succeeded. With the first sign of the serpent and Moses's leprous hand, there were 12 signs altogether. The Passover was killed on the fourteenth day of Abib, at noon. Not one of its bones was to be broken; no stranger was allowed to eat of it. It was to be an exclusive Jewish celebration. This miracle had to be taught from generation to generation; one way was by memorializing it in the first feast of the Jewish Year. (Exodus 12:43-45)

Immediately following the Passover, the Feast of

Unleavened Bread was proclaimed the fifteenth day of the first month, Abib. The Feast of Unleavened Bread meant that people could not put any leaven in their bread during the seven days of the feast. The feast began with a call to worship and on the last day there was another call to worship. Each day of the feast, a Burnt Offering was offered unto the Lord. Although the feast was a time of joy and happiness, it was spiritual.

Some of these feasts could not be celebrated in the Wilderness. The Feast of Harvest was one of them. When Israel first possessed the Promised Land and planted all their fruit trees, they could not reap them until the fifth year. The first three years after planting, the fruits were designated, uncircumcised and required that time for cleansing. In the fourth year after planting, the fruits were said to be holy and were to be dedicated to the Lord. They should not be reaped until the fifth year (Leviticus 19:23-25). This does not seem to apply to unplanted crops the Children of Israel inherited when they first possessed the land. Verse 10 of Leviticus 23 seems to indicate that the law of Leviticus 19:23-25 did not apply. The only condition seems to be that before they ever considered eating the fruits, was to offer a Wave Offering during the Feast of Harvest.

Fifty days from the Feast of Harvest, the Feast of Weeks was to be celebrated. Four offerings were to be offered: a Burnt Offering, a Meat Offering, the Sin Offering, and the Drink Offering. The Feast of the Trumpets was to be celebrated the first day of the seventh month. It was a celebration of victories over adversities: that was their life story. That day the sound of the trumpets was heard everywhere as the Children of Israel rejoiced in the goodness of the Lord. The Sin offering, the Burnt Offering, the Meat Offering, and the Drink offering were offered.

The Day of Atonement was to be celebrated on the tenth day of the Seventh Month. It was more a spiritual feast than literal. It was a time of cleansing and spiritual renewal, a time when the High Priest made an Atonement for himself and family, the congregation, the Tabernacle and its instrument. Aaron offered two offerings for himself and family and two offerings for the congregation: a Sin offering and a Burnt offering.

The Feast of Tabernacles was to be celebrated the fifteenth day of the Seventh Month. It was to last for seven days; all the Children of Israel were to dwell in booths seven days to remind future generations that their forefathers lived in booths in the Wilderness after God brought them from the land of Egypt. The Feast of Tabernacles was a time of great joy and rejoicing. Many sacrifices of Burnt Offering, Meat Offering, Drink Offering, and Sin Offering were offered during each day. The Burnt Offering of 13 bullocks, 2 rams, and 14 lambs was reduced to 7 bullocks the seventh day. The rams and the lambs were not reduced.

These feasts were spiritual and holy and they certainly distinguished Israel from all other nations. However, Israel were not to think themselves superior to other nations.

CHAPTER 17
The Year of Jubilee, Leviticus 25

At the end of the rain there was a rainbow. This is a metaphor for the astounding experiences Israel had during their journey in the Wilderness and what they were expecting to have in the Promised Land. If those experiences were not written in the Bible, I would not have believed any of them; but I know everyone is true, as the Bible is true. Were not some of those experiences paradoxical? Did not some of them reveal God's infinite mercy and love? Did not some of those experiences show the worst and the best in man?

Yet the Year of Jubilee had a very personal message for the poor who had sold their lands and to others who became servants. To them, it meant an end to sorrow and the beginning of a new experience of joy and hope.

The first step toward the Year of Jubilee was the Sabbatical Year.

The Sabbatical Year, Lev. 25:1-7:

Every seventh day was a Sabbath, a day of rest unto the Lord. Every seventh year was to be a year of rest for the land unto the Lord: the Children of Israel were not to work their land. They should not reap their field, everything was to be at rest. However, they all would benefit from the harvest of the Sabbatical Year the following year.

1 And the Lord spoke unto Moses in Mount Sinai, saying,

2 Speak unto the children of Israel, and say unto them, When ye come into the land which I give you, then shall the land keep a Sabbath unto the Lord.

3 Six years thou shalt sow thy field, and six years thou shat prune thy vineyard, and gather in the fruit thereof;

4 But in the seventh year shall be a Sabbath of rest unto the land, a Sabbath for the Lord: thou shalt neither sow thy field, nor prune thine vineyard.

5 That which groweth of its own accord of thy harvest thou shalt not reap, neither gather the grapes of thy vine undressed: for it is a year of rest unto the land.

6 And the Sabbath of the land shall be meat for you; for thee, and for thy servant, and for thy maid, and for thy hired servant, and for thy stranger that sojourns with thee.

7 And for thy cattle, and for the beast that are in thy land, shall all the increase thereof be meat.

Year of Jubilee, Lev. 25:8-55:

The Year of Jubilee fulfilled the hope and dream of all the poor. It was a time of joy for them. This joy began with them but quickly permeated the whole nation because when the poor were relieved of their sorrow, there could only be national Jubilee. On the Day of Atonement its proclamation was made.

The Year of Jubilee was also a year of rest when people were not allowed to sow and reap; yet they would benefit the following year. The liberties gained from the Year of Jubilee are spelled out in verses 13-55. Verses 8-12 describe the year itself.

8 And thou shalt number seven Sabbaths of years unto thee, seven times seven years; and the space of the seven Sabbaths of years shall be unto thee forty and nine years.

9 Then shalt thou cause the trumpet of the Jubilee to sound on the tenth day of the seventh month, in the day of atonement shall ye make the trumpet sound throughout all

your land. *The trumpet was used for different purposes.*

10 And ye shall hallow the fiftieth year, and proclaim liberty throughout all the land unto the inhabitants thereof: it shall be a jubilee unto you; and ye shall return every man unto his possession, and ye shall return every man unto his family.

11 A Jubilee shall that fiftieth year be unto you: ye shall not sow, neither reap that which groweth of itself in it, nor gather the grapes in it of thy vine undressed.

12 For it is the Jubilee; it shall be holy unto you: ye shall eat the increase thereof out of the field.

Blessings of the Jubilee, Lev. 25:13-55:
1. Land Redemption, verses 13-19:

13 In the year of Jubilee ye shall return every man unto his possession.

Verse 13 is an emphatic statement and does not suggest nor imply any conditions for the return of the previously held properties to their rightful owners. Verses 14-19 clearly state the normal land transactions after the Year of Jubilee. The exchange should be determined on the number of years remained after the Jubilee when the transaction occurred. More years meant the buyer had to pay more money; and fewer years meant that he would pay less. It depended on the number of crops that the buyer could reap from the time of the transaction to the time of the next Jubilee.

If buyer and seller followed the rules of land transactions, God would bless the land and the people would be prosperous.

14 And if you sell aught unto thy neighbor, or buy aught of your neighbor's hand, ye shall not oppress one another:

15 According to the number of years after the Jubilee thou shalt buy of thy neighbor, and according unto the number of years of the fruits he shall sell unto thee:

16 According to the multitude of years thou shalt

increase the price thereof, and according to the fewness of years thou shalt diminish the price of it: for according to the number of years of the fruits doth he sell unto thee.

17 Ye shall not therefore oppress one another; but thou shalt fear thy God: I am the Lord your God.

18 Wherefore ye shall do my statutes, and keep my judgments, and do them; and ye shall dwell in the land in safety.

19 And the land shall yield her fruit, and ye shall eat your fill, and dwell therein in safety.

2. Blessings of the Sabbatical Year, verses 20-23:

Verses 20-23 answer quite adequately the question as to how the people were to go about the Sabbatical Year.

20 And if ye say, What shall we eat the seventh year? Behold we shall not sow, nor gather in our increase:

21 Then will I command my blessings upon you in the sixth year, and it shall bring forth fruit for three years.

God's promise of blessing their harvests three times more the sixth year was a promise in which they could believe. God never fails to keep a promise. Furthermore, they would reap the crops of the Sabbatical Year the following year to the ninth year. As God was always faithful to them, He also wanted them to be faithful and obedient to Him. The Year of Jubilee, the nature of the land transactions, and their provision of redemption indicate that the ownership of the land was God's. Everyone was to be grateful for the privilege of using it for its natural benefits.

22 And if ye shall sow the eighth year, and eat yet of old fruit until the ninth year; until her fruits come in ye shall eat of the old store

23 The land shall not be sold for ever: for the land is mine; for ye are strangers and sojourners with me.

3. Land Redemption by a Close Relative, verses 24-28:

Verses 24-28 explain the provision of land redemption for those who were very poor. When someone was too poor and

unable to redeem his land, then his closest relative had the first opportunity. If no relative was available, the land would remain with the buyer until the Year of Jubilee. If the poor brother was going to redeem it himself, he would count the years remaining before the Jubilee and repay for those years since the buyer already paid for those remaining years and did not have the benefit of those years. In essence, redeeming the land did not involve the total purchase price the buyer paid because he would have enjoyed the benefits of many years of the purchase by farming the land. Only the years that he did not use the land would be the redemption price. The Land Redemption was more complicated than first thought.

24 And in all the land of your possession ye shall grant a redemption for the land.

25 If thy brother be waxen poor, and hath sold away some of his possession, and if any of his kin come to redeem it, then shall he redeem that which his brother sold.

26 And if the man have none to redeem it, and himself be able to redeem it;

27 Then let him count the years of the sale thereof, and restore the over-plus unto the man to whom he sold it; that he may return to his possession.

28 But if he be not able to restore it to him, then that which is sold shall remain in the hand of him that hath bought it until the year of Jubilee: and in the Jubilee it shall go out, and he shall return to his possession.

4. House Redemption, verses 29-34:

Land redemption was not the only benefit of the Jubilee, there was also the benefit of redeeming one's house. Verses 29-34 explain. There are two scenarios with respect to the house and each is treated differently. The house that was sold in a walled city, and the house that was sold in a city not walled were treated differently. The house of the walled city could only be redeemed within one year. If it was not redeemed then, the provision of the Jubilee did not apply. The house of the un-walled city was treated as a field and if not redeemed before the Jubilee, would return to the seller in the Jubilee. Nevertheless, there was a distinction with the Levites: they could redeem the houses of the walled cities anytime. If they were not redeemed, they would return to them in the Jubilee.

29 And if a man sell a dwelling house in a walled city, then he may redeem it within a whole year after it is sold; within a full year he may redeem it.

30 And if it be not redeemed within the space of a full year, then the house that is within the walled city shall be established forever to him that bought it throughout his generations: it shall not go out in the Jubilee.

31 But the houses of the villages which have no wall round about them shall be counted as the fields of the country: they may be redeemed, and they shall go out in the Jubilee.

32 Notwithstanding the cities of the Levites, and the houses of the cities of their possession, may the Levites redeem at any time.

33 And if a man purchase of the Levites, then the house that was sold, and the city of his possession, shall go out in the year of Jubilee: for the houses of the cities of the Levites are their possession among the children of Israel.

34 But the field of the suburbs of their cities may not be sold; for it is their perpetual possession.

5. Relief to the Poor, verses 35-46:

Verses 35-46 explain special treatment of the poor. Indeed, loving thy neighbor as thyself was at the heart of the Jubilee. The Jubilee could be called the Social Compact with the poor. They benefited from it like no one else.

35 And if thy brother be waxen poor, and fallen in decay with thee; then thou shalt relieve him: yea though he be a stranger, or a sojourner; that he may live with thee.

It did not matter whether the poor were Hebrew or strangers, the relief should apply equally. God is the God of all mankind, whether acknowledged or not. The fact that a stranger or heathen made the first step to associate with God's people was sufficient condition for God's blessings.

36 Take thou no usury of him, or increase: but fear thy God; that thy brother may live with thee.

37 Thou shalt not give him thy money upon usury, nor lend him thy victuals for increase.

38 I am the Lord your God, which brought you forth out of the land of Egypt, to give you the land of Canaan, and to be your God.

Generous financial consideration was not to be the only expression of kindness; it should be accompanied with social acceptance by which one's neighbor became one's brother.

39 And if your brother that dwells by you be waxen poor, and be sold unto thee; thou shalt not compel him to serve as a bond servant:

There was a difference between a hired servant and a bond servant. A hired servant served for six years and was freed the seventh year. A bond servant served beyond seven years. If one became a hired servant two years before the Year of Jubilee, he would have to be released during the Jubilee without serving the six years of a hired servant. A bond servant was much more complicated. All that a bond servant acquired during the time of serving his master belonged to his master: it included his children. And if an understanding of leaving was reached with his master, then he would not be entitled to his wife and children; he had to leave empty-handed. The opposite was the case with the hired servant.

40 But as an hired servant, and as a sojourner, he shall be with thee, and shall serve thee unto the year of jubilee:

41 And then shall he depart from thee, both he and his children with him, and shall return unto his own family, and

unto the possession of his fathers shall he return.

42 For they are my servants which I brought forth out of the land of Egypt: they shall not be sold for bondmen.

43 Thou shalt not rule over him with rigor; but shalt fear thy God.

In the eye of the Law the Hebrew master was to see his Hebrew servant as his brother, and treat him accordingly. If the Hebrew master had the need for bond men and bond maids he should acquire them from other nations.

44 Both thy bondmen, and thy bondmaids, which thou shalt have, shall be of the heathen that are round about you; of them shall ye buy bondmen and bondmaids.

45 Moreover of the children of the strangers that do sojourn among you, of them shall ye buy, and of their families that are with you, which they begat in your land: and they shall be your possession.

46 And ye shall take them as an inheritance for your children after you, to inherit them for a possession; they shall be your bondmen forever: but over your brethren the children of Israel, ye shall not rule one over another with rigor.

6. Redeeming the Poor from the Rich Stranger, verses 47-55:

47 And if a sojourner or stranger wax rich by you, and your brother that dwells by him wax poor, and sell himself unto the stranger or sojourner by you, or to the stock of the stranger's family:

48 After that he is sold he may be redeemed again; one of his brethren may redeem him:

49 Either his uncle, or his uncle's son, may redeem him, or any that is nigh of kin unto him of his family may redeem him; or if he be able, he may redeem himself.

50 And he shall reckon with him that bought him from the year that he was sold to him unto the year of jubilee: and the price of his sale shall be according to the number of

years, according to the time of an hired servant shall it be with him.

Like lands and houses, the redemption of a person depended on the numbers of years remaining before the Jubilee. When more years remained before the Jubilee, the price of redemption was more; fewer years meant less price. In a case of the maximum years, then one might have to repay the full price.

51 If there be yet many years behind, according unto them he shall give again the price of his redemption out of the money that he was bought for.

52 And if there remain but few years unto the year of jubilee, then he shall count with him, and according unto his years shall he give him again the price of his redemption.

53 And as a yearly hired servant shall he be with him: and the other **shall not rule with rigor** over him in thy sight.

54 And if he be not redeemed in these years, then he shall go out in the year of jubilee, both he, and his children with him.

55 For unto me the children of Israel are servants; they are my servants whom I brought forth out of the land of Egypt: I am the Lord your God.

SUMMARY

The Year of Jubilee brought a joyous conclusion to all land transactions and all person to person transaction as related to masters and servants. Not only the poor benefited from the Year of Jubilee, but the whole nation of Israel. It began with blowing of the trumpets on the Day of Atonement. The Year of Jubilee was to be observed every fifty years. Since it was declared on the tenth day of the Seventh Month, there were only five months remaining in the year. It also meant that there were only seven months of rest instead of a full year.

As the Sabbath was important for the Children of Israel to observe every week, the Sabbath of years was equally important; both were to be a time of rest unto the Lord. The Sabbath of years was primarily for the rest of the land. The Children of Israel were not to plant nor reap their fields during the Sabbath of years. These periods of rest were to test Israel's obedience. God's promises of blessings depended on their obedience. They should not expect to be blessed while disobeying God's commandments.

The Sabbatical Year was emphasized because it offered the truest test of Israel's obedience. The question as to what would have happened during that year of rest was answered by God's promise of blessing their harvest three times more the sixth year. Moreover, they would still have the fruits of the seventh year to begin the eighth year.

The redemption of land and house was separate, but was based on the same principle of the Jubilee. This was a reduced price of redemption depending on the number of years that remained before the Jubilee. The redeemer would pay a less price than when the land or house was first sold. The redemption of land or house could be done by a relative whose property was to be redeemed. The Year of Jubilee, the nature of the land transactions, and their provision of redemption indicated that the ownership of the land was God's. Everyone was to be grateful for the privilege of using it for its natural benefits. If for some reason a person could not redeem his land, in the Year of jubilee every man regained his possession without condition.

Property Redemption was not the only kind; there was redemption of a more personal nature as in the case of a person selling himself to another person or becoming a bond servant. In any of these cases, one became the property of the other. A hired servant was quite a different situation. After he had served six years, was released the seventh year.

If he had only served for two years and it was the year of Jubilee, he would be set at liberty. *A bond servant served beyond seven years. A bond servant was much more complicated.* All that a bond servant acquired during the time of serving his master belonged to his master: it included his children. And if an understanding of leaving was reached with his master, then he would not be entitled to his wife and children; he had to leave empty-handed. The provisions or the blessings of the Year of Jubilee did not apply to the bond servant—he was the property for life and the inheritance of his master's children. In the Year of jubilee the hired servant returned with his family and to his possession.

By the principle of the Year of Jubilee, one never paid the full price of redemption. This stands in clear contrast to Jesus Christ our Redeemer who paid the full price for our Redemption. Greater yet, our Jubilee is for all eternity.

CHAPTER 18
Things To Remember, Leviticus 26-27

Chapters 26 and 27 complete the Book of Leviticus. These two chapters are the conclusion. The words of the conclusion of such an important Book were critical to the survival of Israel. The admonitions, the blessings, the warnings, the promise of mercy, and the pronouncements could not be overlooked by a people whose life depended on the words of God.

The Admonition, Lev. 26:1-3:

1 Ye shall make you no idols nor graven image, neither rear you up a standing image, neither shall ye set up any image of stone in your land, to bow down unto it: for I am the Lord your God.

2 Ye shall keep my Sabbaths and reverence my sanctuary: I am the Lord.

3 If ye walk in my statutes, and keep my commandments, and do them;

God looked through time and saw Israel's propensity for the unknown gods, their desire for the things of other nations, and their reluctance to keep the Sabbath. He admonished them to incline their heart to His commandments. Their obedience to God's commandments would determine their future.

Promised Blessings of Obedience, Lev. 26:4-13:
 1. Prosperity in the Field 26:4-5:

4 Then I will give you rain in due season, and the land shall yield her increase, and trees of the field shall yield their fruit.

5 And your threshing shall reach unto the vintage, and the vintage shall reach unto the sowing time: and ye shall eat your bread to the full, and dwell in your land safely.

2. Peace and Protection, 26:6-8

6 And I will give peace in the land, and ye shall lie down, and none shall make you afraid: and I will rid evil beast out of the land, neither shall the sword go through your land.

7 And ye shall chase your enemies, and they shall fall before you by the sword.

8 And five of you shall chase a hundred, and a hundred of you shall put ten thousand to flight: and your enemies shall fall before you by the sword.

3. Population Growth, 26:9-10:

9 For I will have respect unto you, and make you fruitful, and multiply you, and establish my covenant with you.

10 And ye shall eat old store, and bring forth the old because of the new.

4. The Promise of God's Abiding Presence, 26:11-13:

11 And I will set my tabernacle among you: and my soul shall not abhor you.

12 And I will walk among you, and will be your God, and ye shall be my people.

13 I am the Lord your God, which brought you forth out of the land of Egypt, that ye should not be their bondmen; and I have broken the bands of your yoke, and made you go upright.

Warnings of Disobedience, Lev. 26:14-46:

14 But if ye will not harken unto me, and will not do all these commandments;

15 And if ye shall despise my statutes, or if your soul abhor my judgments, so that ye will not do all my

commandments, but that ye break my covenants:

1. Appointment of Terror, 26:16-17:

16 I also will do this unto you; I will even appoint over you terror, consumption, and the burning ague, that shall consume the eyes, and cause sorrow of heart: and ye shall sow your seed in vain, for your enemies shall eat it.

17 And I will set my face against you, and ye shall be slain before your enemies: they that hate you shall reign over you; and you shall flee when none pursues you.

This punishment carried with it physical impairment, poverty, and death. If Israel refused to repent, God would increase their punishment seven times greater than before.

2. Sevenfold Punishment, 26:18-20:

18 And if ye will not yet for all this harken unto me, then I will punish you seven times more for your sins.

19 And I will break the pride of your power; and I will make your heaven as iron, and your earth as brass:

20 And your strength shall be spent in vain: for your land shall not yield her increase, neither shall the trees of the land yield their fruits.

By this sevenfold punishment, Israel would lose national power, and be driven into the deepest depth of poverty. If they still refused to repent, God would increase their punishment by seven times the number of plagues they experienced before.

3. Sevenfold Plagues, 26:21-22:

21 And if ye walk contrary unto me, and will not harken unto me; I will bring seven times more plagues upon you according to your sins.

22 I will also send wild beast among you, which shall rob you of your children, and destroy your cattle, and make you few in number; and your high ways shall be desolate.

In addition, the plagues would deprive them of their children, deplete their source of wealth, and reduce significantly their population. If they continued not to live by their covenant with their God, He would further punish them seven times more than before.

4. Sevenfold Punishment for sins, 26:23-26:

23 And if ye will not be reformed by me by these things, but will walk contrary unto me;

24 Then will I also walk contrary unto you, and will punish you yet seven times for your sins.

25 And I will bring a sword upon you, that shall avenge the quarrel of my covenant: and when ye are gathered together within your cities, I will send the pestilence among you; and ye shall be delivered into the hand of the enemy.

26 And when I have broken the staff of your bread, ten women shall bake your bread in one oven, and they shall deliver you your bread again by weight: and ye shall eat, and not be satisfied.

In this sevenfold punishment, among other things, they would experience famine, such as they had never experienced before. If they continued on their path to destruction, God would chastise them seven times greater for their sins than He would have normally chastised them.

5. Sevenfold Chastisement for their sins, 26:27-39:

27 And if ye will not for all this harken unto me, but walk contrary unto me;

28 Then I will walk contrary unto you also in fury; and I, even I, will chastise you seven times for your sins.

29 And ye shall eat the flesh of your sons, and the flesh of your daughters shall ye eat.

30 And I will destroy your high places, and cut down your images, and cast your carcasses upon the carcasses of your idols, and my soul shall abhor you.

This punishment could not be worse. No one would like to see a mother and a father eating their children. It got hopeless: their carcasses would be thrown upon their idols. And God would turn away His eyes from looking at them. Then they would become an astonishment to their enemies.

Worst, they would be scattered among their enemies, and they would show them no mercy. Their punishment for disobedience would be more than what they could bear.

31 And I will make your cities waste, and bring your sanctuaries unto desolation, and I will not smell the savor of your sweet odors.

32 And I will bring the land into desolation: and your enemies which dwell therein shall be astonished at it.

33 And I will scatter you among the heathen, and will draw out a sword after you: and your land shall be desolate, and your cities waste.

34 Then shall the land enjoy her Sabbaths, as long as it lies desolate, and ye be in your enemies' land; even then shall the land rest, and enjoy her Sabbaths.

35 As long as it lies desolate it shall rest; because it did not rest in your Sabbaths, when ye dwelt upon it.

36 And upon them that are left alive of you I will send a faintness into their hearts in the lands of their enemies; and the sound of a shaken leaf shall chase them; and they shall flee, as a fleeing from a sword; and they shall fall when none pursues.

37 And they shall fall one upon another, as it were before a sword, when none pursues: and ye shall have no power to stand before your enemies.

38 And ye shall perish among the heathen, and the land of your enemies shall eat you up.

39 And they that are left of you shall pine away in their iniquity in your enemies' lands; and also in the iniquities of their fathers shall they pine away with them.

Four times Israel was warned of the seven fold punishment. It meant that God would punish them 7 more times than normal for all their sins of disobedience. The Divine investment of love and mercy in Israel was too great for them not to have been equally punished. It meant that they were blessed at least 7 times above other nations.

The punishment had to be proportional to their incredible blessings. However it was not over, God had to look far, wide and deep into the infinity of His mercy to be able to promise them the hope of mercy.

The Promise of Mercy, Lev. 26:40-46:

The promise of mercy awaits Israel but they must first repent of all the sins they have committed against their God.

40 If they shall confess their iniquity, and the iniquity of their fathers, with the trespass which they have trespassed against me, and that also they have walked contrary unto me;

41 And that also I have walked contrary unto them, and have brought them into the land of their enemies; if then their uncircumcised hearts be humbled, and they then accept of the punishment of their iniquity:

42 Then will I remember my covenant with Jacob, and also my covenant with Isaac, and also my covenant with Abraham will I remember; and I will remember the land.

Israel had broken their Covenant with God countless times. They could only be considered for mercy on the strength of the Covenant with their fathers. God remembered how faithful and obedient Abraham, Isaac, and Jacob were. Abraham was called the friend of God; he was willing to offer up Isaac a Burnt Sacrifice unto the Lord. Isaac was faithful and obedient to his father and to God. Jacob wrestled with the angel and would not let him go until he blessed him. These patriarchs pleased God by their faith and obedience. God thought about the great fellowship He had with them and the Covenant He made with them. Their children knew of it; yet they provoked Him to anger. Therefore for their fathers' sake, God promised them mercy.

43 The land also shall be left of them, and shall enjoy her Sabbaths, while she lies desolate without them: and they shall accept of the punishment of their iniquity: because

even because they despised my judgments, and because their soul abhorred my statutes.

Israel had crossed the line of Divine justice many times but never one time had they crossed the line of Divine mercy for there is no line to Divine mercy. This was their only salvation.

44 And yet for all that, when they be in the land of their enemies, I will not cast them away, neither will I abhor them, to destroy them utterly, and to break my covenant with them: for I am the Lord their God.

45 But I will for their sakes remember the covenant of their ancestors, whom I brought forth out of the land of Egypt in the sight of the heathen, that I might be their God: I am the Lord.

Israel's relationship with God gives us a vivid picture of what Divine mercy looks like. We would be completely unable to describe in words the greatness and infinity of God's mercy. Israel's experience of God's mercy is the very best description.

46 These are the statutes and judgments and laws, which the Lord made between him and the children of Israel in Mont Sinai by the hand of Moses.

Pronouncements, Lev. 27:

These pronouncements have dealt with the vows which Israel made unto the Lord. A man might vow himself unto the Lord for a specific purpose, his animal, his house, or his field. They have also dealt with tithing.

1. With Respect to Persons, 27:1-8:

1 And the Lord spoke unto Moses, saying,

2 Speak unto the children of Israel, and say unto them, When a man shall make a singular vow, the persons shall be for the Lord by thy estimation.

When a person made a vow of himself to God or a vow of a thing, he or that thing became God's. A vow was of one's free will and sometimes a sacrifice was offered to enforce it

(Leviticus 22:21). A charge was set by the Law which had to be paid to the treasure. This was a way also to make such vow a practical reality.

3 And thy estimation shall be of the male from twenty years old even unto sixty years old, even thy estimation shall be fifty shekels of silver, .5 pound, after the shekel of the sanctuary.

4 And if it be a female, then thy estimation shall be thirty shekels.

5 And if it be from five years old even unto twenty years old, then thy estimation shall be of the male twenty shekels, and for the female ten shekels.

6 And if it be from a month old even unto five years old, then thy estimation shall be of the male five shekels of silver, and for the female thy estimation shall be three shekels of silver.

7 And if it be from sixty years old and above; if it be a male, then thy estimation shall be fifteen shekels, and for the female ten shekels.

This estimation or charge was based on gender and age. For some, it was more and for others it was less. This charge was paid to the priest. In the rare occasion they wanted to break their vow, they had to pay to the priest the equivalent of their estimation with the addition of a fifth. All the estimations were declared in the Law. The exception was when someone was too poor, the priest would make an estimation of him. There were some other cases when the priest had to make an estimation.

8 But if he be poorer than thy estimation, then he shall present himself before the priest, and the priest shall value him; according to his ability that vowed shall the priest value him.

2. With Respect to Beasts, 27:9-13: 9 And if it be a beast, whereof men bring an offering unto the Lord, all that any man giveth of such unto the Lord shall be holy.

10 He shall not alter it, nor change it, a good for a bad: and if he shall at all change beast for beast, then it and the exchange thereof shall be holy.

11 And if it be any unclean beast, of which they do not offer a sacrifice unto the Lord, then he shall present the beast before the priest:

12 And the priest shall value it, whether it be good or bad: as you value it, who art the priest, so shall it be.

13 But if he will at all redeem it, then he shall add a fifth part there unto thy estimation.

In the case of the animal, there was a provision of redemption by which it could be bought back for its value with the addition of a fifth.

3. With Respect to Houses, 27:14-15:

14 And when a man shall sanctify his house to be holy unto the Lord, then the priest shall estimate it, whether it be good or bad: as the priest shall estimate it, so shall it stand.

15 And if he that sanctified it will redeem his house, then he shall add the fifth part of the money of thy estimation unto it, and it shall be his.

The same principle of the animal applied to the house. The person would have to add a fifth to the value of the house in order to buy it back.

4. With Respect to Fields, Lev. 27:16-25:

16 And if a man shall sanctify unto the Lord some part of a field of his possession, then thy estimation shall be according to the seed thereof: an homer of barley seed shall be valued at fifty shekels of silver, .5 pound.

17 If he sanctify his field from the year of jubilee, according to thy estimation it shall stand.

18 But if ye sanctify his field after the jubilee, then the priest shall reckon unto him the money according to all the years that remain, even unto the year of jubilee, and it shall be abated from thy estimation.

If the field was given over to the Lord after the Jubilee, its estimate of value depended on the number of years remaining before the next jubilee.

19 And if he that sanctified the field will in any wise redeem it, then he shall add the fifth part of the money of thy estimation unto it, and it shall be assured to him.

20 And if he will not redeem the field, or if he have sold the field to another man, it shall not be redeemed anymore.

21 But the field, when it goes out in the jubilee, shall be holy unto the Lord, as a field devoted; the possession thereof shall be the priest's.

22 And if a man sanctify unto the Lord a field which he hath bought, which is not of the fields of his possession;

23 Then the priest shall reckon unto him the worth of thy estimation, even unto the year of jubilee: and he shall give thine estimation in that day, as a holy thing unto the Lord.

24 In the year of jubilee, the field shall return unto him of whom it was bought, even to him to whom the possession of the land did belong.

25 And all the estimation shall be according to the shekel of the sanctuary: twenty gerahs, .4 ounce, shall be the shekel.

5. With Respect to General Law of Vows unto the Lord, 27:26-29:

26 Only the firstling of the beasts, which should be the Lord's firstling, no man shall sanctify it; whether it be ox or sheep: it is the Lord's.

The firstlings of the animals belonged to the Lord; a person could not vow unto the Lord something that was already His.

27 And if it be of an unclean beast, then ye shall redeem it according to thine estimation, and shall add a fifth part of it thereto: or if it be not redeemed, then it shall be sold according to thy estimation.

If someone vowed an animal unto the Lord and it happened to be unclean, he had an obligation to redeem it. He had to add a fifth to its value to redeem it.

28 Notwithstanding no devoted thing that a man shall devote unto the Lord of all that he hath, both of man and beast, and of the field of his possession, shall be sold or redeemed: every devoted thing is most holy unto the Lord.

When someone made a vow unto the Lord, it should be final; one should think carefully before making a vow.

Animals which were considered unclean should be redeemed but after they were redeemed should be put to death. The exceptions to a vow should never become the rule.

29 None devoted, which shall be devoted of men, shall be redeemed; but shall surely be put to death.

6. With Respect to Tithes, 27:30-34:

30 And all the tithe of the land, whether of the seed of the land, or of the fruit of the tree, is the Lord's: it is holy unto the Lord.

The first fruits of the land were to be God's tithes, that is to say the first fruits which one acquired belonged to God. In regular circumstances, a tenth of what one acquires belongs to the Lord. If for some reason some one failed in this obligation, he should add a fifth thereto when paying it.

31 And if a man will at all redeem aught of his tithes, he shall add thereto the fifth part thereof.

32 And concerning the tithe of the herd, or the flock, even of whatsoever passes under the rod, the tenth shall be holy unto the Lord (meaning one of every ten of the herd belonged to the Lord).

The counting of animals was done in ancient times with a rod with a marking ink. The tenth animal would be marked: that one would be the tithe unto the Lord.

33 He shall not search whether it be good or bad, neither shall he change it: and if he change it at all, then both it and the change thereof shall be holy; it shall not be redeemed. *This animal should for no reason be exchanged. However if for some reason it was exchanged, it would still be holy.*

34 These are the commandments, which the Lord

commanded Moses for the Children of Israel in Mont Sinai.

The life and the existence of Israel depended on these pronouncements more than anything else.

SUMMARY

This Divine admonition was for good reason. The First Commandment is about loving God and personal devotion to Him. It was important that in the conclusion of Leviticus this Commandment was re-emphasized. Loving God was a condition for all Divine blessings. People were not paid to love God; it was to be a voluntary duty of the heart in recognition of the privilege of life which came from God. To be pouring out abundance of Divine blessings on someone in spiritual darkness would be an encouragement to continue living in sin and darkness. That someone would not be helped thereby. Fellowship with God is important to one's existence. Fellowship is encouraged by obedience to God's commandments. Again, obedience is not something that can be forced; can only be encouraged.

God made promises of blessings of obedience to Israel. The paradox of it all is that Israel would dearly want those blessings, but would not want to obey God. Some of these blessings were the blessing of prosperity, the blessing of Divine protection from natural dangers, the blessing of victory over the enemies, and the blessing of God's abiding presence among them. What other blessing could they have asked of God?

One of the marvelous things about God is that He always gives man a clear choice and the consequences of making the wrong choice. In the conclusion of Leviticus, God strongly warned Israel of the consequences of not living by the Covenant which He made with them. Four times in His warning, He used the term, "seven times punishment for their sins". God would punish them seven times above the normal punishment. This would be the proportional punishment to all the blessings with which God's people were blessed.

Why would God punish his people more than anyone else? One could answer by saying to whom much is given much is expected. However, we must acknowledge the limitation of our capacity to understand all the ways of an infinite God and admit that we do not know. What we do know is that there is a time for Divine justice when God will be compelled to take Divine action, the kind no recipient will like. This is not the case with Divine mercy because there is no limit to the length and width, the height, and depth of Divine mercy. This was the only salvation of Israel.

THE BOOK OF NUMBERS

EXPRESSES DIVINE

ORDER,

RESPONSIBILITY

ACCOUNTABILITY

- *Numbering of the People, Numbers 1-4, 26*

- *Questions of Adultery and Vows, Numbers 5-6*

- *The Offerings of the Princes and the Levites, Numbers 7-8*

- *Journey from Mount Sinai to Paran, Numbers 9-12*

- *Spies Sent to Canaan, Numbers 13-14*

- *Looking Ahead But Going Backward, Numbers 15-17; 20:1-13*

- *The Priesthood and Purification..., Numbers 18-19*

- *Israel Marches Forward, Numbers, 20:14- 25:1-18*

- *Moses Prepares to Handover Leadership, Numbers 27-33:*

- *National Borders and Cities for the Levites, Numbers 34-36*

CHAPTER 19
The Numbering of The People, Numbers 1-4; 26

The Book of Exodus expresses the omnipotence of God, as we have seen in the historic circumstances of the Exodus of the Children of Israel from the bondage of Egypt and in their miraculous experiences in their journeys to Mount Sinai. The Book of Leviticus expresses the holiness of God, as we have seen expressed in the offerings of Atonement, the ceremonies, and statutes of the Law. The Book of Numbers, now under review, expresses order, responsibility, and accountability.

Order is a Divine attribute and is reflected in all of nature, from the cosmic structure to the atom, the smallest unit of matter. It comes to us, therefore, as no surprise that Divine order is reflected in God's relationship with the Children of Israel. Indeed, we would have been rather surprised were this Divine attribute not reflected in His relationship with Israel. If there were no other circumstance that demanded order, the circumstance of the Wilderness certainly demanded it.

It is not strange that in the case of God's relationship with Israel in the Wilderness, order began with the numbering, numbering, and the numbering again of the Children of Israel. This order can be seen in the very way and time numbering was done, in the encamping of the tribes around the Tabernacle, and in their forward march towards the Promised Land.

In the concept of order is also the concept of responsibility and accountability. It is obvious that order demands responsibility and accountability because responsibility and accountability are to be the ends of order, order being the means. The organizing tendency of the human mind is a mere reflection of Divine order. God justly demanded order, responsibility, and accountability of Israel, as He demands of every one of us today.

Numbering began with the heads of the tribes; Moses and Aaron numbered the Children of Israel at God's command.

Heads of Tribes, Num. 1:1-17

1 And the Lord spoke unto Moses in the wilderness of Sinai, in the tabernacle of the congregation, on the first day of the second month, in the second year after they were come out of the land of Egypt, saying,

2 Take ye the sum of all the congregation of the children of Israel, after their families, by the house of their fathers, with the number of their names, every male by their polls;

3 From twenty years old and upward, all that are able to go forth to war in Israel: thou and Aaron shall number them by their armies.

It took the Children of Israel three months from the time they crossed the Red Sea to reach Sinai where they remained, built, and erected the Tabernacle. Most of the laws were given in Sinai. Here Moses was commanded to number only those who were able to go to war; women and children and those under 20 years were not numbered.

Moses, Aaron, and the heads of the tribes, and the princes numbered the tribes, beginning with the tribe of Reuben. The tribe of Levi was not numbered for the purpose of the army. The numbers of the tribes are listed from verses 18-46.

4 And with you there shall be a man of every tribe; everyone head of the house of his fathers.

5 And these are the names of the men that stand with

you: of the tribe of Reuben; Elizur the son of Shedeur.

6 Of Simeon; Shelumiel the son of Zurishaddai.

7 Of Judah; Nahshon the son of Amminadab.

8 Of Issachar; Nethaneel the son Zuar.

9 Of Zebulun; Eliab the son of Helon.

10 Of the children of Joseph: of Ephraim; Elishama the son of Ammihud: of Manasseh; Gamaliel the son of Pedahzur.

11 Of Benjamin; Abidan the son of Gideoni.

12 Of Dan; Ahiezer the son of Ammishaddai.

13 Of Asher; Pagiel the son of Ocran.

14 Of Gad; Eliasaph the son Deuel.

15 Of Naphtali; Ahira the son of Enan.

16 These were the renowned of the congregation, princes of the tribes of their fathers, heads of thousands in Israel.

17 And Moses and Aaron took these men which are expressed by their names.

Their Numbers, Num. 1:18-46

1. Reuben, 46,500

18 And they assembled all the congregation together on the first day of the second month, and they declared their pedigrees after their families, by the house of their fathers, according to the number of the names, from twenty years old and upward, by their polls.

19 As the Lord commanded Moses, so he numbered them in the wilderness of Sinai.

20 And the children of Reuben, Israel's eldest son, by their generation, after their families, by the house of their fathers, according to the number of the names, by their polls, every male from twenty years old and upward, all that were able to go forth to war;

21 Those that were numbered of them, even of the tribe of Reuben, were forty and six thousand and five hundred.

2. Simeon, 59,300

22 Of the children of Simeon, by their generation, after their families, by the house of their fathers, those that were numbered of them, according to the number of their names, by their polls, every male from twenty years old and upward, all that were able to go forth to war;

23 Those that were numbered of them, even of the tribe of Simeon, were fifty and nine thousand and three hundred.

3. Gad, 45,650

24 Of the children of Gad, by their generations after their families, by the house of their fathers, according to the number of the names, from twenty years and upward, all that were able to go forth to war;

25 Those that were numbered of them, even of the tribe of Gad, were forty and five thousand six hundred and fifty.

4. Judah, 74,600

26 Of the children of Judah, by their generations, after their families, by the house of their fathers, according to the number of the names, from twenty years old and upward, all that were able to go forth to war;

27 Those were numbered of them, even of the tribe of Judah, were three score and fourteen thousand and six hundred.

5. Issachar, 54,400

28 Of the children of Issachar, by their generations, after their families, by the house of their fathers, according to the number of the names, from twenty years old and upward, all that were able to go forth to war;

29 Those that were numbered of them, even of the tribe of Issachar, were fifty and four thousand and four hundred.

6. Zebulun, 57,400

30 Of the children of Zebulun, by their generations, after their families, by the house of their fathers, according to the number of the names, from twenty years old and upward, all that were able to go forth to war;

31 Those that were numbered of them, even of the tribe

of Zebulun, were fifty and seven thousand and four hundred.

7. Ephraim, 40,500

32 Of the children of Joseph, namely, of the children of Ephraim, by their generations, after their families, by the house of their fathers, according to the number of the names, from twenty years old and upward, all that were able to go forth to war;

33 Those that were numbered of them, even of the tribe of Ephraim, were forty thousand and five hundred.

8. Manasseh, 32,200

34 Of the children of Manasseh, by their generations, after their families, by the house of their fathers, according to the number of the names, from twenty years old and upward, all that were able to go forth to war;

35 Those that were numbered of them, even of the tribe of Manasseh, were thirty and two thousand and two hundred.

9. Benjamin, 35,400

36 Of the tribe of Benjamin, by their generations, after their families, by the house of their fathers, according to the number of the names, from twenty years old and upward, all that were able to go forth to war;

37 Those that were numbered of them, even of the tribe of Benjamin, were thirty and five thousand and four hundred.

10. Dan, 62,700

38 Of the children of Dan, by their generations, after their families, by the house of their fathers, according to the number of the names, from twenty years old and upward, all that were able to go forth to war;

39 Those that were numbered of them, even of the tribe of Dan, were threescore and two thousand and seven hundred.

11. Asher, 41,500

40 Of the children of Asher, by their generations, after

their families, by the house of their fathers, according to the number of the names, from twenty years old and upward, all that were able to go forth to war;

41 Those that were numbered of them, even of the tribe of Asher, were forty and one thousand and five hundred.

12. Naphtali, 53,400

42 Of the children of Naphtali, throughout their generations, after their families, by the house of their fathers, according to the number of the names, from twenty years old and upward, all that were able to go forth to war;

43 Those that were numbered of them, even of the tribe of Naphtali, were fifty and three thousand and four hundred.

44 These are all those that were numbered, which Moses and Aaron numbered, and the princes of Israel, being twelve men: each one was for the house of his fathers.

45 So were all those that were numbered of the children of Israel, by the house of their fathers, from twenty years old and upward, all that were able to go forth to war in Israel;

46 Even all that were numbered were six hundred thousand and three thousand five hundred and fifty. (603,550)

The Levites were not numbered for the purpose of the army because they were to be appointed to the service of the Tabernacle and were to encamp immediately around the Tabernacle.

The Levites, Num. 1:47-54:

47 But the Levites after the tribe of their fathers were not numbered among them.

48 For the Lord had spoken unto Moses, saying,

49 Only thou shalt not number the tribe of Levi, neither take the sum of them among the children of Israel:

50 For thou shalt appoint the Levites over the tabernacle of testimony, and over all the vessels thereof, and over all the things that belong to it: they shall bear the tabernacle, and

the vessels thereof; and they shall minister unto it, and shall encamp round about the tabernacle.

51 And when the tabernacle sets forward, the Levites shall take it down: and when the tabernacle is to be pitched, the Levites shall set it up: and the stranger that cometh nigh shall be put to death.

52 And the children of Israel shall pitch their tents, every man by his own camp, and every man by his own standard, throughout their hosts.

53 But the Levites shall pitch round about the tabernacle of testimony, that there be no wrath upon the congregation of the children of Israel: and the Levites shall keep the charge of the tabernacle of testimony.

54 And the children of Israel did according to all that the Lord commanded Moses, so did they.

The appointment of the Levites to the ministry of the Tabernacle was a Divine order. They were also to encamp around the Tabernacle of Testimony, close to the Holy of Holies. This was God's way and had to be followed. To do otherwise would be a sin which would incur death and God's wrath on the congregation of Israel.

The other tribes were to encamp with the Tabernacle as their center, in the order commanded by God.

Camping of the Tribes, Num. 2:1-34:

1 And the Lord spoke unto Moses and unto Aaron, saying,

2 Every man of the children of Israel shall pitch by his own standard, with the ensign of their father's house: far off about the tabernacle of the congregation shall they pitch.

There was to be sufficient space between the Levites who closely surrounded the Tabernacle and the other tribes.

East Side:

3 And on the east side toward the rising of the sun shall they of the standard of the camp of Judah pitch throughout

their armies: and Nahshon the son of Amminadab shall be captain of the children of Judah.

The tribe of Judah was to encamp at the east of the Tabernacle with its standard or banner. Every tribe had its own banner which was to be exhibited. The tribe of Joseph was divided into two: Ephraim, and Manasseh; thus replacing the Levites who were not numbered among the army. The location of Judah indicated a position of leadership. Though each tribe had its own banner, two other tribes were under the command of Judah and they encamped nearest to him. It is remarkable that the tribe of Judah hand 74,600 soldiers, twice as many as some of the other tribes.

The order of the encamping of the tribes reveals the command structure, with Judah the head. The other 9 tribes were under three other commands headed by Elizur of the tribe of Reuben, Elishama of the tribe of Ephraim, and Ehiezer of the tribe of Dan.

4 And his host, and those that were numbered of them, were three score and fourteen thousand and six hundred.

5 And those that do pitch next unto him shall be the tribe of Issachar: and Nethaneel the son of Zuar shall be captain of the children of Issachar.

6 And his host, and those that were numbered thereof, were fifty and four thousand and four hundred.

7 Then tribe of Zebulun: and Eliab the son of Helon shall be captain of the children of Zebulun.

8 And his host, and those that were numbered thereof, were fifty and seven thousand and four hundred.

9 All that were numbered in the camp of Judah were a hundred thousand and four score thousand and six thousand and four hundred, throughout their armies. These shall first set forth. (*186,400*)

The South Side:
10 On the south side shall be the standard of the camp

of Reuben according to their armies: and the captain of the children of Reuben shall be Elizur the son of Shedeur.

11 And his host, and those that were numbered thereof, were forty and six thousand and five hundred.

12 And those which pitch by him shall be the tribe of Simeon: and the captain of the children of Simeon shall be Shelumiel the son of Zurishaddai.

13 And his host, and those that were numbered of them, were fifty and nine thousand and three hundred.

14 Then the tribe of Gad, and the captain of the sons of Gad shall be Eliasaph the son of Reuel.

15 And his host, and those that were numbered of them, were forty and five thousand and six hundred and fifty.

16 All that were numbered in the camp of Reuben were a hundred thousand and fifty and one thousand and four hundred and fifty, throughout their armies. And they shall set forth in the second rank. (*151,450*)

17 Then the tabernacle of the congregation shall set forward with the camp of the Levites in the midst of the camp: as they camp, so shall they set forward, every man in his place by their standards.

All those who were not numbered – women and children, and the very old who could not go to war were the congregation. In fact they were the majority; they followed behind the Levites. This was the only time the army was distinguished from the congregation; at all other times it was recognized as a part of the congregation of Israel.

The West Side:

18 On the west side shall be the standard of the camp of Ephraim according to their armies: and the captain of the sons of Ephraim shall be Elishama the son of Ammihud.

19 And his host, and those that were numbered of them, were forty thousand and five hundred.

20 And by him shall be the tribe of Manasseh: and the captain of the children of Manasseh shall be Gamaliel the

son of Pedahzur.

21 And his host, and those that were numbered of them, were thirty and two thousand and two hundred.

22 Then the tribe of Benjamin: and the captain of the sons of Benjamin shall be Abidan the son of Gideoni.

23 And his host, and those that were numbered of them, were thirty and five thousand and four hundred.

24 All that were numbered of the camp of Ephraim were a hundred thousand and eight thousand and an hundred throughout their armies. And they shall go forward in the third rank. *(108,100)*

Ephraim and Manasseh the sons of Joseph camped together. Joseph and Benjamin were the sons of Rachel, one of the two wives of Jacob; the other wife was Leah. These three tribes continued the natural closeness.

The North Side:

25 The standard of the camp of Dan shall be on the north side by their armies; and the captain of the children of Dan shall be Ehiezer the son of Ammishaddai.

26 And his host, and those that were numbered of them, were three score and two thousand and seven hundred.

27 And those that encamp by him shall be the tribe of Asher: and the captain of the children of Asher shall be Pagiel the son of Ocran.

28 And his host, and those that were numbered of them, were forty and one thousand and five hundred.

29 Then the tribe of Naphtali: and the captain of the children of Naphtali shall be Ahira the son of Enan.

30 And his host, and those that were numbered of them, were fifty and three thousand and four hundred.

31 All they were numbered in the camp of Dan were a hundred thousand and fifty and seven thousand and six hundred. They shall go hindmost with their standards. *(157, 600) (603,550, total)*

32 These are those which were numbered of the children

of Israel by the house of their fathers: all those that were numbered of the camps throughout their hosts six hundred thousand and three thousand and five hundred and fifty.

33 But the Levites were not numbered among the children of Israel; as the Lord commanded Moses.

34 And the children of Israel did according to all that the Lord commanded Moses: so they pitched by their standards, and so they set forward, every one after their families, according to the house of their fathers.

If you were a teacher and wanted to know the attendance of your class, you could easily know by counting the empty chairs, once you knew the total number of chairs in your class room. But the counting of the Children of Israel in the Wilderness was not like counting children in a class room. The people were scattered all over the Wilderness in their tents and some were attending their flocks. The task of getting the correct numbering was overwhelming and it was a great accomplishment. It took the diligence of Moses, Aaron, and the princes, and the co-operation of every one. The lesson here for us as Christians is that much more can be done in unity and co-operation than by a single effort of 1,000 years.

The numbering of the Levites was to be done separately and for a different purpose. It presented the most accurate equation and exchange with the firstborn. The Passover was predicated on the death of the firstborn of man and beast in the land of Egypt. This miracle witnessed the deliverance of Israel from bondage. From that point in time, the Lord claimed the firstborn of man and beast in Israel as His own.

After the counting all the other tribes, it was then time to count the Levites. The numbering of the Levites had to be comparable to the numbering of the firstborn, which was numbered from a month old and upward.

The Exchange of Levites for the First Born, Num. 3

1 These also are the generations of Aaron and Moses in

the day that the Lord spoke with Moses in Mount Sinai.

2 And these are the names of the sons of Aaron; Nadab the first born, and Abihu, Eleazar, and Ithamar.

3 These are the names of the sons of Aaron, the priests which were anointed, whom he consecrated to minister in the priest's office.

4 And Nadab and Abihu died before the Lord, when they offered strange fire before the Lord, in the wilderness of Sinai, and they had no children: and Eleazar and Ithamar ministered in the priest's office in the sight of Aaron their father.

5 And the Lord spoke unto Moses, saying,

6 Bring the tribe of Levi near, and present them before Aaron the priest, that they may minister unto him.

This command of the Lord was fulfilled in chapter 8 in a special dedication ceremony and was acknowledged by the whole congregation of Israel. They all knew of the duties and responsibilities of the Levites.

7 And they shall keep his charge, and the charge of the whole congregation, to do the service of the tabernacle.

8 And they shall keep all the instruments of the tabernacle of the congregation, and the charge of the children of Israel, to do the service of the tabernacle.

9. And thou shalt give the Levites unto Aaron and to his sons: they are wholly given unto him out of the children of Israel.

10 And thou shalt appoint Aaron and his sons, and they shall wait on their priest's office: and the stranger that cometh near shall be put to death.

Though Aaron's sons were anointed to the priesthood, only Aaron was anointed High Priest who would serve for life. After his death his oldest son would succeed him.

11 And the Lord spoke unto Moses, saying,

12 And I, behold, I have taken the Levites from among the children of Israel instead of the first born that opens

the matrix among the children of Israel: therefore the Levites shall be mine.

13 Because all the first born are mine; for on the day that I smote all the first born in the land of Egypt I hallowed all the first born in Israel, both man and beast: mine shall they be: I am the Lord.

Age of Numbering of a Month, Num. 3:14-51:

14 And the Lord spoke unto Moses in the wilderness of Sinai, saying,

15 Number the children of Levi after the house of their fathers, by their families: every male from a month old and upward shalt thou number them.

16 And Moses numbered them according to the word of the Lord, as he was commanded.

The tribe of Levi was headed by three brothers who were the fathers of the Levites. The descendants of each of the fathers were assigned to a specific duty. The three brothers that headed the tribe of Levi remind us of the Trinity of the Godhead, Father, Son, and Holy Spirit. Moses, Aaron, and Miriam were the descendants of Kohath.

Gershonites, 7,500; Pitched Westward, Num. 3:17-22:

17 And these were the sons of Levi by their names; Gershon, and Kohath, and Merari.

18 And these are the names of the sons of Gershon by their families; Libni, and Shimiei.

19 And the sons of Kohath by their families; Amram, and Izehar, Hebron, and Uzziel.

20 And the sons of Merari by their families; Mahli, and Mushi, These are the families of the Levites according to the house of their fathers.

21 Of Gershon was the family of the Libinites, and the family of the Shimites: these are the families of the Gershonites.

22 Those that were numbered of them, according to the

number of all the males, from a month old and upward, even those that were numbered of them were seven thousand and five hundred.

The males that were numbered of the Gershonites from a month old were 7,500; females were not numbered. The Gershonites pitched closest to the Tabernacle of Testimony, the Holy of Holies.

Position of the Gershonites, Num. 3:23-26:

23 The families of the Gershonites shall pitch behind the Tabernacle westward.

24 And the chief of the house of the father of the Gershonites shall be Eliasaph the son of Lael.

25 And the charge of the sons of Gershon in the tabernacle of the congregation shall be the tabernacle, and the tent, the covering thereof, and the hanging for the door of the tabernacle of the congregation,

26 And the hanging of the court, and the curtain for the door of the court, which by the tabernacle, and by the altar round about, and the cords of it for all the service thereof.

The Gershonites were responsible for setting up and taking down the Tabernalce and the Court.

The Kohathites 8,600; Pitched Southward, Num.3:27-32:

27 And of Kohath was the family of the Amramites, and the family of the Izeharites, and the family of the Hebronites, and the family of the Uzzielites: these are the families of the Kohathites.

28 In the number of all males from a month old and upward, were eight thousand and six hundred, keeping the charge of the sanctuary.

29 The families of the sons of Kohath shall pitch on the side of the tabernacle southward.

30 And the chief of the house of the father of the families of the Kohathites shall be Elizaphan the son of Uzziel.

31 And their charge shall be the ark, and the table, and the candlestick, and the altars, and the vessels of the sanctuary wherewith they minister, and the hanging, and all the service thereof.

32 And Eleazar the son of Aaron the priest shall be chief over the chief of the Levites, and have the oversight of them that keep the charge of the sanctuary.

The Kohathites had the charge of the holy things.

The Merarites 6,200; Pitched Northward, Num. 3:33-37:

33 Of Merari was the family of the Mahlites, and the family of the Mushites: these are the families of Merari.

34 And those that were numbered of them, according to the number of all males, from a month old and upward, were six thousand and two hundred.

35 And the chief of the house of the father of the families of Merari was Zuriel the son of Abihail: these shall pitch on the side of the tabernacle northward.

36 And under the custody and charge of the sons of Merari shall be the boards of the tabernacle, and the bars thereof, and the pillars thereof, and the sockets thereof, and all the vessels thereof, and all that serve thereto,

37 And the pillars of the court round about, and their sockets, and their pins, and their cords.

38 But those that encamp before the tabernacle toward the east, even before the tabernacle of the congregation eastward, shall be Moses, and Aaron and his sons, keeping the charge of the sanctuary for the charge of the children of Israel; and the stranger that cometh nigh shall be put to death.

Moses, Aaron and his sons encamped at the east of the Tabernacle because they were the leaders of the Children of Israel. Farther east was the camp of Judah; they were the leaders of the tribes of the army.

Number of Levites, 22,000, 3:39-41:

39 All that were numbered of the Levites, which Moses and Aaron numbered at the commandment of the Lord, throughout their families, all the males from a month old and upward, were twenty and two thousand.

40 And the Lord said unto Moses, Number all the first born of the males of the children of Israel from a month old and upward, and take the number of their names.

41 And thou shalt take the Levites for me (I am the Lord) instead of all the first born among the children of Israel; and the cattle of the Levites instead of all the firstlings among the cattle of the children of Israel.

Number of the Firstborn, 22,273, 3:42-45:

42 And Moses numbered as the Lord commanded him, all the firstborn among the children of Israel.

43 And all the firstborn males by the number of names, from a month old and upward, of those that were numbered of them, were twenty and two thousand two hundred and three score and thirteen.

44 And the Lord spoke unto Moses, saying,

45 Take the Levites instead of all the firstborn among the children of Israel, and the cattle of the Levites instead of their cattle; and the Levites shall be mine: I am the Lord.

The numbering of the firstborn and the numbering of the Levites show an amazing result. The firstborn were more than the Levites by only 273 persons. There was to be an exchange of the firstborn by the Levites. Taking the Levites instead of all the firstborn of the other Tribes was the wise decision, considering it was for the purpose of the Ministry. Already, Moses and Aaron and his sons who were from the tribe of Levi were serving in the Ministry. For the sake of unity, it was better to anoint one tribe for the Ministry than the firstborn which were from all the other tribes. There was only one problem which was that there were 273 more firstborn than the Levites. This problem would be solved by redeeming the 273 firstborn. A price had to be paid for buying them back from the Lord and the redemption money had to be paid into the treasury of the Tabernacle.

Redemption of the Firstborn, 273, Num. 3:46-51:

46 And for those that shall be redeemed of the two hundred and three score and thirteen of the firstborn of the children of Israel, which are more than the Levites;

47 Thou shalt even take five shekels apiece by the poll, after the shekel of the sanctuary shalt thou take them: (the shekel is twenty gerahs:)

48 And thou shalt give the money, wherewith the odd number of them is to be redeemed, unto Aaron and to his sons.

49 And Moses took the redemption money of them that were over and above them that were redeemed by the Levites:

50 Of the firstborn of the children of Israel took he the money, a thousand three hundred and three score and five shekels, after the shekel of the sanctuary:

51 And Moses gave the money of them that were redeemed unto Aaron and to his sons, according to the word of the Lord, as the Lord commanded Moses.

It is not clear if the redemption money was to be made in silver or gold. I would assume it was to be paid in silver. A thousand three hundred and sixty-five shekels of silver or gold seems to be a lot of money. But at 100 shekels to the pound (weight), it amounted to just 13.5 pounds of silver or gold.

All the Levites were dedicated to the Ministry of the Tabernacle but they could not begin service until the age of 30 years and upward. Thus it was important to number those who were qualified to begin service. They were to be numbered according to the house of their fathers: Gershon, Kohath, and Merari. These are the fathers of the Levites. These three fathers remind us of the Holy Trinity.

Age of Numbering the Levites for Service, 30 to 50 years, Numbers 4

One had to be 30 years old before entering public office. This law was true in time of Christ. That was the reason He began His ministry at the age 30 years.

The Kohathites 2,750, Num. 4:1-20:

1 And the Lord spoke unto Moses and unto Aaron, saying,

2 Take the sum of the sons of Kohath from among the sons of Levi, after their families, by the house of their fathers,

3 From thirty years old and upward even until fifty years old, all that enter into the host, to do the work of the tabernacle of the congregation.

The sons of Kohath were assigned to the most holy things, including the Ark of the Covenant. Moses, Aaron and his sons were from the house Kohath. Aaron and his sons would therefore cover the holy things when the Tabernacle was to relocate.

4 This shall be the service of the sons of Kohath in the tabernacle of the congregation about the most holy things:

5 And when the camp sets forward, Aaron shall come, and his sons, and they shall take down the covering veil, and cover the ark of the testimony with it:

The covering of blue cloth was commonly used in covering the holy things of the Tabernacle. Blue symbolizes holiness, Divinity.

6 And shall put thereon the covering of badgers' skins, and shall spread over it a cloth wholly of blue, and shall put it in the staves thereof.

7 And upon the table of showbread they shall spread a cloth of blue, and put thereon the dishes, and the spoons, and the bowls, and covers to cover withal: and the continual bread shall be thereon:

8 And they shall spread upon them a cloth of scarlet, and cover the same with covering of badgers' skins, and shall put in the staves thereof.

9 And they shall take a cloth of blue, and cover the candlestick of the light, and his light, and his lamps, and his tongs, and his snuff-dishes, and all the oil vessels thereof, wherewith they minister unto it.

10 And they shall put it and all the vessels thereof within a covering of badgers' skins, and shall put it upon a bar.

11 And upon the golden altar they shall spread a cloth of blue, and cover it with a covering of badgers' skins, and shall put to the staves thereof:

12 And they shall take all the instruments of ministry, wherewith they minister in the sanctuary, and put them in a cloth of blue, and cover them with a covering of badgers' skins, and shall put them on a bar:

13 And they shall take away the ashes from the altar, and spread a purple cloth thereon:

14 And they shall put upon it all the vessels thereof, wherewith they minister about it, even the censers, the flesh hooks, and the shovels, and the basins, all the vessels of the altar; and they shall spread upon it a covering of badgers' skins, and put to the staves of it.

After Aaron and his sons had covered all the holy things and had everything ready for relocation, the sons of Kohath came and carried them to the next location.

15 And when Aaron and his sons have made an end of covering the sanctuary, and all the vessels of the sanctuary, as the camp is to set forward; after that the sons of Kohath shall come to bear it: but they shall not touch any holy thing, lest they die. These things are the burden of the sons of Kohath in the tabernacle of the congregation.

Eleazar who was next in line for the High Priesthood was given special responsibility.

16 And to the office of Eleazar the son of Aaron the priest

pertains the oil for the light, and the sweet incense, and the daily meat offering, and the anointing oil, and the oversight of all the tabernacle, and of all that therein is, in the sanctuary, and in the vessels thereof.

17 And the Lord spoke unto Moses and unto Aaron, saying,

18 Cut ye not off the tribe of the families of the Kohathites from among the Levites:

19 But thus do unto them, that they may live, and not die, when they approach unto the most holy things: Aaron and his sons shall go in, and appoint them every one to his service and to his burden:

20 But they shall not go in to see when the holy things are covered, lest they die.

The Gershonites 2,630, Num. 4:21-28:

21 And the Lord spoke unto Moses, saying,

22 Take also the sum of the sons of Gershon, throughout the houses of their fathers, by their families;

23 From thirty years old and upward until fifty years old shalt thou number them; all that enter in to perform the service, to do the work in the tabernacle of the congregation.

24 This is the service of the families of the Gershonites, to serve, and for burdens.

25 And they shall bear the curtains of the tabernacle, and the tabernacle of the congregation, his covering, and the covering of the badgers' skins that is above it, and the hanging for the door of the tabernacle of the congregation,

26 And the hangings of the court, and the hanging for the door of the gate of the court, which is by the tabernacle and by the altar round about, and their cords, and all the instruments of their service, and all that is made of them: so shall they serve.

27 At the appointment of Aaron and his sons shall be all the service of the sons of the Gershonites, in all their

burdens, and in all their service: and ye shall appoint unto them in charge all their burdens.

28 This is the service of the families of the sons Gershon in the tabernacle of the congregation: and their charge shall be under the hand of Ithamar the son of Aaron the priest.

Ithamar the younger son of Aaron had the charge of the Gershonites. Here again we can see the order and accountability in everything.

The Merarites 3,200, Num. 4:29-33:

29 As for the sons of Merari, thou shalt number them after their families, by the house of their fathers;

30 From thirty years old and upward even unto fifty years old shalt thou number them, every one that enters into the service, to do the work of the tabernacle of the congregation.

31 And this is the charge of their burden, according to all their service in the tabernacle of the congregation; the boards of the tabernacle, and the bars thereof, and the pillars thereof, and the sockets thereof,

32 And the pillars of the court round about, and their sockets, and their pins, and their cords, with all their instruments, and with all their service: and by name ye shall reckon the instruments of the charge of their burden.

33 This is the service of the families of the sons of Merari, according to all their service, in the tabernacle of the congregation, under the hand of Ithamar the son of Aaron the priest.

34 And Moses and Aaron and the chief of the congregation numbered the sons of the Kohathites after their families, and after the house of their fathers,

35 From thirty years old and upward even unto fifty years old, every one that enters into the service, for the work in the tabernacle of the congregation:

36 And those that were numbered of them by their families were two thousand seven hundred and fifty.

37 These were they that were numbered of the families of the Kohathites, all that might do service in the tabernacle of the congregation, which Moses and Aaron did number according to the commandment of the Lord by the hand of Moses.

38 Those that were numbered of the sons of Gershon, throughout their families, and the house of their fathers,

39 From thirty years old and upward even unto fifty years old, every one that enters into the service, for the work in the tabernacle of the congregation,

40 Even those that were numbered of them, throughout their families, by the house of their fathers, were two thousand and six hundred and thirty.

41 These are they that were numbered of the families of the sons of Gershon, of all that might do service in the tabernacle of the congregation, whom Moses and Aaron did number according to the commandment of the Lord.

42 And those that were numbered of the families of the sons of Merari, throughout their families, by the house of their fathers,

43 From thirty years old and upward even unto fifty years old, every one that enters into the service, for the work in the tabernacle of the congregation,

44 Even those that were numbered of them after their families, were three thousand and two hundred,

45 These be those that were numbered of the families of the sons of Merari, whom Moses and Aaron numbered according to the word of the Lord by the hand of Moses.

46 All those were numbered of the Levites, whom Moses and Aaron and the chief of Israel numbered, after their families, and after the house of their fathers,

47 From thirty years old and upward even unto fifty years old, every one that came to do the service of the ministry, and the service of the burden in the tabernacle of the congregation,

48 Even those that were numbered of them, were eight thousand and five hundred and fourscore (8,580).

49 According to the commandment of the Lord they were numbered by the hand of Moses, every one according to his service, and according to his burden: thus were they numbered of him, as the Lord commanded Moses.

This was the first time of numbering the Children of Israel. It was done in Sinai after a year in the Wilderness. Absent from this numbering were the female. The army was 603,550; the Levites were 22,000. If all the women and children were numbered, there would have been more than 2,000,000 people.

In keeping with our objective of reviewing subjects of like nature together, we have here included the second numbering of the Children of Israel, which was done approximately 38 years after the first numbering in the Plains of Moab. Except for Caleb and Joshua all those who were numbered in Sinai all perished in the Wilderness because of their disobedience and unbelief. This numbering was of the children of the disobedient and unbelieving Israelites. God had promised that their disobedience would prevent them from entering the Promised Land.

God calls for the numbering of the new generation. The numbering began with the oldest son. It proved that the old generation died in the wilderness.

The Numbering Again of the Children of Israel, Numbers 26

1 And it came to pass after the plague, that the Lord spoke unto Moses and unto Eleazar the son of Aaron the priest, saying,

2 Take the sum of all the congregation of the children of Israel, from twenty years old and upward, throughout their fathers' house, all that are able to go to war in Israel.

3 And Moses and Eleazar the priest spoke with them in

the plains of Moab by Jordan near Jericho, saying,

4 Take the sum of the people from twenty years old and upward; as the Lord commanded Moses and the children of Israel, which went forth out of the land of Egypt.

1. Reuben, 43,730, 26:5-11:

5 Reuben, the eldest son of Israel: the children of Reuben, Hanoch of whom cometh the families of the Hanochites: of Pallu, the family Palluites:

6 Of Hezron, the family of the Hezronites: of Carmi, the family of the Carmites.

7 These are the families of the Reubenites: and they that were numbered of them were forty and three thousand and seven hundred and thirty.

8 And the sons of Pallu; Eliab.

9 And the sons of Eliab; Nemuel, and Dathan, and Abiram. This is that Dathan and Abiram, which were famous in the congregation, who strove against Moses and against Aaron in the company of Korah, when they strove against the Lord: *(43,730 compared with 46,500, first numbering).*

10 And the earth opened her mouth and swallowed them up together with Korah, when that company died, what time the fire devoured two hundred and fifty men: and they became a sign.

11 Notwithstanding the children of Korah died not.

2. Simeon, 22,200, 26:12-14:

12 The sons of Simeon after their families: of Nemuel, the family of the Nemuelites: of Jamin, the family of the Jaminites: of Jachin, the family of the Jachinites: *(22,200 compared with 59,300, first numbering).*

13 Of Zerah, the family of the Zarhites: of Shaul, the family of the Shaulites.

14 These are the families of the Simeonites, twenty and two thousand and two hundred.

3. Gad, 40,500, 26:15-18:

15 The children of Gad after their families: of Zephon, the family of the Zephonites: of Haggi, the family of the Haggites: of Shuni, the family of the Shunites: *(40,500 compared 45,650, first numbering).*

16 Of Ozni, the family of the Oznites: of Eri, the family of the Erites:

17 Of Arod, the family of the Arodites: of Areli, the family of the Arelites.

18 These are the families of the children of Gad according to those that were numbered of them, were forty thousand and five hundred.

4. Judah, 76,500, Num. 26:19-22:
19 The sons of Judah were Er and Onan: and Er and Onan died in the land of Canaan.

20 And the sons of Judah after their families were; of Shelah, the family of the Shelanites: of Pharez, the family of the Pharzites: of Zerah, the family of the Zarahites. *(76,500 compared with 74,600, first numbering).*

21 And the sons of Pharez were; of Hezron, the family of the Hezronites: of Hamul, the family of Hamulites.

22 These are the families of Judah according to those that were numbered of them, three score and sixteen thousand and five hundred.

5. Issachar, 64,300, 26:23-25:
23 Of the sons of Issachar after their families: of Tola, the family of the Tolaites: of Pua, the family of the Punites:

24 Of Jashub, the family of the Jashubites: of Shimron, the family of the Shimronites. *(64,300 compared with 54,400, first numbering).*

25 These are the families of Issachar according to those that were numbered of them, three score and four thousand and three hundred.

6. Zebulun, 60,500, Num.26:26-27:

26 Of the sons of Zebulun after their families: of Zered, the family of the Sardites: of Elon, the family of Elonites: of Jahleel, the family of the Jahleelites.

27 These are the families of the Zebulunites according to those that were numbered of them, threescore thousand and five hundred. *(60,500 compared with 57,400, first numbering).*

7. Manasseh, 52,700, 26:28-34:

28 The sons of Joseph after their families were Manasseh and Ephraim.

29 Of the sons of Manasseh: Machir, the family of the Machirites: and Machir begat Gilead: of Gilead come the family of the Gileadites.

30 These are the sons of Gilead: of Jeezer, the family of the Jeezerites: of Helek, the family of the Helekites:

31 And of Asriel, the family of the Asrielites: and of Shechem, the family of the Shechemites:

32 And of Shemida, the family of the Shemidaites: and of Hepher, the family of the Hepherites.

33 And Zelophehad the son of Hepher had no sons, but daughters: and the names of the daughters of Zelophehad were Mahlah, and Noah, Hogla, Milcah, and Tirza. *(52,700 compared with 32,200, first numbering).*

34 These are the families of Manasseh, and those that were numbered of them, fifty and two thousand and seven hundred.

The tribe of Manasseh had a substantial increase.

8. Ephraim, 32,500, 26:35-37:

35 These are the sons of Ephraim after their families: of Shuthelah, the family of the Shuthalhites: of Becher, the family of the Bechrites: of Tahan, the family of the Tahanites. *(32,500 compared with 40,500, first numbering)*

36. And these are the sons of Shuthelah: of Eran, the family of the Eranites.

37 These are the families of the sons of Ephraim according to those that were numbered of them, thirty and

two thousand and five hundred. These are the sons of Joseph after their families.

9 Benjamin, 45,600, 26:38-41:

38 The sons of Benjamin after their families: of Bela, the family of the Belaites: of Ashbel, the family of the Asbelites: of Ahiram, the family of the Ahiramites:

39 Of Shupham, the family of the Shuphamites: of Hupham, the family of the Huphamites. *(45,600 compared with 35,400, first numbering)*

40 The sons of Bela were Ard and Naaman: of Ard, the family of the Ardites: and of Naaman, the family of the Naamites.

41 These are the sons of Benjamin after their families: and they that were numbered of them were forty and five thousand and six hundred.

10. Dan, 64,400, 26:42-43:

42 These are the sons of Dan after their families: of Shuham, the family of the Shuhamites. These are the families of Dan after their families.

43 All the families of the Shuhamites, according to those that were numbered of them, were threescore and four thousand and four hundred.
(64,400 compared with 62,700, first numbering).

11. Asher, 53,400, 26:44-47:

44 Of the children of Asher after their families: of Jimna, the family of the Jimnites: of Jesui, the family of the Jesuites: of Beriah, the family of the Beriites.

45 Of the sons of Beriah: of Heber, the family of the Heberites: of Malchiel, the family of the Malchielites. *(53,400 compared with 41,500, first numbering)*

46 And the name of the daughter of Asher was Sarah.

47 These are the families of the sons of Asher according to those that were numbered of them; who were fifty and three thousand and four hundred.

12. Naphtali, 45,400, 26:48-50:

48 Of the sons of Naphtali after their families: of Jahzeel, the family of the Jahzeelites: of Guni, the family of the Gunites:

49 Of Jezer, the family of the Jerzerites: of Shillem, the family of the Shillemites.

50 These are the families of Naphtali according to their families: and they that were numbered of them were forty and five thousand and four hundred.
(45,400 compared with 53,400, first numbering).

51 These were the number of the children of Israel, six hundred thousand and a thousand seven hundred and thirty. (601,730 compared with 603,550, first numbering).

52 And the Lord spoke unto Moses, saying,

53 Unto these the land shall be divided for an inheritance according to the number of names.

54 To many thou shalt give more inheritance, and to few thou shalt give the less inheritance: to every one shall his inheritance be given according to those that were numbered of him.

55 Notwithstanding the land shall be divided by lot: according to the names of the tribes of their fathers they shall inherit.

56 According to the lot shall the possession thereof be divided between the many and few.

57 And these are they that were numbered of the Levites after their families: Gershon, the family of the Gershonites: of Kohath, the family of the Kohathites: of Merari, the family of the Merarites.

58 These are the families of the Levites: the family of the Libnites, the family of the Hebronites, the family of the Mahlites, the family of the Mushites, the family of the Korathites. And Kohath begat Amram.

59 And the name of Amram's wife was Jochebed, the daughter of Levi, whom her mother bare to Levi in Egypt: and she bare unto Amram, Aaron and Moses, and Miriam

their sister.

60 And unto Aaron was born Nadab, and Abihu, Eleazar, and Ithamar.

61 And Nadab and Abihu died, when they offered strange fire before the Lord.

62 And those that were numbered of them were twenty and three thousand, all males from a month old and upward: for they were not numbered among the children of Israel, because there was no inheritance given them among the children of Israel. *(23,000 compared with 22,000, first numbering).*

63 These are they that were numbered by Moses and Eleazar the priest, who numbered the children of Israel in the plains of Moab by Jordan near Jericho.

64 But among these there was not a man of them whom Moses and Aaron the priest numbered, when they numbered the children of Israel in the wilderness of Sinai.

65 For the Lord said of them, They shall surely die in the wilderness. And there was not left a man of them save Caleb the son of Jephunneh, and Joshua the son of Nun.

SUMMARY

The Book of Numbers derived its name from the numbering of the Children of Israel. Order, responsibility, and accountability demanded this numbering. The Levites were not numbered with the other tribes. They were, however, numbered and then exchanged for all the firstborn in Israel and assigned to the Ministry of the Tabernacle. The firstborn of Israel was a gift of the Passover to the Lord. In the night of the Passover when the Lord killed all the firstborn of man and beast in Egypt, He claimed all the firstborn in Israel as His. When the firstborn was counted, there were 22,273 of them; the number of the Levites when counted was 22,000. The extra number of the firstborn had to be redeemed at the price commanded by the Lord. After the redemption of the 273 firstborn, the Levites were dedicated to the service of the Tabernacle, to serve the whole congregation of Israel.

They camped around the Tabernacle while Moses, Aaron and his sons dwelled in front of the Tabernacle. The congregation of women, children, and the elderly dwelled next to the Levites Then the armies of the tribes of Israel encamped around the Levites in their respective order. The armies of Judah, Issachar, and Zebulun of 186,409 encamped east of the Tabernacle. The armies of Reuben, Simeon, and Gad of 151, 450 encamped south of the Tabernacle. The armies of Ephraim, Manasseh, and Benjamin of 108,100 encamped west of the Tabernacle. The armies of Dan, Asher and Naphtali of 157,600 encamped north of the Tabernacle

Numbering implies order, responsibility, and accountability. It also implies value. The things God created are important to Him; therefore they are numbered. The stars are numbered, the angels, and human beings. Because Israel, God's chosen people, were important, they were numbered. But the second numbering was important for another reason. It was to confirm God's promise that the generation that was numbered in Mount Sinai would be denied the blessing of inheriting the Promised Land because of its disobedience and unbelief. Israel was a type of the Church; the members of Christ's Church are all numbered not my man, but by God Himself and their names are written in the Book of Life.

The second numbering shows a decrease of 1,820 from 603,550 to 601,730 in the army and an increase of 1,000 Levites, from 22,000 to 23,000. Those of the army were numbered from 20 years old and upward; the Levites were numbered from a month old and upward. For the service of the Ministry of the Tabernacle, the Levites began to serve at age 30 years old and upward. Women and children were not numbered. The land was to be divided among the 624,730 people. Amazingly, all the Children of Israel were pleased with their inheritance.

CHAPTER 20

Questions of Leprosy, Adultery and Vows, Numbers 5-6

God's children were called to holiness because God is holy. Yet things that were common to other nations had invaded the life of the Children of Israel and checked their natural progress to a life of holiness. Why should issues of leprosy, adultery, failures of vows be identified with the people of God? All these things happened to show that they are, nevertheless, normal human beings who like all others inherited a fallen nature. However, these very issues and circumstances, by their very nature, pointed to the provision of Atonement as the solutions to the problems and the answers to these perplexing questions.

Leprosy, Num. 5:1-4

1 And the Lord spoke unto Moses, saying,

2 Command the children of Israel that they put out of the camp every leper, and every one that hath an issue, and whosoever is defiled by the dead:

3 Both male and female shall ye put out, without the camp shall ye put them; that they defile not their camps, in the midst whereof I dwell.

The disease of Leprosy had plagued the Children of Israel for a long time. The shame associated with the disease was even greater than the pain. It called for abandonment from society without exception. The leper was not allowed to participate in the regular life of the Nation. He was put outside the camp of the congregation of Israel. The only company the leper had, were those that were defiled by the dead. The reason for the isolation of the leper and the defiled was because of the abiding presence of God. God was dwelling among the people and they had to live by His principles of holiness.

God could have prevented the disease of leprosy but he did not. The Bible says, "All things work together for good to them that love the Lord". Even Leprosy could be used to turn one's heart to the Lord, one who was going astray from God. Not in all cases the Children of Israel obeyed the Lord but in this case they did. It was rather difficult for them to isolate the lepers and the defiled. But God does not always ask His children to do the easiest of things. It requires faith and obedience. God takes pleasure in watching us obey Him. He is a perfect God and His will for us is better than ours.

4 And the children of Israel did so, and put them out without the camp: as the Lord spoke unto Moses, so did the children of Israel.

Confession, Num. 5:5-10:

5 And the Lord spoke unto Moses, saying,

6 Speak unto the children of Israel, When a man or a woman shall commit any sin that men commit, to do a trespass against the Lord, and that person be guilty;

7 Then they shall confess their sin which they have done: and he shall recompense his trespass with the principal thereof, and add unto it the fifth part thereof, and give unto him against whom he hath trespassed.

Confession is good for the soul; it frees the guilty conscience and allows for the renewal of fellowship with man and God. But in most cases, confession alone is not good enough: it must be followed with acts of contrition. In this case the trespasser must recompense the offended and add a fifth thereto. Whether or not the offended is recompensed, the trespasser had to offer to the priest a ram for his atonement. If no one was found to whom the recompense be made, the trespasser had to pay the amount to the priest.

8 But if the man have no kinsman to recompense the trespass unto, let the trespass be recompensed unto the Lord, even to the priest; beside the ram of the atonement, whereby an atonement shall be made for him.

9 And every offering of all the holy things of the children of Israel, which they bring unto the priest, shall be his.

10 And every man's hallowed things shall be his: whatsoever any man giveth the priest, it shall be his.

Adultery, Num. 5:11-31

This is the case of a man who suspects his wife of adultery and is jealous about her. He and his wife had to follow the procedure as commanded by the Lord. He had to take his wife to the priest with his jealousy offering and had to follow the mediation of the priest. Jealousy is a most deadly sin. The Atonement is the answer to all sins, including the sin of adultery.

11 And the Lord spoke unto Moses, saying,

12 Speak unto the children of Israel, and say unto them, If any man's wife go aside, and commit a trespass against him,

13 And a man lie with her carnally, and it be hid from the eyes of her husband, and be kept close, and she be defiled, and there be no witness against her, neither she be taken with the manner;

14 And the spirit of jealousy come upon him, and he be jealous of his wife, and she be not defiled:

15 Then shall the man bring his wife unto the priest, and he shall bring her offering for her, the tenth part of an ephah of barley meal; he shall pour no oil upon it, nor put frankincense thereon; for it is an offering of jealousy, an

offering of memorial, bringing iniquity to remembrance.

The Jealousy Offering was treated differently from other offerings, for example, the Meat Offering. Oil and frankincense did not apply to the jealousy offering, but to the Meat Offering.

Holy Water:

16 And the priest shall bring her near, and set her before the Lord:

17 And the priest shall take holy water in an earthen vessel; and of the dust that is in the floor of the tabernacle the priest shall take, and put it into the water:

18 And the priest shall set the woman before the Lord, and uncover the woman's head, and put the offering of memorial in her hands which is the jealousy offering: and the priest shall have in his hand the bitter water that causes the curse:

19 And the priest shall charge her by an oath, and say unto the woman, If no man have lain with thee, and if thou hast not gone aside to uncleanness with another instead of thy husband, be thou free from this bitter water that causes the curse:

20 But if thou hast gone aside to another instead of thy husband, and if thou be defiled, and some man have lain with thee beside thine husband:

21Then the priest shall charge the woman with an oath of cursing, and the priest shall say unto the woman, The Lord make thee a curse and an oath among thy people, when the Lord doth make thy thigh to rot, and thy belly to swell;

22 And this water that causes the curse shall go into thy bowels, to make thy belly to swell, and thy thigh to rot: And the woman shall say, Amen, amen.

The holy water was intended to be a blessing as well as a curse. The dust from the floor of the Tabernacle caused the holy water to be bitter and gave it the potential to cause a curse. If the wife was guilty of adultery, the water would become bitter and would cause her belly to swell and her thigh to rot. If she was innocent, she would be free from the curse of the bitter water and would be able to have children.

23 And the priest shall write these curses in a book, and he shall blot them out with the bitter water:

24 And he shall cause the woman to drink the bitter water that causes the curse: and the water that causes the curse shall enter into her, and become bitter.

Before the wife is given the bitter water to drink, the priest offers the Jealousy Offering unto the Lord.

The Jealousy Offering:

25 Then the priest shall take the jealousy offering out of the woman's hand, and shall wave the offering before the Lord, and offer it upon the altar:

26 And the priest shall take an handful of the offering, even the memorial thereof, and burn it upon the altar, and afterward shall cause the woman to drink the water.

27 And when he hath made her to drink the water, then it shall come to pass, that, if she be defiled, and have done trespass against her husband, that the water that causes the curse shall enter into her, and become bitter, and her belly shall swell, and her thigh shall rot: and the woman shall be a curse among her people.

28 And if the woman be not defiled, but be clean; then she shall be free, and shall conceive seed.

29 This is the law of jealousy, when a wife goes aside to another instead of her husband, and is defiled.

30 Or when the spirit of jealousy cometh upon him, and he be jealous over his wife, and shall set the woman before the Lord, and the priest shall execute upon her all this law.

31 Then shall the man be guiltless from iniquity, and this woman shall bear her iniquity.

This law of jealousy was good because it guaranteed true results as to innocence or guilt. It also served as a warning to those that had intentions to commit adultery. The adulteress carries the mark and shame of the guilt of adultery for the rest of her life.

Vows of the Nazarite, Num. 6:1-27:

Any vow between the Lord and a person was sacred and should be honored. When a man took the vow of the Nazarite, he could not cut his hair or shave his beard until his vow to the Lord was fulfilled. There were other conditions he had to meet. These are not conditions for us to explain away; instead, they are to be accepted at face value. One should think twice before making avow unto the Lord.

Separation from Strong Drink, Num. 6:1-5:

1 And the Lord spoke unto Moses, saying,

2 Speak unto the children of Israel and say unto them, When either man or woman shall separate themselves to vow a vow of a Nazarite, to separate themselves unto the Lord:

3 He shall separate himself from wine and strong drink, and shall drink no vinegar of wine, or vinegar of strong drink, neither shall he drink any liquor of grapes, nor eat moist grapes, or dried.

4 All the days of his separation shall he eat nothing that is made of the vine, from the kernels even to the husk.

5 All the days of the vow of his separation there shall no razor come upon his head: until the days be fulfilled, in the which he separates himself unto the Lord, he shall be holy, and shall let the locks of the hair of his head grow.

Separation from Dead Bodies, Num. 6:6-12:

6 All the days that he separates himself unto the Lord he shall come at no dead body.

7 He shall not make himself unclean for his father, or for his mother, or for his brother, or for his sister, when they die: because the consecration of his God is upon his head.

8 All the days of his separation he is holy unto the Lord.

The Law required that the priests be not defiled with the body of the dead because of the anointing of the Lord upon them. Here the Nazarite was required not to be defiled with the body of the dead because the consecration of God was upon his head. If anyone died accidentally by him, the possibility to be defiled increased; and in such case that he was defiled, he had to shave his head and bring an offering to the priest.

9 And if any man die very suddenly by him, and he hath defiled the head of his consecration; then he shall shave his head in the day of his cleansing, on the seventh day shall he shave it.

10 And on the eighth day he shall bring two turtles, or two young pigeons, to the priest, to the door of the tabernacle of the congregation:

11 And the priest shall offer the one for a sin offering, and the other for a burnt offering, and make an atonement for him, for that he sinned by the dead, and shall hallow his head that same day.

Because he accidentally defiled his consecration, he had the opportunity to re-consecrate himself unto the Lord; but the days before the time of his recommitment would not be counted unto him.

12 And he shall consecrate unto the Lord the days of his separation, and shall bring a lamb of the first year for a trespass offering: but the days that were before shall be lost, because his separation was defiled.

Fulfillment of Vow, Num. 6:13-21:

When the Nazarite normally fulfilled his vow, He had to follow the procedure of the Law and offer those sacrifices required of him.

13 And this is the law of the Nazarite, when the days of his separation are fulfilled: he shall be brought unto the door of the tabernacle of the congregation:

Making a vow unto the Lord was a decision of the heart, but it involved much effort and determination. However, the vow of the Nazarite was not legally fulfilled until he offered all the sacrifices required under the Law. To mark the formal fulfillment of his vow, he had to offer a Sin Offering, a Burnt Offering, a Peace Offering, and a Meat Offering with its Drink Offering.

14 And he shall offer his offering unto the Lord, one he lamb of the first year without blemish for a burnt offering, and one ewe lamb of the first year without blemish for a sin offering, and one ram without blemish for peace offerings.

15 And a basket of unleavened bread, cakes of fine flour mingled with oil, and wafers of unleavened bread anointed with oil, and their meat offering, and their drink offerings.

16 And the priest shall bring them before the Lord, and shall offer his sin offering, and his burnt offering:

17 And he shall offer the ram as a sacrifice of peace offerings unto the Lord, with the basket of unleavened bread: the priest shall offer also his meat offering, and his drink offering.

The offerings were only part of the ceremony of fulfillment of the Nazarite's vow; the shaving of his head and its offering up unto the Lord expressed complete fulfillment of his vow unto the Lord.

18 And the Nazarite shall shave the head of his separation at the door of the tabernacle of the congregation, and shall take the hair of the head of his separation, and put it in the fire which is under the sacrifice of the peace offerings.

19 And the priest shall take the sodden shoulder of the ram, and one unleavened cake out of the basket, and one unleavened wafer, and shall put them upon the hands of the Nazarite, after the hair of his separation is shaven:

20 And the priest shall wave them for a wave offering before the Lord: this is holy for the priest, with the wave

breast and heave shoulder: and after that the Nazarite may drink wine.

21 This is the law of the Nazarite who hath vowed, and of his offering unto the Lord for his separation, beside that that his hand shall get: according to the vow which he vowed, so he must do after the law of his separation.

Only after the Children of Israel fully obeyed the Lord, His blessings would rest upon them. Therefore, obedience was the secret of their prosperity.

22 And the Lord spoke unto Moses, saying,

23 Speak unto Aaron and unto his sons, saying, On this wise ye shall bless the children of Israel, saying unto them,

24 The Lord bless thee, and keep thee:

25 The Lord make his face shine upon thee, and be gracious unto thee:

26 The Lord lift up his countenance upon thee, and give thee peace.

27 And they shall put my name upon the children of Israel; and I will bless them.

SUMMARY

The Children of Israel did not live with their problems; they found a way to solve them because God was their Problem Solver. The disease of leprosy was a problem with which they had lived but God was able to rid them of their leprosy. The shame associated with the disease was even greater than the pain. It called for abandonment from society without exception. The leper was not allowed to participate in the regular life of the nation. He was put outside the camp of the congregation of Israel. The only company the leper had were those that were defiled by the dead.

God could have prevented the disease of leprosy but he did not. Even Leprosy could be used to turn one's heart to the Lord, one who was going astray from God. Not in all cases the Children of Israel obeyed the Lord but in this case they did. It was rather difficult for them to isolate the lepers and the defiled. But God does not ask His children to do the easiest of things; but at all times it requires faith and obedience. God takes pleasure in watching us obey Him.

God's children were required not to be perfect, but to be holy. At times they had problems with adultery and even with jealousy of adultery. There was a stigma attached to adultery that was greater than that of leprosy. There was the instance in which an adulterous woman's belly could be swollen for the rest of her life and become a curse; yet by the nature of this curse, adultery could be prevented in Israel.

A vow was a sacred commitment between a person and his God, it should always be honored; yet there were circumstances just waiting by to render them meaningless. It was as though one was powerless to pursue the desire of the heart and willing to return to the arms of despair. Yet with God, the problem of a vow was not too difficult to solve; and He had placed the solution within the reach of all those who wanted to fulfill the desire of their heart.

CHAPTER 21
The Offerings of The Princes And The Levites, NUMBERS, 7-8

At the end of the first year in the Wilderness, the Children of Israel constructed the Tabernacle and dedicated it unto the Lord. It was equally important that the princes of the Children of Israel and the Levites be dedicated to the Lord. The princes were to serve in the capacity of captains of the armies of Israel. The Levites were to serve in the capacity of spiritual leaders. The ceremonies of dedication were of themselves a spiritually moving experience to all of Israel. The nation united as one with God their Immortal King.

The twelve princes were to each offer their offerings on behalf of their respective tribes. The Levites were to offer the offering of themselves to the Lord on behalf of the congregation of Israel.

The Offering of the Princes, Numbers, 7

Each prince was to offer four of the principal offerings of atonement in the same proportion. These princes were to offer their offerings in the order of their encampment around the Tabernacle. Each prince had a separate day to offer his offering. Manasseh and Ephraim the two sons of Joseph became two tribes; the Levites who were taken by the Lord instead of the firstborn were not represented by the princes. Before they had offered their offerings, they gave a gift to the Levites, verses 1-9.

1 And it came to pass on the day that Moses had fully set

up the tabernacle, and had anointed it, and sanctified it, and all the instruments thereof, both the altar and all the vessels thereof, and had anointed them, and sanctified them:

2 That the princes of Israel, heads of the house of their fathers, who were the princes of the tribes, and were over them that were numbered, offered:

3 And they brought their offerings before the Lord, six covered wagons and twelve oxen; a wagon for two of the princes, and for each one an ox: and they brought them before the tabernacle.

4 And the Lord spoke unto Moses, saying,

5 Take it of them that they may be to do the service of the tabernacle of the congregation; and thou shalt give them unto the Levites, to every man according to his service.

These gifts were given to the Levites to do the service of the Tabernacle, namely to transport the Tabernacle to its next destination. It seems the Merarites were given more of the gifts because they were more in number than the Gershonites: 3,200 compared with 2,630 Gershonites.

6 And Moses took the wagons and the oxen, and gave them unto the Levites.

7 Two wagons and four oxen he gave unto the sons of Gershon, according to their service:

8 And four wagons and eight oxen he gave unto the sons of Merari, according to their service, under the hand of Ithamar the son of Aaron the priest.

The Kohathites were not given any of the gifts from the princes because they were assigned to the most holy things such as the Ark of the Covenant and the Mercy Seat, which could not be transported in the wagons. They had to carry them on their shoulders. Moses and Aaron were from the family of the Kohathites (Numbers 3: 17-19, 30-32; 4: 4-15). The Kohathites were appointed to carry the most holy things. As head of the nation, Moses was also High Priest.

.9 But unto the sons of Kohath he gave none: because

the service of the sanctuary belonging unto them was that they should bear upon their shoulders.

10 And the princes offered for dedicating of the altar in the day that it was anointed, even the princes offered their offering before the altar.

11 And the Lord said unto Moses, They shall offer their offering, each prince on his day, for the dedicating of the altar. *(See Exodus 29:36-37)*

1. Judah, Num.7: 12-17:

Meat Offering vs.12-14:

12 And he that offered his offering the first day was Nahshon the son of Amminadab, of the tribe of Judah:

13 And his offering was one silver charger, the weight thereof was an hundred and thirty shekels (100 S = 1pound; 1Shekel = .4 ounce), one silver bowl of seventy shekels, after the shekel of the sanctuary; both of them were full of fine flour mingled with oil for a meat offering:

14 One spoon of ten shekels of gold, full of incense:

The incense was used with the Meat Offering.

Burnt Offering v. 15

15 One young bullock, one ram, one lamb of the first year, for a burnt offering:

Sin Offering, v. 16,

16 One kid of the goats for a sin offering:

Peace Offering, v. 17,

17 And for a sacrifice of peace offerings, two oxen, five rams, five he goats, five lambs of the first year: this was the offering of Nahshon the son of Amminadab.

Judah was the leader of the tribes that encamped east of the Tabernacle; he offered first and Issachar and Zebulun offered after.

2. Issachar, 7: 18-23

18 On the second day Nethaneel the son of Zuar, prince of Issachar, did offer:

Meat Offering, vs. 19-20,

19 He offered for his offering one silver charger, the weight whereof was one hundred and thirty shekels, one silver bowl of seventy shekels, after the shekel of the sanctuary; both of them full of fine flour mingled with oil for meat offering:

20 One spoon of gold of ten shekel, full of incense:

Burnt Offering, v. 21,

21 One young bullock, one ram, one lamb of the first year, for a burnt offering:

Sin Offering, v. 22,

22 One kid of the goats for a sin offering:

Peace Offering, v.23

23 And for a sacrifice of peace offerings, two oxen, five rams, five he goats, five lambs of the first year: this was the offering of Nethaneel the son of Zuar.

3. Zebulun, 7:24-29

24 On the third day Eliab the son of Helon, prince of the children of Zebulun, did offer:

Meat Offering, vs. 25-26,

25 His offering was one silver charger, the weight whereof was an hundred and thirty shekels, one silver bowl of seventy shekels, after the shekel of the sanctuary; both of them full with fine flour mingled with oil for a meat offering:

26 One golden spoon of ten shekels, full of incense:

Burnt Offering, v. 27,

27 One young bullock, one ram, one lamb of the first year, for burnt offering:

Sin Offering, v. 28,

28 One kid of the goats for a sin offering:

Peace Offering, v. 29,

29 And for a sacrifice of peace offerings, two oxen, five rams, five he goats, five lambs of the first year: this was the offering of Eliab the son of Helon.

4. Reuben, 7:30-35

Reuben encamped south of the Tabernacle; he was the

leader of the tribes that encamped with him south of the Tabernacle. He offered first and Simeon and Gad followed after.

30 On the fourth day Elzur the son of Shedeur, prince of the children of Reuben, did offer:

His Meat Offering, Num. 7: 31-32,

31 His offering was one silver charger of the weight of an hundred and thirty shekels, one silver bowl of seventy shekels, after the shekel of the sanctuary; both of them full of fine flour mingled with oil for a meat offering:

32 One golden spoon of ten shekels, full of incense:

Burnt Offering, v. 33,

33 One young bullock, one ram, one lamb of the first year, for a burnt offering:

Sin Offering, v. 34,

34 One kid of the goats for a sin offering:

His Peace Offering, v. 35,

35 And for a sacrifice of peace offerings, two oxen, five rams, five he goats, five lambs of the first year: this was the offering of Elizur the son of Shedeur.

The response of the princes to the dedication of the Tabernacle by their offerings shows the unity as one nation under God and the determination to follow God in obedience to His commandments. With God as their Leader, victory was theirs.

5. Simeon Num. 7: 36-41

36 On the fifth day Shelumiel the son of Zurishaddai, prince of the children of Simeon, did offer:

His Meat Offering, vs. 37-38,

37 His offering was one silver charger, the weight whereof was an hundred and thirty shekels, one silver bowl of seventy shekels, after the shekel of the sanctuary; both of them full of fine flour mingled with oil for a meat offering:

38 One golden spoon of ten shekels, full of incense:

His Burnt Offering, v. 39,

39 One young bullock, one ram, one lamb of the first year, for a burnt offering:

 His Sin Offering, v. 40,

40 One kid of the goats for a sin offering:

His Peace Offering, v. 41,

41 And for a sacrifice of peace offerings, two oxen, five rams, five he goats, five lambs of the first year: this was the offering of Shelumiel the son of Zurishaddai.

6. Gad, Num. 7:42-47

42 On the sixth day Eliasaph the son of Deuel, prince of the children of Gad, offered:

 His Meat Offering, vs. 43-44,

43 His offering was one silver charger of the weight of an hundred and thirty shekels, a silver bowl of seventy shekels, after the shekel of the sanctuary; both of them full of fine flour mingled with oil for a meat offering:

44 One golden spoon of ten shekels, full of incense:

 His Burnt Offering, v. 45,

45 One young bullock, one ram, one lamb of the first year, for a burnt offering:

His Sin Offering, v. 46,

46 One kid of the he goats for a sin offering:

His Peace Offering, v. 47,

47 And for a sacrifice of peace offerings, two oxen, five rams, five he goats, five lambs of the first year: this was the offering of Eliasaph the son of Deuel.

7. Ephraim, Num. 7: 48-53

Ephraim was the leader of the tribes that encamped west of the Tabernacle; he offered first and Manasseh and Benjamin followed.

48 On the seventh day Elishama the son of Ammihud, prince of the children of Ephraim, offered:

His Meat offering, vs. 49-50,

49 His offering was one silver charger, the weight whereof was an hundred and thirty shekels, one silver charger of

seventy shekels, after the shekel of the sanctuary; both of them full of fine flour mingled with oil for a meat offering:

50 One golden spoon of ten shekels, full of incense:

His Burnt Offering, v. 51,

51 One young bullock, one ram, one lamb of the first year, for a burnt offering:

His Sin Offering, v. 52,

52 One kid of the goats for a sin offering:

His Peace Offering, v. 53,

53 And for a sacrifice of peace offerings, two oxen, five rams, five he goats, five lambs of the first year: this was the offering of Elishama the son of Ammihud.

8. Manasseh, Num. 7: 54-59

54 On the eighth day offered Gamaliel the son of Pedahzur, prince of the children of Manasseh:

His Meat Offering, vs. 55-56,

55 His offering was one silver charger of the weight of an hundred and thirty shekels, one silver bowl of seventy shekels, after the shekel of the sanctuary; both of them full of fine flour mingled with oil for a meat offering:

56 One golden spoon of ten shekels, full of incense:

His Burnt Offering, v. 57,

57 One young bullock, one ram, one lamb of the first year, for a burnt offering:

His Sin Offering, v. 58,

58 One kid of the goats for a sin offering:

His Peace Offering, v. 59,

59 And for a sacrifice of peace offerings, two oxen, five rams, five he goats, five lambs of the first year: this was the offering of Gamaliel the son of Pedahzur.

9. Benjamin, Num. 7: 60-65

60 On the ninth day Abidan the son of Gideoni, prince of the children of Benjamin, offered:

His Meat Offering, vs. 61-62,

61 His offering was one silver charger, the weight whereof was an hundred and thirty shekels, one silver bowl of seventy shekels, after the shekel of the sanctuary; both of them full of fine flour mingled with oil for a meat offering:

62 One golden spoon of ten shekels, full of incense:

His Burnt Offering, v. 63,

63 One young bullock, one ram, one lamb of the first year, for a burnt Offering:

His Sin Offering, v. 64,

64 One kid of the goats for a sin offering:

His Peace Offering, v. 65,

65 And for a sacrifice of peace offerings, two oxen, five rams, five he goats, five lambs of the first year: this was the offering of Abidan the son of Gideoni.

10. Dan, Num. 7: 66-71

Dan was the leader of the tribes that encamped north of the Tabernacle; he offered first and Asher and Naphtali followed

66 On the tenth day Ahiezer the son of Ammishaddai, prince of the children of Dan, offered:

His Meat offering, vs. 67-68,

67 His offering was one silver charger, the weight whereof was an hundred and thirty shekels, one silver bowl of seventy shekels, after the shekel of the sanctuary; both of them full of fine flour mingled with oil for a meat offering:

68 One golden spoon of ten shekels, full of incense:

His Burnt Offering, v. 69,

69 One young bullock, one ram, one lamb of the first year, for a burnt offering:

His Sin Offering, v. 70,

70 One kid of the goats for a sin offering:

His Peace Offering, v. 71,

71 And for a sacrifice of peace offerings, two oxen, five rams, five he goats, five lambs of the first year: this was the offering of Ahiezer the son of Ammishaddai.

11. Asher, Num. 7: 72-77

72 On the eleventh day Pagiel the son of Ocran, prince of the children of Asher, offered:

His Meat Offering, vs. 73-74,

73 His offering was one silver charger, the weight whereof was an hundred and thirty shekels, one silver bowl of seventy shekels, after the shekel of the sanctuary; both of them full of fine flour mingled with oil for a meat offering:

74 One golden spoon of ten shekels, full of incense:

His Burnt Offering, v. 75,

75 One young bullock, one ram, one lamb of the first year, for a burnt offering:

His sin Offering, v. 76,

76 One kid of the goats for a sin offering:

His Peace Offering, v. 77,

77 And for a sacrifice of peace offerings, two oxen, five rams, five he goats, five lambs of the first year: this was the offering of Pagiel the son of Ocran.

12. Napthtali, Num. 7: 78-83

78 On the twelfth day Ahira the son of Enan, prince of the children of Napthali, offered:

His Meat Offering, vs. 79-80,

79 His offering was one silver charger, the weight whereof was an hundred and thirty shekels, one silver bowl of seventy shekels, after the shekel of the sanctuary; both of them full of fine flour mingled with oil for a meat offering:

80 One golden spoon of ten shekels, full of incense:

His Burnt Offering, v. 81,

81 One young bullock, one ram, one lamb of the first year, for a burnt offering:

His Sin Offering, v. 82,

82 One kid of the goats for a sin offering:

His Peace Offering, v. 83,

83 And for a sacrifice of peace offerings, two oxen, five

rams, five he goats, five lambs of the first year: this was the offering of Ahira the son of Enan.

Summary of the Offerings, Num. 7: 84-88

84 This was the dedication of the altar, in the day when it was anointed, by the princes of Israel: twelve chargers of silver, twelve silver bowls, twelve spoons of gold:

85 Each charger of silver weighing an hundred and thirty shekels *(about 1.3pounds x 12 = 16 pound, the weight of the chargers)*, each bowl seventy *(.66 x12 = 7.9 pound, the weight of the bowls)*: all the silver vessels weighed two thousand and four hundred shekels, after the shekel of the sanctuary *((about 24 pounds, the weight of the silver vessels)*:

86 The golden spoons were twelve, full of incense weighing ten shekels a piece, after the shekel of the sanctuary: all the gold of the spoons was an hundred and twenty shekels *(about 1 and 1/5 pound, the weight of the golden spoons)*.

87 All the oxen for the burnt offering were twelve bullocks, the rams twelve, the lambs of the first year twelve, with their meat offering: and the kids of the goats for sin offering, twelve.

88 And all the oxen for the sacrifice of the peace offerings were twenty and four bullocks, the rams sixty, the goats sixty, the lambs of the first year sixty. This was the dedication of the altar, after that it was anointed.

Each of the twelve princes offered identical offerings on the appointed day of their dedication. Each offered a Meat Offering, a Burnt Offering, a Sin Offering, and a Peace Offering. These offerings established the right spiritual relationship they needed to have with God their Commander-in-Chief. They above all others needed this relationship because they were the ones entrusted with the defense of the nation and they needed God by their side ever moment in battle. A dedicated army to the Lord was unbeatable.

The Offerings of The Princes And The Levites

Missing from the offerings of the princes was the Trespass Offering. The Trespass Offering was to be offered for a sin caused by ignorance to what one should have known. The Trespass Offering was another kind of Sin Offering; since the Sin Offering was offered there was no need for the Trespass Offering.

The four principal offerings, the Sin Offering, the Burnt the Meat Offering, and The Peace Offering represented the different aspects of Atonement. The Sin Offering represented the forgiveness of sins; the Burnt Offering represented right relationship with God; the Meat Offering represented fellowship with God; and the Peace Offering represented peace with God. The fact that these offerings were offered together indicates complete wholeness of body, soul, and spirit.

After the forgiveness of sins, one's relationship with God was changed. After a portion of the Meat Offering was poured upon the Burnt Altar, unto God, the Priest ate the rest in the holy place, signifying fellowship with God. In this act he represented the whole congregation, meaning that those on whose behalf the Meat Offering was offered were in fellowship with God. If one was in fellowship, then one was at peace with God as represented by the Peace Offering.

It took 12 days of dedication of the princes and at the end God was well pleased.

89 And when Moses was gone into the tabernacle of the congregation to speak with him, then he heard the voice of one speaking unto him from off the mercy seat that was upon the ark of testimony, from between the two cherubim: and he spoke unto him.

What could have been more rewarding to the spiritual leader of the nation of Israel than, at the end of a job well done, to hear God's voice of approval. God had kept His promise to Moses. In Exodus 25:22 God promised that He would speak to Moses from above the Mercy Seat. Is God still speaking to His servants? What was the last time that you heard His voice?

The Offering of the Levites of Themselves, Numbers 8

1 And the Lord spoke unto Moses, saying,

2 Speak unto Aaron, and say unto him, When thou lightest the lamps, the seven lamps shall give light over against the candlestick.

3 And Aaron did so; he lighted the lamps over against the candle stick, as the Lord commanded Moses.

4 And this work of the candlestick was of beaten gold, unto the shaft thereof, unto the flowers thereof, was beaten work: according to the pattern which the Lord shown Moses, so he made the candlestick.

5 And the Lord spoke unto Moses, saying,

The Lord had told Moses that the Levites were His own; He had taken them instead of the firstborn and reminded him a number of times. The idea of exchanging the Levites for the firstborn was conceived in God's mind the day He destroyed all the firstborn of man and beast in the land of Egypt. The exchange had formally occurred with the dedication of the Levites and the offering of themselves unto God for the spiritual service of the Children of Israel.

6 Take the Levites from among the children of Israel, and cleanse them.

7 And thus shalt thou do unto them, to cleanse them: Sprinkle water of purifying upon them, and let them shave all their flesh, and let them wash their clothes, and so make themselves clean.

The Levites had to be first separated from the Children of Israel by the cleansing of water, followed by the offering of the Sin Offering, and the Burnt Offering.

8 Then let them take a young bullock with his meat offering, even fine flour mingled with oil, and another young bullock shalt thou take for a sin offering.

The Offerings of The Princes And The Levites

The Meat Offering was to be offered with the Burnt Offering. One of the bullocks was to be offered for the Sin Offering and the other for the Burnt Offering.

9 And thou shalt bring the Levites before the tabernacle of the congregation: and thou shalt gather the whole assembly of the children of Israel together:

10 And thou shalt bring the Levites before the Lord: and the children of Israel shall put their hands upon the Levites:

The dedication and the offering of the Levites were to be a national event. This would gain them national recognition of their service to God and the congregation.

11 And Aaron shall offer the Levites before the Lord for an offering of the children of Israel, that they may execute the service of the Lord.

Aaron was accustomed to offering all the offerings of the Law, but for the first time he was offering one of the tribes of Israel as an offering unto the Lord. This would have to be one of the most moving spiritual experience the Children of Israel ever had as they watched more 22, 000 of their brethren surrender their lives completely to the Lord.

12 And the Levites shall lay their hands upon the heads of the bullocks: and thou shalt offer the one for a sin offering, and the other for a burnt offering, unto the Lord, to make an atonement for the Levites.

13 And thou shalt set the Levites before Aaron, and before his sons, and offer them as an offering unto the Lord.

14 Thus shalt thou separate the Levites from among the children of Israel: and the Levites shall be mine.

15 And after that shall the Levites go in to the service of the tabernacle of the congregation: and thou shalt cleanse them, and offer them for an offering.

After the ceremony of the dedication and offering of the Levites of themselves unto the Lord, they were ready to do the service of the Tabernacle.

The Lord explains the reason for the exchange of the

Levites for the firstborn:

16 For they are wholly given unto me from among the children of Israel; instead of such as open every womb, even instead of the firstborn of all the children of Israel, have I taken them unto me.

17 For all the firstborn of the children of Israel are mine, both man and beast: on the day that I smote every firstborn in the land of Egypt I sanctify them for myself.

18 And I have taken the Levites for all the firstborn of the children of Israel.

19 And I have given the Levites as a gift to Aaron and to his sons from among the children of Israel, to do the service of the children of Israel in the tabernacle of the congregation, and to make an atonement for the children of Israel: that there be no plague among the children of Israel, when the children of Israel come nigh unto the sanctuary.

Moses was always faithful and obedient to the commandments of God:

20 And Moses, and Aaron, and all the congregation of the children of Israel did to the Levites according unto all that the Lord commanded Moses concerning the Levites, so did the children of Israel unto them.

21 And the Levites were purified, and they washed their clothes; and Aaron offered them as an offering before the Lord; and Aaron made an atonement for them to cleanse them.

22 And after that went the Levites in to do the service in the tabernacle of the congregation before Aaron, and before his sons: as the Lord had commanded Moses concerning the Levites, so did they unto them.

The Retirement Age of the Levites, 50 years, Num. 8:23-26:

23 And the Lord spoke unto Moses, saying,

24 This is what belongs unto the Levites: from twenty

and five years old and upward they shall go in to wait upon the service of the tabernacle of the congregation:

25 And from the age of fifty years they shall cease waiting upon the service thereof, and shall serve no more.

26 But shall minister with their brethren in the tabernacle of the congregation, to keep the charge, and shall do no service. Thus shalt thou do to the Levites touching their charge.

SUMMARY

It took the Children of Israel three months to arrive at Sinai where they remained for more than nine months. There the Tabernacle was built and dedicated to the Lord. The Law and its commandments were there given, not all at once, but during that time. The dedication of the twelve princes and the offering of the Levites of themselves unto the Lord brought a successful end to the dedication of the Tabernacle.

The twelve princes each offered their offerings unto the Lord in the order they encamped around the Tabernacle. The twelve tribes they represented were divided into four divisions. Judah and his division encamped east of the Tabernacle and offered their offerings first. Then followed Reuben and his division that were encamped south of the Tabernacle. After Reuben, followed Ephraim and his division that were encamped west. Dan and his division that encamped north of the Tabernacle offered their offering. Each prince was given a day to offer his offering: a total of twelve days. These ceremonies brought the nation together in oneness of purpose.

The offering of each prince was identical. Each prince offered a Meat Offering of fine flour, oil, and incense; a Burnt Offering of one young bullock, a ram, and a lamb of the first year; a Sin Offering of one kid; and a Peace Offering of two oxen, five rams, five he goats, and five lambs of the first year.

Under God, the security of the nation was entrusted to these princes and their armies. These offerings put them in right relationship with God their Commander-in-Chief. On the battlefield, they needed God at their side.

The dedication and the offering of the Levites of themselves in complete surrender to the Lord was moving as it was unique. On the day of their dedication, 22,000 Levites separated themselves unto the Lord. This was the first offering of its kind to the Lord. As part of their dedication they were purified by water, by shaving the hair off their bodies and by washing their clothes. Then Aaron offered on their behalf a Sin offering of a bullock, a Burnt Offering of one bullock, and the Meat Offering of fine flour and oil.

The Lord had told Moses that the Levites were His own; He had taken them instead of the firstborn and reminded him a number of times. The idea of exchanging the Levites for the firstborn was conceived in God's mind the day He destroyed all the firstborn of man and beast in the land of Egypt. The exchange finally and formally occurred with the dedication of the Levites and the offering of themselves unto God for the spiritual service of the Children of Israel.

CHAPTER 22

Journey From Mount Sinai, Numbers 9-12

The Children of Israel had been dwelling at Mount Sinai for more than nine months; it took them three months to get to Sinai. They were now preparing to go forward to the Promised Land and it was time to commemorate the Passover. There were questions of clarification about the Passover and other issues that demanded immediate attention. Before going forward, these issues had to be addressed.

The Passover, Num. 9:1-5:

1 And the Lord spoke unto Moses in the wilderness of Sinai, in the first month of the second year after they were come out of the land of Egypt, saying,

2 Let the children of Israel keep the Passover at his appointed season.

3 In the fourteenth day of this month, at even, ye shall keep it in his appointed season: and according to all the ceremonies thereof, shall ye keep it.

4 And Moses spoke unto the children of Israel that they should keep the Passover.

5 And they kept the Passover on the fourteenth day of the first month at even in the wilderness of Sinai: according to all that the Lord commanded Moses, so did the children of Israel.

Israel kept the Passover at the appointed time but there were questions of cleansing that needed to be addressed.

Question of Cleansing, Num. 9: 6-13:

6 And there were certain men that were defiled by the dead body of a man, that they could not keep the Passover on that day: and they came before Moses and before Aaron on that day:

7 And those men said unto him, We are defiled by the dead body of a man: wherefore are we kept back, that we may not offer an offering of the Lord in his appointed season among the children of Israel?

In response, Moses inquired of the Lord for an answer. Verses 8-13 give the answer:

8 And Moses said unto him, Stand still, and I will hear what the Lord will command concerning you.

9 And the Lord spoke unto Moses, saying,

10 Speak unto the children of Israel, saying, If any man of you or your posterity shall be unclean by reason of a dead body, or be in a journey afar off, yet he shall keep the Passover unto the Lord.

11. The fourteenth day of the second month at even they shall keep it, and eat it with unleavened bread and bitter herbs.

12 They shall leave none of it unto the morning, nor brake any bone of it: according to all the ordinances of the Passover they shall keep it.

Being unclean by touching the body of the dead was not a reason not to keep the Passover according to its ordinance. The question was an important one and Moses sought the answer from the Lord.

13 But the man that is clean, and is not in a journey, and forbears to keep the Passover, even the same soul shall be cut off from among his people: because he brought not the offering of the Lord in his appointed season, that man shall bear his sin.

There was another question; it had to do with the participation of strangers in the Passover.

Stranger Participation in the Passover, Num. 9:14

14 And if a stranger shall sojourn among you, and will keep the Passover unto the Lord; according to the ordinance of the Passover and according to the manner thereof, so shall he do: ye shall have one ordinance, both for the stranger, and for him that was born in the land.

The answers to these questions were important and could not be delayed because they had to do with a man's soul.

In the Wilderness Divine guidance was absolutely necessary. A pillar of cloud was the evidence.

The Cloud of Divine Guidance, Num. 9: 15-23:

The cloud of Divine guidance was one of the great blessings Israel enjoyed during their forty years in the Wilderness. It was the assurance that God was always watching over them and directing their every step. By this blessing they knew when to remain and when to go forward and where.

Verses 15-23 present a word picture of what is meant to lean on the Everlasting Arms of God and what is also meant that man shall not live by bread alone but by every word that proceeds from the mouth of the Living God. Indeed, at the commandment of God the Children of Israel rested in their tents and at the commandment of God they journeyed forward to the Promised Land.

15 And on the day that the tabernacle was reared up the cloud covered the tabernacle, namely the tent of the testimony: and at even there was upon the tabernacle as it were the appearance of fire, until the morning.

The cloud of fire was a symbol of purity; but it is evident that they did not allow the holy fire to burn the dross of unbelief and disobedience from their heart and soul.

16 So it was always: the cloud covered it by day, and the appearance of fire by night.

17 And when the cloud was taken up from the tabernacle, then after that the children of Israel journeyed: and in the place where the cloud abode, their the children of Israel pitched their tents.

18 At the commandment of the Lord the children of Israel journeyed, and at the commandment of the Lord they pitched: as long as the cloud abode upon the tabernacle they rested in their tents.

19 And when the cloud tarried long upon the tabernacle many days, then the children of Israel kept the charge of the Lord, and journeyed not.

20 And so it was, when the cloud was a few days upon the tabernacle; according to the commandment of the Lord they abode in their tents, and according to the commandment of the Lord they journeyed.

21 And so it was, when the cloud abode from even unto the morning, and that the cloud was taken up in the morning, then they journeyed: whether it was by day or by night that the cloud was taken up, they journeyed.

22 Or whether it were two days, or a month, or a year, that the cloud tarried upon the tabernacle, remaining thereon, the children of Israel abode in their tents, and journeyed not: but when it was taken up, they journeyed.

23 At the commandment of the Lord they rested in their tents, and at the commandment of the Lord they journeyed: they kept the charge of the Lord, at the commandment of the Lord by the hand of Moses.

The Church today is very much alike the Church in the Wilderness. The only difference is that in our Wilderness the Holy Spirit guides us; and we can choose to allow Him to burn the dross from our lives, or we can choose to allow them to remain our greatest barrier to the rich blessings of Grace.

The Trumpets, Num. 10:1-10:
Before the Children of Israel journeyed from Sinai, they

were given by God the ordinance of the trumpets. They were to make two trumpets of silver to be used for different purposes. With these two trumpets, they were given the different codes for their sounds. These trumpets in a way were used as weapons against their enemies.

1 And the Lord spoke unto Moses, saying,

2 Make you two trumpets of silver; of a whole piece shalt thou make them: that you may use them for the calling of the assembly, and for the journeys of the camps.

The blowing of the two trumpets simultaneously meant the assembly of the whole congregation at the door of the Tabernacle. The first sound of both trumpets meant the coming together of the people. These two trumpets symbolize the trumpets of the Lord, which shall call away the waiting Church. In 1Thessalonians 4:16-17, we read, "For the Lord Himself shall descend from Heaven with a shout, with the voice of the arch angel, and with the trump of God: and the dead in Christ shall rise first: Then we which are alive shall be caught up together with them in the clouds, to meet the Lord in the air: and so shall we ever be with the Lord". This corresponds to the sound of the first trumpet in the Wilderness. The Church in the Wilderness assembled at the door of the Tabernacle and was ready to go. The difference is that we will not be assembled at the Church door and ready to go; we will be gone, we will caught up to meet the Lord Jesus Christ in the air.

The Rapture of the Church will be unknown to the world; they will be fast asleep, in deep sleep! But the world will soon be awaken for in 2 Thessalonians 1:7-10 we read, " And to you who are troubled rest with us, when the Lord Jesus shall be revealed from heaven with his mighty angels,

In flaming fire taking vengeance on them that know not God, and that obey not the Gospel of our Lord Jesus Christ:

Who shall be punished with everlasting destruction from the presence of the Lord, and from the glory of His power when He shall come to be glorified in His saints, and be admired in all them that believe (because our testimony among you was believed) in that day". It means that the world will only hear the sound of the last trumpet. This is what is going to happen.

3 And when they shall blow with them, all the assembly shall assemble themselves to thee at the door of the tabernacle of the congregation.

The blowing of one trumpet was a code to the princes of the armies of Judah to be assembled before the Tabernacle. The sound of one trumpet was an alarm to the captains of the armies of Israel and they would respond accordingly.

As Christians, there is another way we can look at the sounds of the trumpet. As Israel marched to the sound of the trumpet, we must march to the sound of God's trumpet, but we must know the code of the sounds. If we do not know the code, we will not know when it is the trumpet of our fleshly desires calling us and will find ourselves doing again the things of the past. God had done everything to make Israel His chosen people.

4 And if they blow but with one trumpet, then the princes which are heads of the thousands of Israel, shall gather themselves unto thee.

5 When ye blow an alarm, then the camps that lie on the east parts shall go forward.

6 When ye blow an alarm the second time, then the camps that lie on the south side shall take their journey: they shall blow an alarm for their journeys.

7 But when the congregation is to be gathered together, ye shall blow, but ye shall not sound an alarm.

It was the responsibility of the sons of Aaron to blow the trumpets of Israel. They were to blow the trumpets also for the purposes in verses 8-10. Moses who was the Commander-in-Chief would give the order to blow the trumpets.

8 And the sons of Aaron, the priest, shall blow with the

trumpets; and they shall be to you for an ordinance forever throughout your generations.

9 And if ye go to war in your land against the enemy that oppresses you, then ye shall blow an alarm with the trumpets; and ye shall be remembered before the Lord your God and ye shall be saved from your enemies.

10 Also in the day of your gladness, and in your solemn days, and in the beginnings of your months, ye shall blow with the trumpets over your burnt offerings, and over the sacrifices of your peace offerings; that they may be to you for a memorial before your God: I am the Lord your God.

After the trumpets were made, the Children of Israel were ready and prepared to begin their journey from Sinai. They began their journey in the order they camped around the Tabernacle with the armies of Judah leading. In many ways Juda had distinguished themselves in their nation.

Israel Begin Their Forward March, Num. 10: 11-36

For the sake of order, they appointed the heads of the tribes.

11And it came to pass on the twentieth day of the second day of the second month, in the second year, that the cloud was taken up from off the tabernacle of the testimony.

12 And the children of Israel took their journeys out of the wilderness of Sinai; and the cloud rested in the wilderness of Paran.

The Tabernacle would be erected at Paran next, where the cloud of the Lord rested. Verses 13-28 explain the order in which the armies of Israel journeyed: the order in which they encamped around the Tabernacle.

13 And they first took their journey according to the commandment of the Lord by the hand of Moses.

14 In the first place went the standard of the camp of the children of Judah according to *their armies: and over his host was Nahshon the son of Amminadab*

15 And over the host of the tribe of the children of

Issachar was Nethaneel the son Zuar.

16 And over the house of the tribe of the children Zebulun was Eliab the son of Helon.

17 And the tabernacle was taken down; and the sons of Gershon and the sons of Merari set forward, bearing the tabernacle.

18 And the standard of the camp of Reuben set forward according to their armies: and over his host was Elizur the son of Shedeur.

19 And over the house of the tribe of the children of Simeon was Shelumiel the son of Zurishaddai.

20 And over the house of the tribe of the children Gad was Elisaph the son of Deuel.

21 And the Kohathites set forward, bearing the sanctuary: and the other did set up the tabernacle against they came. *(This means that the Gershonites and the Merarites set up the Tabernacle before they came so that the holy things carried by the Kohathites could be placed in their respective order in the Tabernacle.)*

22 And the standard (*banner*) of the camp of the children of Ephraim set forward according to their armies: and over his host was Elishama the son of Ammihud.

23 And over the house of the tribe of the children of Manasseh was Gamaliel the son of Pedahzur.

24 And over the house the tribe of the children of Benjamin was Abidan the son of Gideoni.

25 And the standard of the camp of the children of Dan set forward, which was the rearward of all the camps throughout their hosts: and over his host was Ahiezer the son of Ammishhaddai.

26 And over the house of the tribe of the children of Asher was Pagiel the son of Ocran.

27 And over the house of the tribe of the children of Naphtali was Ahira the son Enan.

28 Thus were the journeyings of the children of Israel

according to their armies, when they set forward.

Verses 29-32 state an earnest plead of Moses to Hobab, his brother-in-law, to join them in their journey to the Promised Land. His plead fell on deaf hears because Hobab wanted none of Moses's faith promise. Hobab chose to walk by sight and not by faith. To him it was too much a sacrifice to make. So Hobab went back to his familiar neighborhood. It reminds us of those who would like the blessings of eternal life, but when they count the high cost of discipleship, they choose the **blessings of the Here and Now instead.**

29 And Moses said unto Hobab, the son of Raguel the Midianite, Moses Father-in-law, We are journeying unto the place of which the Lord said, I will give it you: come thou with us, and we will do thee good: for the Lord hath spoken good concerning Israel.

30 And he said unto him, I will not go; but I will depart to mine own land, and to my kindred.

31 And he said, Leave us not, I pray thee; for as much as thou knowest how we are to camp in the wilderness, and thou mayest be to us instead of eyes.

32 And it shall be, if thou goest with us, yea, it shall be, that what goodness the Lord shall do unto us, the same will we do unto thee.

Nothing that Moses could say would have influenced him. And nothing that God could have said would influence Hobab because he wanted no part of a life of faith.

33 And they departed from the mount of the Lord three day's journey: and the ark of the covenant of the Lord went before them in the three days' journey, to search out a resting place for them.

34 And the cloud of the Lord was upon them by day, when they went out of the camp.

The disappointment with Hobab did not stop Moses from praising God:

35 And it came to pass, when the ark set forward, that

Moses said, Rise up, Lord, and let thine enemies be scattered; and let them that hate thee flee before thee.

36 And when it rested, he said, Return, O Lord, unto the many thousands of Israel.

The Paradox of the Journey, the Rebellion, Num.11:1-9

It would appear there was a missing gap of information between verse 36 of chapter 10 and verse 1 of chapter 11. It seems Paran was intended to be the next meaningful stop for Israel after leaving Sinai (verse12 Of chapter 10). Paran is on the map on page 67 but Taberah and Kibroth-hat-taavah are not on the map, page 67. Hazeroth seems to be their third stop before they arrived at Paran, their real destination. Hezeroth is south of the Wilderness of Paran; so, Taberah and Kiboth-hat-taavah would have to be south of Hezeroth.

It seems, therefore, that when the people arrived at Taberah they murmured against God and Moses. The paradox is that after Moses expressed such hope and pleasure with the early stage of the journey, out of nowhere, unexpectedly the people complained.

1 And when the people complained, it displeased the Lord: and the Lord heard it; and his anger was kindled; and the fire of the Lord burnt among them, and consumed them that were in the uttermost part of the camp.

2 And the people cried unto Moses; and when Moses prayed unto the Lord, the fire was quenched.

3 And he called the name of the place Taberah: because the fire of the Lord burnt among them.

It is not clear what the first murmur was about, but we know what the second murmur was about. Murmuring was like a second nature to them. During the first three months of their journey in the Wilderness, they murmured for the same thing (Exodus 16). But they did not learn anything about faith in God or they were too arrogant to go to Moses in humility and ask him to intercede with God on their behalf. A year after, their arrogant attitude remained unchanged. The worse thing about their attitude was that it would finally lead to their destruction in the Wilderness because later God promised that not one of them would inherit the Promised Land.

They had forgotten that God had provided them with quails from the sea and Manna from Heaven. The quails had ceased but they still had the Manna and were no longer satisfied with it.

4 And the mixed multitude that was among them fell a-lusting: and the children of Israel also wept again, and said, Who shall give us flesh to eat?

5 We remember the fish, which we did eat in Egypt freely; the cucumbers, and the melons, and the leeks, and the onions, and the garlic:

6 But now our soul is dried away: there is nothing at all, beside this manna before our eyes.

7 And the manna was coriander seed, and the color thereof as the color of bdellium.

8 And the people went about, and gathered it, and ground it in mills, or beat it in a mortar, and baked it in pans, and made cakes of it: and the taste of it was as the taste of fresh oil.

9 And when the dew fell upon the camp in the night, the manna fell upon it.

They murmured against Moses and against God but none of it was justified because they still had an abundance of the Manna and the cloud of Divine guidance every day.

Moses was justified with his displeasure of them but, unlike them, he took it to the Lord and unburdened his soul before the Lord.

Moses' Displeasure, Num. 11:10-16:

10 Then Moses heard the people weep throughout their families, every man in the door of his tent: and the anger of

the Lord was kindled greatly; Moses also was displeased.

11 And Moses said unto the Lord, Wherefore hast thou afflicted thy servant? And wherefore have I not found favor in Your sight, that You lay the burden of all this people upon me?

12 Have I conceived all this people? Have I begotten them, that should say unto me, Carry them in thy bosom, as a nursing father bears the sucking child, unto the land where You swore unto their fathers?

Moses' burden for his people was overwhelming: it was just too much for him to bear. In his zeal and love for the people, he thought that he was the one to provide for their desire for flesh, not remembering that God was the abundant Provider.

13 Whence should I have flesh to give unto all this people? For they weep unto me, saying, Give us flesh, that we may eat.

14 I am not able to bear all this people alone, because it is too heavy for me.

15 And if thou deal thus with me, kill me, I pray thee, out of hand, If I have found favor in thy sight; and let me not see my wretchedness.

It was just too much for Moses: he was still a lump of clay blessed and favored by God. He thought it was a favor and honor if God would instantly call him Home instead of staying around and losing God's favor. This desire was quite the opposite of when he prayed to see the face of God. Yet God understood, took some of the spiritual burden from him, and provided flesh for His children. Yet the provision of flesh would not stop the murmuring among them.

God's Tabernacle was always the meeting place for God and His children. There was no better meeting place. Today God's house of worship is still the best meeting place for God and the Believers. There can be no excuses for not meeting with God at the designated place of worship. Burdens are lifted, problems are solved, and lives are transformed there.

16 And the Lord said unto Moses, Gather unto me seventy men of the elders of Israel, whom you know to be the elders of the people, and officers over them; and bring them unto the tabernacle of the congregation, that they may stand there with thee.

17 And I will come down and talk with thee there: and I will take of the spirit which is upon thee, and will put it upon them; and they shall bear the burden of the people with thee, that thou bear it not thyself alone.

Moses' Prayer Was Answered, Num.11:18-30

18 And say thou unto the people, Sanctify yourselves against tomorrow, and ye shall eat flesh: for ye have wept in the ears of the Lord, saying, Who shall give us flesh to eat? For it was well with us in Egypt: therefore the Lord will give you flesh, and ye shall eat.

19 Ye shall not eat one day, nor two days, nor five days, neither ten days, nor twenty days;

20 But even a whole month, until it come out at your nostrils, and it be loathsome unto you: because that ye have despised the Lord which is among you, and have wept before him, saying, Why came we forth out of Egypt?

21 And Moses said, The people, among whom I am, are six hundred thousand footmen; and thou hast said, I will give them flesh, that they may eat a whole month.

22 Shall the flocks and the herds be slain for them, to suffice them? Or shall all the fish of the sea be gathered together for them, to suffice them?

23 And the Lord said unto Moses, Is the Lord's hand waxed short? Thou shalt see now whether my word shall come to pass unto thee or not.

Moses was still in amazement but he believed God and gave the word of God to the people: Moses did not know everything about God. He was still learning. Life is a learning process for everyone

24 And Moses went out, and told the people the words of the Lord, and gathered the seventy men of the elders of the people, and set them round about the tabernacle.

25 And the Lord came down in a cloud, and spoke unto him, and took of the spirit that was upon him, and gave it unto the seventy elders: and it came to pass, that, when the spirit rested upon them, they prophesied, and did not cease.

26 But there remained two of the men in the camp, the name of the one was Eldad, and the name of the other was Medad: and the spirit rested upon them; and they were of them that were written, but went not out unto the tabernacle: and they prophesied in the camp.

27 And there ran a young man, and told Moses, and said, Eldad and Medad do prophesy in the camp.

28 And Joshua the son of Nun, the servant of Moses, one of his young men, answered and said, My Lord Moses, Forbid them.

29 And Moses said unto him, Do you envy for my sake? Would God all the Lord's people were prophets, and that the Lord would put his spirit upon them!

30 And Moses gat him into the camp, he and the elders of Israel.

The Word of God Fulfilled, Num. 11: 31-35:

31 And there went forth a wind from the Lord, and brought quails from the sea, and let them fall by the camp, as it were a day's journey on this side, and as it were a day's journey on the other side, round about the camp, and as it were two cubits high upon the face of the earth.

32 And the people stood up all that day, and all that night, and all the next day, and they gathered the quails: he that gathered least gathered ten homers: and they spread them all abroad for themselves round about the camp.

33 And while the flesh was yet between their teeth, ere it

was chewed, the wrath of the Lord was kindled against the people, and the Lord smote the people with a very great plague.

God fulfilled His word of providing flesh for the people; but in His anger He destroyed many of the murmurers. What happened in chapter 11 amounted to a rebellion against God. A rebellion against God was always met with a degree of Divine anger, which always resulted in the death of many.

34 And he called the name of that place Kibroth-hat-taavah: because there they buried the people that lusted.

35 And the people journeyed from Kibroth-hat-taavah unto Hazeroth.; and abode at Hazeroth.

Rebellion Again, Num. 12: 1-16

1 And Miriam and Aaron spoke against Moses because of the Ethiopian woman whom he had married: for he had married an Ethiopian woman.

2 And they said hath the Lord indeed spoken only by Moses? Hath he not spoken also by us? And the Lord heard it.

3 (Now the man Moses was very meek, above all the men which were upon the face of the earth.)

4 And the Lord spoke suddenly unto Moses, and unto Aaron, and unto Miriam, Come out ye three unto the tabernacle of the congregation. And the three came out.

This is another example of the Tabernacle being the meeting place for God and His people. Some people stay away from the House of Worship at the time when they needed to be there. At times of problems and troubles people need to be in God's House. There was a problem in the family of Moses, not one he created, but Aaron his brother and Miriam his sister. It was definitely a rebellion against God. God had to instantly intervene before it became a national catastrophe. Verses 1- 4 address the serious nature of the problem.
A Rebuke to Aaron and Miriam, Num. 12:5-10:

5 And the Lord came down in the pillar of cloud, and stood in the door of the tabernacle, and called Aaron and Miriam: and they both came forth.

6 And he said, Hear now my words: If there be a prophet among you, I the Lord will make myself known unto him in a vision, and will speak to him in a dream.

God did not only come to Moses' defense, but He spoke highly of him and sharply rebuked Aaron and Miriam.

7 My servant Moses is not so, who is faithful in all mine house.

8 With him will I speak mouth to mouth, even apparently, and not in dark speeches; and the similitude of the Lord shall he behold: wherefore then were ye not afraid to speak against my servant Moses?

The mistake Aaron and Miriam made was that they saw Moses as their blood brother and not as the anointed Prophet of God. Moreover, Moses was the only Prophet with whom He spoke face to face and the only Prophet that saw His likeness. And God was not pleased with Aaron and Miriam. They had interfered with something bigger than their human minds could grasp because Moses' marriage of the Ethiopian woman was a type of Christ's marriage to the Gentile Believers, His Church. Though the Church is comprised of Jewish Believers, it is predominantly of Gentile Believers.

9 And the anger of the Lord was kindled against them; and he departed.

10 And the cloud departed from off the tabernacle; and, behold, Miriam became leprous, white as snow: and Aaron looked upon Miriam, and, behold she was leprous.

Aaron confessed the folly of their ways and turned to Moses for help for he was not in a position to intercede on behalf of Miriam.

Aaron's Confession, Num. 12:11-15:

11 And Aaron said unto Moses, Alas, my lord, I beseech thee, lay not the sin upon us, wherein we have done foolishly, and wherein we have sinned.

12 Let her not be as one dead, of whom the flesh is half consumed when he cometh out of his mother's womb.

13 And Moses cried unto the Lord, saying, Heal her now, O God, I beseech thee.

Moses' response was human but God's response was Divine. There is a difference between the human nature and the Divine nature. The human nature of Moses showed forgiveness; the Divine nature of God required responsibility and accountability of Miriam — the distinction could not be clearer.

14 And the Lord said unto Moses, If her father had spit in her face, should she not be ashamed seven days? Let her be shut out from the camp seven days, and after that let her be received in again.

15 And Miriam was shut out from the camp seven days: and the people journeyed not till Miriam was brought in again.

The number 7 is a Divine number; it is used by God; we do not know all the reasons He uses it. Here Miriam' leprosy was to remain on her for 7 days. That was a lesson she would never forget. And there is something else —God has a way of teaching us by object lessons for that's the best way for us to remember things.

16 And afterward the people removed from Hazeroth, and pitched in the wilderness of Paran.

Finally the people arrived at the Wilderness of Paran that was first mentioned in verse 12 of chapter 10. The impression was that after leaving Sinai they would immediately arrive at the Wilderness of Paran where the guiding cloud was seen.

SUMMARY

The journey of the Children of Israel to the Wilderness of

Paran began well, but did not continue as one would have expected. Before leaving they celebrated the Passover and there were some questions of some issues related to the Passover, which Moses answered. These questions had to do with the participation in the Passover by those who were defiled by touching the body of the dead and by those who were strangers. People who were defiled by touching the dead and those who were strangers could not participate in the Passover.

The Children of Israel were guided by a pillar of cloud. After the Tabernacle was built and dedicated to the Lord, the pillar of cloud remained over it as long as it was erected. When the Tabernacle was taken down for their journey, the pillar of cloud went ahead and settled where the Tabernacle was next to be pitched.

While the Children of Israel were at Sinai, they were commanded to make two trumpets of silver. These trumpets were to be used to call the Assembly of Israel before the Tabernacle, to call the princes of the armies to the Tabernacle, and to cause the armies to march forward. The priests were to blow these trumpets in the midst of war, during the feasts of the Lord, at the beginnings of the months, and over the offerings unto the Lord. The priests were given a code for the sounds of the trumpets, which was known to the people.

The cloud of Divine guidance went ahead and rested in the Wilderness of Paran. What should have been a blessed journey to the Wilderness of Paran happened to be a most disappointing expectation. At Taberah, on their way to the Wilderness of Paran the people complained and God was displeased. Therefore the fire of the Lord consumed many of them. It only stopped when Moses prayed for them. The people then journeyed to Kibroth-hat-taavah but they did not leave the murmuring behind: it became worse. This time they were dissatisfied with the Manna and were asking for flesh with a rebellious attitude. They were too arrogant to go to Moses and respectfully ask him to intercede with God on their behalf. Instead, they murmured against him and against God. Unlike them, Moses went to God with his burden and the burden of the people and unburdened his soul before God.

God promised that He would give them their desire but they might not be altogether happy. "And while the flesh was yet between their teeth, ere it was chewed, the wrath of the Lord was kindled against the people, and the Lord smote the people with a very great plague". A rebellion against God was always met with a degree of Divine anger, which always resulted in the death of many.

The people left Kibroth-hat-taavah and journeyed to Hazeroth. Here another rebellion was waiting to happen, only this time it was not a rebellion of the congregation— it was a rebellion of Moses' own brother and sister against him for marrying an Ethiopian woman.

This rebellion had the potential of ripping the whole congregation of Israel apart. God had to quickly intervene to prevent it. The mistake Aaron and Miriam made was that they saw Moses as their blood brother and not as the anointed Prophet of God. Moreover, Moses was the only Prophet with whom He spoke face to face and the only Prophet that saw His likeness. And God was not pleased with Aaron and Miriam. They had interfered with something bigger than their human minds could grasp because Moses' marriage of the Ethiopian woman was a type of Christ's marriage to the Church which is predominantly comprised of Gentile Believers.

Miriam was covered with leprosy as the consequence of her rebellion against Moses. Moses response to Miriam's leprosy showed forgiveness; God required of Miriam, responsibility and accountability for her sin.

CHAPTER 23
Spies Sent To Canaan, Numbers 13-14

We do not know how long a time it took the Children of Israel to journey from Sinai to the Wilderness of Paran. However, we are sure that whatever was the time, it would not change the time they spent in the Wilderness. The command of the Lord came expressly to Moses in the Wilderness of Paran to send spies to Canaan. Moses obeyed and it took 40 days for the spies to spy out Canaan and to return with their report. It must be emphasized that the spies were sent after the Children of Israel had spent more than a year in the Wilderness. This time of 40 days would only have been the time since the spies were sent and the possible time they could have conquered Canaan from the point in time at the Wilderness of Paran. It is often talked about in the Church World that it could have taken only 40 days to conquer Canaan. But the question is, From what point in time and from what location?

Because the Children of Israel failed to conquer Canaan in 40 days, every day of their failure became a year. Thus the Day A Year Principle was established. Bear in mind that this Day A Year Principle took into account the year before the spies were sent. Therefore the exact time was really 39 years. In this chapter the focus will be on the causes of their failure and the consequences.

The Command to Spy the Land of Canaan, Num. 13:1-20

1 And the Lord spoke unto Moses, saying,

2 Send thou men, that they may search the land of Canaan, which I give unto the children of Israel: of every tribe of their fathers shall ye send a man, everyone a ruler among them.

3 And Moses by the commandment of the Lord sent them from the wilderness of Paran: all those men were heads of the children of Israel.

God's command to spy out the Promised Land was a reassurance of His faithfulness and power to fulfill His promise made to Abraham, Isaac, Jacob and to them. They should not expect to possess the Promised Land by their own strength, but by their faith in Him and by their obedience to His word. Moses had no doubt that God would fulfill His Promise; he quickly obeyed and sent the heads of the tribes.

The Spies Sent, Num. 13:4-16

4 And these were their names: of the tribe of Reuben, Shammua the son of Zaccur.

5 Of the tribe of Simeon, Shaphat the son of Hori.

6 Of the tribe of Judah, Caleb the son of Jephunneh.

7 Of the tribe of Issachar, Igal the son of Joseph.

8 Of the tribe of Ephraim, Oshea the son of Nun.

9 Of the tribe of Benjamin, Palti the son of Raphu.

10 Of the tribe of Zebulun, Daddiel the son of Sodi.

11 Of the tribe of Joseph, namely, of the tribe of Manasseh, Gaddi the son of Susi.

12 Of the tribe of Dan, Ammiel the son of Gemmalli.

13 Of the tribe of Asher, Sethur the son of Michael.

14 Of the tribe of Naphtali, Nahbi the son of Vophsi.

15 Of the tribe of Gad, Geuel the son of Machi.

16 These are the names of the men which Moses sent to spy out the land. And Moses called Oshea the son of Nun Joshua.

The Purpose, Num. 13:17-20:

The purpose of spying the Land was to relieve the Children of Israel of their curiosity and fear, and to inspire faith in God who brought them to the threshold of their inheritance.

17 And Moses sent them to spy out the land of Canaan, and said unto them, Get you up this way southward, and go up into the mountain:

By going to the mountain, they would have a panoramic view of the land and make their search easier. As Christians, we need to go as often as we can to the mountain top of faith where we can view the whole realm of the possibilities of Grace. This should inspire us instead of discouraging us.

18 And see the land, what it is; and the people that dwell therein, whether they be strong or weak, few or many.

19 And what the land is that they dwell in, whether it be good or bad; and what cities they be that they dwell in, whether in tents, or in strongholds;

20 And what the land is, whether it be fat or lean, whether there be wood therein, or not. And be ye of good courage, and bring of the fruit of the land. Now the time was the time of the first ripe grapes.

Moses knew that the inhabitants of the Canaan were not going to invite them into their cities and fields to give them – there was going to be strong resistance, but God would give them the victory.

Area of Search, Num. 13:21-24:

21 So they went up, and searched the land from the wilderness of Zin unto Rehob, as men come to Hamath.

22 And they ascended by the south, and came unto Hebron; where Ahiman, Sheshai, and Talmai, the children of Anak were. (Now Hebron was buit seven years before Zoan in Egypt.)

23 And they came unto the brook of Eshcol, and cut down from thence a branch with one cluster of grapes, and

they bare between two upon a staff; and they brought of the pomegranates, and of the figs.

24 The place was called the brook of Eshcol, because of the cluster of grapes which the children of Israel cut down from thence.

Though the search was extensive and was a good one, only three of the places are located on the map on page 67: the Wilderness of Paran, the Wilderness of Zin, and Hebron. There was no better time to do the search because it was the time of harvest. They ended their search and were on their way home with the report.

Report of the Spies, Num. 13:25-33:

25 And they returned from searching of the land after forty days.

26 And they went and came to Moses, and to Aaron, and to all the congregation of the children of Israel, unto the wilderness of Paran, to Kadesh; and brought back word unto them, and to all the congregation, and showed them the fruit of the land.

Ten of the princes began to give their report to Moses and the congregation. And so far it was good, but then they had faith problem — they actually recognized their own inability to conquer Canaan. They had forgotten it was not to be by their own might but by faith in God. They allowed the impossibilities caused by their fear to overwhelm them; and so created fear in the whole congregation of Israel. It is clear that these ten spies were motivated by fear.

27 And they told him and said, We came to the land whither thou sent us, and surely it flows with milk and honey; and this is the fruit of it.

28 Nevertheless the people be strong that dwell in the land, and the cities are walled, and very great: and moreover we saw the children of Anak there.

29 The Amalekites dwell in the land of the south: and the

Hittites, and the Jebusites, and the Amorites, dwell in the mountains: and the Canaanites dwell by the sea, and by the coast of Jordan.

Though the land was perfect for them, their faith was imperfect. That was why their report was filled with every possible reason they could not conquer the land instead of all the reasons they could conquer the land. When Christians fail to exercise their faith, they begin to make excuses for not doing what they know God wants them to do. The effect of this is the same as it was with the Children of Israel— fear, discouragement, and rebellion in the Church.

There was another report from one of the other two princes:

30 And Caleb stilled the people before Moses, and said, Let us go up at once, and possess it; for we are well able to overcome it.

Caleb had the faith, saw the possibility and urgency to claim their inheritance in the Lord, but he was only one voice of twelve. The destructive seed of fear and doubt was already sown in the congregation and had taken root. All they could think of were the great giants of Anak but not the Great God who divided the Red Sea.

31 But the men that went up with him said, We be not able to go up against the people; for they are stronger than we.

32 And they brought up an evil report of the land which they had searched unto the children of Israel, saying, The land, through which we have gone to search it, is a land that eats up the inhabitants thereof; and all the people that we saw in it are men of great stature.

33 And there we saw the giants, the sons of Anak, which come of the giants: and we were in our own sight as grasshoppers, and so we were in their sight.

When there was a report that compared God's children as grass-hoppers with any other nation, you knew that was an *evil report coming from the **kingdom of darkness**. No one had to tell you that there would be serious consequences of such evil report.*

Consequences of the Evil Report, Num. 14

1 And all the congregation lifted up their voice, and cried, and the people wept that night.

2 And all the children of Israel murmured against Moses and against Aaron: and the whole congregation said unto them, Would God that we had died in the land of Egypt! Or would God we had died in this wilderness!

3 And wherefore hath the Lord brought us unto this land, to fall by the sword, that our wives and our children should be a prey? Were it not better for us to return to Egypt?

The evil report of the ten princes caused the entire congregation of Israel to murmur against Aaron and Moses. And while they were murmuring against them they were also murmuring against God. Then they entered into that death wish attitude and wanted to die. Suddenly they wanted to make themselves a leader to take them back to Egypt; yet they had the greatest Leader. It did not take very much for them to show their true nature of fear, disobedience, and rebellion. It got the attention of Moses and Aaron and brought to light the true leadership of Moses. While everyone else lost faith in God, Moses' faith grew stronger.

The Test of True Leadership, Num. 14:4-20:

4 And they said one to another, Let us make a captain, and let us return into Egypt.

5 Then Moses and Aaron fell on their faces before all the assembly of the congregation of the children of Israel.

Moses and Aaron did not join the rebellion but, instead, they fell on their faces before God because they knew that He was bigger than the circumstances they faced. As always, in times of turmoil, uncertainty, and confusion, Moses turned to the One who called him to lead His people. He would prefer to have died than to forsake his people; he was always the intercessor, the mediator between the people and God.

The people provoked God because they did not allow the miracles to bring them closer to God. Their behavior proved that they were not even thankful to God. God was justly angry.

Joshua then joined Caleb and gave the people the true report. They could not believe what they were seeing and hearing from the people.

6 And Joshua the son of Nun, and Caleb the son of Jephunneh, which were of them that searched the land, rent their clothes:

7 And they spoke unto all the company of the children of Israel, saying, The land which we passed through to search it, is an exceeding good land.

8 If the Lord delight in us, then he will bring us into this land, and give it to us; a land which flows with milk and honey.

9 Only rebel not against the Lord, neither fear ye the people of the land; for they are bread for us: their defense is departed from them, and the Lord is with us: fear them not.

This was the true report: it was a land flowing with milk and honey ready to transfer land ownership to the Children of Israel. But the people chose to believe the evil report and they rejected the good report of Caleb and Joshua. It became so bad that God had to quickly intervene to control the rebellion. Rebellion was one of the bad seeds sowed by Satan in the heart of man.

10 But all the congregation bade stone them with stones. And the glory of the Lord appeared in the tabernacle of the congregation before all the children of Israel.

Stoning was a gesture of disrespect; that was how adulterers and blasphemers were treated. There was nothing worse they could have thought of doing to Aaron and Moses.

11 And the Lord said unto Moses, How long will this people provoke me? And how long will it be ere they believe me, for all the signs which I have shown among them?

God made Moses the greatest offer of his life but his love for his brethren would not allow him to accept; it did not matter how many times the people murmured against him. Would we love to that degree after they had tried to stone us?

Moses was not carried away by this great offer from God. Instead, it caused him to pray the greatest prayer of his life. It was not great because of the eloquence and the wisdom expressed by Moses, but because of the abundance of his love it expressed and reverence for and faith in God.

12 I will smite them with the pestilence, and disinherit them, and will make of thee a great nation and mightier than they.

13 And Moses said unto the Lord, Then the Egyptians shall heart it, (for You brought up this people in Your might from among them;)

14 And they will tell it to the inhabitants of this land: for they have heard that thou Lord art among this people, that thou Lord art seen face to face, and that Your cloud stands over them, and that You go before them, by day time in a pillar of cloud, and in a pillar of fire by night.

15 Now if thou shalt kill all this people as one man, then the nations which have heard the fame of thee will speak saying,

16 Because the Lord was not able to bring this people into the land which he swore unto them, therefore he hath slain them in the wilderness.

17 And now, I beseech thee, let the power of my Lord be great, according as thou hast spoken, saying,

18 The Lord is longsuffering and of great mercy, forgiving iniquity and transgression, and by no means clearing the guilty, visiting the iniquity of the father upon the children of

the third and fourth generation.

19 Pardon, I beseech thee, the iniquity of this people according to the greatness of thy mercy, and as thou hast forgiven this people, from Egypt even until now.

20 And the Lord said, I have pardoned according to thy word:

God forgave the people of this great sin but could not prevent the consequences of their disobedience and rebellion. Just as the principle of sin was established, so was the principle of its consequence, they cannot be prevented. To prevent them means that sin would no longer be sin. Notwithstanding, the consequence of spiritual death can be prevented by the provision of Redemption. This is what God's breach of promise is saying.

God's Breach of Promise, Num.14:21-39:

21 But as truly as I live, all the earth shall be filled with the glory of the Lord.

22 Because all those men which have seen my glory, and my miracles, which I did in Egypt and in the wilderness, and have tempted me now these ten times and have not harkened unto my voice;

23 Surely they shall not see the land which I swore unto their fathers, neither shall any of them that provoked me see it.

God's forgiveness did not prevent the consequence to those who rebelled against His word of seeing the Promised Land but not inheriting it. Caleb and Joshua inherited the Promised Land because they were not involved in the sin of disobedience and rebellion.

24 But my servant Caleb because he had another spirit with him, and hath followed me fully, him will I bring into the land where into he went; and his seed shall possess it.

Verses 25-39 explain why the consequences of the great sin of rebellion had to be charged to the rebellious ones.

Moses was commanded to declare the consequences to the people and he did. They would return into the wilderness and wandered until their carcasses remained behind. Then their children would inherit the Promised Land.

25 (Now the Amalekites and the Canaanites dwelt in the valley.) Tomorrow turn you, and get you into the wilderness by the way of the Red Sea.

The map on page 67 shows only their journey of the first year.

26 And the Lord spoke unto Moses and unto Aaron, saying,

27 How long shall I bear with this evil congregation, which murmur against me? I have heard the murmurings of the children of Israel, which they murmur against me.

They would receive their death wish:

28 Say unto them, As truly as I live, says the Lord, as ye have spoken in mine ears, so will I do to you:

29 Your carcasses shall fall in this wilderness; and all that were numbered of you, according to your whole number, from twenty years old and upward, which have murmured against me,

30 Doubtless ye shall not come into the land, concerning which I swore to make you dwell therein, save Caleb the son of Jephunneh, and Joshua the son of Nun.

Their children would inherit the Promised Land instead of their rebellious parents:

31 But your little ones, which ye said should be a prey, them will I bring in, and they shall know the hand which ye have despised.

Their carcasses would be wasted in the Wilderness. For that to happen, they would spend 39 more years in the Wilderness.

32 But as for you, your carcasses, they shall fall in this wilderness.

33 And your children shall wander in the wilderness forty

years, and bear your whoredom, until your carcasses be wasted in the wilderness.

34 After the number of the days in which ye searched the land, even forty days, each day for a year, shall ye bear your iniquities, even forty years, and ye shall know my breach of promise.

The consequences of the rebellion would not remain a secret but common knowledge to parents and children and a silent memorial to the nation of Israel.

35 I the Lord have said, I will surely do it unto all this evil congregation, that are gathered together against me: in this wilderness they shall be consumed, and there they shall die.

36 And the men, which Moses sent to search the land, who returned, and made all the congregation to murmur against him, by bringing up a slander upon the land,

With regards to the ten princes who delivered the evil report to Moses and the congregation, they faced the consequence of death immediately – consequences of sin cannot be prevented!

37 Even those men that did bring up the evil report upon the land, died by the plague before the Lord.

38 But Joshua the son of Nun, and Caleb the son of Jephunneh, which were of the men that went to search the land, lived still.

39 And Moses told these sayings unto all the children of Israel: and they mourned greatly.

Learning of the consequences of their rebellion, the people mourned greatly but there was no evidence they ever repented of their sins. The evidence was that they became more rebellious as seen in their determination to go up against the Amalekites against the command of Moses. Obedience was one lesson they never learned

The People's Response, Num.14: 40-45:

40 And they rose up early in the morning, and gat them

up into the top of the mountain, saying, Lo, we are here, and will go up unto the place which the Lord hath promised: for we have sinned.

41 And Moses said, Wherefore now do ye transgress the commandment of the Lord? But it shall not prosper.

42 Go not up, for the Lord is not among you; that ye be not smitten before your enemies.

43 For the Amalekites and the Canaanites are there before you, and ye shall fall by the sword: because ye are turned away from the Lord, therefore the Lord will not be with you.

Moses knew that the Lord was not among them and that their new found courage was not a substitute for God's presence. He refused to bless their effort with his presence and with the Ark of the Covenant.

44 But they presumed to go up unto the hill top: nevertheless the ark of the covenant of the Lord, and Moses departed not out of the camp.

45 Then the Amalekites came down, and the Canaanites which dwelt in that hill, and smote them, and discomfited them, even unto Hormah.

Their chastisement by the Amalekites was an early consequence of their sin of rebellion. There is some truth to the statement of being grasshoppers because without God's presence with them, they were grasshoppers in the presence of the Amalekites.

SUMMARY

The Children of Israel journeyed from Sinai to the Wilderness of Paran. After arriving, God commanded them to send spies to Canaan. This was to reassure them of His faithfulness and power to fulfill the promise He made to Abraham, Isaac, Jacob, and to them. They should not expect to possess the Promised Land by their own strength but by their faith in God and by their obedience to His word. Moses quickly obeyed and sent twelve princes of the tribes.

The search was extensive. They searched from the Wilderness of Zin to Rehob, to Hebron, to the Brook of Eschol among other places. At the Brook of Eschol, the spies cut down a branch of grapes; they also took with them pomegranates and figs. After forty days the spies returned and gave their repot to Moses and the congregation of Israel. Ten of the twelve spies gave an evil report, saying that there were giants in the land and they were like grasshoppers compared with them; they would be unable to conquer the land. When a report compared God's children as grass hoppers to another nation, it was enough to tell you it had to be evil.

However, two of the spies, Caleb and Joshua gave a good report saying, "The land which we passed through to search it, is an exceeding good land. If the Lord delight in us, then he will bring us into this land, and give it to us; a land which flows with milk and honey. Only rebel not against the Lord, neither fear ye the people of the land; for they are bread for us: their defense is departed from them, and the Lord is with us: fear them not". This was the true report but the people chose to believe the evil report and they rejected the good report of Caleb and Joshua. The report given by the ten spies was so evil that when Caleb and Joshua herd it, they rent their clothes. They must have wandered if they saw the same places and the same people.

Besides showing the power of words, the evil report had three notable consequences. First, it caused a national rebellion: the entire congregation of Israel rebelled against, Aaron, Moses, and God. Later they claimed to repent, but there was no evidence of it because they insisted on going to fight the Amalekites against the advice of Moses. They were instantly defeated and quickly learned they could not possess the Promised Land by their own strength. The second consequence of the evil report was that it showed the great leadership of Moses. When Moses saw the rebellion and confusion, he fell on his face before the Lord and pleaded for mercy and forgiveness on behalf the rebellious people. He refused the greatest offer of his life, when God promised to make of him a greater nation than Israel, and chose instead that God pardoned His people.

The third consequence of the evil report of the spies was God's breach of promise. Though He took the Children of Israel to the threshold of Canaan, He did not allow that rebellious generation to inherit the land. The 40 days of spying the land was translated into forty years of wandering in the Wilderness. The children, and not the rebellious parents, inherited the Promised Land. They wandered in the wilderness until they all perished and their carcass wasted.

The Children of Israel were pardoned as the Lord told Moses but the consequences of their sins could not be prevented.

CHAPTER 24

Looking Ahead But Going Backwards, Numbers 15-17; 20:1-13

In the previous chapter God told the Children of Israel to go back into the Wilderness by the way of the Red Sea. The paradox of this is that they were not only going backward in their journey but more so, spiritually as well. Still, in attitude, they were looking ahead but their actions indicated otherwise. The text explains this paradox.

Attitude of Looking Ahead, Numbers 15:

1 And the Lord spoke unto Moses, saying,

2 Speak unto the children of Israel, and say unto them, When ye be come into the land of your habitations, which I give unto you,

3 And will make an offering by fire unto the Lord, a burnt offering, or a sacrifice in performing a vow, or in a freewill offering, or in your solemn feasts, to make a sweet savor unto the Lord, of the herd, or of the flock:

4 Then shall he that offers his offering unto the Lord bring a meat offering of a tenth deal of flour mingled with the fourth part of an hin of oil.

5 And the fourth part of an hin of wine for a drink offering shalt thou prepare with the burnt offering or sacrifice, for one lamb.

6 Or for a ram, thou shalt prepare for a meat offering two tenth deals of flour mingled with the third part of an hin of oil.

7 And for a drink offering thou shalt offer the third part of an hin of wine, for a sweet savor unto the Lord.

8 And when you prepare a bullock for a burnt offering, or for a sacrifice in performing a vow, or peace offerings unto the Lord:

9 Then shall ye bring with a bullock a meat offering of three tenth deals of flour mingled with half an hin of oil.

10 And thou shalt bring for a drink offering half an hin of wine, for an offering made by fire, of a sweet savor unto the Lord.

11 Thus shall it be done for one bullock, or for one ram, or for a lamb, or a kid.

12 According to the number that thou shalt prepare, so shall ye do to every one according to their number.

God was here addressing the future generation through Moses because the rebellious generation was not going to inherit the Promised Land. The offerings of the Lord were important to their spiritual survival as a nation. The emphasis was on the proportion of the Meat Offerings to the sacrificial offerings of the bullock, the ram, and the lamb. The amount increased for the bullock. The Meat Offering and the Drink Offering were offered with other offerings

The ordinance of these offerings applied to strangers also, implying that righteousness applies to all nations.

13 All that are born of the country shall do these things after this manner, in offering an offering made by fire, of sweet savor unto the Lord.

14 And if a stranger sojourn with you, or whosoever be among you in your generations, and will offer an offering made by fire, of a sweet savor unto the Lord; as ye do, so he shall do.

15 One ordinance shall be both for you of the congregation, and also for the stranger that sojourns with you, an ordinance forever in your generations: as ye are, so shall the stranger be before the Lord.

16 One law and one manner shall be for you, and for the stranger that sojourns with you.

It was also important to offer a Heave Offering unto the Lord of their first fruits of the land. By this offering they acknowledged God as the source of their blessings. The Old Economy of the Law demonstrates that is a new lesson to be learned from giving to the Lord.

17 And the Lord spoke unto Moses, saying,

18 Speak unto the children of Israel, and say unto them, When ye come into the land wither I bring you,

19 Then it shall be, that, when ye eat of the bread of the land, ye shall offer an heave offering unto the Lord.

20 Ye shall offer up a cake of the first of your dough for an heave offering: as ye do the heave offering of the threshing floor, so shall ye heave it.

21 Of the first of your dough ye give unto the Lord an heave offering in your generations.

It was possible to forget some of the commandments and, therefore, failed to do them. Failure to do what one ought to have done was a sin of omission. There was a provision made for the sin of omission.

The Sin of Omission, Num.15:22-31

22 And if ye have erred, and not observed all these commandments, which the Lord hath spoken unto Moses,

23 Even all that the Lord hath commanded you by the hand of Moses, from the day that the Lord commanded Moses, and henceforward among your generations;

24 Then it shall be, if aught be committed by ignorance without the knowledge of the congregation, that all the congregation shall offer one young bullock for a burnt offering, and his drink offering, according to the manner, and one kid of the goats for a sin offering.

25 And the priest shall make an atonement for all the congregation of the children of Israel, and it shall be forgiven

them; for it is ignorance: and they shall bring their offering a sacrifice made by fire unto the Lord, and their sin offering before the Lord, for their ignorance:(Ignorance was never an excuse to sin.)

26 And it shall be forgiven all the congregation of the children of Israel, and the stranger that sojourns among them; seeing all the people were in ignorance.

27 And if any soul sin through ignorance, then he shall bring a she goat of the first year for a sin offering.

28 And the priest shall make an atonement for the soul that sins ignorantly, when he sins by ignorance before the Lord, to make an atonement for him; and it shall be forgiven him.

29 Ye shall have one law for him that sins through ignorance, both for him that is born among the children of Israel, and for the stranger that sojourns among them.

30 But the soul that doeth aught presumptuously, whether he be born in the land, or a stranger, the same reproaches the Lord; and that soul shall be cut off from among his people.

31 Because he hath despised the word of the Lord, and hath broken his commandments, that soul shall utterly be cut off; his iniquity shall be upon him.

What Happened to the Man Found Breaking the Sabbath, Num.15:32- 37:

32 And while the children of Israel were in the wilderness, they found a man that gathered sticks upon the Sabbath Day.

33 And they that found him gathering sticks brought him unto Moses and Aaron, and to all the congregation.

Some would criticize those who brought the Sabbath breaker to Moses and the congregation. They needed not be criticized because they were doing the right thing. Sin should not be condoned by God's children. Moses felt it was something for which to seek Divine guidance and he did.

34 And they put him in ward, because it was not declared what should be done to him.

35 And the Lord said unto Moses, The man shall be surely put to death: all the congregation shall stone him with stones without the camp.

36 And all the congregation brought him without the camp, and stoned him with stones, and he died, as the Lord commanded Moses.

The Lord made the decision to put the man to death because it was the right thing to do. Thousands of people were waiting to gather sticks and would have done so if the Sabbath breaker went unpunished. A people that were always inclined to sin should not be encouraged.

A constant reminder of the commandments would be helpful to prevent the people from sinning:

37 And the Lord spoke unto Moses, saying,

38 Speak unto the children of Israel, and bid them that they make them fringes in the borders of their garments throughout their generations, and that they put upon the fringe of the borders a ribbon of blue:

39 And it shall be upon you for a fringe, that ye may look upon it, and remember all the commandments of the Lord, and do them; and that ye seek not after your own heart and your own eyes, after which ye use to go a-whoring:

40 That ye may remember, and do all my commandments, and be holy unto your God.

41 I am the Lord your God which brought you out of the land of Egypt, to be your God: I am the Lord your God.

The commandments could not be written on the fringes in the borders of their garments; but by looking on the blue ribbon, they would be reminded of the commandments. It would give them a consciousness of wanting to do what was right. The color blue signifies holiness.

The reminder of the commandments and offerings was a way of putting the Children of Israel in the right attitude. But the actions of Korah and his company suggested that the Children of Israel were going backwards while looking ahead. Korah's action of wrestling the leader-ship of Israel and replacing Moses with renowned men who had no spiritual experience was a giant step backward.

Going Backward, the Rebellion of Korah, Number 16

1 Now Korah the son of Izhar, the son of Kohath, the son of Levi, and Dathan and Abiram, the sons of Eliab, and On the son of Peleth, sons of Reuben, took men:

This rebellion was not accidental; it was carefully planned. Korah, Datham and Abiram gained the confidence and willingness of 250 of the most powerful princes of the congregation to replace the leadership of Moses by confronting him face to face. One thing that must not be overlooked is that these men were master appeasers, telling the congregation how holy they were —they did not need Moses and Aaron. In their craftiness, they were trying to get the entire congregation of Israel to rebel against Moses and to choose them instead.

Today it is not different. Groups of Church members formed and rebelled against their pastors. Pastors conspire with Church members to divide the Church. These groups may have accomplished their goals but will not prosper.

2 And they rose up before Moses, with certain of the children of Israel, two hundred and fifty princes of the assembly, famous in the congregation, men of renown:

3 And they gathered themselves together against Moses and against Aaron, and said unto them, Ye take too much upon you, seeing all the congregation are holy, every one of them, and the Lord is among them: wherefore then lift ye up yourselves above the congregation of the Lord?

This was an outrageous and sinful charge against Moses.

Moses's Response, Num. 16: 4-27

4 And when Moses heard it, he fell upon his face:

5 And he spoke unto Korah and unto all his company, saying, Even tomorrow the Lord will show who are his, and who is holy; and will cause him to come near unto him: even him whom he hath chosen will he cause to come near unto him.

By falling on his face before the Lord, Moses did not only show humility, but he set the supreme example for all Israel, as well as for Christian followers and leaders alike. We all need Divine guidance particularly at times of trouble and confusion. If we follow his example, we will be victorious in life and in death.

6 This do; Take you censers, Korah, and all his company;

7 And put fire therein, and put incense in them before the Lord tomorrow: and it shall be that the man whom the Lord doth choose, he shall be holy: ye take too much upon you, ye sons of Levi.

Moses did not procrastinate; he quickly dealt with the problem at hand and thereby prevented a national disaster. Most of the problems we face are due to our procrastination.

8 And Moses said to Korah, Hear, I pray you, ye sons of Levi:

9 Does it seem but a small thing unto you, that the God of Israel hath separated you from the congregation of Israel, to bring you near to himself to do the service of the tabernacle of the Lord, and to stand before the congregation to minister unto them?

10 And he hath brought thee near to him, and all thy brethren the sons of Levi with thee: and seek ye the priesthood also?

11 For which cause both thou and all thy company are gathered together against the Lord: and what is Aaron, that ye murmur against him?

Moses emphasized the honor and privilege given the Levites to serve the congregation spiritually and the serious nature of Korah's rebellion, he being a Levite.

12 And Moses sent to call Dathan and Abiram, the sons of Eliab: which said, We will not come up:

13 Is it a small thing that thou hast brought us up out of a land flowing with milk and honey, to kill us in the wilderness, except thou make thyself altogether a prince over us?

14 Moreover thou hast not brought us into a land that flows with milk and honey, or given us inheritance of fields and vineyards: wilt thou put out the eyes of these men? We will not come up.

Here, Dathan and Abiram repeated their sinful charge against Moses. Moses did not allow himself to be intimidated because he was filled with the Spirit of God. They were the ones who were afraid because they did not stand on the side of truth and righteousness.

15 And Moses was very wroth, and said unto the Lord, Respect not thou their offering: I have not taken one ass from them, neither have I hurt one of them.

16 And Moses said unto Korah, Be thou and all thy company before the Lord, thou, and they, and Aaron tomorrow:

17 And take every man his censer, and put incense in them, and bring ye before the Lord every man his censer, two hundred and fifty censers; thou also, and Aaron, each of you his censer.

18 And they took every man his censer, and put fire in them, and laid incense thereon, and stood in the door of the tabernacle of the congregation with Moses and Aaron.

Korah, Dathan, and Abiram were looking for trouble, not realizing that sometimes you cannot back away from it because sometimes there will be someone who will accept the challenge. That someone was Moses. It was a fallacy for them to think that they had the congregation on their side because only God's truth could keep the congregation on their side. The evidence was shown when God appeared on the scene and everyone was silent and confounded except Moses and Aaron.

19 And Korah gathered all the congregation against them unto the door of the tabernacle of the congregation: and the glory of the Lord appeared unto all the congregation.

20 And the Lord spoke unto Moses and unto Aaron, saying,

21 Separate yourselves from among this congregation, that I may consume them in a moment.

Korah and his company were about to be destroyed and he did not know it. It was not only his company of 250 princes but the entire congregation. They were not spared Divine judgment but the congregation was spared through Moses' intercession. This judgement of Korah was the first of its kind in Israel's history.

22 And they fell upon their faces and said, O God, the God of the spirits of all flesh, shall one man sin, and wilt thou be wroth with all the congregation?

23 And the Lord spoke unto Moses, saying,

24 Speak unto the congregation, saying, Get you up from about the tabernacle of Korah, Dathan, and Abiram.

25 And Moses rose up and went unto Dathan and Abiram; and the elders of Israel followed him.

26 And he spoke unto the congregation, saying, Depart, I pray you, from the tents of these wicked men, and touch nothing of theirs, lest ye be consumed in all their sins.

27 So they got up from the tabernacle of Korah, Dathan, and Abiram, on every side: and Dathan and Abiram came out, and stood in the door of their tents, and their wives, and their sons, and their little children.

There was a separation of the congregation from the evil company of Korah, Dathan, and Abiram. God would not destroy the wicked with the righteous. These wicked men almost caused the destruction of the entire congregation. They had to be consumed, not by fire this time but by the Earth itself in order to spare the congregation.

In verses 28-35 Moses puts his leadership to the Divine test. This test would also test the leadership of Korah as to whether it was of God. The test of leadership is not an every day occurrence. But in life, it does happen from time to time under rear circumstances.

Test of Leadership, Num. 16: 27-50

28 And Moses said, Hereby ye shall know that the Lord sent me to do all these works; for I have not done them of mine own mind.

29 If these men die the common death of all men or if they be visited after the visitation of all men, then the Lord hath not sent me.

30 And if the Lord make a new thing, and the earth open her mouth, and swallow them up, with all that appertain unto them, and they go down quick into the pit; then ye shall understand that these men have provoked the Lord.

31 And it came to pass, as he had made an end of speaking all these words, that the ground clave asunder that was under them:

32 And the earth opened her mouth, and swallowed them up, and their houses, and all the men that appertained unto Korah, and all their goods.

33 They, and all that appertained to them, went down alive into the pit, and the earth closed upon them: and they perished from among the congregation.

34 And all Israel that were round about them fled at the cry of them: for they said, Lest the earth swallow us up also.

35 And there came out a fire from the Lord, and consumed the two hundred and fifty men that offered incense.

Korah and his company did not pass the leadership test – they all perished.

36 And the Lord spoke unto Moses, saying

37 Speak unto Eleazar the son of Aaron the priest, that he take up the censers from out of the burning, and scatter thou the fire yonder; for they are hallowed.

38 The censers of these sinners against their own souls, let them make them broad plates for a covering of the altar: for they offered them before the Lord, therefore they are hallowed: and they shall be a sign unto the children of Israel.

39 And Eleazar the priest took the brazen censers, wherewith they that were burnt had offered; and they were made broad plates for a covering of the altar:

40 To be a memorial unto the children of Israel, that no stranger, which is not of the seed of Aaron, come near to offer incense before the Lord; that he be not as Korah, and as his company: as the Lord said to him by the hand of Moses.

The plates of covering made from the censers of Korah and his company were to memorialize their evil deed to warn anyone who would desire to usurp the spiritual authority of the priesthood.

41 But on the morrow all the congregation of the children of Israel murmured against Moses and against Aaron, saying, Ye have killed the people of the Lord.

The constant murmurings of the people show that sin has a constant rebellious nature and if given the chance, will violate all rules and regulations of God and man. Righteousness cannot co-exist with sin. It must be completely obliterated from the face of the Universe. That day is fast approaching.

42 And it came to pass, when the congregation was gathered against Moses and against Aaron, that they looked toward the tabernacle of the congregation: and, behold, the cloud covered it, and the glory of the Lord appeared.

43 And Moses and Aaron came before the tabernacle of the congregation.

44 And the Lord spoke unto Moses, saying,

45 Get you up from among this congregation, that I may consume them as in a moment. And they fell upon their faces.

As their leader, Moses saw their potential; and although they often thought of stoning him, he would not give up on them. He believed that there were no boundaries surrounding Divine mercy.

46 And Moses said unto Aaron, Take a censer, and put fire therein from off the altar, and put on incense, and go quickly unto the congregation, and make an atonement for them: for there is wrath gone out from the Lord; the plague is begun.

47 And Aaron took as Moses commanded, and ran into the midst of the congregation; and, behold, the plague was begun among the people: and he put on incense, and made an atonement for the people.

There is power in atonement. More than fourteen thousand died but it speared the lives of some 2,000,000 of the congregation. If the Atonement under the Law was so powerful, how much more is the Atonement under Grace?

48 And he stood between the dead and the living; and the plague was stayed.

49 Now they that died in the plague were fourteen thousand and seven hundred, beside them that died about the matter of Korah.

50 And Aaron returned unto Moses unto the door of the tabernacle of the congregation: and the plague was stayed.

With all that Moses had been through with the congregation, you would have thought that was nothing more to prove. The Children of Israel were still demanding proofs.

Proof of Aaron's Priesthood, the Miracle of His Rod, Numbers 17

1 And the Lord spoke unto Moses, saying,

2 Speak unto the children of Israel, and take of every one of them a rod according to the house of their fathers, of all their princes according to the house of their fathers twelve rods: write thou every man's name upon his rod.

3 And thou shalt write Aaron's name upon the rod of Levi: for one rod shall be for the head of the house of their fathers.

The Tabernacle was the place of God's abiding presence, a place where God communicated with His people. All spiritual matters had to be taken to the Tabernacle, doubts and fears, sins and forgiveness, healing and cleansing. This time Aaron's rod and also the rods of the doubters were to be taken there.

4 And thou shalt lay them up in the tabernacle of the congregation before the testimony, where I will meet with you.

5 And it shall come to pass, that the man's rod, whom I shall choose, shall blossom: and I will make to cease from me the murmurings of the children of Israel, whereby they murmur against you.

6 And Moses spoke unto the children of Israel, and every one of their princes gave him a rod apiece, for each prince, one according to their fathers' house, even twelve rods: and the rod of Aaron was among their rods.

7 And Moses laid up the rods before the Lord in the tabernacle of witness.

8 And it came to pass, that on the morrow Moses went into the tabernacle of witness; and, behold, the rod of Aaron for the house Levi was budded and brought forth buds, and bloomed blossoms, and yielded almonds.

The miracle of Aaron's rod shows that spiritual matters must be treated with a sense of urgency. The memorialization of that miracle was to remind succeeding generations that God did walk with their forefathers in the Wilderness and fed them for forty years.

9 And Moses brought forth all the rods from before the Lord unto all the children of Israel: and they looked, and took every man his rod.

10 And the Lord said unto Moses, Bring Aaron's rod again before the testimony, to be kept for a token against the rebels; and thou shalt quite take away their murmurings from me, that they die not.

11 And Moses did so: as the Lord commanded him, so did he.

12 And the children of Israel spoke unto Moses, saying, Behold, we die, we perish, we all perish.

13 Whosoever cometh anything near unto the tabernacle of the Lord shall die: shall be consume with dying?

Verse 13 alone sums up the attitude of the people and shows why God concluded that they all perish in the Wilderness and not be allowed into the Promised Land.

Numbers 20:1-13 was transferred to this chapter because of its particular relevance. It speaks about another rebellion by the Children of Israel. We cannot forget that rebellion began with Lucifer because of selfish ambition.

Rebellion Again, Number 20:1-13

1 Then came the children of Israel, even the whole congregation, into the desert of Zin in the first month: and the people abode in Kadesh; and Miriam died there, and was buried there.

The people had just buried Miriam a few days ago and should be thinking about their eternal souls. They did not do that because they began murmuring again.

2 And there was no water for the congregation: and they gathered themselves together against Moses and against Aaron.

3 And the people chide with Moses, and spoke, saying, Would God that we had died when our brethren died before the Lord!

4 And why have ye brought up the congregation of the Lord into this wilderness, that we and our cattle should die there?

5 And wherefore have ye made us to come up out of Egypt, to bring us unto this evil place? It is no place of seed, or figs, or vines, or of pomegranates; neither is there any water to drink.

Human behavior for the most part can be predicted. On the other hand, sometimes it cannot be predicted. Not so with the Children of Israel, their behavior could always be predicted with precision. Under certain circumstances, you could tell what they would do and what they would say and how. Many years before, they had faced a similar situation and their reaction was identical. History has shown that they did not learn anything of faith from that experience. Moses and Aaron had to be on their faces again, asking for God's mercy for their lives. It is about the seventh time the term, falling on their faces, is used in connection with their murmurs.

6 And Moses and Aaron went from the presence of the assembly unto the door of the tabernacle of the congregation, and they fell upon their faces: and the glory of the Lord appeared unto them.

Moses' plead was heard and God promised them water.

Water from the Rock, Num. 20:7-13:

7 And the Lord spoke unto Moses, saying,

8 Take the rod and gathered the assembly together, thou, and Aaron thy brother, and speak ye unto the rock before their eyes; and it shall give forth his water, and thou shalt bring forth to them water out of the rock: so thou shalt give the congregation and their beast drink.

9 And Moses took the rod from before the Lord, as he commanded him.

10 And Moses and Aaron gathered the congregation together before the rock, and he said unto them, Hear now,

ye rebels; must we fetch you water out of this rock?

After thirty-nine years Moses was still using his rod to work miracles. He was commanded to take his rod with him and to speak to the rock; but he smote the rock twice. "Must we fetch you water out of this rock" was the one term he regretted using. The term somewhat elevated him to the same level of God. And although he was God's friend, he could never be an equal with God. Carrying the burden of a rebellious and unthankful people for nearly 40 years, impacted his emotions and caused him to speak foolishly —it was a sin. God forgave him but He did not prevent the consequence of that sin of Moses.

11 And Moses lifted up his hand, and with his rod he smote the rock twice: and the water came out abundantly, and the congregation drank, and their beasts also.

12 And the Lord spoke unto Moses and Aaron, Because ye believed me not, to sanctify me in the eyes of the children of Israel, therefore ye shall not bring this congregation into the land which I have given them.

13 This is the water of Meribah; because the children of Israel strove with the Lord, and he was sanctified in them.

SUMMARY

Sometimes boisterous winds blow between one's desire and its fulfillment. This can cause unfulfilled desires. It was what the Children of Israel experienced, looking forward but going backwards. This was the dominant characteristic of their 40 year experience of the Wilderness. Looking at it, still deeper was the desire to please self instead of God. This was the same desire of our fore-parents, Adam and Eve. Further still, it caused the first rebellion of Lucifer. As always, there was an optimistic outlook of the future but when it is met with the forces of circumstances, the result is always a backward march.

God's address through Moses to the Children of Israel was to set a positive future outlook for the succeeding generations. He spoke of the offerings they were to offer in the Promised Land, the equality of the Law, the provision for the sin of omission, and the reminder of the blue ribbon of the commandments. God had done everything possible to fulfill His promise of giving them the land of Canaan; they needed to do their part, largely obeying His word.

With the rebellion of Korah, the whole picture of the future outlook was changed. There was no justifiable reason for his rebellion or any other rebellion. The sad thing about these rebellions was that the Children of Israel were always rebelling against the only persons who could help them and their problems. They were rebelling against God, Moses, and Aaron. Korah's attempt to replace the leadership of Moses with his own was a giant step backwards for all of Israel. The congregation was forgiven for its part but the consequences could not be prevented. Korah and his company were consumed and more than 14,000 members of the congregation were consumed by fire from the Lord. It was Moses against whom they rebelled interceded on their behalf and stopped the destruction of lives.

It seems the cure of Atonement was not enough to check the rebellious nature of the Children of Israel. What happened at the water Meribah happened about 39 years before. The miracle of Aaron's rod shows that their rebellious nature could not be satisfied by water but they would not give God the freedom to satisfy it with His righteousness and love. The miracle rod of Aaron would remind succeeding generations for years to come that their fore-fathers provoked the Lord their God forty years in the Wilderness.

CHAPTER 25
The Priesthood And Purification, Numbers 18-19

The Priesthood was at the heart of Israel's Theocracy. The goal of the Priesthood was to keep the people holy. The offerings of Atonement were dedicated to this purpose. The purification by the Red Heifer, a cleansing process, was added to the purification of the Children of Israel. Because of the importance of the Priesthood, special privileges were given to the priests. Some of those privileges are explained in this chapter as well as the process of purification by the Red Heifer.

Privileges of the Priesthood, Num. 18

First came the duties and responsibilities, verses 1-7. Though the priesthood was limited to Aaron and his descendants, the whole tribe of Levites were to be their assistants.

1 And the Lord said unto Aaron, Thou and thy sons and thy father's house with thee shall bear the iniquity of the sanctuary: and thou and thy sons with thee shall bear the iniquity of your priesthood.

2 And thy brethren also of the tribe of Levi, the tribe of thy father, bring thou with thee, that they may be joined unto thee, and minister unto thee: but thou and thy sons with thee shall minister before the tabernacle of witness.

The offerings represented the sins for which the people were to be forgiven. These were offerings of mediation by the priests between God and the people. These offerings were, therefore, representations of blessings as well as sins. The representation of sin is here described as iniquity of the sanctuary. Aaron, his sons, and the Levites were to bear the spiritual weight of the people; only Aaron and his sons or descendants were to bear the spiritual weight of the priesthood.

3 And they shall keep thy charge, and the charge of all the tabernacle: only they shall not come nigh the vessels of the sanctuary and the altar, that neither they, nor ye also die.

4 And they shall be joined unto thee, and keep the charge of the tabernacle of the congregation, for all the service of the tabernacle: and a stranger shall not come nigh unto you.

5 And ye shall keep the charge of the sanctuary, and the charge of the altar: that there be no wrath any more upon the children of Israel.

6 And I, behold, I have taken your brethren the Levites from among the children of Israel: to you they are given as a gift for the Lord, to do the service of the tabernacle of the congregation.

7 Therefore thou and thy sons with thee shall keep your priest's office for everything of the altar, and within the veil; and ye shall serve: I have given your priest's office unto you as a service of gift: and the stranger that cometh nigh shall be put to death.

With respect to the priesthood, all others except Aaron and his descendants were barred. Due to the overwhelming duties of the priesthood, Aaron and his sons were given special privileges: all that remained of the offerings that were offered was given to Aaron and his sons. These provisions were to be eaten in the holy place. Eating of the holy things was no ordinary blessing of the priests.

8 And the Lord spoke unto Aaron, Behold, I also have given thee the charge of mine heave offerings of all the hallowed things of the children of Israel; unto thee have I given them by reason of the anointing, and to thy sons, by an ordinance forever.

9 This shall be thine of the most holy things, reserved from the fire: every oblation of theirs, every meat offering of theirs, and every sin offering of theirs, and every trespass offering of theirs, which they shall render unto me, shall be most holy for thee and for thy sons.

10 In the most holy place shalt thou eat it; every male shall eat it: it shall be holy unto thee.

The participation of the priests by eating of the allotted offerings represented fellowship with God. And since the priests represented God and the people, the people were also in fellowship with God.

There was no mention of the Burnt Offering because it was to be wholly burnt.

11 And this is thine; the heave offering of their gift, with all the wave offerings of the children of Israel: I have given them unto thee, and to thy sons and to thy daughters with thee, by a statute forever: every one that is clean in thy house shall eat of it.

The daughters of the priest were to also participate in the offerings allotted to the priest.

Furthermore,

12 All the best of the oil, and all best of the wine, and of the wheat, the first fruits of them which they shall offer unto the Lord, them have I given thee.

13 And whatsoever is first ripe in the land, which they shall bring unto the Lord, shall be thine; every one that is clean in thine house shall eat of it.

14 Everything devoted in Israel shall be thine.

15 Everything that opens the matrix in all flesh, which they bring unto the Lord, whether it be of men or beasts

shall be thine: nevertheless the firstborn of man shalt thou surely redeem, and the firstling of unclean beasts shalt thou redeem.

All the firstborn of man and beast in Israel belonged to the Lord; they had to be redeemed, except the first born of cow, sheep, and goat. These were to be offered as Burnt offerings to the Lord.

16 And those that are to be redeemed from a month old shalt thou redeem, according to thy estimation, for the money of five shekels, after the shekel of the sanctuary, which is twenty gerahs.

17 But the firstling of a cow, or the firstling of a sheep, or the firstling of a goat, thou shalt not redeem; they are holy: thou shalt sprinkle their blood upon the altar, and shalt burn their fat for an offering made by fire, for a sweet savor unto the Lord.

18 And the flesh of hem shall be thine, as the wave breast and as the right shoulder are thine.

The blessing of the Covenant of Salt was also given to Aaron and his sons:

19 All the heave offerings of the holy things, which the children of Israel offer unto the Lord, have I given thee, and thy sons and thy daughters with thee, by a statute forever: it is a covenant of salt for ever before the Lord unto thee and to thy seed with thee.

20 And the Lord spoke unto Aaron, Thou shalt have no inheritance in their land, neither shalt thou have any part among them: I am thy part and thine inheritance among the children of Israel.

By not allotting any inheritance in the Promised Land to the priests, they would be completely dedicated to God's service.

The Levites were singled out for their own blessings for their services. They were to be examples of Believers who live by faith. Many are challenged by a life of faith.

The Blessings of the Levites, Num. 18:21-25

21 And, behold, I have given the children of Levi all the tenth in Israel for an inheritance, for their service which they serve, even the service of the tabernacle of the congregation.

22 Neither must the children of Israel henceforth come nigh the tabernacle of the congregation, lest they bear sin, and die.

23 But the Levites shall do the service of the tabernacle of the congregation, and they shall bear their iniquity: it shall be a statute forever throughout your generations, that among the children of Israel they have no inheritance.

24 But the tithes of the children of Israel, which they offer as an heave offering unto the Lord, I have given to the Levites to inherit: therefore I have said unto them, Among the children of Israel they shall have no inheritance.

25 And the Lord spoke unto Moses, saying,

All the tithes of the Children of Israel were given to the Levites as their inheritance. From their tithes, they would give a tenth unto the Lord to Aaron, the Anointed Priest. The thing about giving is that it makes Divine worship tangible and personal. We must make giving to the Lord a part of our lives.

Tithe of Tithes, Num. 18:26-32:

26 Thus speak unto the Levites, and say unto them, When ye take of the children of Israel the tithes which I have given you from them for your inheritance, then ye shall offer up an heave offering of it for the Lord, even a tenth part of the tithe.

27 And this your heave offering shall be reckoned unto you, as though it were the corn of the threshing-floor, and as the fullness of the winepress.

28 Thus ye also shall offer an heave offering unto the Lord of all your tithes, which ye receive of the children of Israel; and ye shall give thereof the Lord's heave offering to

Aaron the priest.

29 Out of all your gifts ye shall offer every heave offering of the Lord, of all the best thereof, even the hallowed part thereof out of it.

30 Therefore thou shalt say unto them, When ye have heaved the best thereof from it, then it shall be counted unto the Levites as the increase of the threshing-floor, and as the increase of the wine press.

The tithes of the Levites would be like any other tithe, a tenth of what they received. God will not settle for second best; He requires the best from us and gives the best to His children. He gave us Heaven's best when He sent His only Son to die for our Redemption.

31 And ye shall eat it in every place, ye and your households: for it is your reward for your service in the tabernacle of the congregation.

32 And ye shall bear no sin by reason of it, when ye have heaved from it the best of it: neither shall ye pollute the holy things of the children of Israel, lest ye die.

Purification by the Red Heifer, Num. 19

The purification by the Red Heifer was primarily for those who were defiled by the body of the dead, a bone of a man, and a grave. The defiled person lost access to the Tabernacle because his defilement would cause defilement to the Tabernacle. It cannot be denied that purification is a part of holiness.

The perfect Red Heifer was to be chosen:

1 And the Lord spoke unto Moses and unto Aaron saying,

2 This is the ordinance of the law which the Lord hath commanded, saying, Speak unto the children of Israel, that they bring thee a red heifer without spot, wherein there is no blemish, and upon which never came yoke:

3 And ye shall give her unto Eleazar the priest that he may bring her forth without the camp, and one shall slay her

before his face.

The Red Heifer was to play an important role in the sanctification of Israel. Because God's presence abode in the camp, anything that had any defilement, even the provision of cleansing had to be dealt with without the camp.

The sprinkling of the blood of the Red Heifer before the Tabernacle of the congregation signified the external nature of the cleansing. It was not performed by the priest.

4 And Eleazar the priest shall take of her blood with his finger and sprinkle of her blood directly before the tabernacle of the congregation seven times:

5 And one shall burn the heifer in his sight; her skin, and her flesh, and her blood, with her dung, shall he burn:

6 And the priest shall take cedar wood, and hyssop, and scarlet, and cast it into the midst of the burning of the heifer.

Cedar wood and hyssop were known to be cleansing agents. They were cast into the burning Red Heifer, becoming thereby a part of the purification process.

The priest and anyone else involved in the provision of the purification became unclean for that day.

7 Then the priest shall wash his clothes, and he shall bathe his flesh in water, and afterward he shall come into the camp, and the priest shall be unclean until the even.

8 And he that burns her shall wash his clothes in water, and bathe his flesh in water, and shall be unclean until the even.

9 And a man that is clean shall gather up the ashes of the heifer, and lay them up without the camp in a clean place, and it shall be kept for the congregation of the children of Israel for a water of separation: it is a purification for sin.

10 And he that gathers the ashes of the heifer shall wash his clothes, and be unclean until the evening: and it shall be unto the children of Israel, and unto the stranger that

sojourns among them, for a statute forever.

The Purpose, Num. 19: 11-16

11 He that touches the dead body of any man shall be unclean seven days.

12 He shall purify himself with it on the third day, and on the seventh day he shall be clean: but if he purify not himself the third day, then the seventh day he shall not be clean.

13 Whosoever touches the dead body of any man that is dead, and purifies not himself, defiles the tabernacle of the Lord; and that soul shalt be cut off from Israel: because the water of separation was not sprinkled upon him, he shall be unclean; his uncleanness is yet upon him.

14 This is the law when a man dies in a tent: all that come into the tent, and all that is in the tent, shall be unclean seven days.

15 And every open vessel, which hath no covering bound upon it, is unclean.

16 And whosoever touches one that is slain with a sword in the open fields, or a dead body, or a bone of a man, or a grave, shall be unclean seven days.

Application, Num. 19: 17-22:

17 And for an unclean person they shall take of the ashes of the burnt heifer of purification for sin, and running water shall be put thereto in a vessel:

18 And a clean person shall take hyssop, and dip in the water, and sprinkle it upon the tent, and upon all the vessels, and upon the persons that were there, and upon him that touches a bone, or one slain, or one dead, or a grave:

19 And the clean person shall sprinkle upon the unclean on the third day, and on the seventh day: he shall purify himself, and wash his clothes, and bathe himself in water,

and shall be clean at even.

20 But the man that shall be unclean, and shall not purify himself, that soul shall be cut off from among the congregation, because he hath defiled the sanctuary of the Lord: the water of separation hath not been sprinkled upon him; he is unclean.

21 And it shall be a perpetual statute unto them, that he that sprinkles the water of separation shall wash his clothes; and he that touches the water of separation shall be unclean until even.

22 And whatsoever the unclean person touches shall be unclean; and the soul that touches it shall be unclean until even.

SUMMARY

The material blessings accorded to the priests clearly showed the righteousness of God. The priests were God's servants chosen and anointed to offer unto God the holy offerings of Atonement on behalf of the Children of Israel. They were the mediators between God and the people. As God expected faithful service of the priests, He gave them an abundance of the best blessings. Verses 9-14 of chapter 18 enumerate those blessings:

9 This shall be thine of the most holy things, reserved from the fire: every oblation of theirs, every meat offering of theirs, and every sin offering of theirs, and every trespass offering of theirs, which they shall render unto me, shall be most holy for thee and for thy sons.

10 In the most holy place shalt thou eat it; every male shall eat it: it shall be holy unto thee.

11 And this is thine; the heave offering of their gift, with all the wave offerings of the children of Israel: I have given them unto thee, and to thy sons and to thy daughters with thee, by a statute forever: every one that is clean in thy

house shall eat of it.

12 And the best of the oil, and all best of the wine, and of the wheat, the first fruits of them which they shall offer unto the Lord, them have I given thee.

13 And whatsoever is first ripe in the land, which they shall bring unto the Lord, shall be thine; every one that is clean in thine house shall eat of it.

14 Everything devoted in Israel shall be thine.

The Covenant of Salt is another name for the material blessings given to the priests. The Levites were blessed with all the tithes of the Children of Israel. From the tithes they received, they paid a tenth to the High Priest.

Death is a natural part of human life and is treated of such. In the case of the Children of Israel, one could be defiled by touching the body of the dead, in which case had to be cleansed by the purification of the Red Heifer. What therefore was natural to other people became a cause of defilement to the Children of Israel. Touching the body of the dead could not be prevented— people naturally died in their tents and people died at wars.

A perfect Red Heifer was killed outside the camp in the presence of the priest. Its entire body was burnt to ashes and then secured in a clean vessel. Anyone who had anything to do with this provision of purification became unclean for the day, even the person who applied its cleansing to another. Some of the ashes of the Red Heifer and some running water were put in a clean vessel and then applied to the person or thing to be cleansed. When a person was defiled by the dead, the water of purification was to be applied the third and the seventh day. After the seventh day, the cleansing was complete. God's presence was abiding among the Children of Israel; therefore, they could not only be holy in name but also in their daily lives.

CHAPTER 26

Israel Marches Forward, Numbers 20:14-Chap.25:18

At the water of Meribah Moses and Aaron displeased the Lord. Moses was told to speak to the rock; he smote the rock twice with his rod instead. Then he spoke unwisely by calling the Children of Israel rebels and by not glorifying God as the only source of the material needs of His children. By using the term, "Must we fetch you water out of this rock", he lifted himself above the people and assumed power which only belonged to God. At that moment, he did not realize what he had done, but later fully understood that he sinned and that it was serious enough to prevent him from leading Israel into the Promised Land. He put all that behind him and was ready to go forward.

Message Sent to the King of Edom, Num. 20:14-17

14 And Moses sent messengers from Kadesh unto the king of Edom, Thus says thy brother Israel, You know all the travail that hath befallen us:

15 How our fathers went down into Egypt, and we have dwelt in Egypt a long time; and the Egyptian vexed us, and our fathers:

16 And when we cried unto the Lord, he heard our voice, and sent an angel, and hath brought us forth out of Egypt

531

and, behold, we are in Kadesh a city in the uttermost of thy border:

17 Let us pass, I pray thee, through thy country: we will not pass through the fields, or through the vineyards, neither will we drink of the water of the wells: we will go by the king's high way, we will not turn to the right hand nor to the left, until we have passed thy borders

Edom's Response, Num. 20:18-21

18 And Edom said unto him, Thou shalt not pass by me, lest I come out against thee with the sword.

19 And the children of Israel said unto him, We will go by the high way: and if I and my cattle drink of thy water, then I will pay for it: I will only, without doing anything else, go through on my feet.

20 And he said, Thou shalt not go through. And Edom came out against him with much people, and with a strong hand.

21 Thus Edom refused to give Israel passage through his border: wherefore Israel turned away from him

Moses' earnest plead fell on deaf hears; Israel had to find another way to Mount Hor.

From Kadesh to Mount Hor, Num. 20:22-29:

22 And the children of Israel, even the whole congregation, journeyed from Kadesh, and came unto mount Hor.

23 And the Lord spoke unto Moses and Aaron in mount Hor, by the coast of the land of Edom, saying,

Moses' request to the king of Edom was well stated. The people of Edom were the descendant of Esau. Esau was the older brother of Jacob; the children of Edom were their brethren. But they had grown miles apart. Their spiritual interest was not the same. Because of that they were more enemies than they were brethren. The spiritual desire of the Children of Jacob and the material desire of Esau made their descendants two distinct peoples. The choices these two sons made, made all the difference in their destiny.

There is no doubt that the people of Esau had lost their humanity because granting them safe passage was the human thing to do; the descendants of Esau did the opposite because of their spiritual blindness.

These two peoples represent the peoples of the world today. Of course, there are only two: the one representing the Believers and the other representing the non-Believers. While the Believers show understanding towards the unsaved, the unsaved (Esau) will show no understanding towards the Believers. Christians should not expect to benefit from an understanding from the people of the world.

24 Aaron shall be gathered unto his people: for he shall not enter into the land which I have given unto the children of Israel, because he rebelled against my word at the water of Meribah.

25 Take Aaron and Eleazar his son, and bring them up unto mount Hor:

26 And strip Aaron of his garments, and put them upon Eleazar his son: And Aaron shall be gathered unto his people, and shall die there.

No one has the slightest doubt that the Lord forgave Aaron of his sin at the water of Meribah. However, God's forgiveness did not prevent the consequence of the sin. God did not allow him to enter the Promised Land

27 And Moses did as the Lord commanded: and they went up into mount Hor in the sight of all the congregation.

28 And Moses stripped Aaron of his garments, and put them upon Eleazar his son; and Aaron died there in the top of mount Hor: and Moses and Eleazar came down from the mount.

29 And when all the congregation saw that Aaron was dead, they mourned for Aaron thirty days, even all the house of Israel. *Aaron lived a full life of service to God and his*

people, and was buried in Mount Hor, and mourned by the Children of Israel. He was 83 years old when he stood before Pharaoh and 123 years old when he died. If it can be said that someone died in an honorable way, it could be said of Aaron. God told him the day he was going to die and the place he would be buried. Not many of us will know the time of our death and where. It was also an honor that his son Eleazar succeeded him as the High Priest.

The loss of Aaron was real but there was a greater problem awaiting them.

Israel warred with the King of Canaan, Num. 21:1-3

1 And when king Arad the Canaanite, which dwelt in the south, heard tell that Israel came by the way of the spies; then he fought against Israel, and took some of them prisoners.

2 And Israel vowed a vow unto the Lord, and said, If thou wilt indeed deliver this people into my hand, then I will utterly destroy their cities.

3 And the Lord harken to the voice of Israel, and delivered up the Canaanites; and they utterly destroyed them and their cities: and he called the name of the place Hormah.

Engaging the journey wearied Israelites in an unexpected war was not a very nice welcome by King Arad of Canaan. Worse yet, he had taken some of them prisoners. One would ask, Why did God allow that? God allows many things to happen because it is not His job to prevent people from doing what they have chosen to do. The good thing was that the Children of Israel turned to God for help and He did. But would their victory over the Canaanites inspire their faith in God to greater things?

From Mount Hor to Compass Edom, Num. 21:4-9:

4 And they journey from mount Hor by the way of the

Red Sea, to compass the land of Edom: and the soul of the people was much discouraged because of the way.

5 And the people spoke against God, and against Moses, Wherefore have ye brought us up out of Egypt to die in the wilderness? For there is no bread, neither is there any water; and our soul loaths this light bread.

The people were weary, tired, and hungry. Nevertheless, that did not justify their murmuring against Moses. God showed His displeasure by commanding serpents to punish them. Using the serpents was a sad reminder of the fact that the problems with the human race began with the serpent, and not with Moses. Many people began to die; then they realized it was not Moses' fault: it was theirs.

6 And the Lord sent fiery serpents among the people, and they bit the people; and much people of Israel died.

7 Therefore the people came to Moses, and said, We have sinned, for we have spoken against the Lord, and against thee; pray unto the Lord, that he take away the serpents from us. And Moses prayed for the people.

8 And the Lord said unto Moses, Make thee a fiery serpent, and set it upon a pole: and it shall come to pass, that every one that is bitten, when he looks upon it, shall live.

9 And Moses made a serpent of brass, and put it upon a pole, and it came to pass, that if a serpent had bitten any man, when he beheld the serpent of brass, he lived.

God used the serpent of brass to bring restoration of life to those who were dying. But first, their healing was to be by believing not in the serpent of brass but in the One who commanded it to be made. This serpent of brass was to be a symbolic lesson, symbolizing Christ who by dying on the Cross would effect complete restoration of life to mankind.

The faith healing stopped the plague of death among the Children of Israel. The people realized and repented of their sins. They were ready to go forward.

Journeys to Mount Pisgah Num. 21:10-20:

Israel's journey to Mount Pisgah saw a number of stops along the way. While they were at Mount Pisgah, Israel fought two wars.

10 And the children of Israel set forward, and pitched in Oboth.

11 And they journeyed from Oboth, and pitched at Ijeabarim, in the wilderness which is before Moab, toward the sun rising.

12 From thence they removed, and pitched in the valley of Zared.

13 From thence they removed, and pitched on the other side of Arnon, which is in the wilderness that cometh out of the coast of the Amorites: for Arnon is the border of Moab, between Moab and the Amorites.

14 Wherefore it is said in the book of the wars of the Lord, What he did in the Red Sea, and in the brooks of Arnon,

15 And at the stream of the brooks that goes down to the dwelling of Ar, and lies upon the border of Moab.

16 And from thence they went to Beer: that is the well whereof the Lord spoke unto Moses, Gather the people together, and I will give them water.

17 Then Israel sang this song, Spring up, O ye well; sing ye unto it:

18 The princes dug the well, the nobles of the people digged it, by the direction of the lawgiver, with their staves. And from the wilderness they went to Mattanah:

19 And from Mattanah to Nahaliel: and from Nahaliel to Bamoth:

20 And from Bamoth in the valley, that is in the country of Moab, to the top of Pisgah, which looks **toward Jeshimon**.

1. War with the King of the Amorites, Num. 21:21-31:

21 And Israel sent messengers unto Sihon king of the Amorites, saying,

22 Let me pass through thy land: we will not turn into the fields, or into the vineyards; we will not drink of the waters of the well: but we will go along by the king's high way, until we be past thy borders.

23 And Sihon would not suffer Israel to pass through his border: but Sihon gathered all his people together, and went out against Israel into the wilderness: and he came to Jahaz, and fought against Israel.

24 And Israel smote him with edge of the sword, and possessed his land from Arnon unto Jabbok , even to the children of Ammon: for the border of the children of Ammon was strong.

25 And Israel took all these cities: and Israel dwelt in all these cities of the Ammorites in Heshbon, and in all the villages thereof.

26 For Heshbon was the city of Sihon the king of the Amorites, who had fought against the former king of Moab, and taken all his land out of his hand, even unto Arnon.

The war with the Amorites was not something Israel wanted. They respectfully asked the Amorites for passage and were told, No. The Amorites used their request as an excuse to fight against them. The war did not go as they expected because they were defeated by the armies of the Lord and their cities were taken. This was another victory for Israel; every victory was important to their survival. That is why it is important that Christians do not allow themselves to be defeated by the enemies. Did you stop to think that some Christians never recover from defeat?

27 Wherefore they that speak in proverbs say, Come into Heshbon, let the city of Sihon be built and prepared:

28 For there is a fire gone out of Heshbon, a flame from the city of Sihon: it hath consumed Ar of Moab and the lords of the high places of Arnon.

29 Woe to thee, Moab! Thou art undone, O people of Chemosh: he hath given his sons that escaped, and his daughters, into captivity unto Sihon king of the Amorites.

30 We have shot at them; Heshbon is perished even unto Dibon, and we have laid them waste even unto Nophath, which reacheth unto Medeba.

31 Thus Israel dwelt in the land of the Amorites.

These nations of Canaan were un-Godly; they had done abominable things in God's sight. That was why it was God's plan to replace them with the Children of Israel. There is something common with human nature – people do not learn from their mistakes or the mistakes of others. What happened to Arad the king of the Canaanites, also happened to Sihon King of the Amorites.

The King of Basham would follow their example and would also share the same fate.

2. War with OG King of Bashan, Num. 21:32-35

32 And Moses sent to spy out Jaazer, and they took the villages thereof, and drove out the Amorites that were there.

33 And they turned and went up by the way of Bashan: Og the king of Bashan went out against them, he, and all his people, to the battle of Edrei.

34 And the Lord said unto Moses, Fear him not: for I have given him into thy hand, and all his people, and his land; and thou shalt do to him as thou didst unto Sihon king of the Amorites, which dwelt at Heshbon.

35 So they smote him, and his sons, and all his people, until there were none left him alive: and they possessed his land.

At Shittim, the Plains of Moab, Numbers 22:1-4:

While being at Shittim, in the Plains of Moab, a number of consequential events occurred affecting Israel.

22:1 And the children of Israel set forward, and pitched in the plains of Moab on this side Jordan by Jericho.

2 And Balak the son of Zippor saw all that Israel had done to the Amorites.

King Balak did not want a free favor from the Prophet; his servants loaded themselves with rewards for the Prophet. But Balaam had to do exactly as the King requested in order to get the rewards. More accurately, Balaam was a diviner, which was not the same as one of the Old Testament Prophets – he could be bought as will be proven.

3 And Moab was sore afraid of the people, because they were many: and Moab was distressed because of the children of Israel.

4 And Moab said unto the elders of Midian, Now shall this company lick up all that round about us, as the ox licks up the grass of the field. And Balak the son of Zippor was king of the Moabites at that time.

Balak the King of Moab saw what Israel had done to the nations that made war with them. He decided to do things differently. Balak was a king who wanted to see the destruction of Israel at all cost and consulted Balaam the Prophet. On the other hand, Balaam was determined to please man and God at the same time. That was a difficult thing to do.

Balak the King of Moab Consults with the Prophet Balaam, Num. 22:5-11:

5 He sent messengers therefore unto Balaam the son of Beor to Pethor, which is by the river of the land of the children of his people, to call him, saying, Behold, there is a people come out from Egypt: behold, they cover the face of the earth, and they abide over against me:

6 Come now therefore, I pray thee, curse me this people; for they are too mighty for me: peradventure I shall prevail, that we might smite them, and that I may drive them out of the Land: for I wot that he whom you blesse is blessed, and he whom you curse is cursed.

Balak's message to Balaam conveyed a sense of despair and urgency. He learned from the defeat of the other kings that fought against Israel that he could not naturally defeat the common enemy of the nations of Canaan; he needed supernatural help. It was most urgent because Israel was on his borders and he felt helpless. Whereas the Prophet was famous for his deeds, I would personally question his spiritual genuineness as it relates to character. God's prophets are not known for blessing and cursing others. They are known for declaring God's truth to His people in an effort to turn them from unrighteousness to God. It was personally gratifying to Balaam to be recognized by the King of Moab as having special powers of blessing and cursing. Because that was so appealing to him he would, no doubt, want to prove his power to King Balak. As a prophet he would want to please God. The situation presented a great and unique temptation for him. He could not please God and King Balak at the same time. In the end Balaam would displease himself.

7 And the elders of Moab and the elders of Midian departed with the rewards of divination in their hand; and they came unto Balaam, and spoke unto him the words of Balak.

8 And he said unto them, Lodge here this night, and I will bring you word again, as the Lord shall speak unto me: and the princes of Moab abode with Balaam.

9 And God came unto Balaam, and said, What men are these with thee?

10 And Balaam said unto God, Balak the son of Zippor, king of Moab, hath sent unto me, saying,

11 Behold, there is a people come out of Egypt, who cover the face of the earth: come now, curse me them; peradventure I shall be able to overcome them, and drive them out.

Balaam delivered Balak's message to God and returned the answer. But it was not the answer Balaam nor Balak was

expecting.

God intervenes, Num. 22:12-27:

12 And God said unto Balaam, Thou shalt not go with them; thou shalt not curse the people: for they are blessed.

13 And Balaam rose up in the morning, and said unto the princes of Balak, Get you into your land: for the Lord refuses to give me leave to go with you.

14 And the princes of Moab rose up, and they went unto Balak, and said, Balaam refuses to come with us.

Balak was not satisfied with Balaam's answer and insisted on getting the answer he wanted.

15 And Balak sent yet again princes, more, and more honorable than they.

16 And they came to Balaam, and said to him, Thus says Balak the son of Zippor, Let nothing, I pray thee, hinder thee from coming unto me:

17 For I will promote thee unto very great honor, and I will do whatsoever you say unto me: come therefore, I pray you, curse me this people.

18 And Balaam answered and said unto the servants of Balak, If Balak would give me his house full of silver and gold, I cannot go beyond the word of the my God, to do less or more.

Balaam said the right thing but then did the wrong thing, by insisting on trying to get God to change His mind. God had told him he could not curse the Children of Israel because He had blessed them. Balaam did not want to take, "No" for an answer. Simply, he wanted to be praised and be held in high esteem by King Balak. He should have ended the dialogue with Balak there and then. It is an axiom that one cannot serve two masters simultaneously. But Balak thought he could.

19 Now therefore, I pray you, tarry ye also here this night, that I may know what the Lord will say unto me more.

Balak was very determined to get his desired answer.

20 And God came unto Balaam at night, and said unto him, If the men come to call thee, rise up, and go with them; but yet the word which I shall say unto thee, that shalt thou do.

21 And Balaam rose up in the morning, and saddled his ass, and went with the princes of Moab.

22 And God's anger was kindled because he went: and the angel of the Lord stood in the way for an adversary against him, Now he was riding upon his ass, and his two servants were with him.

God had already told Balaam not go with Balak's servant. God then gave him his desire to prove a point that He required obedience to His command.

23 And the ass saw the angel of the Lord standing in the way, and his sword drawn in his hand: and as the ass turned aside from out of the way, and went into the field: Balaam smote the ass, to turn her into the way.

24 But the angel of the Lord stood in a path of the vineyards, a wall being on his side, and a wall on that side.

25 And when the ass saw the angel of the Lord, she thrust herself unto the wall, and crushed Balaam's foot against the wall: and he smote her again.

26 And the angel of the Lord went further, and stood in a narrow place, where there was no way to turn either to the right or to the left.

27 And when the ass saw the angel of the Lord, she fell down under Balaam: and Balaam's anger was kindled, and he smote the ass with a staff.

It was Balaam's will to go with King Balak's servant, not God's. The answer God gave Balaam when he first enquired of Him was final; there was nothing more to be said. There are two ways to learn from God, by obedience, and by chastisement. Many have chosen to learn by chastisement; Prophet Balaam was one of them. God sent an angel to oppose him in his erroneous way. God opened the eyes of the ass to see the angel, yet Balaam's eyes were blinded by the rewards of unrighteousness to the extent that he could not see the angel of the Lord.

*Being blinded by the error of his way, Balaam smote his ass three times. The third time, the **dumb ass** had some compelling questions for him.*

The Dumb Ass Speaks Num. 22:28-41

28 And the Lord opened the mouth of the ass, and she said unto Balaam, What have I done unto thee, that thou hast smitten me these three times?

29 And Balaam said unto the ass, Because thou hast mocked me: I would there were a sword in mine hand, for now would I kill thee.

30 And the ass said unto Balaam, Am not I your ass, upon which thou hast ridden ever since I was thine unto this day? Was I ever want to do so unto thee? And He said, Nay.

Did Balaam ever communicate with an ass before? Did he not realize it was not a normal thing for an ass to be talking and asking the most logical questions of a prophet? There was an angel standing in his way.

He finally came to his senses:

31 Then the Lord opened the eyes of Balaam, and he saw the angel of the Lord, standing in the way, and his sword drawn in his hand: and he bowed his head and fell flat on his face.

Balaam was unable to answer the question asked of him by the ass, so he was not able to answer the questions asked by the angel.

32 And the angel of the Lord said unto him, Wherefore hast thou smitten thine ass these three times? Behold, I went out to withstand thee, because thy way is perverse before me:

33 And the ass saw me and turned from me these three

times: unless she had turned from me, surely now also I had slain thee, and save her alive.

34 And Balaam said unto the angel of the Lord, I have sinned; for I knew not that you stood in the way against me: now therefore, if it displeases thee, I will get me back again.

Balaam's repentance was not about the perverseness of his ways. It was about the fact that the ass spared his life from the destruction of the angel and he unwittingly smote him three times. The angel showed him a sign that he should not go to King Balak. Why would the angel change his mind after, and would want him to go? The truth is that Balaam still wanted to have his own way, and not God's way. Simply, he was unrepentant. Balaam still had a deep desire for the honor of men and wanted that honor more than anything else.

35 And the angel of the Lord said unto Balaam, Go with the men: but only the word that I shall speak unto thee, that thou shalt speak. So Balaam went with **the princes** of Balak.

36 And when Balak heard that Balaam was come, he went out to meet him unto a city of Moab, which is in the border of Arnon, which is in the utmost coast.

37 And Balak said unto Balaam, Did I not earnestly send unto thee to call thee? Wherefore you came not unto me? Am I not able indeed to promote you to honor?

God wanted Balaam to know that He was his real Master and not King Balak; Balaam could go, since he was insisting but had to speak God's words.

38 And Balaam said unto Balak, Lo, I am come unto thee: have I now any power at all to say anything? The word that God puts in my mouth, that shall I speak.

39 And Balaam went with Balak, and they came unto Kirjath-huzoth.

40 And Balak offered oxen and sheep, and sent to Balaam, and to the princes that were with him.

41 And it came to pass on the morrow, that Balak took Balaam, and brought him up into the high places of Baal,

that thence he might see the utmost part of the people.

*The efforts Balaam made to be in the presence of King Balak in the high places of Baal did not worth it because being there, he recognized how powerless he was and **how almighty** God was— he had to say what God wanted him to say. This reminds us of the story of Mordecai and Haman. Haman who was Mordecai's greatest enemy had to announce Mordecai's promotion in the streets of the Persian Kingdom. Balaam's insistence on trying to get God to curse Israel lets us know on whose side he was and he had to say what God told him. Balaam was doing everything in his power to improve the fortunes of King Balak. One could clearly see that if Balaam could curse Israel he would.*

Balaam Blesses Israel, Numbers 23-24:

1 And Balaam said unto Balak, Build me here seven altars, and prepare me here seven oxen and seven rams.

2 And Balak did as Balaam had spoken; and Balak and Balaam offered on every altar a bullock and a ram.

3 And Balaam said unto Balak, Stand by thy burnt offering, and I will go: peradventure the Lord will come to meet me: and whatsoever he shows me I will tell thee. And he went to an high place.

4 And God met Balaam: and he said unto him, I have prepared seven altars, and I have offered upon every altar a bullock and a ram.

5 And the Lord put a word in Balaam's mouth, and said, Return unto Balak, and thus thou shalt speak,

6 And he returned unto him, and, lo, he stood by his burnt sacrifice, he, and all the princes of Moab.

First Occasion of Blessing Israel, Num. 23:7-10:

7 And he took up his parable, and said, Balak the king of Moab hath brought me from Aram, out of the mountains of

the east, saying, Come, curse me Jacob, and come defy Israel.

8 How shall I curse, whom God hath not cursed? Or how shall I defy, whom the Lord hath not defied?

9 For from the top of the rocks I see him, and from the hills I behold him: lo, the people shall dwell alone, and shall not be reckoned among the nations.

10 Who can count the dust of Jacob, and the number of the fourth part of Israel? Let me die the death of the righteous, and let my last end be like his!

These words were spoken by Balaam but they were God's words of blessings on Israel. The present population of Israel is 7,000,000 — they are living in the land of Israel. But there are untold millions of the Children of Israel living in other countries. God's words of blessings are final, cannot be reversed. There are millions of people living in the world who do not realize that they are the Children of Israel —they have lost their identity.

Furthermore, there are more Israelis living in other countries than those who are living in the Holy Land. Their destiny is far greater than they even realize. One day soon all will realize it. King Balak was told by prophecy and still he did not realize the magnitude of it. And many of their enemies, like King Balak, are not aware of the awesome destiny that awaits Israel.

Balak's Reponse, Num.23:11-14

11 And Balak said unto Balaam, What hast thou done unto me? I took thee to curse mine enemies, and, behold, thou hast blessed them altogether.

12 And he answered and said, Must I not take heed to speak that which the Lord hath put in my mouth?

13 And Balak said unto him, Come, I pray thee, with me to another place, from whence you may see them: you

shall see but the utmost part of them, and shalt not see them all: and curse me them from thence.

14 And he brought him into the field of Zophim, to the top of Pisgah, and built seven altars, and offered a bullock and a ram on every altar.

Balaam, like King Balak, was determined to reverse God's blessings on His people. This was something they could not do because the blessings were already given. The offerings of the seven bullocks and seven rams upon the seven altars could not reverse the Divine blessings of Israel. The gifts and calling of God are without repentance.

The Prophet Balaam continued to try to defeat God's plan of blessings because he was unconnected with them. He was speaking about them with no passion nor desire nor optimism; and he never expressed the desire of being a part of the **Blessed People***. He was just like an instrument of music, projecting the sound but not connected.*

Second Occasion of Blessing Israel, Num.23:15-24

15 And he said unto Balak, Stand here by thy burnt offering, while I meet the Lord yonder.

16 And the Lord met Balaam, and put a word in his mouth, and said, Go again unto Balak, and say thus,

17 And when he came to him, behold, he stood by his burnt offering, and the princes of Moab with him. And Balak said unto him, What hath the Lord spoken?

18 And he took up his parable, and said, Rise up, Balak and hear; harken unto me thou son of Zippor:

19 God is not a man, that he should lie, neither the son of man, that he should repent: hath he said, and shall he not do it? Or hath he spoken, and shall he not make it good?

20 Behold, I have received commandment to bless: and he hath blessed: and I cannot reverse it.

21 He hath not beheld iniquity in Jacob, neither hath he

seen perverseness in Israel; the Lord his God is with him, and the shout of a king is among them.

22 God brought them out of Egypt; he hath as it were the strength of an unicorn.

23 Surely there is no enchantment against Jacob, neither is there any divination against Israel: according to this time, it shall be said of Jacob and of Israel, What hath God wrought?

24 Behold, the people shall rise up as a great lion, and lift up himself as a young lion: he shall not lie down until he eat of the prey, and drink the blood of the slain.

This pronouncement of Divine blessings was pointing in Israel's direction, but not in Balak's direction as he would have liked. He had to be trembling when he heard that Israel was unstoppable and would not rest until he destroyed his enemies. He knew he was one of those enemies. Why? He made himself one and demonstrated that fact beyond any doubt.

Balak's Response, Num.23:25-27

25 And Balak said unto Balaam, Neither curse them at all, nor bless them at all.

26 But Balaam answered and said unto Balak, Told not I thee, saying, All that the Lord speaks, that I must do?

27 And Balak said unto Balaam, Come, I pray thee, I will bring thee unto another place; peradventure it will please God that you may curse me them from thence.

28 And Balak brought Balaam unto the top of Peor, that looks toward Jeshimon

It is strange that the Prophet was saying the right things but was always doing the wrong things without realizing, because he never refused King Balak's invitations to curse Israel. Balaam realized that God would never curse Israel on behalf of King Balak or any other nation; he was in a serious way playing mind games with King Balak. Such behavior was not a characteristic of a genuine Old Testament prophet like Moses, Isaiah, or Jeremiah.

Third Occasion of Blessing Israel, Num. 23:29-24:1-9:

29 And Balaam said unto Balak, Build me here seven altars, and prepare me here seven bullocks and seven rams.

30 And Balak did as Balaam had said, and offered a bullock and a ram on every altar.

24:1 And when Balaam saw that it pleased the Lord to bless Israel, he went not, as at other times, to seek for enchantments, but he set his face toward the wilderness.

2 And Balaam lifted up his eyes, and he saw Israel abiding in his tents according to their tribes; and the spirit of God came upon him.

3 And he took up his parable and said, Balaam the son of Beor hath said, and the man whose eyes are open hath said:

4 He hath said which heard the words of God, which saw the vision of the Almighty, falling into a trance, but having his eyes open:

5 How goodly are thy tents, O Jacob, and thy tabernacles, O Israel!

6 As the valleys are they spread forth, as gardens by the river's side, as trees of lign aloes which the Lord hath planted, and as cedar trees beside the waters.

7 He shall pour the water out of his buckets, and his seed shall be in many waters, and his king shall be higher than Agag, and his kingdom shall be exalted.

8 God brought him forth out of Egypt; he hath as it were the strength of an unicorn: he shall eat up the nations his enemies, and shall break their bones, and pierce them through with his arrows.

9 He couched, he lay down as a lion: and as a great lion, who shall stir him up? Blessed is he that blesses you, and

cursed is he that curses you.

This blessing speaks of the abundance of Israel's prosperity and their numerical growth; it also speaks of military strength. Their military strength was what caused King Balak great fear. "His seed shall be in many waters" suggests the world- wide locations of the Children of Israel (verse 7). The prophetic King references Christ the Millennium King. The smart thing then was to be Israel's friends.

Balak's Response, Num. 24:10-14:

10 And Balak's anger was kindled against Balaam, and he smote his hands together: and Balak said unto Balaam, I have called thee to curse mine enemies, and, behold, thou hast altogether blessed them these three times.

11 Therefore now flee thou to thy place: I thought to promote thee to great honor; but, lo, the Lord has kept you back from honor.

Balak eventually lost control of the situation and the whole argument for wanting Balaam to curse Israel. What do we do when our desires and wishes are not granted? Do we replace them with anger and despair?

12 And Balaam said unto Balak, Spoke I not also to your messengers which you sent unto me, saying,

13 If Balak would give me his house full of silver and gold, I cannot go beyond the commandment of the Lord, to do either good or bad of mine own mind; but what the Lord says, that will I speak.

14 And now, behold, I go unto my people: come therefore and I will advertise thee what this people shall do to thy people in the latter days.

The King and The Prophet had both given up. King Balak could not get the Prophet to curse Israel; the Prophet became discouraged and did not offer any more sacrifices on the altar of King Balak. They went their separate ways. Before they

did, the Prophet gave his departing words:

Fourth Occasion of Blessing Israel, Num.24:15-25

15 And he took his parable, and said, Balaam the son of Beor hath said, and the man whose eyes are open hath said:

16 He hath said which heard the words of God, and knew the knowledge of the most High, Which saw the vision of the Almighty, falling into a trance, but having his eyes open:

17 I shall see him but not now: I shall behold him but not nigh: there shall come a star out of Jacob, and a Scepter shall rise out of Israel, and shall smite the corners of Moab, and destroy all the children of Seth.

18 And Edom shall be a possession, Seir also shall be a possession for his enemies; and Israel shall do valiantly.

19 Out of Jacob shall come he that shall have dominion, and shall destroy him that remains of the city.

20 And when he looked on Amalek, he took up his parable, and said, Amalek was the first of the nations; but his latter end shall be that he perish forever.

21 And he looked on the Kenites, and took up his parable, and said, Strong is thy dwelling place, and you put your rest in a rock.

22 Nevertheless the Kenite shall be wasted, until Asshur shall carry thee away captive.

23 And he took up his parable, and said, Alas, who shall live when God doeth this!

24 And ships shall come from the coast of Chittim, and shall afflict Asshur, and shall afflict Eber, and he also shall perish forever.

25 And Balaam rose up, and went and returned to his place: and Balak also went his way.

Balaam used his departing words to confirm what he already knew. He was powerless to add to or subtract from God's word. God's word is the truth and will outlast the

Universe.

Israel Being Overcome by Sin and Idolatry, Numbers 25

The Children of Israel were overcome at a time when they had secured a series of outstanding victories. This was a most unlikely time, as they should be praising God, giving the enemy no opportunity to pierce their defenses. They remained in the plains of Moab for a considerable amount of time after defeating some of the enemies. They were overcome on two fronts: committing fornication with the Moabites and by sacrificing to Baal-peor. Peor was a high mountain where sacrifices were made to Baal the god of the Moabites; hence the name Baal-peor.

The Double Sin of Fornication and Idolatry, Num.25:1-3

1 And Israel abode in Shittim, and the people began to commit whoredom with the daughters of Moab.

2 And they called the people to the sacrifices of their gods.

3 And Israel joined himself unto Baal-peor: and the anger of the Lord was kindled against Israel.

At a time when the Children of Israel were on the threshold of their inheritance, they became careless and allowed an opening in their defenses. The sins of adultery and idolatry carried the death sentence. The sins of the individuals were the sins of the whole nation. With sin in their lives they were defenseless against their enemies. The enemies knew that the way to defeat them was to get them to sin against their God. The worst thing about sins of this nature was they incurred the anger of God. When a Holy God is made angry there will be consequences. Death is the ultimate consequence.

The people looked to Aaron and Moses for help but they could not prevent the consequences; they could only limit them by their intercession.

Consequences of Their Sins, Num.25:4-18

4 And the Lord said unto Moses, Take all the heads of the people, and hang them up before the Lord against the sun, that the fierce anger of the Lord may be turned away from Israel.

There were consequences of death by the fire of the Lord from His fierce anger. Everyone caught in those sins were killed. Killing some of their brethren was not something they wanted to do; they had no choice if they wanted to spare the whole congregation.

5 And Moses said unto the judges of Israel, Slay ye everyone his men that were joined unto Baal-peor.

6 And, behold, one of the children of Israel came and brought unto his brethren a Midianitish woman in the sight of Moses, and in the sight of all the congregation of the children of Israel, who were weeping before the door of the tabernacle of the congregation.

7 And when Phinehas, the son of Eleazar, the son of Aaron the priest, saw it, he arose up from among the congregation, and took a javelin in his hand;

8 And he went after the man of Israel into the tent, and thrust both of them through, the man of Israel, and the woman through her belly. So the plague was stayed from the children of Israel.

9 And those that died in the plague were twenty and four thousand.

The action of Phinehas the son the Priest was righteously inspired. It certainly stopped the plague of death among the congregation and described the calamity better than any words could.

10 And the Lord spoke unto Moses, saying,

11 Phinehas, the son of Eleazar, the son of Aaron the priest, hath turned my wrath away from the children of

Israel, while he was zealous for my sake among them, that I consumed not the children of Israel in my jealousy.

God's jealousy is not like man's jealousy. One should not try to explain it for it cannot be explained. We know it is real; we saw the result, more than twenty four thousand people were destroyed. The holiness under the Law was based on Divine justice;under Grace is based on Divine mercy.

12 Wherefore say, Behold, I give unto him my covenant of peace.

13 And he shall have it, and his seed after him, even the covenant of an everlasting priesthood; because he was zealous for his God, and made an atonement for the children of Israel.

Phinehas' covenant of peace means that his descendants would be priests as long as the nation of Israel exists.

14 Now the name of the Israelite that was slain, even that was slain with the Midianitish woman, was Zimri, the son of Salu, a prince of a chief house among the Simeonites.

15 And the name of the Midianitish woman that was slain was Cozbi, the daughter of Zur; he was head over a people,
and of a chief house in Midian.

18 For they vex you with their wiles, wherewith they have beguiled you in the matter of Peor, and in the matter of Cozbi, the daughter of a prince of Midian, their sister, which was slain in the day of the plague for Peor's sake.

The Children of Israel were entrapped by their enemies at a time when they should have been praising God for the great victories He had given them before. These were not merely sins of choice, but sins of rebellion against God. The evidence was the 24000 people who died in the plague. The holiness under the Law required Divine justice.

Footnote: Numbers 26 is transferred to chapter 19 where it is treated; Numbers 29 is transferred to chapter 16, The Yearly Feast; Numbers 20:1-13 transferred to chapter, 24. These transfers were made to complete the subject matter of those chapters.

Israel Marches Forward

SUMMARY

The Strife at Meribah was behind the Children of Israel and they were ready to go forward with their journey. Moses sent a warm message to the king of Edom, expecting a positive response. He showed no humanity to the Children of Israel. He did not care to hear about their years of bondage in Egypt, neither their long and weary journeys. He did not care to be reminded of their family history. His army was ready to stop them by force if necessary. Moses had to find another way to continue their journey.

In addition to all the problems Moses and the Children of Israel had faced, the sudden declaration of the death of Aaron had caused a great burden to Moses and the Children of Israel. The Lord commanded Moses to take Aaron, his brother and priest to Mount Hor where he was to die and be buried. He was to be striped of the priestly garment and be placed upon his son, Eleazar. That very day of Aaron's death, his son was made priest. Aaron's death was accepted in a spirit of national unity. The congregation mourned his death for thirty days. And the forward march continued.

King Arad of Canaan was not happy about their famous new neighbors and took matters into his own hands. He warred with Israel and took many of them prisoners. They turned to the Lord and asked for His help. Then Israel defeated them and utterly destroyed their cities. The joy of their victory did not last very long; as they journeyed by the way of Mount Hor, they became wearied and went back to their old habit of murmuring. As usual, they murmured against those whom they needed most, Aaron Moses, and God. God was displeased and sent serpents to bite them. Many of them died. They recognized their sins and turned again to Moses and God for forgiveness and healing.
God commanded Moses to make a serpent of brass and to

put it upon a pole that those who were stung by the serpents could be healed by looking at it. The Brazen Serpent was to be a point of faith contact. The source of their healing was God. Yet the Brazen Serpent was symbolic of the Son of God who would be lifted up on the Cross for the healing and Atonement of mankind. Christ referenced this story in one of His declarations of His Messiah-ship.

The Children of Israel healed and restored continued with their journey to Mount Pisgah.From there, they sent message to King Sihon of the Amorites asking for permission to pass by his borders. He refused and came out with his army against them. Israel defeated them and took all their cities.

As the Children of Israel were close by the land of Bashan, Og the king came with his army and engaged them. They defeated Og and took his land. When the Children of Israel were in right relationship with God, they were victorious. For Israel, it was not over: there were yet more wars to be fought and there was always the unexpected. The nations of Canaan heard the fame of Israel and were terrified. King Balak of Moab was one of those kings.

The story of King Balak and Prophet Balaam shows the human side of both men. Both were determined in their own way. Balak was determined to defeat Israel not on the battlefield, but by a curse by the Prophet Balaam. Prophet Balaam was determined to live up to his reputation of cursing and blessing whomsoever he pleased. This time it was a little different for the Prophet because an angel was in his way. The story also shows God used a prophet of a different nation to reveal His sovereignty to a heathen king. It is doubtful as to whether King Balak benefited from the revelation of God. It is also doubtful as to whether Prophet Balaam learned that it was hard for him to resist the will of God. His prophecies with respect to Israel's survival and destiny were not his wishes nor desire. The Prophet failed to transcend the threshold of national perception where he would have been clearly recognized as a prophet of truth, representing Universal righteousness, not national boundaries.

God's message is universal that's why it was given through him to Israel, to Moab and to all the nations of Canaan. The universal nature of God's message was to make His prophet universal. But a prophet can try to limit God's message to his own national borders. When he does, he has lost sight of his High Calling as was in the case of Balaam. He it was that counseled the Moabites to entice the Children of Israel into fornication and idolatry. And instead of dying with the righteous as he once wished, he was slain among the Midianites. He was the prophet who knew and saw the destiny of others but not his own.

CHAPTER 27

Moses Prepares To Handover Leadership, Numbers 27-33

As Moses prepares to handover leadership to young Joshua, there were some urgent matters which demanded his attention. It was important for him to bring all these matters to a final conclusion and to settle all remaining questions before charging Joshua with the leadership of the Nation. Since Moses had been leading the Nation for approximately forty years, a smooth transition of leadership demanded sometime of preparation for himself, for his successor, and for the Nation as a whole.

There were matters that would be better dealt with by Moses than a new successor. His knowledge of the Law was beyond question, perfect; his relationship with God was all that was humanly possible.

Questions of the Daughters of Zelophehad, Num.27:1-6

1 Then came the daughters of Zelophehad, the son of Hepher, the son of Gilead, the son of Machir, the son of Manasseh of the families of Manasseh the son of Joseph: and these are the names of his daughters; Mahlah, Noah, and Hoglah, and Milcah, and Tirza.

2 And they stood before Moses, and before Eleazar the priest, and before the princes of all the congregation, by the door of the tabernacle of the congregation, saying,

3 Our father died in the wilderness, and he was not in the company of them that gathered themselves together

against the Lord in the company of Korah; but he died in his own sin, and had no sons.

The courage of the daughters of Zelophehad is admirable. Their father died leaving them no brothers. In those days the voices of women were silent as it were: they did not have much say, if any at all, in the affairs of the nation. Everything was left up to the men. They realized their inheritance was at stake and that they had to speak up load and clear. They went to the door of the Tabernacle and presented their case to Moses and the congregation.

Because of the importance of their case and its unique nature, Moses brought it before the Lord.

4 Why should the name of our father be done away from his family, because he hath no son? Give unto us therefore a possession among the brethren of our father.

5 And Moses brought their cause before the Lord.

6 And the Lord spoke unto Moses, saying,

The Zelophehad Law Num. 27: 7-11:

7 The daughters of Zelophehad speak right: thou shalt surely give them a possession of an inheritance among their father's brethren; and thou shalt cause the inheritance of their father to pass on to them.

8 And thou shalt speak unto the children of Israel, saying, If a man die, and have no son, then ye shall cause his inheritance to pass unto his daughter.

9 And if he have no daughter, then thou shalt give his inheritance unto his brethren.

10 And if he have no brethren, then ye shall give his inheritance unto his father's brethren.

11 And if his father have no brethren, then ye shall give his inheritance unto his kinsman that is next to him of his family, and he shall possess it: and it shall be unto the children of Israel a statute of judgment, as the Lord commanded Moses.

Justice was done to the daughters of Zelophehad and because of the righteousness of their cause a statute was instituted for those who had similar causes. As Christians, we must have the courage to speak out for just causes. If these causes are beyond the limits of the Church, then the larger society can move to action to effect the needed social justice.

Moses Views the Promised Land, Num.27:12-17

12 And the Lord said unto Moses, Get thee up into this mount Abarim, and see the land which I have given unto the children of Israel.

13 And when thou hast seen it, thou also shall be gathered unto thy people, as Aaron thy brother was gathered.

14 For ye rebelled against my commandment in the desert of Zin, in the strife of the congregation, to sanctify me at the water before their eyes: that is the water of Meribah in Kadesh in the wilderness of Zin.

The Lord told Moses the reason he would not lead the Children of Israel into the Promised Land. Moses recognized his failure at the water at Meribah to give God the glory in the presence of the congregation. Moses accepted his fate but was more concerned about the future of the Children of Israel. In expressing his concern for the future of the Children of Israel, he revealed his true heart, a heart after the heart of Christ. There were times when God wanted to consume the entire nation, when Moses stood between God and the congregation and pleaded with God for mercy and forgiveness for the people. He would have sacrificed his life for the congregation because God placed that love within his heart for them. We need spiritual leaders like Moses today to love the souls of men, not the material things the world has to offer.

15 And Moses spoke unto the Lord saying,

16 Let the Lord, the God of the spirits of all flesh, set a man over the congregation,

17 Which may go out before them, and which may go in before them, and which may lead them out, and which may bring them in; that the congregation of the Lord be not as sheep which have no shepherd.

Joshua Chosen to Succeed Moses, Num. 27:18-23

18 And the Lord said unto Moses, Take thee Joshua the son of Nun, a man in whom is the spirit, and lay thine hand upon him;

19 And set him before Eleazar the priest, and before all the congregation; and give him a charge in their sight.

20 And thou shalt put some of thine honor upon him, that all the congregation of the children of Israel may be obedient.

21 And he shall stand before Eleazar the priest, who shall ask counsel for him after the judgment of the Urim before the Lord: at his word shall they go out, and at his word they shall come in, both he, and all the children of Israel with him, even all the congregation.

22 And Moses did as the Lord commanded him: and he took Joshua, and set him before Eleazar the priest, and before the congregation:

23 And he laid his hands upon him, and gave him a charge, as the Lord commanded by the hand of Moses.

God chose Joshua to succeed Moses. Joshua was Moses faithful minister who with Caleb gave the congregation a good report after spying the land of Canaan. Joshua was filled with the Spirit of God and, therefore, had all the qualities of leadership to lead Israel. He was consecrated by Moses in the presence of the congregation and charged with the leadership of Israel.

The Children of Israel were on the borders of Canaan and were preparing to possess the land any time. Some of the offerings and memorials could only be done in their new country. It was important to commit these offerings to memory.

Emphases on the Offerings and the Memorials, 28:1-8

1 And the Lord spoke unto Moses, saying,

2 Command the children of Israel, and say unto them, My offering, and my bread for my sacrifices made by fire, for a sweet savor unto me, shall ye observe to offer unto me in their due season.

The offerings were not to be offered at times of their own choice; they were to be offered at their appointed times in accordance with their ordinance. Any failure meant the offerings would not be accepted. Some of these offerings were to be offered with the Memorials of the Lord. Three appointed times for the Burnt Offerings and three of the feasts are herein mentioned.

The Daily Burnt Offerings Num. 28:3-8

3 And thou shalt say unto them, This is the offering made by fire which ye shall offer unto the Lord; two lambs of the first year without spot day by day, for a continual burnt offering.

4 The one lamb shalt thou offer in the morning, and the other lamb shalt thou offer at even.

5 And a tenth part of an ephah of flour for a meat offering, mingled with the fourth part of an hin of beaten oil.

6 It is a continual burnt offering, which was ordained in mount Sinai for a sweet savor, a sacrifice made by fire unto the Lord.

7 And the drink offering thereof shall be the fourth part of an hin for the one lamb: in the holy place shalt thou cause the strong wine to be poured unto the Lord for a drink offering.

8 And the other lamb shalt thou offer at even: as the meat offering of the morning, and as the drink offering thereof, thou shalt offer it, a sacrifice made by fire, a sweet

savor unto the Lord.

The Burnt Offering was the only sacrificial offering completely burned on the Burnt Altar. With the daily Burnt Offerings of two lambs, one in the morning and the other in the evening, a Meat Offering and a Drink offering were offered. The Meat Offering and the Drink offering were offered with other offerings too. The Burnt Offering that was offered at evening typified Christ who was crucified in the evening. These two lambs were spotless, signifying the Spotless Lamb of God.

The Burnt Offering of the Sabbath Day, Num. 28:9-10

9 And on the Sabbath day two lambs of the first year without spot, and two tenth deals of flour for a meat offering, mingled with oil, and the drink offering thereof:

10 This is the burnt offering of every Sabbath, beside the continual burnt offering, and his drink offering.

On the Sabbath two additional lambs were offered with their Meat Offering and their Drink offering

The Monthly Burnt Offering, Num. 28:11-15

11 And in the beginnings of your months ye shall offer a burnt offering unto the Lord; two young bullocks, and one ram, seven lambs of the first year without spot;

12 And three tenth deals of flour for a meat offering, mingled with oil, for one bullock; and two tenth deals of flour for a meat offering, mingled with oil, for one ram;

13 And a several tenth deal of flour mingled with oil for a meat offering unto one lamb; for a burnt offering of a sweet savor, a sacrifice made by fire unto the Lord.

14 And their drink offerings shall be half an hin of wine, unto a bullock, and the third part of an hin unto a ram, and the fourth of an hin unto a lamb: this is the burnt offering of every month throughout the months of the year.

15 And one kid of the goats for a sin offering unto the Lord shall be offered, beside the continual burnt offering, and his drink offering.

The Monthly Burnt Offerings involved more sacrifices: two bullocks, one ram, and seven lambs with their Meat offerings and Drink Offerings, besides the daily Burnt Offerings.

The Passover, 28:16:

And in the fourteenth day of the first month is the Passover of the Lord.

For the Passover, only one spotless lamb was killed by each household in accordance with its ordinance. It was to remind them of the death of the first born of man and beast when the Lord passed over the land of Egypt and delivered them from bondage. Then followed the Feast of Unleavened Bread.

The Feast of Unleavened Bread, Num. 28:17-25:

17 And in the fifteenth day of this month is the feast: seven days shall unleavened bread be eaten.

18 In the first day shall be an holy convocation; ye shall do no manner of servile work therein:

19 But ye shall offer a sacrifice made by fire for a burnt offering unto the Lord; two young bullocks, and one ram, and seven lambs of the first year: they shall be unto you without blemish:

20 And their meat offering shall be of flour mingled with oil: three tenth deals shall ye offer for a bullock, and two tenth deals for a ram;

21 A several tenth deal shalt thou offer for every lamb, throughout the seven lambs:

22 And one goat for a sin offering, to make an atonement for you.

23 Ye shall offer these beside the burnt offering in the morning, which is for a continual burnt offering.

24 After this manner ye shall offer daily, throughout the seven days, the meat of the sacrifice made by fire, of a sweet savor unto the Lord: it shall be offered beside the continual burnt offering, and his drink offering.

25 And on the seventh day ye shall have an holy convocation; ye shall do no servile work.

The Feast of Unleavened Bread was associated with the Passover. It began the day after the Passover. It lasted seven days and began with a solemn assembly and a Burnt Offering of two bullocks, one ram, seven lambs with their Meat Offering and Drink Offering. Besides, a male goat for a Sin Offering was to be offered. The Daily Burnt Offerings continued. During the seven days all these offerings were to be offered.

The distinction between the Passover and the Week of Unleavened Bread is that the Passover is to be observed one day; the Week of Unleavened Bread is to be observed seven days. The importance of these feasts cannot be overstated. They should be committed to memory.

The Feast of the First Fruits, Pentecost, Num. 28:26-31

26 And in the day of the first fruits, when ye bring a new meat offering unto the Lord, after your weeks be out, ye shall have an holy convocation; ye shall do no servile work.

27 But ye shall offer the burnt offering for a sweet savor unto the Lord; two young bullocks, one ram, seven lambs of the first year;

28 And their meat offering of flour mingled with oil, three tenth deals unto one bullock, two tenth deals unto one ram,

29 A several tenth deal unto one lamb, throughout the seven lambs;

30 And one kid of the goats to make an atonement for you.

31 Ye shall offer them beside the continual burnt offering, and his meat offering, (they shall be unto

you without blemish) and their drink offering.

A similar Burnt Offering to the ones offered during the Feast of Unleavened Bread was to be offered for the Feast of Weeks (Pentecost).(Leviticus 23:15-21). A male goat was also offered as a Sin Offering. The daily Burnt Offerings continued as before. The Feast of Weeks(Pentecost, Leviticus 23:15-21), differs from the Feast of the First Fruits of Leviticus 23:10-14 and the First Fruits of Leviticus 19:23-25. The First Fruits of Leviticus 23:10-14 was to be celebrated in Canaan, also the First Fruits of Leviticus 19:23-25 and Leviticus 23:15-21.

Leviticus 23:10-14 clearly states that when the Children of Israel reaped the first harvest in Canaan they were to offer their first fruits unto the Lord. In truth, this account is independent of any of the other two accounts. From the Sabbath after the Wave Offering in Canaan of the First Fruits, fifty days should be counted and then a new offering was to be offered unto the Lord (Pentecost)

"The First Fruits" of Leviticus 19:23-25 suggest something altogether different. This account plainly says the first fruits would not be ready to be offered until the fifth year after the fruit trees were planted. The account characterizes the fruits as being uncircumcised and needed such time for purification. In the fourth year the fruits would be holy and should not be eaten. They should remain un-harvested in that way God would be honored. The fifth year was to be the time for Israel to enjoy the fruits of their labor and to celebrate the Feast of the First Fruits after planting the fruit trees. This time of sanctification was needed for the fruits

Questions of Vows, Num. 30

Vows were sacred with the Children of Israel and were to be kept as unto the Lord. Vows were made by men as well as women unto the Lord. Most vows were established by the Peace Offering. This involved the priest and showed the serious nature of vows. In the vows which we will now consider, we shall see how certain conditions could void the vows of others.

Consent of the Father, Num. 30:1-5:

1 And Moses spoke unto the heads of all the tribes concerning the children of Israel, saying, This is the thing which the Lord hath commanded.

2 If a man vow a vow unto the Lord, or swear an oath to bind his soul with a bond; he shall not break his word, he shall do according to all that proceeds out of his mouth.

Verses 1-2 state emphatically that vows are to be kept and must not be taken lightly. However, there are some conditions that could cause a vow to be nullified.

3 If a woman also vow a vow unto the Lord, and bind herself by a bond, being in her father's house in her youth;

4 And her father hear her vow, and her bond wherewith she hath bound her soul, and her father shall hold his peace at her: then all her vows shall stand, and every bond wherewith she hath bound her soul shall stand.

5 But if her father disallow her in the day that he hears; not any of her vows, or of her bonds wherewith she hath bound her soul, shall stand: and the Lord shall forgive her because her father disallowed her.

A father could nullify her daughter's vow if he heard when she was making it and then expressed his disagreement. But if he heard it and remained silent, she could fulfill her vow.

Consent of the Husband, Num. 30: 6-16:

6 And if she had at all an husband, when she vowed, or uttered aught out of her lips, wherewith she bound her soul;

7 And her husband heard it, and held his peace at her in the day that he heard it: then her vows shall stand, and her bonds wherewith she bound her soul shall stand.

8 But if her husband disallowed her on the day that he heard it; then he shall make her vow which she vowed, and

that which she uttered with her lips, wherewith she bound her soul, of none effect: and the Lord shall forgive her.

9 But every vow of a widow, and of her that is divorced, wherewith they bound their souls, shall stand against her.

10 And if she vowed in her husband's house, or bound her soul by a bond with an oath;

11 And her husband heard it, and held his peace at her, and disallowed her not: then all her vows shall stand, and every bond wherewith she bound her soul shall stand.

12 But if her husband hath utterly made them void on the day he heard them; then whatsoever proceeded out of her lips concerning her vows, or concerning the bond of her soul, shall not stand: her husband hath made them void; and the Lord shall forgive her.

13 Every vow, and every binding oath to afflict the soul, her husband may establish it, or her husband may make it void.

14 But if her husband altogether hold his peace at her from day to day; then he establishes all her vows, or all her bonds, which are upon her: he confirms them, because he held his peace at her in the day that he heard them.

15 But if he shall in any ways make them void after that he hath heard them; then he shall bear her iniquity.

16 These are the statutes which the Lord commanded Moses, between a man and his wife, between the father and his daughter, being yet in her youth in her father's house.

A husband had the power to void the vow of his wife if when he heard it being made, expressed his disapproval. If he heard it and remained silent, he consented.

Before Moses handed over the leadership of Israel to Joshua he had a big assignment to perform.

War with the Midianites, Numbers 31

1 And the Lord spoke unto Moses, saying

2 Avenge the children of Israel of the Midianites: afterward shalt thou be gathered unto thy people.

3 And Moses spoke unto the people, saying, Arm some of yourselves unto the war, and let them go against the Midianites, and avenge the Lord of Midian.

4 Of every tribe a thousand, throughout all the tribes of Israel, shall ye send to the war.

5 So they were delivered out of the thousands of Israel, a thousand of every tribe, twelve thousand armed for war.

6 And Moses sent them to the war, a thousand of every tribe, them and Phinehas the son of Eleazar the priest, to the war, with the holy instruments, and the trumpets to blow in his hand.

From Israel's prospective it was to be a holy war. Though Israel had more than 600,000 in the army only twelve thousand were chosen, a thousand from each tribe. Phinehas was sent to blow the holy trumpets. The victory was not to be won by Israel's military might but by God's own might as symbolized by the holy trumpets and the small army.

Defeat and Victory, Num. 31:7-24:

7 And they warred against the Midianites, as the Lord commanded Moses; and they slew all the males.

8 And they slew the kings of Midian, beside the rest of them that were slain; namely, Evi and Rekem, and Zur, and Hur, and Reba, five kings of Midian: "Balaam" also the son of Beor they slew with the sword.

Twelve thousand men went against five kings of Midian. This indicates that the armies of Midian were great in number, many more than the twelve thousands of Israel's army. The fact that these five kings were killed describes beyond words the greatness of Israel's victory.

9 And the children of Israel took all the women of Midian captives, and their little ones, and took the spoil of all their cattle, and all their flocks, and all their goods.

10 And they burnt all the cities wherein they dwelt, and all their goodly castles, with fire.

11 And they took all the spoil, and all the prey, both of men and beasts.

12 And they brought the captives, and the prey, and the spoil, unto Moses, and Eleazar the priest, and unto the congregation of the children of Israel, unto the camp at the plains of Moab.

13 And Moses, and Eleazar the priest, and all the princes of the congregation, went forth to meet them without the camp.

14 And Moses was wroth with the officers of the host, with the captains over thousands, and captains over hundreds, which came from the battle.

15 And Moses said unto them, Have ye saved all the women alive?

16 Behold, these caused the children of Israel, through the counsel of Balaam, to commit trespass against the Lord in the matter of Peor, and there was a plague among the congregation of the Lord.

Moses laid the blame on Balaam for the 24,000 people of the congregation who were destroyed by the fire of the Lord for the sins of idolatry and fornication with the Moabites. The true character of Balaam came to light because he it was that counseled Balack against the Children Israel, which led to idolertry and fornication. If Balaam was a holy prophet, he would not be killed with the unrighteous.

It was difficult for a prophet to order the death of anyone but Moses had to do what was necessary to preserve the spiritual wellbeing of Israel

17 Now therefore kill every male among the little ones, and kill every woman that hath known a man by lying with him.

18 But all the women children that have not known a man by lying with him, keep alive for yourselves.

19 And do ye abide without the camp seven days: whosoever hath killed any person, and whosoever hath touched any slain, purify both yourselves and your captives on the third day, and on the seventh day.

20 And purify all your raiment, and all that is made of skins, and all work of goats' hair, and all things made of wood.

The purification of the Red Heifer applied to all the men that returned from the war (Numbers 19). It was easy for things to become chaotic after such great victory over the Midianites but Moses made sure the camp remained holy by applying the purification of the Red Heifer

21 And Eleazar the priest said unto the men of war which went to the battle, This is the ordinance of the law which the Lord commanded Moses;

22 Only the gold, and the silver, the brass, the iron, the tin, and the lead,

23 Everything that may abide the fire, ye shall make it go through the fire, and it shall be clean: nevertheless it shall be purified with the water of separation: and all that abides not the fire ye shall make go through the water.

24 And ye shall wash your clothes on the seventh day, and ye shall be clean, and afterward ye shall come into the camp.

The fire was another method of purification, which was necessary to purify some of the spoils. But those things would also be cleansed by the water of purification of the Red Heifer. To have the abiding presence of God, the whole congregation and the camp had to be holy.

The Rewards of Victory, Num. 31:25-54

25 And the Lord spoke unto Moses, saying,

26 Take the sum of the prey that was taken, both of man and beast, thou, and Eleazar the priest, and the chief fathers of the congregation:

27 And divide the prey into two parts; between them that took the war upon them, who went out to battle, and between all the congregation:

28 And levy a tribute unto the Lord of the men of war who went out to battle: one soul of five hundred, both of the persons, and of the beeves, and of the asses, and of the sheep:

29 Take it of their half, and give it to Eleazar the priest, for an heave offering of the Lord.

30 And of the children of Israel's half, thou shalt take one portion of fifty, of the persons, of the beeves, of the asses, and of the flocks, of all manner of beasts, and give them unto the Levites, which keep the charge of the tabernacle of the Lord.

The rewards of victory were to be divided equally between the congregation and the men who went to war. They were to pay a tribute to the Lord and the congregation was to pay a tribute as well. The tribute of the army was to be paid to Eleazar the priest as a Heave Offering. The Heave Offering would be the Priest's portion of the spoil. The tribute of the congregation was to be given to the Levites for their service to the Tabernacle.

31 And Moses and Eleazar the priest did as the Lord commanded Moses.

32 And the booty, being the rest of the prey which the men of war had caught, was six hundred thousand and seventy thousand and five thousand sheep,

33 And three score and twelve thousand beeves,

34 And three score and one thousand asses,

35 And thirty and two thousand persons in all, of women that had not known man by lying with him.

This was the spoil divided among the congregation and the men who went to war and from which the Lord's tribute was paid. The division was as follows:

36 And the half, which was the portion of them that went

out to war, was in number three hundred thousand and seven and thirty thousand and five Hundred sheep:

37 And the Lord's tribute of the sheep was six hundred and three score and fifteen (*That was 1/500th of the sheep*).

38 And the beeves were thirty and six thousand; of which the Lord's tribute was three score and twelve (*That was 1/500th of the beeves*).

39 And the asses were thirty thousand and five hundred; of which the Lord's tribute was three score and one (*That was 1/500th*).

40 And the persons were sixteen thousand; of which the Lord's tribute was thirty and two persons (*That was 1/500th*)

41 And Moses gave the tribute, which was the Lord's heave offering, unto Eleazar the priest, as the Lord commanded Moses.

42 And of the children's half, which Moses divided from the men that warred,

43 (Now the half that pertained unto the congregation was three hundred thousand and thirty thousand and seven thousand and five hundred sheep,

44 And thirty and six thousand beeves,

45 And thirty thousand asses and five hundred,

46 And sixteen thousand persons;)

47 Even of the children of Israel's half, Moses took one portion of fifty, both of man and of beast, and gave them unto the Levites, which kept the charge of the tabernacle of the Lord; as the Lord commanded Moses.

48 And the Officers which were over thousands of the host, the captains of thousands, and the captains of hundreds, came near unto Moses:

49 And they said unto Moses, Thy servants have taken the sum of the men of war which are under our charge, and there lacks not one man of us.

The greatness of the miracle was that not one of the soldiers died in the war, for which the captains were extremely thank-

ful to the Lord. As the victory was great for Israel so was the defeat great for the Midianites. Indeed the wages of sin is death. And when a man dies he loses everything. This was true of the Midianites. As an expression of gratitude, the captains brought an offering unto the Lord.

50 We have therefore brought an oblation for the Lord, what every man hath gotten, of jewels of gold, chains, and bracelets, rings, earrings, and tablets, to make an atonement for our souls before the Lord.

51 And Moses and Eleazar the priest took the gold of them, even all wrought jewels.

52 And all the gold of the offering that they offered up to the Lord, of the captains of thousands, and of the captains of hundreds, was sixteen thousand seven hundred and fifty shekels. *(the equivalent of 167.5 pounds of gold).*

53 (For the men of war had taken spoil, every man for himself.)

54 And Moses and Eleazar the priest took the gold of the captains of thousands and of hundreds, and brought it into the tabernacle of the congregation, for a memorial for the children of Israel before the Lord.

In doing so, Moses places the true value on material things. Moses, unlike Balaam, could not be bought by gold or by anything earthly. He did not take much or little from the great amount of spoil of war. He laid the offering of gold upon the altar of the Lord, realizing that his reward in heaven was far greater than anything earthly. He set a sublime example for all Christians of the world to follow. Today many Christians have allowed material things to rob them of a more enduring reward. In the end such Christians will lose everything. Material things are only to be used in a way to glorify God the Giver of all blessings. One of the best ways is by sharing with others.

The Inheritance of Reuben, Gad, and Half the Tribe of Manasseh, Num. 32

Just before the Children of Israel entered into the Promised Land and just before the departure of Moses to his eternal home, Reuben, Gad, and half the tribe of Manasseh came before him with a request for their inheritance to be given them on the other side of Jordan where they were dwelling since the military victories over some of the neighboring countries.

Those lands were favorable for cattle farming and would be most suited for them since they were cattle farmers. They presented their request, expecting an immediate answer.

Request Presented, Num. 32: 1- 5

1 Now the children of Reuben and the children of Gad had very great multitude of cattle: and when they saw the land of Jazer, and the land of Gilead, that, behold, the place was a place for cattle;

2 And the children of Gad and the children of Reuben came and spoke unto Moses, and to Eleazar the priest, and unto the princes of the congregation, saying,

3 Ataroth and Dibon, and Jazer, and Nimrah, and Hesbon, and Elealeh, and Shebam, and Nebo, and Beon,

4 Even the country which the Lord smote before the congregation of Israel, is a land for cattle, and thy servants have cattle:

5 Wherefore, said they, if we have found grace in thy sight let this land be given unto thy servants for a possession and bring us not over Jordan.

Their request was sincere and was presented to Moses in the presence of the congregation, just the way Christian business should be conducted. Today Christian business is conducted for the most part in deep secrecy. Being the wise and experienced leader Moses was, he listened carefully before reminding them of recent history.

Moses's Response Num. 32: 6-15:

6 And Moses said unto the children of Gad and to the children of Reuben, Shall your brethren go to war, and shall ye sit here?

7 And wherefore discourage the heart of the children of Israel form going over into the land which the Lord hath given them?

8 Thus did your fathers, when I sent them from Kadesh-barnea to see the land.

9 For when they went up into the valley of Eshcol, and saw the land, they discouraged the heart of the children of Israel, that they should not go into the land which the Lord had given them.

10 And the Lord's anger was kindled the same time, and he swore, saying,

11 Surely none of the men that came up out of the land of Egypt, from twenty years old and upward, shall see the land which I swore unto Abraham, unto Isaac, and unto Jacob; because they have not wholly followed me.

12 Save Caleb the son of Jephunneh the Kenzite, and Joshua the son of Nun: for they have wholly followed the Lord.

13 And the Lord's anger was kindled against Israel, and he made them wander in the wilderness forty years, until all the generation, that had done evil in the sight of the Lord, was consumed.

14 And, behold, ye are risen up in your fathers' stead, an increase of sinful men, to argument the fierce anger of the Lord toward Israel.

15 For if ye turn away from after him, he will yet again leave them in the wilderness; and ye shall destroy all this people.

Moses' first response was well said; but Reuben listened carefully and responded.

An Explanation from Reuben, Num. 2:16-19:

16 And they came near unto him, and said, We will build sheep folds for our cattle, and cities for our little ones:

17 But we ourselves will go ready armed before the children of Israel, until we have brought them unto their place: and our little ones shall dwell in the fenced cities because of the inhabitants of the land.

18 We will not return to our houses, until the children of Israel have inherited every man his inheritance.

19 For we will not inherit with them on yonder side Jordan, or forward; because our inheritance is fallen to us on this side Jordan eastward.

After fully understanding their motives and their purpose of national unity, Moses granted their request on the condition that Reuben and his brethren will join the other tribes to evict the enemies from the land the other side of Jordan.

Inheritance Received, Num. 32:20-42

20 And Moses said unto them, If ye will do this thing, if ye will go armed before the Lord to war,

21 And will go all of you armed over Jordan before the Lord, until he hath driven out his enemies from before him,

22 And the land be subdued before the Lord: then afterward ye shall return, and be guiltless before the Lord, and before Israel; and this land shall be your possession before the Lord.

23 But if ye will not do so, behold, ye have sinned against the Lord: and be sure your sin will find you out.

24 Build you cities for your little ones, and folds for your sheep; and do that which hath proceeded out of your *mouth*.

Moses was satisfied that Reuben and his brethren were committed to the defense of Israel and gave them his blessing. Moses made plain to the Priest and the other leaders of the congregation the conditions on which Reuben, Gad, and the half tribe of Manasseh received their possession of the east of Jordan. These tribes were happy to receive their lots east of of Jordan

25 And the children Gad and the children of Reuben spoke unto Moses, saying, Thy servants will do as my lord commands.

26 Our little ones, our wives, our flocks, and all our cattle, shall be there in the cities of Gilead:

27 But thy servants will pass over, every man armed for war, before the Lord to battle, as my lord says.

28 So concerning them Moses commanded Eleazar the priest, and Joshua the son of Nun, and the chief fathers of the tribes of the children of Israel:

29 And Moses said unto them, If the children of Gad and the children of Reuben will pass with you over Jordan, every man armed to battle, before the Lord, and the land shall be subdued before you; then ye shall give them the land of Gilead for a possession:

30 But if they will not pass over with you armed, they shall have their possession among you in the land of Canaan.

31 And the children of Gad and the children of Reuben answered, saying, As the Lord hath said unto thy servants, so will we do.

32 We will pass over armed before the Lord into the land of Canaan, that the possession of our inheritance on this side Jordan may be ours.

33 And Moses gave unto them, even to the children of Gad, and to the children of Reuben, and half the tribe of Manasseh the son of Joseph, the kingdom of Sihon king of the Amorites, and the kingdom of Og king of Bashan, the land, with cities thereof in the coasts, even the cities of the country round about.

34 And the children of Gad built Dibon, and Ataroth, and Aroer,

35 And Atroth, Shophan, and Jaazer, and Jogbehah,

36 And Beth-nimrah, and Beth-haran, fenced cities: and

folds for sheep.

37 And the children of Reuben built Heshbon, and Elealeh, and Kirjathaim,

38 And Nebo and Baal-meon, (their names being changed,) and Shibmah: and gave other names unto the cities which they builded.

39 And the children of Machir the son of Manasseh went to Gilead, and took it, and dispossessed the Amorite which was in it.

40 And Moses gave Gilead unto Machir the son of Manasseh; and he dwelt therein.

41 And Jair the son of Manasseh went and took the small towns thereof, and called them Havoth-jair.

42 And Nobah went and took Kenath, and the villages thereof, and called it Nobah, after his own name.

Reuben, Gad, and the half tribe of Manasseh proved themselves worthy of their inheritance by quickly building new cities and expelling the enemies that had remained in other areas.

The Journeys of the Children of Israel, Numbers 33

The journeys of the Children of Israel, to a great degree, reflect the Christian experience. The destination points of each of the many journeys brought a new realization of life to the Children of Israel. It is, indeed, a sad reality that many of them who journeyed from Egypt and witnessed the signs and wonders never experienced the final journey into the Promised Land. For those who did not experience that final journey, it was all in vain. The lesson Christians can learn from the experienced of those who failed to enter into the Promised Land is that we must overcome fear; let go of unbelief, and depend on the abundance of God's grace.

Most of the destination points of these journeys are not on the maps. They were written by Moses for succeeding generations to emphasize how disobedience and unbelief

could rob them of God's abundant blessings and how life would be less complicated when faith was placed in God.

The journeys herein highlight the main destination points recognized on the map on page 67; they are the journeys of the first year.

Journey from Rameses to the Red Sea, Num. 33:1-8:

1 These are the journeys of the children of Israel, which went forth out of the land of Egypt with their armies under the hand of Moses and Aaron.

2 And Moses wrote their goings out according to their journeys by the commandment of the Lord: and these are their journeys according to their goings out.

3 And they departed from Rameses in the first month, Abib, on the fifteenth day of the first month; on the marrow after the Passover the children of Israel went out with an high hand in the sight of all the Egyptians.

4 For the Egyptians buried all their first born, which the Lord had smitten among them: upon their gods also the Lord executed judgment.

5 And the children removed from Rameses, and pitched in Succoth.

6 And they departed from Succoth, and Pitched in Etham, which is in the edge of the wilderness.

7 And they removed from Etham, and turned again unto Pi-hahiroth, which is before Baal-zephon: and they pitched before Migdol.

8 And they departed from before Pi-hahiroth, and passed through the midst of the sea into the wilderness, and went three days' journey in the wilderness of Etham, and pitched at Marah.

Rameses was where the Children of Israel were living since their fathers went to Egypt 430 years before the Exodus. Rameses is on the map; it is nearer to the Mediterranean Sea than the Red Sea. If they had gone by the way of the

Mediterranean Sea, their journey would have been less than forty days. Succoth their next stop is on the map but Etham, Pihahiroth, and Baal-zephon, are not on the map. Marah is south of Succoth and north of Elim. Marah is also close to the Red Sea. At Marah they had an experience with bitter water.

Journey from the Red Sea to Sinai, Num. 33:9-15:

9 And they removed from Marah, and came unto Elim: and in Elim were twelve fountains of water, and three score and ten palm trees; and they pitched there.

10 And they removed from Elim, and encamped by the Red sea.

11 And they removed from the Red sea, and encamped in the wilderness of Sin.

12 And they took their journey out of the wilderness of Sin, and encamped in Dophkah.

13 And they departed from Dophkah, and encamped in Alush.

Elim is relatively close to the Red Sea, also the Wilderness of Sin. Dophkah and Alush are not on the map, Rephidim was another place of experience. It is also near the Red Sea on the map. The Wilderness of Sinai was where the Ten Commandments were given and from where God appeared and spoke to all Israel in Mount Sinai. Sinai is on the map.

14 And they departed from Alush, and ecamped at Rephidim, where was no water for the people to drink.

15 And they departed from Rephidim, and pitched in the wilderness of Sinai.

Journey from Sinai to the Wilderness of Zin, Kadesh, Num. 33:16-36:

16 And they removed from the desert of Sinai, and pitched at Kibroth-hattaavah.

Kibroth-hattaavah was another place of notable experience.

There the Lord consumed many of the people who lusted after flesh. While they were eating, the anger of the Lord destroyed many of them. Hazeroth is north of Sinai and south of Paran. It is also close to the Red Sea. Rithmah, Rimon-parez, Libnah, Rissah, Kehelathah, Mount Shapher, Haradah, Makheloth, Tahath, and many other of these place are not on the map. These were the names of their jorneys before they had turned back in the Wilderness.

17 And they departed from Kibroth-hattaavah, and encamped at Hazeroth.

18 And they departed from Hazeroth, and pitched at Rithmah.

19 And they departed from Rithmah, and pitched at Rimon-parez.

20 And they departed from Rimon-parez, and pitched in Libnah.

21 And they removed from Libnah, and pitched at Rissah.

22 And they removed from Rissah, and pitched at Kehelathah.

23 And they went from Kehelathah, and pitched in mount Shapher.

24 And they removed from mount Shapher, and encamped in Haradah.

25 And they removed from Haradah, and pitched in Makheloth.

26 And they removed from Makheloth, and encamped at Tahath.

27 And they departed from Tahath, and pitched at Tarah.

28 And they removed from Tarah, and pitched in Mithcah.

29 And they removed from Mithcah, and pitched in Hashmonah.

30 And they departed from Hashmonah, and encamped

at Moseroth.

31 And they departed from Moseroth, and pitched in Bene-jaakan.

32 And they removed from Bene-jaakan, and encamped at Hor-hagidgad.

33 And they went from Hor-hagidgad, and pitched in Jotbathah.

34 And they removed from Jotbathah, and encamped at Ebronah.

35 And they departed from Ebronah, and encamped at Ezion-geber.

36 And they removed from Ezion-geber, and pitched in the wilderness of Zin, which is Kadesh.

Journey from Kadesh to the Plains of Moab by Jordan, Num. 33: 37-56:

Here they returned to Kadesh in the Wilderness of Zin about thirty nine years after the spies were sent into Canaan. Kadesh and the Wilderness of Zin are on the map. Kadesh is south of Canaan. On the map on page 67, Kadesh-barnea is south of the Wilderness of Zin.

37 And they removed from Kadesh, and pitched in mount Hor, in the edge of the land of Edom.

38 And Aaron the priest went up into mount Hor at the commandment of the Lord, and died there, in the fortieth year after the children of Israel were come out of the land of Egypt, in the first day of the fifth month.

39 And Aaron was an hundred and twenty and three years old when he died in mount Hor.

40 And king Arad the Canaanite, which dwelt in the south in the land of Canaan, heard of the coming of the children of Israel.

41 And they departed from mount Hor, and pitched in Zalmonah.

42 And they departed from Zalmonah, and pitched in Punon.

43 And they departed from Puon, and pitched in Oboth.

44 And they departed from Oboth, and pitched in Ijeabarim, in the border of Moab

45 And they departed from Iim, and pitched in Dibongad.

46 And they removed from Dibongad, and encamped in Almon-diblathaim, before Nebo.

47 And they removed from Almon-diblathaim, and pitched in the mountains of Abarim, before Nebo.

 None of the above named places is on the map. Moab, Jordan, and Jericho are on the map

48 And they departed from the mountains of Abarim, and pitched in the plains of Moab, by Jordan near Jericho.

49 And they pitched by Jordan, from Beth-jeshimoth even unto Abel-Shittim in the plains of Moab.

Moses' Departing Words, Num. 33:50-56:

The departing words of the holy Prophet came to Israel from the Plains of Moab. In these words is an exhortation of love for God, obedience, and courage. There is also a strong warning of failure to obey the commandments of God.

50 And the Lord spoke unto Moses in the plains of Moab by Jordan near Jericho, saying,

51 Speak unto the children of Israel, and say unto them, When ye are passed over Jordan into the land of Canaan;

52 Then ye shall drive out all the inhabitants of the land from before you, and destroy all their pictures, and destroy all their molten images, and quite pluck down all their high places:

53 And ye shall dispossess the inhabitants of the land, and dwell therein: for I have given you the land to possess it.

54 And ye shall divide the land by lot for an inheritance among your families: and to the more ye shall give the more inheritance, and to the fewer ye shall give the less

inheritance: every man's inheritance shall be in the place where his lot falls; according to the tribes of your fathers ye shall inherit.

55 But if ye will not drive out the inhabitants of the land from before you; then it shall come to pass, that those which ye let remain of them shall be pricks in your eyes, and thorns in your sides, and shall vex you in the land wherein ye dwell.

56 Moreover it shall come to pass, that I shall do unto you, as I thought to do unto them.

SUMMARY

This chapter bears testimony to the point in Moses' life when he was required to hand over the leadership of the Children of Israel to a successor. After leading the Nation forty years, adequate time of preparation was needed in order to successfully hand over the leadership to a successor. There were certain issues better addressed by Moses than by the new successor. There was the request from the daughters of Zelophehad. Some of the laws could not be fulfilled until the Children of Israel had taken possession of the Promised Land. The offerings and the feasts of memorials had to be reemphasized. The heart of Israel's Theocracy was embodied in these offerings. The spiritual life of the Nation depended on these offerings.

The defeats and destructions of some of the neighboring nations were led by Moses. That was the right thing to do instead of committing such awesome responsibilities to a new successor. The victory over the Midianites was most memorable not only from the consideration of the enormous amount of spoils, but also from the consideration that not one of the men who went to war against the enemy was killed. The death of Aaron the anointed priest was a great blow to the Children of Israel. However, they responded with grace and optimism. The immediate consecration of his son, Eleazar, as his successor showed the critical role of the High Priest. It was reassuring that Eleazar was prepared to assume the responsibility.

The 40 year journey of the Children of Israel had many destination points, most of which had unforgettable experiences: times of anguish of soul and spirit, fear and unbelief, defeats and victories, and miracles. Out of each of these experiences, there was some lesson to be learned. In the end, God's faithfulness and mercies were revealed. From Rameses, the point of beginning, through the Red Sea to Kadesh and back, that, of itself, was the greatest of all miracles. The congregation of Israel was more than 2,000,000 at all times living in the Wilderness without the benefits of modern convenience. And having to keep their camp holy to welcome the holy presence of God was a human and Divine accomplishment of the greatest order. There was a sadness which could not be hoped to be expressed in words is the fact that all those who began this long and miraculous journey never reached the Promised Land.

God's promise of giving the land of the nations of Canaan to the Children of Israel had Divine justification. The nations of Canaan were wholly corrupt and had no intentions of changing from their sinful ways of idolatry and sexual perversions. God had given them 430 years to amend their ways and turn to Him in righteousness. They proved to be hopeless; they, therefore, became vessels of wrath fitted for destruction— they had to be removed from the land that it could be given to the Children of Israel who would establish righteousness and the honor of God. As the privileges of Israel were great, so were the responsibilities. God expected them to do well for failure would not be accepted.

The journey of the Children of Israel was a long one with many destination points. It was both literal and spiritual.

Ours is a spiritual one with many experiences which are our destination points. Like them, we must use these destination points to renew us spiritually as we await the imminent return of Christ.

CHAPTER 28
National Borders And Cities For The Levites, Numbers 34-36

It was important for the Children of Israel to know their national borders. These borders identified their land rights and also identified them as a nation. They placed certain restrictions on them on the one hand; and on the other hand, gave them the right of possession of those lands within their borders. Knowing their borders they would possess all those lands and defend them as well.

The Levites were the servants of all the people and were not to be given their inheritance in the manner of the other tribes. Instead, the other tribes were to each give to them cities and suburbs from their inheritance. The discussion of the subject matter by Moses was a guarantee that the land was already theirs because God was going to lead them into it.

God described the national borders; they could not have expected more

National Borders, Num. 34

1 And the Lord spoke unto Moses, saying,

2 Command the children of Israel, and say unto them, When ye come into the land of Canaan; (this is the land that shall fall unto you for an inheritance, even the land of Canaan with the coast thereof:)

God expected the Children of Israel to possess every square foot of the land within the borders He declared and to defend it. All the border marks cannot be identified of the maps. Nevertheless, with those borders which can easily be identified and with the map of their dominion, the extent of their dominion is easily recognized.

Southern and Western Borders, Num. 34: 3-6

3 Then your south quarter shall be from the wilderness of Zin along by the coast of Edom, and your south border shall be the outmost coast of the salt sea eastward:

4 And your border shall turn from the south to the ascent of Akrabbim, and pass on to Zin: and the going forth thereof shall be from the south to Kadesh-barnea, and shall go unto Hazar-addar, and pass on to Azmon:

5 And the border shall fetch a compass from Azmon unto the river of Egypt, and the goings out of it shall be at the sea.

6 And as for the western border, ye shall even have the great sea for a border: this shall be your west border.

On the map on page 600, the Wilderness of Zin, the Coast of Edom, and the Salt Sea are shown. Kades-Barnea and the river of Egypt, (the Wadi of Egypt), are also shown. The Great Sea, the Mediterranean Sea is the Western border is shown on both maps.

Northern and Eastern Borders Num. 34: 7-12:

7 And this shall be your north border: from the great sea (Mediterranean) ye shall point out for you mount Hor:

8 From mount Hor ye shall point out your border unto the entrance of Hamath; and the goings forth of the border shall be to Zedad:

9 And the border shall go on to Ziphron, and the goings out of it shall be at Hazarenan: this shall be your north border.

10 And ye shall point out your east border from Hazarenan to Shepham:

11 And the coast shall go down from Shepham to Riblah, on the east side of Ain; and the border shall descend, and shall reach unto the side of the sea of Chinnereth eastward:

12 And the border shall go down to Jordan, and the goings out of it shall be at the salt sea: this shall be your land with the coast thereof round about.

Dominion of the Twelve Tribes

From north of the Mediterranean Sea, eastward, Mount Hor (Mount Hermon), Chinnereth (Kinnereth), Jordan, and the Salt Sea can be recognized.

13 And Moses commanded the children of Israel, saying, This is the land which ye shall inherit by lot, which the Lord

commanded to give unto the nine tribes, and to the half tribe:

14 For the tribe of the children of Reuben according to the house of their fathers, and the tribe of the children Gad according to the house of their fathers, have received their inheritance; and half the tribe of Manasseh have received their inheritance.

15 The two tribes and the half tribe have received their inheritance on this side Jordan near Jericho eastward, toward the sun rising.

Reuben, Gad, and the half tribe of Manasseh already received their inheritance east of Jordan and divided it by lots. The land distribution by casting of lots was a fair and just way. The priests and the princes were to ensure that every man received his inheritance. Notwithstanding, God was the permanent Owner. That was why every seven years the land was to be at rest to honor the Lord. One reason for removing Israel from their inheritance was that they did not allow the land to rest its Sabbatical Year.

The Responsibility for Dividing the Land, Num. 34:16-29

16 And the Lord spoke unto Moses, saying,

17 These are the names of the men which shall divide the land unto you: Eleazer the priest, and Joshua the son of Nun.

18 And ye shall take one prince of every tribe, to divide the land by inheritance.

19 And the names of the men are these: of the tribe of Judah, Caleb the son of Jephunneh.

20 And of the tribe of the children of Simeon, Shemuel the son of Ammihud.

21 Of the tribe of Benjamin, Elidad the son of Chislon.

22 And the prince of the tribe of the children of Dan, Bukki the son of Jogli.

23 The prince of the children of Joseph, for the tribe

of the children of Manasseh, Hanniel the son of Ephod.

24 And the prince of the tribe of the children of Ephraim, Kemuel the son of Shiphtan.

25 And the prince of the children of Zebulun, Elizaphan the son of Parnach.

26 And the prince of the tribe of the children of Issachar, Paltiel the son of Azzan.

27 And the prince of the tribe of the children of Asher, Ahihud the son of Shelomi.

28 And the prince of the tribe of the children of Naphtali, Pedahel the son of Ammihud.

29 These are they whom the Lord commanded to divide the inheritance unto the children of Israel in the land of Canaan.

The Inheritance of the Levites, Num. 35:1-34:

The inheritance of the Levites was treated differently. Because they were wholly given to the Lord instead of the first born of the Children of Israel, God used them to serve the other tribes in the service of the Tabernacle. Therefore each of the tribes was to give cities and suburbs form their inheritance to the Levites. It was to be done fairly.

1 And the Lord spoke unto Moses in the plains of Moab by Jordan near Jericho, saying,

2 Command the children of Israel, that they give unto the Levites of the inheritance of their possession cities to dwell in; and ye shall give also unto the Levites suburbs for the cities round about them.

3 And the cities shall they have to dwell in; and the suburbs of them shall be for their cattle, and for their goods, and for all their beasts.

4 And the suburbs of the cities, which ye shall give unto the Levites, shall reach from the wall of the city and outward a thousand cubits round about.

The suburbs should be measured 1500 feet from each city. The area of the suburb was to be 3,000 x 3000 square feet: an area of 206 acres. They were to be given forty-two cities with their suburbs, besides six cities of Refuge for the man slayer. This shows the just manner everyone was given his inheritance.

5 And ye shall measure from without the city on the east side two thousand cubits, and on the south side two thousand cubits, and on the west side two thousand cubits, and on the north side two thousand cubits; and the city shall be in the midst: this shall be to them the suburbs of the cities.

Cities of Refuge, Num. 35:6-15

6 And among the cities which ye shall give unto the Levites there shall be six cities for refuge, which ye shall appoint for the man slayer that he may flee thither: and to them ye shall add forty and two cities.

7 So all the cities which ye shall give to the Levites shall be forty and eight cities: them shall ye give with their suburbs.

8 And the cities which ye shall give shall be of the possession of the children of Israel: from them that have many ye shall give many; but from them that have few ye shall give few: every one shall give of his cities unto the Levites according to his inheritance which he inherits.

9 And the Lord spoke unto Moses, saying,

10 Speak unto the children of Israel, and say unto them, When ye be come over Jordan into the land of Canaan.

These cities of refuge were for the safety of those who killed someone accidentally. They were to remain in these cites until the death of the High Priest. The judgment by the congregation was to determine innocence or guilt as to manslaughter or murder, but not freedom from the City of Refuge.

11 Then ye shall appoint you cities to be cities of refuge for you; that the slayer may flee thither, which kills any person at unawares.

12 And they shall be unto you cities for refuge from the avenger; that the manslayer die not, until he stand before the congregation in judgment.

13 And of these cities which ye shall give six cities shall ye have for refuge.

14 Ye shall give three cities on this side Jordan, and three cities shall ye give in the land of Canaan, which shall be cities of refuge.

15 These six cities shall be a refuge, both for the children of Israel, and for the stranger, and for the sojourner among them: that every one that kills any person unawares may flee thither.

The cities of Refuge were not limited to the Children of Israel; they were for the sojourner and strangers as well. The Law defines who was a man slayer and who was a murderer. By this definition, the congregation of Israel could render a true verdict.

Distinction between Accidental Killing and Murder, Num. 35:16-23:

16 And if he smite him with an instrument of iron, so that he die, he is a murderer: the murderer shall surely be put to death.

17 And if he smite him with throwing a stone, wherewith he may die, and he die, he is a murderer: the murderer shall surely be put to death.

18 And if he smite him with an hand-weapon of wood, wherewith he may die, and he die, he is a murderer: the murderer shall surely be put to death.

19 The revenger of blood himself shall slay the murderer: when he meets him, he shall slay him.

20 But if he thrust him of hatred, or hurl at him by laying of wait, that he die;

21 Or in enmity smite him with his hand, that he die: he that smote him shall surely be put to death; for he is a murderer: the revenger of blood shall slay the murderer, when he meets him.

22 But if he thrust him suddenly without enmity, or have cast upon him anything without laying of wait,

23 Or with any stone, wherewith a man may die, seeing him not, and cast it upon him, that he die, and was not his enemy, neither sought his harm:

Judgment by the Congregation, Num. 35:24-34:

24 Then the congregation shall judge between the slayer and the revenger of blood according to these judgments:

25 And the congregation shall deliver the slayer out of the hand of the revenger of blood, and the congregation shall restore him to the city of his refuge, whither he was fled: and he shall abide in it unto the death of the of the high priest, which was anointed with the holy oil.

26 But if the slayer shall at any time come without the border of the city of his refuge, whither he was fled;

27 And the revenger of blood find him without the borders of the city of his refuge, and the revenger of blood the slayer; he shall not be guilty of blood.

28 Because he should have remained in the city of his refuge until the death of the high priest: but after the death of the high priest the slayer shall return into the land of his possession.

29 So these things shall be for a statute of judgment unto you throughout your generations in all your dwellings.

These judgments were to be executed without fear or favor. One should not be allowed to buy his way out from God's righteous judgments. By allowing the murderer to go

free, the land would be polluted by blood and could only be cleansed, not by the blood sacrifices but by the blood of the murderer. One witness could not secure a conviction of guilt.

30 Whoso kills any person, the murderer shall be put to death by the mouth of witnesses: but one witness shall not testify against any person to cause him to die.

31 Moreover ye shall take no satisfaction for the life of a murderer, which is guilty of death: but he shall be surely put to death.

32 And ye shall take no satisfaction for him that is fled to the city of refuge, that he should come again to dwell in the land, until the death of the priest.

33 So ye shall not pollute the land wherein ye are: for blood defiles the land: and the land cannot be cleansed of the blood that is shed therein, but by the blood of him that shed it.

34 Defile not therefore the land which ye shall inhabit, wherein I dwell: for I the Lord dwell among the children of Israel.

The things done in other nations were not permitted to be practiced by Israel because the Holy God was dwelling among them. In a nation of more than 2,000,000 people new laws were instituted as circumstances dictated. So a law was instituted to deal with land ownership.

Questions of Land Transfers, Num. 36

1 And the chief fathers of the families of the children of Gilead, the son of Machir, the son of Manasseh, of the families of the sons of Joseph, came near, and spoke before Moses, and before the princes, the chief fathers of the children of Israel:

2 And they said, The Lord commanded my lord to give the land for an inheritance by lot to the children of Israel: and my lord was commanded by the Lord to give the inheritance

of Zelophehad our brother unto his daughters.

3 And if they be married unto any of the sons of other tribes of the children of Israel, then shall their inheritance be taken from the inheritance of our fathers, and shall be put to the inheritance of the tribe whereto they are received: so shall it be taken from the lot of our inheritance.

4 And when the Jubilee of the children of Israel shall be, then shall their inheritance be unto the inheritance of the tribe whereto they are received: so shall their inheritance be taken away from the inheritance of the tribe of our fathers.

This was rather a pertinent question, and demanded an answer.

5 And Moses commanded the children of Israel according to the word of the Lord, saying, The tribes of the sons of Joseph hath said well.

6 This is the thing which the Lord doth command concerning the daughters of Zelophehad, saying, Let them marry to whom they think best; only to the family of the tribe of their fathers shall they marry.

7 So shall not the inheritance of the children of Israel remove from tribe to tribe: for every one of the children of Israel shall keep himself to the inheritance of the tribe of his fathers.

8 And every daughter, that possesses an inheritance in any tribe of the children of Israel, shall be wife unto one of the family of the tribe of her father, that the children of Israel may enjoy every man the inheritance of his fathers.

9 Neither shall the inheritance remove from one tribe to another tribe; but every one of the tribes of the children of Israel shall keep himself to his own inheritance.

10 Even as the Lord commanded Moses, so did the daughters of Zelophehad:

11 For Malah, Tirza, and Hogla, and Milcah, and Noah the daughters of Zelophehad were married unto their fathers' brothers' sons:

12 And they were married into the families of the sons of Manasseh the son of Joseph, and their inheritance remained in the tribe of the family of their father.

The answer to the landownership question was answered. Daughters who inherited lands of their tribe should marry to members of their own tribe. This prevented landownership from going from tribe to tribe.

13 These are the commandments and the judgments, which the Lord commanded by the hand of Moses unto the children of Israel in the plains of Moab by Jordan near Jericho.

<u>Duplicate Map of the First Year's Journey in the Wilderness</u>

The journey is marked by the red line

SUMMARY

For forty years, the Children of Israel had been living in the Wilderness. They had come to the Plains of Jordan where Reuben, Gad, and Half the Tribe of Manasseh received their inheritance. They were on the threshold of the Promised Land when Moses spelled out the borders of their inheritance. These borders defined the land and gave them their land rights. Knowing their borders meant that they should possess every square foot of their land and defend it. The map on page 591 shows the dominion of the twelve tribes with the Mediterranean Sea as their western border.

It was still a formidable task to divide their new land among the 2,000,000 or more people equitably. The method of doing that was by casting lots. This was a well proven method of achieving their ends. It was the responsibility of the priests, Joshua, and the twelve princes to ensure that every man received His inheritance.

The inheritance of the Levites was to be given by a different method than the general one used among the nine and a half remaining tribes. These tribes were to give from their inheritance 42 cities to the Levites in addition to 6 cities of refuge. These cities of refuge were to be a place of safety for anyone who accidentally killed another. They were to remain in these cities of refuge until the death of the High Priest. There was to be the judgment by the Congregation to determine innocence or guilt of the murderer. The murderer would be put to death, but the man slayer would be sent to one these cities of refuge.

The transfer of land ownership is a normal part of society. But Israel was not like any other society. They were a Theocracy: they were to do things differently. One way of dealing with the transfer of land ownership from tribe to tribe was that daughters who gained their fathers' inheritance should marry within their own tribes. In that way, the inheritance of one tribe would not be transferred to another. The lesson is that God is faithful to His promises. Therefore we must be faithful in serving Him.

At this point each of the twenty-eight chapters of this book has been summarized and 174,864 words have been used. However, in concluding I wish to look at the *Riddle of Time.* This is for a good reason.

The Riddle of Time

Our first Calendar was the calendar of Genesis chapter 1. It was a 7 day Calendar— "And the evening and the morning were the first day". With this, we could count to a billion days and more or we could count to eternity for that matter. Day and night were the only marks of time. While this Calendar had the capacity to calculate infinite measure of time, we poor human beings needed to look at time in a more finite manner. Thus we were compelled to adopt other time marks in order to divide, add, and subtract time.

In early civilization the Moon provided some very solid time marks. We were able to calculate the days and nights from one New Moon to the other, from New Moon to Full Moon, and from Full Moon to the Waning Phase. Though these time marks helped man to divide time, they had the capacity for infinite measures of time because one could count a billion New Moons and continue to count without an end in sight. Simply, though these time marks were greatly helpful, they did not solve all the problems for man's practical purposes.

Another division of time became necessary. Twelve new moons were added together as one period of time, called the Lunar Year. Still this was not all we needed to know about Earth's time because it did not complete the 365 1/4 days of the Calendar Year or the 364 days of the Enochic Calendar Year.

As early as the Seventh Generation from Adam, Enoch the Prophet was given a Calendar Year of 364 days by the Arch Angel Uriel with its revealed science. In the Enochic Calendar, the year is divided into 12 months of 30 days each. These months are divided into four seasons. These 12 months added to 360 days, meeting the scientific requirement of the 360 degree circle. An extra day was added to four of the months for the purpose of separating each of the four seasons. This resulted into the Calendar Year of 364 days.

Today, the World Calendar has 365 1/4 days in the regular year and 366 days in the Leap Year which is every 4 years. The difference between the two Calendars is infinitesimal, a difference of one and a quarter day. Modern science says the Earth makes one revolution around the Sun within 365 1/4 days. The four quarters are added to make an extra day every four years. There is very little difference between the two Calendars, but I would choose the Enochic Calendar as the better of the two.

There remains, however, a little problem not with any of the two Calendars, but with the choice of beginning of the year. What is the month of beginning? A nation can choose any of the 12 months as the beginning of its year. Israel did not have a choice; God made that choice for them. God expressly said to them, "Abib (April) shall be the beginning of your year". This beginning marked the event of their freedom from the bondage of Egypt. It is suggested that the beginning of the Egyptian year was June 21. This beginning was based on the appearance of the yearly cycle of the star, Sirius. Abib, the month of beginning of Israel's Calendar, also marks the beginning of the Cosmic Year and it is the beginning of Spring. The choice of beginning of Israel's year could not be better. March is suggested as the month of beginning of the Roman Calendar (date of information, April 19, 2013).

Since the English word for Abib is April, we ought to celebrate Easter in April instead of March.

Israel was to celebrate two great events in the month: the Passover on the 14 day, and the Feast of Unleavened Bread of 7 days, beginning the 15th day to the 22nd day. The Passover symbolizes Christ our Passover Lamb. Accordingly, Christ was to be crucified on the 14th day of Abib (April) at evening and not one of His bones would be broken. This symbolic prophecy was fulfilled by Christ 2000 years ago. Sacred record shows that on the night before His Crucifixion He kept the Passover with His Disciples, was crucified in the evening, and rose the Sunday morning following. The religious authority hastily removed Christ's body from the Cross because it was getting close to the preparation of the Sabbath.

Christ's death and resurrection did not span 3 days of 24 hours each, but did stretch across Friday, Saturday, to Sunday. March 31 of the year, 2013, Easter Sunday was celebrated worldwide. This calculation of Easter Sunday is very inaccurate. The Roman calculation of Easter should be replaced and Easter should always be celebrated in the month of April. There was no way Christ could escape the legal and symbolic prophecy of the Law. Christ had to be crucified on the 14th day of Abib (April) and because of that Easter had to be on the Sunday following. Christians ought to be celebrating Easter according to God's command in the Bible and not according the command of Rome.

Celebrating Easter March 31st did not mean that Christians would lose their salvation or their souls. Now we have solved the *Riddle of Time* to this point. Time itself demands of us that we show the reverence due to the symbolic prophecy of Christ our Passover Lamb and celebrate Easter the precise time.

The indispensable truth of these Three Books is that God wanted to have a personal relationship with His people,

Israel and everyone. He had this relationship with Abraham, Isaac, and Jacob. This is the only reason He is called the GOD of Abraham, Isaac, and Jacob. In Egypt Israel as a nation did not have this personal relationship with their God. The Divine judgment executed upon Pharaoh and Egypt was one way of accomplishing this end. But the Wilderness Experience was the only way that Israel could understand and experience God's holiness

INDEX OF SUBJECTS

INDEX OF SUBJECTS

INDEX OF SUBJECTS

Expression of gratitude,
575

Eleazar, the priest 575,
587

F

First sign to Pharaoh,
43-44, 74, 364
Freedom from bondage
82
Fight between two
men, 116
Feast of Unleavened
 Bread, 122, 201, 364
Feast of Ingathering, 123
Frame of the Tabernacle,
143, 216
First mention of the
Peace Offering…, 164
Feast of Weeks, 202, 366
Freewill Offering, 359-360
Forty days of communication
204
Fragrance of grace, 219
Feast of the Tabernacles
370

Firstborn of man and
 beast are the Lord's, 70
Fearsome holiness of
 God, 114
First fruits, 120, 122
Finger of God, 176
Feast of First Fruits,
 122, 566
Fine linen, 152
Fillets of silver, 146, 147,
 221
Further action of
sanctification, 189
Feast of Harvest, 365
Feast of Trumpets, 368
Five of the Ten
 Commandments, 347
Fire of Molech, 323
Fiftieth Year, 385
Fulfillment of vows, 449

G

God's name, 28
God's message to
Pharaoh, 35
Great judgments, 43
Golden vials of
wrath, 45
God's miraculous
provision, 94
God's omnipresent
nature, 114
Golden Altar of Incense,

God's guarantee, 39
Greater spiritual status
 of Moses, 42
God's schedule, 43
Grievous murrain, 51
God' ultimatum, 61
God's true intentions, 106
God's approval, 190
Gate of the Court, 147
Gifts of the people, 157
General law of the

INDEX OF SUBJECTS

INDEX OF SUBJECTS

T